"This collection of wonderful wr_____ _____ personal, and compelling. Stoke _____ book. Like me, you'll be comfort_____ God were reading over my shoulder."

Michael Messenger, Executive VP, World Vision Canada

"A soul-stirring spiritual refill of this beloved modern classic! Don't be mistaken—these aren't frothy tales boasting syrupy platitudes: these homegrown stories capture both the grit and inspiring reality of Canadians who live out their faith, seeing God at work in their lives and the world around them."

Michelle Nagle, Executive Director, Women Alive

"With moments of humour, struggle, romance, courage, heartache, and ultimately hope, *A Second Cup of Hot Apple Cider* is rich with buoyant prose and wondrous poetry… From slices of real life to flights of fancy, this cup runneth over with chapter after chapter of great reading."

Martin Smith, President, GMA Canada

"Several of these authors have shared their personal faith journey on my *100 Huntley Street* interview couch. Their writer's craft is as soul-warming as curling up in a handmade afghan with a fireside mug of cider. Whatever the season of the year, or the season of your life—whether for your own nurture, or as a hug from heaven for a friend—the publishers have given us a refreshing refill of Canadiana at its best!"

Moira Brown, Co-Host of *100 Huntley Street* and regular participant on *Full Circle* daily television shows

"This book is easy to pick up and tough to put down. You'll love these stories of love, faith, and hope. Thank God for second helpings!"

Phil Callaway, bestselling author of *To Be Perfectly Honest*

"The writers in this book share their finely-honed stories with an honesty and vulnerability that touches a universal chord in readers. Whether the setting is a remote farm on the Prairies, a First Nations community in Canada's Far North, a multi-cultural kindergarten in Toronto, a lonely highway in Nova Scotia, an isolation ward of a children's hospital, a blinding snowstorm in Québec, or a crammed church auditorium in British Columbia—you'll find these stories lingering in your mind as fresh evidences of God's grace."

Ginger Kolbaba, Founding Editor of Kyria.com, Christianity Today International; author of *Desperate Pastors' Wives*

"Like a heart-to-heart conversation with a close friend, *A Second Cup of Hot Apple Cider* draws us into the intimacy of relationship with one another and our Creator. As you traverse this wonderful collection of significant moments in the lives of ordinary people, you'll be inspired by God's extraordinary grace. Enjoy. You'll be warmed and filled."

Karen Bjerland, President and CEO, FaithLife Financial

"The stories are a strong sampling of the talents of… writers who exemplify the character and perseverance that has been instrumental in the success of the growth of Christian literature in our country in the past decade. The writers in this new collection constantly exhibit standards of excellence in communicating the Christian message in a Canadian context."

Larry Willard, Co-Owner, Faith Family Books & Gifts, Toronto; Owner and Publisher, Castle Quay Books Canada and BayRidge Books

"*A Second Cup of Hot Apple Cider* is a delightful read. This heartwarming and comforting anthology is just what we need to remind ourselves that God is willingly present in every facet of our lives. Well done!"

Karen Burke, Director of JUNO Award winning Toronto Mass Choir; Professor of Music, York University

"The wise man of Israel observed that there is no end of making books. Not that there are too many books, but that books must be selected with great care—they should be "goads and nails," provocative and assuring. *A Second Cup of Hot Apple Cider* will stir some of your complacent reveries, but will be an anchor to understand eternal values."

August H. Konkel, PhD, President, Providence College and Seminary

"Day after day, as we live our lives, we're creating new stories. *A Second Cup of Hot Apple Cider* is a well-written collection of short pieces that reflect this reality. I identified with many of the characters, and found the stories inspiring and motivating. I highly recommend this volume."

Lando Klassen, bookseller (38 years), House of James, Abbotsford, B.C.

"You'll find stories to tug at your heart and inspire you, stories that will make you smile, and stories that might just fill your eyes with tears. For this is a book that explores the human condition—how we as people suffer and how we celebrate. The works are culled from both the imagination, and from real life, as it is lived by Canadians who know their God… You just might find your own faith renewed."

Patricia Paddey, Senior Producer, Listen Up TV; writer on faith issues for Canada's Christian and mainstream media

"This book is great food for the soul, with practical applications to help navigate life's daily challenges and turbulences. It gives hope for those in despair and helps to build the faith of its readers. Its engaging writers make a deep impact as they articulate their individual experiences simply yet profoundly—enabling all levels of readers to appreciate the stories and draw their own life lessons. This comforting and encouraging book should be in every home, library, church, and school."

Pauline Christian, President, Black Business and Professional Association; one of Canada's Top 20 Women in 2010 as selected by *Women's Post*; recipient of African Canadian Achievement Award for Business

"Who doesn't always need a second cup? And this is one cup worth reaching for. From a host of talented writers who serve rich words, wrap your hands around a volume that will not only warm you right through, but strengthen you for the road ahead. A perfectly inspiring read."

Ann Voskamp, author of *One Thousand Gifts: A Dare to Live Fully Right Where You Are* and the blog A Holy Experience

"A refreshing taste of life—its challenges and joys, disappointments and small victories. Its genuine honesty encourages us that we are not alone in the challenges and struggles we all share."

Jean Chamberlain Froese, MD, recipient of the Royal College of Physicians and Surgeons of Canada's Teasdale-Corti Humanitarian Award; Executive Director, Save the Mothers program (East Africa)

"I've been drawn back to this book many times. The stories touched me deeply and I envision myself using them as sermon illustrations in the coming days. I enjoyed it tremendously and will highly recommend this easy-reading book to my colleagues."

Alex Pacis, WorldTeam Canada Field Director; Executive Director of Church Planting Ministries Inc.; Chairman of the Board of Emmanuel Relief and Rehabilitation Philippines

"This anthology is a beautiful offering by an array of gifted Canadian Christian writers. You will be inspired and comforted by the heartwarming stories, soothing words, and uplifting experiences shared from varied perspectives by these godly women and men. This book offers refreshing encouragement to the very depths of your mind and spirit!"

Audrey Meisner, Co-Host, *It's a New Day* television program; author

This book is dedicated to
Raymond and Lois Nelles
in tribute to their exceptional support
of Canadian writers who are Christian

A Second Cup of
Hot Apple Cider

Words to Stimulate the Mind
and Delight the Spirit

Edited by

N. J. Lindquist
Wendy Elaine Nelles

That's Life! Communications

A Second Cup of Hot Apple Cider

That's Life! Communications
Box 487, Markham, ON L3P 3R1, Canada
905-471-1447
www.thatslifecommunications.com
thats-life@rogers.com

Cover design by Ingrid Paulson, Ingrid Paulson Design
Interior layout and design by N. J. Lindquist

Photo illustrations were acquired from iStockphoto, with the exception of the photo on page 166, which was taken by Jamie Self Photography (www.jamieself.com).

Printed in Canada.

Library and Archives Canada Cataloguing in Publication

A second cup of hot apple cider : words to stimulate the mind and delight the spirit / edited by N.J. Lindquist, Wendy Elaine Nelles.

Also issued in electronic format.

ISBN 978-0-9784963-1-9

1. Inspiration--Religious aspects--Christianity. 2. Christian life--Anecdotes. 3. Spiritual life--Anecdotes. 4. Canadian literature (English)--Christian authors. I. Lindquist, N. J. (Nancy J.), 1948-II. Nelles, Wendy E

BV4515.3.S44 2011   242   C2011-900435-6

Table of Contents

Foreword

Ellen Vaughn

What a great book! Cozy reading that's warming like apple cider, but also energizing like the best caffeine! *A Second Cup of Hot Apple Cider* will give you a refreshing lift and a change of perspective, perhaps when you need it most.

Ah, there's nothing like the pleasure of reading a good book.

But it's a pleasure many of us put off because, you know, we're just too busy. Too many things must get done. I must check off all those items on my to-do list… so maybe I'll make time to sit down and read tomorrow. Or the tomorrow after that.

Social commentators say that we live in a "time-crunched culture." Psychologists, noting the rising stress levels of people who try to fill each moment and do too much in too little time, diagnose "hurry sickness"… which the rest of us call "multitasking."

The problem is, a 24/7 mindset of constant "productivity" makes us less productive than ever. Constant "doing" affects our "being." Running the "everydayathon" wearies not just our bodies but our souls, and somewhere along the production line of accomplishing a hundred different tasks each day, we can become hollow people.

That's why reading is not just a pleasure, but a duty for those who want to swim against the quick tide of the churning world around us. Reading takes time. Though such a thing as "speed reading" exists, the notion, actually, is oxymoronic. Absorbing reading demands a purposefully slower pace. It requires our full attention.

In return, reading is generous with its gifts.

Good books give us fresh vistas. They take us places we've never been. They can transport us beyond ourselves, beyond our pinched schedule and cramped concerns, to a place where we stretch and connect with others. For even though reading is a solitary endeavor, it joins us together in community.

This book is a perfect example. Its stories remind us that we're not alone. They inspire, for when we read of people who have faced formidable obstacles and overcome them, we begin to believe we just might be able to conquer our own challenges.

And when we laugh and weep and ponder over these well-wrought stories, something invisible, intrinsic, and powerful leaps off the pages and into our lives. It reminds us that we are part of something bigger than ourselves. It gives us strength.

Reading can enrich, ennoble, motivate, challenge, encourage, and arouse us. That's why you'll want to purposefully stop now and then in your busy days, get a cup of coffee, tea—or yes, hot apple cider—and relish the gifts this fine book offers.

Photo by Col. Douglas Martin, Canadian Forces Public Affairs Attaché. Taken from the roof of the Embassy of Canada in Washington, D.C.

Ellen Vaughn is a *New York Times* bestselling author and inspirational speaker. Her recent collaborative books include *Choosing to SEE*—which spent six weeks on the *New York Times* bestseller list in the autumn of 2010—as well as *Shattered*, *Lost Boy*, and *It's All About Him*. The last debuted at #1 on the *New York Times* nonfiction list in 2007.

Vaughn has also authored *Time Peace* and *Radical Gratitude*. Her award-winning novels are *The Strand* and *Gideon's Torch*, which she co-authored with Chuck Colson. She collaborated with Colson on eight other nonfiction books, including Gold Medallion Award winners *The Body*, *Kingdoms in Conflict*, and *Being the Body*.

Former vice president of executive communications for Prison Fellowship, Vaughn speaks frequently at retreats, conferences, and writers' seminars. She holds a Master of Arts from Georgetown University and a Bachelor of Arts from the University of Richmond. Vaughn and her husband Lee live in the Washington, D.C. area with their teenagers Emily, Haley, and Walker. She enjoys reading, walking, drinking coffee, and staring pensively at the ocean.

www.ellenvaughn.com

Introduction

Would you like to take a break from your busy life, have a heartwarming conversation with a friend, and come away refreshed, encouraged and inspired? *A Second Cup of Hot Apple Cider* was created with you in mind. It's the sequel to the bestselling first volume, *Hot Apple Cider: Words to Stir the Heart and Warm the Soul*, which received an enthusiastic response from thousands of readers.

Inside the pages of this exceptional inspirational anthology, you'll find more than 50 honest stories written from the heart. You can choose from moving true-life experience, thought-provoking drama, light-hearted humour, imaginative fiction or touching poetry—whatever you're in the mood for at the moment.

The short chapters—which each contain a complete story—make it easy for you to pick up the book and read something satisfying and uplifting whenever you have a few minutes... before bed, during coffee breaks, while you're commuting to work, if you're travelling, even when you're under the weather. All the pieces, whether they're talking about everyday incidents or life-changing events, are filled with hope and will raise your spirits.

You can relate to these stories because they're written by your neighbours—real people wrestling with real life, just like you. You'll meet 37 talented writers from across Canada: men and women who represent a wide variety of viewpoints, writing styles, experiences, ages, and backgrounds. You'll be sure to find some new favourites, all of whom will make you smile, shed a tear, think about the deeper meaning in life, and be drawn closer to God.

Are you looking for reassurance that you're not alone? Many readers of the first book told us how much the stories helped them and encouraged them, often when they were going through hard times themselves. *A Second Cup of Hot Apple Cider* will remind you that God is at work in your life, that good will come out of the struggles you face, and that every person matters.

Some of our writers draw from their spirited imaginations and their observations about life's complexities to offer fictional tales or insightful poems that you'll want to linger over. Other storytellers are straightforward and truthful as they share their personal experiences and what they've learned about God's loving faithfulness during life's challenges and joys.

In the pages of *A Second Cup of Hot Apple Cider: Words to Stimulate the Mind and Delight the Spirit,* you will:

- Meet an optimistic man who decides to redo the bathroom as a surprise for his wife;
- Discover how a husband and wife whose marriage has disintegrated learn to value each other;
- See how God used a rickety old stepladder to transform a broken heart;
- Follow along as an empty nester discovers a new purpose in life after the kids grow up;
- Gain insight into God's heart through ordinary things such as rusty junkyard trash, chocolate chip cookies, and a broken bookcase;
- Find out how two young women's holiday road trip to Montréal goes horribly wrong;
- Learn a valuable life lesson from a shark and a minnow;
- Share the heartbreak—and joy—of a woman who discovers she has cancer.

The first book was groundbreaking, introducing readers to excellent writing by Canadian writers who are Christian, all of whom are members of the national association The Word Guild. Many readers have been asking for another serving of this warm and welcoming collection. So unwind with *A Second Cup of Hot Apple Cider,* and let the grace-filled stories surprise you, make you laugh, and inspire you to have a deeper relationship with God.

N. J. Lindquist and *Wendy Elaine Nelles*

The Bulletin Board

Nonfiction

Adele Simmons

I'm standing in a corridor near the bulletin board where marks are posted. It's January, and I'm a student at the University of Lethbridge, Alberta. I'm a psychology major, minoring in biology.

Sheets of paper cover the long cork bulletin board. The page I want is Developmental Psychology 201.

Dr. Miller is the prof. He's good. He isn't just book smart, he's people smart. He bridges the gap of knowledge by checking where we are in our comprehension and taking us, step by clear step, to his point. He explains thoroughly and has high expectations of us.

I should ace the course—I'm an honours student. But I've had some challenges lately.

Students crowd the hall. The keeners jockey to get close to the bulletin board to check their marks. Cheers and curses mingle in the anxious mêlée. As the crowd clears, my best friend, smart Jan, and I find ourselves in the front.

There's her name… Yes! Jan gets an A. She's a humble friend. Smart, but humble. No boasting.

There's my name down with the Ss. I get a C. Humiliating.

Jan wraps a comforting arm around my shoulders. She makes no fuss, but encourages me. "You'll pull it back. He has no idea…"

Dr. Miller notices us in the hall later that day, as Jan and I walk to class. He pauses, then approaches us, his head tipped with intent. He closes in with quick, short strides.

"Nice work," he says to Jan.

Students flow by on both sides of us like rapids coursing around a boulder in the river. Inquisitive eyes question us in passing; they will expect an account of the discussion later.

Dr. Miller turns to me, leans closer and peers into my ashen face. He pokes the books in my arms with a stubby finger and spits his words, "Next time, study."

Quiet tears blur my vision as Jan and I continue down the hall. She knows all. But I can't tell him how my time has been spent over the last several weeks. My days have been consumed with helping my scared little sister settle in Calgary in the Salvation Army home for unwed mothers. I can't tell him I used my bursary money to cover some of my little sister's costs. I can't tell him I'm now grasping for extra work to make ends meet and pay for school.

I certainly cannot tell him about our marathon 2300-mile train ride during the Christmas break. We spent a tense Christmas Day in Lethbridge avoiding strife with our mother, her friends and other relatives. The next morning, we climbed on the train and journeyed for two weeks: first 900 miles west from our home in Lethbridge to see our dad and grandmother in Vancouver, British Columbia, and then another 800 miles straight north up to the small town of Houston to see our elder sister.

Mom had instructed us; they were not to know of the pregnancy. We obeyed. Didn't tell. Bittersweet to see family, an ache in the heart not to be able to share the truth with them.

We would not return to Lethbridge together. From Houston, we travelled 600 miles to Calgary to the Salvation Army home. It was a bonus for us to see family on this trip, but the pretense of an excursion to visit relatives over the Christmas holidays was actually our mother's calculated dodge to cover up my sister's failure to return to high school in January: she went on a trip and didn't come back.

As we travelled, the cry of the train whistle and rumble of steel wheels underscored the rhythm of my sister's tears, my efforts to cheer, and her fearful 15-year-old confidences. On each leg of the journey, we ate from our grocery bag, which contained two-day stashes of peanut butter and strawberry jam sandwiches, crackers, apples and oranges—ritzy Mandarin oranges you only get at Christmas. The aroma of orange peel lingered on our fingers like perfume. We rationed the oranges to last till the end of each ride.

Sleep came in fitful hazes, our chair backs reclined as far as they would go, our feet supported by suitcases, and our coats snugged up under our chins against the cold draft. It was uncomfortable, but much better than riding the bus.

While my sister slept, I stared out the window into the black night of the mountains and let the tears rise. Developmental Psych 201 and other looming January exams badgered my mind, but I knew I was where I needed to be.

The trip was two weeks of too little sleep and too many tears. I wept for her, this beautiful child, my sister. Her fault was craving to hear "I love you." Her mistake was trusting someone who said, "You are wonderful."

When else, in her entire difficult life, had she heard someone say she was wonderful? She was precious and innocent, now painted as sinful. The guilt was our parents', the weapons neglect and abuse. Yes, they too had been abused and neglected. So, the cycle continued.

Now, my pretty little sister was beaten down. Bruised. Scarred. She was paying for their choices. But for God, it would be me.

My own bruises were healing, my bleeding had stopped, and my scars hurt less as I learned about a loving God.

Love. A strange concept. Impossible to understand without experience. God's people reached out to me and loved me into His Kingdom.

They shared hot chicken noodle soup with me, included me in their family picnics, took me camping, sang with me, and prayed over me. Their faith opened my ears and my eyes. And Jesus dawned on me. Slowly, I came to know He is true. Slowly, as the tide comes in, I understood that Jesus came for me, too. Slowly, as the snow melts, my life warmed up. I was not excluded from His promises. At 17, my life changed.

My Christian friends gave me dreams. They guided me to pursue higher education, helped me secure a bursary and loan, encouraged me in my natural strengths of perception, teaching and counselling.

Now, I find myself in the psychology stream at university. But I am armed with a new, growing strength called love. And that love compels me to help my sister.

I get a C in Developmental Psychology that January. By April, I pull up my final grade to a B+. In my heart, I am still an A student.

That same April, my little sister has a baby boy. She gives him away for adoption. But, in her heart, she is still a mother.

The Scavengers

Nonfiction

Judi Peers

At first glance it was only a junkyard, but once I truly began to see, this small plot of ground became a treasure trove.

My daughter Sarah and I were travelling into the countryside early one Saturday morning in search of an estate auction. I was hot on the trail of an antique wheelbarrow, a much-desired prop for my ever-expanding garden. The auctioneers had specifically mentioned one in their newspaper listing. As we neared our destination, we noticed a long procession of parked cars. Assuming this must be it, we pulled over at the side of the road.

"It's just a junkyard," Sarah called to me after running ahead to take a closer look. Seconds later, she was back in the car and we drove on.

The auction we were seeking turned out to be a little further down the road. Several antique dealers and hordes of bidders from the city milled about the beautiful old Victorian home, causing prices to rapidly escalate beyond our meagre budget. The wheelbarrow sold for $350.

On the way home, thinking it might be fun to watch for a while, we stopped at the junkyard auction. Besides, it was a beautiful spring day, a perfect time to flit about the countryside, to wander off the beaten path in search of intrigue and adventure.

The auctioneer had wrapped things up only minutes before our return, but there were lots of people lingering, chatting, and collecting their "junk."

Many people had purchased job lots—small groups of items—and they were willing to sell the things they didn't need.

Before long, I was crazy with excitement. Some of this stuff had tremendous potential.

Sarah and I hunted through wagonloads of scrap metal and old machinery parts. I purchased, very cheaply, wonderful things

I could put to use in my garden: weathered sap buckets, old pails with wooden handles, rusty chains and whippletrees for hanging baskets, aged wooden boxes for planters, etc. A pair of dirty, rusty gears lay discarded on the ground. Upon closer examination, I realized they would make the most amazing candlesticks.

Thus began my lust for rust, my love affair with garden junk. What's more, I discovered one of my neighbours was a kindred spirit. We began foraging into rustic rural areas and nosing around salvage yards in search of hidden treasure.

Sometimes, my husband thinks I've lost my mind. Other people say I'm creative because I can see beyond an object's past and envision a new and purposeful future. I think the ability to do this began out of desperation—my need to decorate a large space on a limited budget. Over the years, however, it has blossomed into a definite preference.

While meticulously arranging a newly acquired piece of "junk" in my garden one day, I thought about a statement I'd heard at a recent Bible study: "Too often, we allow our past to mold and shape our life today."

My mind raced on. If creativity allows me to see the potential that rusty, old junk has to offer, what happens when God looks upon us? He possesses the ultimate in creativity; He is the Creator!

When God looks on His children, He must see us in our full potential—the people we will eventually be. Perfect. Complete. Made whole through the redeeming work of Jesus Christ, who, temporarily laying aside His glory, became like us so we could become like Him.

In my garden, a beat-up, old window frame with flaking green paint can become a unique, yet functional trellis; a worn work boot with a gaping hole is the perfect container for succulent plants; a large rusty spring makes an interesting garden accent; a rusty pulley turns into a work of art.

Can you imagine what *we* could become if we were willing to place our lives completely in God's hands? To live each day in obedience to Him?

Or how we'd treat people if we could see them through God's eyes?

As children of God, our lives ought to be shaped by the future, because God no longer sees our past—He sees our potential!

The "mistake" my daughter and I made by pulling over at the side of the road near the so-called junkyard, provided me with wealth beyond measure. I not only gained inspiration for my garden and my writing, but, of far more importance, I discovered how to look at people through God's eyes. And I realized that God's grace poured into a receptive heart has tremendous transforming power. His work is not limited by human imagination. He is the Creator!

And my daughter? Well… she's now a teacher who loves to use her creativity in the classroom. She too has learned to see beyond what is there—to imagine what one day might be.

Lost: One Green Scarf

Nonfiction

Vilma Blenman

I definitely left it with my coat, but it's definitely not there when I go to leave. I shake out the coat sleeves, look under the rack with its one remaining jacket, and check behind my boots. At the suggestion of one of my group members, I retrace my steps to the large meeting room where we had just finished three hours of volunteer facilitator training. I know it won't be here. I had chosen not to wear it into the room, but I check anyhow. No scarf.

A familiar emotion sweeps over me. It's the fear one feels when suddenly, inevitably, one encounters an acquaintance from one's multi-storied past, but is unsure what to say, knowing it will be either an awkward encounter, or a cathartic one, or both. It's the fear that begins in the lower entrails and moves swiftly up to the rib cage, then upward to the throat, tightening its grip as it climbs. It's the fear that something significant that was, will be no more. Something vital to me is lost.

Just leave, I tell myself. *Just get going. It's only a scarf, for heaven's sake.*

True, it's only a scarf. A vivid green silk and pashmina scarf patterned with trailing black tendrils criss-crossing earthy-brown patches—all three of my comfort colours in one place. A green scarf that makes my brown skin shine when I drape it against my face and neck; a green scarf that goes well with the blacks and browns in my budget-bound wardrobe; a green scarf I spent months hunting for, and finally found for $7.99 at a sidewalk sale; a green scarf my daughter loves to share, and I love to wear.

Gone is that green floral scarf I was beginning to build a loving, fragrant relationship with, fingering its black-brown veins and the laughing, hanging tassels. Now it's just one lost, green scarf.

After five more minutes of searching, I step briskly off the steps of the BFO house down to the sidewalk on Madison Avenue in downtown Toronto. Bereaved Families of Ontario secured this quaint, strategically located house in an older section of the city nestled amidst University of Toronto sorority houses, and turned it into a multi-purpose office and meeting place. I walk quickly towards the Spadina Avenue subway station, clutching my naked throat. Without intending to, I begin to notice people's scarves: some dark, some brightly coloured, some woollen, some cotton— all deftly knotted at the nape, complementing coats, shielding owners from cold.

Déjà vu, grief whispers. *Didn't you notice every mother with a baby after you buried each of your own babies? Didn't you hear your babies' cries in the cry of every child for a year or more after your babies were silent?* It's the way grief travels, a river running its course through a crowded landscape on its way to the open sea, tracing and retracing its paths. It must get to the sea to be the part of the ocean it was meant to be. Let grief go. Let it run through your bloodstream to the heart and race back out to your limbs— oxygen-rich, life-giving, meaning-making grief. Then you'll know you're still alive, still breathing, still being.

Going eastbound on the subway is instinctive. Usually I go all the way to the end of the line at Kennedy Station, but tonight I must remember to change trains at Yonge and Bloor because I'm getting off the subway and taking the above-ground GO commuter train from Union Station. Tonight, I don't have a car parked and waiting for me in Scarborough; my husband needed the car. Tonight is suddenly so different.

Sitting awkwardly on the nearest subway seat, I'm keenly aware of the absence of a scarf, and I feel vulnerable—aware of the absence of not only my two children, but also my friend Jean, gunned down in her own home on New Year's Day by a demented man who drove away with a blood-stained gun as neighbours poured into the street. Wise, beautiful Jean, dying on her clean kitchen floor. And me telling the reporter from Citytv that Jean was a community activist who chose the church as her arena for change. Jean is dead.

And before that, my two brown babies, dead and buried in small white coffins on fine summer days exactly a year apart.

"Arriving at Union, Union Station," the robotic female voice calls out. I stumble off the train, the subway doors closing smoothly behind me. What next? *Climb those stairs and make your way towards the GO Station signs.*

I've never taken the GO train home from here before. This is new. But then, this form of grief is new. *Where the heck do I buy tickets? Ah. Steady now. Get a grip. Follow the signs.*

"One-way ticket to Pickering!" I shout to the man behind the counter as I hand him a ten dollar bill. *Why am I shouting?*

He does not see me, or so it seems. Nothing in his stony nine-to-five expression behind the glass partition acknowledges me. I hear the clink of change in the steel cup and grope for the coins before picking up the ticket he slides simultaneously towards me. He's finished with me now, about to serve the next in line.

"Which platform?" I ask him, panic rising.

"That screen will tell you when the train is arriving," he answers brusquely, pointing to the overhead arrival and departure schedule as if annoyed by my inane question. How was I to know? I've never been here before, never buried babies before, never organized a prayer vigil for a murdered friend. *How insensitive!*

I sit down to wait, then stand up, walk over to another bench. I sit down again, gingerly. Finally my brain decodes the jumble of words and numbers on the screen. The eastbound train arrives at 10:13 p.m.

Breathe. Just breathe.

I take in gulps of air, scented with burnt cinnamon from the fresh-baked cinnamon bun kiosk nearby and the sweat from the teenage boy propped up against the wall playing Nintendo™.

Breathe. Keep breathing.

Even at the worst of times, I'm not prone to hysterics. But this rising torrent is threatening to submerge me. What professional person has an emotional outburst in the middle of Union Station?

Breathe, grieve. Breathe, grieve.

Let air in, let loss out. Let the rhythm lull you the way you rocked babies in the womb. The womb that became their tomb.

Breathe, grieve. Breathe, grieve. You gave love. They gave life lessons. Keep going. Push…

Suddenly a light is flashing on the illuminated sign beside the 10:13 train eastbound to Pickering. People are on the move. The teenage boy picks up his giant knapsack and lumbers off. I pick up my feet and move—up the stairs, into the night air—without my scarf, loss trailing me doggedly.

I know I'm going to cry on the train. I choose a solitary seat, far from the crowd. On such a night, a dark window seat is a woman's best friend. Grief settles down beside me. Tears reappear. Why now, 18 years after the second of the stillborn babies? Why now, when there are two living babies I'm racing home to kiss goodnight?

Forty-two minutes later, I button my coat and brace myself to exit. The green and white GO train sign tells me I've arrived in Pickering. I walk down the exit tunnel and emerge once more into the night air. I find our waiting car easily. He timed my arrival just right. "How was your session tonight?" my husband asks hopefully as I click the seatbelt firmly in place.

"Good," I answer. "Good." I hesitate. *Can I tell him without bursting into tears?* "I lost my green scarf. Or maybe it was stolen. I don't know. I just didn't come home with it."

"Oh dear," he says, his concern echoing my careful tone.

But I say no more, nothing more on the ten-minute drive home. Taking his cue from my silence, he says no more. Talk can come later.

I go upstairs and check on my kids. Just to be sure they're alive. Our eight-year-old is snoring, coiled in his usual pillow-hugging position. Our sixteen-year-old is reading beneath a mound of blankets, her clothes carpeting the floor.

I stumble into our bed and curl into a ball, my knees jabbing into my husband's ribs. "Good night, dear," he mumbles, half-asleep as he turns to kiss me. Then he turns back to his side of the bed.

"Good night," I whisper, taking care he doesn't hear the sound of my tears tumbling over my pillow.

I can kiss that green scarf goodbye. But I'll miss it. I'll miss it every time I put on my coat. I miss my friend. And I miss my babies.

Breathe, grieve. Breathe, grieve. This too, is the rhythm of living.

Dazed

Fiction

Kevin J. Dautremont

She had always slept in the middle of the bed. He could steal some of her warmth—or avoid it—just by rolling one way or another. Lately though, she'd clung to her side of the mattress as tightly as a burr would to a wool blanket. For the past week or so, her warmth wasn't the only thing she'd been unwilling to share.

That evening, Dylan Martinson had showered after finishing his chores. He'd even shaved. When he came into the bedroom, Sarah lay curled in a rigid ball on the far side of the bed. He slid in beside her and laid his hand on her shoulder. "Whatcha doing?"

"Reading."

Reading? She shouldn't be. Just that afternoon, he had hidden the novel she was halfway through.

He tilted his chin to peer over her. *You're kidding me.* The Guinness Book of World Records, 1995 Edition? *A 16-year-old book of trivia! What closet did she dig that out of?* He touched her shoulder again. "Do you want—"

"I'm reading."

He rolled onto his back and stared at the ceiling. The bedside clock snarled in his ear. Five minutes passed. Raising himself up on his elbow, Dylan glared once more at the book in his wife's hands. She continued to stare at the same page. *How could anyone be that interested in the world's largest ball of string?* With a grunt, he rolled into a sitting position and began pulling on his socks.

"What are you doing?" she asked without looking at him.

He finished buttoning his shirt and scooped his jeans up from the floor. "Going to check on the cattle."

The cattle were fine. They had plenty of feed. The water trough was full and unhampered by ice. The animals all looked calm and comfortable. *Nothing to worry about.* He had known that before getting into bed. There had been no need to check them again.

The night was cold. Some parts of the country were feeling the first vestiges of spring, but late February on the Saskatchewan prairie always meant winter, no matter what that stupid groundhog said. As Dylan stood in the doorway of the cattle shed, the yellow ring of his flashlight filtered through the fog created by the breath of 23 bred heifers.

The old bull snorted and plodded to the gate of his pen. The man smiled and shook his head when the bull pawed the ground and stuck his muzzle out through the bars of the gate. The heifers remained aloof and out of reach. "Sorry, old fella. Nothing tonight for you either." He watched as the bull turned back toward the door and lowed softly. It was almost a moan.

"You need more bedding?" Dylan asked as he stepped outside and reached for a bale of straw. Carrying it to the pen, he pulled the twine off to spill the straw over the top of the railing. As the golden strands scattered over the hard-packed ground, the old bull edged forward to nose through the pile. The big Red Angus snorted again and looked up at his owner. The farmer grinned and leaned against the barricade. "You want something else? How about some oats?"

Hanging from a nail by the door was a pail half full of chopped oats. As he moved to take it from its hook, a noise caused him to look up. A pair of yellow eyes in the midst of a small mound of black and grey striped fur gazed down at him from the rafters. Mother Cat. The sound that crept from her throat was half purr, half growl. She blinked twice and yawned to show the fierceness of her bite. The fact that one of her upper fangs was missing ruined the effect.

"Have you been doing your job, Cat?" Dylan asked as he carried the pail to the bull's feed trough. "No mice around?" The cat ignored him and tucked its nose back under its tail. The man frowned and shook his head. "Women."

The bull, at least, was pleased with his efforts and buried his nose in the trough. The beast even allowed Dylan to reach down and rub his forehead.

Replacing the pail on the hook, the farmer stepped back into the night. He closed the door of the shed and turned toward the house. He walked slowly, listening to the playful crunch of the snow under his boots. Coming to a stop, Dylan turned off the flashlight and tipped his head back. He closed his eyes and listened. His dad had always told him that on the coldest of winter nights, if you were still enough, patient enough, you could hear the stars hum. He waited, willing his pulse to slow and holding his breath. *Nothing.*

He opened his eyes and inhaled sharply. The stars seemed nearly within reach. *Stretch out your hands and you might brush a finger through droplets of silver.* A quotation came to him. Thoreau? No, Emerson. "Nature is too thin a screen; the glory of the omnipresent God bursts through everywhere."[1] *And they said two years of university was a waste of time.*

He turned and looked at the house. Darkness filled the bedroom window. *That two years of higher education isn't helping me much now, though, is it?*

The quiet enveloped him and pressed him down toward the snow. He felt so tired. Confused. Dull. Pointless. Like a man discarding a heavy cloak, he shook himself. He looked upward once more, and wisps of steam rose with words no louder than a sigh, "Help me."

One more passage came to him, this one written thousands of years earlier by another bewildered man. "There are three things that are amazing to me, four that I do not understand: the way of an eagle in the sky, the way of a snake on a rock, the way of a ship on the high seas and the way of a man with a maiden."[2]

He spoke again, louder this time, "Not really helpful. I already know that I don't understand. I'm asking for help. Didn't You say if any man lacked wisdom he should ask? Well, hello?"

No hum from the stars and no answers from God.

A sharp wind began to stir. Flecks of snow were stripped from the roof of the cattle shed and flung downward to knife against the back of his neck. He flipped his collar up against the insult and hunched his shoulders. "Thanks. Thanks a lot," he muttered.

As he shuffled toward the house, the wind seemed to whisper in his ear, "Husbands, love your wives, just as Christ loved the church."[3] He stopped and tipped his face upward. "I'm trying," he said, almost shouting now, "Isn't that enough?" The sky was silent. He dipped his chin and moved on.

Dylan took extra care when he entered the house. He beat each drop of snow from his boots before allowing either one across the threshold. The old fleece jacket did not end up flung down over a chair but actually made it into the closet, on a hanger no less. Even his ball cap was sequestered away in its proper hiding spot.

His mind was whirling. *So what's wrong? What did I do that's so terrible?*

Our anniversary? No way. That was almost seven months ago and she'd only been acting strange the last week or two. Besides, he had not only remembered their wedding anniversary but had even arranged a surprise dinner party with family and friends. Sarah had loved it.

Her birthday? It wasn't until later in the spring and hadn't even blipped on the radar yet.

Christmas; what about Christmas? He thought he'd done well. All of the gifts he'd bought were from the list she'd given him and he'd even outspent her for a change. *No problem there.*

The in-laws? No, her mother actually liked him and her dad had just gone ice fishing with him a couple of weeks ago.

What about the boys? Had they done something or said something that made her suddenly hate all carriers of a Y chromosome? Possibly. Last week they'd turned the living room into a disaster area by pulling the couches apart to build a fort right before company arrived. But that's pretty normal. Nah, she'd have told him if they'd done anything truly terrible.

He stepped carefully through the house to peer into the boys' bedroom. The dim light from the kitchen touched their smooth cheeks as they slept. More of Emerson came to him. "There was never a child so lovely but his mother was glad to get him to sleep."[4] He grinned. *No, it isn't the boys. Besides, how awful can a four- and a six-year-old be?*

Dylan moved back to the kitchen and filled the kettle. While the water heated on the stove, he glanced around the room. Sarah hadn't done the dishes. That wasn't like her. She always cleaned up right after supper. He stared at the pile on the counter for a moment. The command from Scripture to love his wife nibbled at the edge of his conscience.

He began to rinse the dishes and stack them in the dishwasher. He finished just as the water boiled and he lifted the kettle from the burner before it had a chance to whistle. The tea steeped in its mug while he quickly wiped down the counters. That done, he looked around the room and shook his head. *No problems in the kitchen. And no clues either. Maybe in the den?*

It wasn't really a den. It had been built as a laundry-slash-sewing room, but the laundry had been moved to the basement and Sarah didn't really like sewing. So it had become her office. She kept the farm's books there, balancing the cheque books, paying the bills, and doing all those things he struggled with and ultimately hated. She was good with numbers and never seemed to mind managing that part of things while he took care of the land and the livestock. He'd thought they made a good team.

He knew the bottom line, of course. Followed the prices of grain, livestock, fuel and fertilizer as closely as anyone. That was why he'd taken the job with the oil company. Maintaining the pumper stations had paid the bills and allowed them to keep farming until things had improved. It was better now. The crops had been good and prices were up. There was still debt but it was manageable for a change. The pressure wasn't so intense anymore. He didn't really need the oil company job now, but the extra money was nice and Sarah didn't seem to mind him being away a couple of days a week. *No, it had to be something else.*

The office was neat but not obsessively so. He stepped up to the bookcase and ran a finger across the rows of spines while he sipped from his mug. *Has she been reading something weird? Some bizarre anti-marriage philosophy?* There didn't seem be anything like that here. *Hey, there's my book on the '72 Summit Series. Canada— Russia. Now that was hockey!* He pulled the volume halfway out but then frowned and pushed it back into place. *Focus, Dylan. This is more important than hockey. Being crunched in the corner by a 6 foot 5 defenseman is nothing. Figuring out women—that's hard.*

He turned to Sarah's desk and began to leaf through the pile of papers. Some bills. A couple of flyers. A note from school about an upcoming field trip. A reminder that the boys were overdue for a checkup at the dentist's. Underneath the papers was something else—a thin hard-covered text. Plain dark green embossed with gold letters. Simple and clean. Innocent even. A high school yearbook. It had to be Sarah's.

Dylan held the book tightly as he walked to the family room. He hadn't known her then, hadn't been part of her life. While she was finishing high school, he'd been coming to the realization that university wasn't for him; farming was. They had met at his cousin's wedding a month after she graduated. A year later, they were married.

Setting his mug on the coffee table, he eased himself down onto the couch and opened the yearbook. The graduating class was two-thirds of the way through, after the lower grades but before the sports teams and school clubs. *There she is, Sarah Stadnik.* He grinned and touched a finger to the page. *She was beautiful then, almost as beautiful as she is now.* His finger moved down the page, tracing the inscription under her picture. Student body president. Co-editor of the student newspaper. Photography club. Honour roll. *Yeah, that sounds like her all right. Gorgeous and smart.*

His eyes moved further down. Her plans for the future were listed next. Her hopes. Her dreams. "I want to study photography and then travel the world as a photo-journalist for a top news agency."

He put the book down and frowned. *Nothing about marriage and kids. And definitely nothing about a struggling mixed farm in the middle of the Canadian West.* His smile faded. *Is that it?*

Dylan looked again at the yearbook. When he'd set it down, something had slipped out from between the back pages. A letter, written on engraved stationery. He opened it and quickly scanned its message. Sarah's ten-year high school reunion was coming up and Jillian Trembley, the chairwoman of the organizing committee, had contacted her for help. *Hmm, Trembley. Sounds familiar.* He turned to the grad pictures once more, and there she was next to Sarah.

His face became grim when he read the inscription beneath her picture. "I'll run my own company and be a millionaire before I'm 30." The letter mocked him from where it lay on the coffee table. Just below Jillian Trembley's scrawled signature, stark and arrogant, shrieked the words, President and CEO, Trembley & Associates.

The clock on the mantle filled the room with its rhythmic ticking. The tea grew cold in his mug. At last, he shook himself.

Getting up, he began to wander through the house. Entering the living room, he reached out to touch the small objects that had become part of their home through the past eight and a half years. A watercolour of Old Québec City they had purchased on their honeymoon. The figurine of a dancing ballerina his parents had given them for their sixth anniversary, prominently displayed even though Sarah hated it. A paper star one of the boys had made at Sunday school. This she loved.

He moved into the dining room and stared at the wall above the buffet. A collage of framed photographs covered the wall. A variety of sizes and styles, they were all photos Sarah had taken over the years—portraits, action shots, scenes from the farm or from trips—each one a frozen memory.

He took down a small one and held it in his hands. Dylan sat holding three-week-old Joshua while two-year-old Nate peered over his dad's shoulder at his new baby brother. The morning light filtered through a window misted with dew to touch their faces. Sarah hadn't posed them. She'd waited until the moment was perfect—light, angle, their expressions, everything. He couldn't help smiling once more at the image. *Yes, this one is definitely my favourite.*

He carried the picture back to the family room and laid it on the coffee table beside the yearbook and the letter. Sitting on the couch, he leaned forward to touch the faces in the photograph, studying them carefully. His finger moved to the yearbook and traced once more the words beneath his wife's graduation photo. He looked again at the images of Josh and Nate. *Have I failed them? Have I failed her?* Wiping his damp face with his hands, he lay back on the couch and stared at the ceiling. He tried, but failed, to stifle a yawn. *Maybe if I closed my eyes… just for a minute.*

Something bright shone on his face. A strong aroma tickled the back of his brain, stretching through his mind like a cat rising from a pool of sunlight. It demanded his attention, his wakefulness. Dylan opened his eyes. Sarah was standing in front of him.

He sat upright on the couch and blinked up at his wife. In her hand, she held a cup of coffee. Without asking, he knew it would be double cream, double sugar—just the way he liked it. He smiled as he took the cup from her.

"You didn't come back to bed last night," she said.

"Sorry, I meant to." He scratched his head and sipped the coffee. "I guess I fell asleep."

She sat on the couch beside him and gestured toward the kitchen. "You didn't have to do the dishes. I would have gotten to them."

"I know you would have," he shrugged, "but I kinda thought it was my turn."

Sarah reached out and touched the objects on the coffee table. "You've been busy."

"Yeah, I guess."

She picked up the yearbook and the letter. "You were looking at these?"

"Yeah, sorry. I didn't mean to pry."

"It's okay. I've been looking at them too. For quite awhile. I guess I've been feeling distracted—I don't know, sort of dissatisfied. Had you noticed?"

"Ah, no, not really." He stared into his mug, the hot liquid as murky as his thoughts. "Well, yeah. I guess I did. A little." He turned and pointed at the yearbook. "I'm sorry."

"For what?"

"For that. Losing your dream. Seeing the world. Being a famous photographer."

"You *had* noticed." Sarah closed the yearbook and picked up the photo of Dylan and the boys. "I've been thinking about things too," she said. "When I woke up this morning and you were gone, it felt as though something were wrong—I don't know, something important. And then I came down and found you here."

"Uh-huh?"

"I saw the things you had out and it made me remember something—something I'd forgotten. While you were snoring on the couch, I did a lot of thinking." She looked into his eyes. "I came to a decision."

"Okay."

"I've decided that this is a pretty good picture." She smiled and set the photo back on the coffee table. "Good enough to have been done by a famous photographer."

"I've always thought so."

"I made another decision as well."

He chewed his bottom lip and placed his cup beside the year-book. "You did?" He braced himself.

"Yes, I did," Sarah said. She reached over and took his hands in hers. "I decided that what was wrong this morning was that I woke up alone. I didn't like that. I decided I like being married, and that I *especially* like being married to you. I also love being a mom. So I made up my mind that I want to keep things just the way they are, because what I have right *here* is my dream. You. The boys. The farm."

Dylan lifted one of her hands to his lips and kissed it softly. "That's good. That's *so* good." He looked into her eyes for a brief moment. "But what convinced you?"

"After you went out last night, I prayed in a way I haven't for a long time." She wiped her eyes. "Then I left it in God's hands. I knew He'd show me what to do. This morning when I saw you here on the couch with the photo, I had my answer. This is where I belong. This is home."

"That's just what I needed to hear. I love you, Sarah Martinson."

"I love you too." She shifted closer to him and laid her head on his shoulder. After a moment, she spoke again, "So, is everything all cleared up now?"

Dylan grinned. "What do you mean by 'everything'? I mean, I think I understand what you were feeling these past few days. But there's still a ton of other stuff about you that I'm totally confused about."

"Never mind," she said as she moved to kiss him. "Let's just keep it that way."

1. Ralph Waldo Emerson, *Lectures and Biographical Sketches, Volume X: The Preacher,* The Philosophy Pages, http://davemckay.co.uk/philosophy/emerson/emerson. php?name=emerson.10.lectures.08 (accessed December 15, 2010).

2. Proverbs 30:18-19

3. Ephesians 5:25

4. Ralph Waldo Emerson, *Essays: Second Series—Experience,* The Philosophy Pages, http://davemckay.co.uk/philosophy/emerson/emerson.php?name=emerson.03. essays2.02 (accessed December 15, 2010).

Fallout

Heather McGillivray

In the event of an emergency
like a fallout
between you and me—
and not just some random
act of annoyance,
remain calm;
proceed to the nearest
storm shelter
the doghouse will do just fine
and barricade yourself inside.

Do not attempt to rectify
the situation on your own.

Once the storm blows over,
pick up the scattered
debris; clear the walkway, and
keeping your dirty boots outside
proceed with caution through
the back entrance.

There, every attempt to put the
pieces back together,
together,
will make for the highest
survival rate.

A Shout in the Dark

Nonfiction

Heidi McLaughlin

"Just keep talking. Don't stop now!" The force of those words, whispered urgently from somewhere behind me in the pitch-black, 2,000-seat auditorium, jolted me out of my confusion and propelled me back to reality. A large audience, sitting somewhere in front of me in the dark, sat nervously wondering what to do and questioning whether or not I would finish my address.

I had been thrilled when organizers asked me to be the keynote speaker at the World Day of Prayer, an ecumenical gathering of people from many churches in my hometown of Kelowna, British Columbia. I carefully prepared my talk on this year's theme, "The Rainbow Colours of Africa," and put together a display of vibrant, hand-picked fabrics. I hoped that the tapestry of multi-hued textiles behind me would provide a powerful illustration of the stories behind my words. But while I was passionately explaining how the colour green depicted new growth and a refreshed spirit through prayer, the room had been thrust into absolute blackness and silence. Everyone wondered, *What happened?*

We didn't know it then, but a power outage due to lightning striking a transformer had hit this part of the city, causing all the lights and technical systems to shut down during our meeting. Caught off-guard in the middle of my speech, I was stunned by this unexpected glitch. How would I find my way out of what felt like a vacuum?

As I struggled to find words to calm my audience, I heard the voice of my friend Carol, the musical director for the event, who was on the stage behind me. "Come on, Heidi," she urged, "you can finish this." Her words spurred me on, giving me the courage to take my next step.

Without a working microphone, I had to shout my words into the heavy blackness. People hurriedly found candles and flashlights, but nothing was able to reveal the beauty of the fabrics that had formed the basis of my talk. Somehow, I finished an abbreviated version of my speech without notes.

Drained and shaking, I stumbled off the stage into the foyer of the large church to find reporters and cameras from the local television station waiting to learn what had happened inside the blackened auditorium. This World Day of Prayer had became a newsworthy affair after our city's newspaper showcased the amount of prayer taking place simultaneously that day in more than 170 countries around the globe.

The reporters seemed curious about how my topic of rainbow colours correlated with the overall "power of prayer" theme, topped by the added drama of losing the power of electricity. Questions were thrust at me:

"What happened in there?"

"What motivated you to keep going?"

"Why didn't you just give up and walk out?"

I told them I was hoping the darkness was only a temporary glitch, and that soon the lights would again illuminate the beautiful colours of Africa. But deep inside my soul, I knew that my friend's words echoing in my brain had been the impetus to keep me going.

Many years earlier, I had learned to pay attention to the power of a friend's voice shouting to me in the middle of the darkness…

On a Thursday evening two weeks before Christmas, a ringing doorbell smashed my perfect Christmas picture into a thousand, unidentifiable pieces. When I opened the door, a policeman spoke words that none of us ever wants to hear.

"Mrs. Conley, I'm so sorry to have to tell you this. Your husband Dick died tonight while he was playing basketball in the high school gym."

My head reeled. Dick had left just a couple of hours before to play his usual Thursday night game with friends in an intramural league. From the time he was old enough to dribble a ball, he had lived and breathed basketball. The sport was the passion of his life.

Although he was general manager of a large modular housing corporation, everything related to basketball—coaching, refereeing, playing, cheering and going to training camps—had been part of our lives for the entire 28 years of our marriage.

Now I was being told that, while he was playing the sport he loved with every fibre of his being, Dick had collapsed and died on the gymnasium floor from heart failure. My heart pounded frantically. Dick was only 49 years old. He'd seemed perfectly healthy. How was this possible?

I longed to scream at the policeman standing on my doorstep, *How can you say those terrible words?* Instead, I looked into his face and, with a shaky voice, I asked, "What do you need me to do?"

Gently, he told me that I needed to go to the morgue to identify the body. Then he added, "You can't do this alone; you'll need to call a friend."

Even though Dick and I had lived in Kelowna for only a year or so, I had made intentional efforts to build friendships by joining a choir, going to a gym, attending a women's retreat, and inviting women to my home for coffee. That night, I needed to shout out to one of my new friends in the darkest moment of my life.

Bea was by my side in a matter of minutes. She drove me to the morgue and held me up when I had to identify the body. She made me tea. Then she sat across from me in my dimly-lit kitchen, looked into my swollen eyes, and quietly said, "Heidi, you need to call your children."

Dick and I had recently become empty nesters, and I missed my grown-up children. They were my heartbeats walking around outside of my body, and I still felt compelled to protect them. This phone call would shatter their lives.

I knew my son Donovan was in the middle of his final exams at the University of Lethbridge, and my daughter Michelle was fully immersed in Christmas activities in her community in Grassy Lake, Alberta.

"I can't," I sobbed. "It will be hard enough for them in the morning. Let them sleep for the rest of the night."

Bea urged, insisted, and then, when I still wouldn't respond, she quietly, lovingly shouted out to me in the blackness of my soul.

"Heidi, you have to call your children *right now*! They will be hurt if they find out their father died and you left them sleeping."

In a stupor, I stumbled to the phone and told my children the most painful news they would ever hear.

The minutes and hours of that long night chipped away in agonizing slow motion. Somewhere in the haze and confusion I heard more words—the sound of my friend calling someone, requesting that a substitute teacher take her class the next morning. An unusual calmness entered my spirit: I would not be alone tomorrow.

As the first rays of sunlight washed over my bedroom window, I stood and watched the morning splash forth in glorious colours over our beautiful mountains. With a gut-wrenching sadness, I turned away, knowing it was time to start shuffling through this unprecedented day.

Within hours, the phone started to ring, and I heard love shouts from across Canada.

"We can't believe what happened! How can we help?"

"We're going to rent a bus from Lethbridge so that we all can come out for the funeral."

"Can we bring meals?"

"How are your children doing?"

"Do you have friends to walk with you through this?"

Oh yes, I had friends: our old faithful friends from all over Alberta and British Columbia, plus the new friendships we had established in Kelowna. They walked through the door in clusters. They answered my phone, put groceries in my fridge, cooked breakfasts, cleaned my bathrooms, drove me around the city, and wrapped their arms around me when I knuckled under the pain and pressure. They were the hands, arms and feet of God to give me the strength and faith to scuffle through one more hour. The beautiful, wise, love-filled shouts of my friends navigated me through the bleak murkiness of my unfamiliar new days.

In Christian circles, many of us liberally throw around the phrase, "We are made for relationships." And we say that the greatest commandment in the Bible tells us to, "Love the Lord your God with all your heart and with all your soul and with all your strength and with all your mind," and, "Love your neighbour as yourself" (Luke 10:27). Those are no longer meaningless clichés or empty words for me; this belief—lived out by my brothers and sisters in Christ by showing up when I needed them—built my faith, held me up, and kept me moving when everything went dark.

Every one of us will experience days when a phone call, a ringing doorbell, or a sentence in the doctor's office has the ugly power to thrust our present normal reality into an undefined tomorrow. Shouts of love in the dark urge us to find the courage to press on.

"Keep going."

"I will walk this journey with you, no matter what."

"When you can't believe any longer, I will believe for you."

"I'm right here."

"Don't give up. It *will* get better."

Those words are like brilliant colours unleashing hope when we are shrouded in murky darkness.

There will be seasons in our life when we are meant to receive these life-giving words, and seasons when we are meant to give them away. But whether we give the words or receive them, there is nothing sweeter than the shout of a friend that helps to build our faith in God when, suddenly, all the lights go out.

Holding His Hand

Nonfiction

Mary Ann Benjamins

Lying on the narrow slab that in the medical field passes for a bed, I can't help but wince as a cold blob of gel hits my stomach. The soft glow of the monitor does little to illumine the closet-sized space we are crammed into. Low lighting might create a soft romantic ambience in any other setting, but with the sterile grey walls and the impersonal hum of computer equipment, this room has the personality of a science lab—which makes me the rat. I struggle not to shift and groan when the probe skates back and forth over my bloated bladder.

The technician is young and our conversation awkward. The previous day I'd felt like the object of one of my kids' lame jokes. ("Mommy, spell 'P-I-G' backwards. Now say 'funny colours.' Got you, Mommy.") Except I *was* peeing in funny colours.

A hypochondriac lurks in my husband's genes and he kept nagging until I finally headed to the emergency room to get things checked out. So, a day later, here I am shivering and half-naked in an acid-green gown on a narrow cot trying to evoke a response from this serious young woman. Having an abdominal ultrasound was not how I planned to celebrate my thirty-first birthday.

With equal amounts of boredom and discomfort, I scrutinize the technician. I crack a few jokes, ineptly trying to elicit reassurance that I'm indeed wasting everyone's time. I can't decide if her stilted responses mean there is something seriously wrong or if I'm just not very funny. The shadows in the room do nothing to help me with my systematic evaluation of her every facial tic. Does the fact that she just looked at the clock mean my time is running out, or is she worried she'll be late for lunch?

The hands on the clock inch forward.

After a while, my discomfort grows to agony as she relentlessly probes my abdomen from every possible angle. Finally, she smiles a tight smile, gives me directions to the bathroom, and informs me the results will be forwarded to my doctor.

I have to be honest; I'm not a pessimist. So it takes less than five minutes out of the dreariness of that room to dispel the ghosts. With my clothes back on and my bladder emptied, the world immediately feels like a better place. Seriously, I feel fine! What could possibly be wrong? At home, over lunch, I endure a pointed interrogation by my husband, "What do you think the technician was thinking?" and questions of like nature. We go around in circles for a minute and then he subsides. If there really is something wrong, I would know, wouldn't I?

I escape and go on with my mom routine.

I have four curly-haired blonds-with-blue-eyes who all want a snack. Jantina, at eight, is the fashion guru of the family, although thankfully she's moved on from matching everything and no longer insists on dressing in purple from head to foot. Six-year-old Derek, whose mischievous eyes remind me of the constantly changing sea, has already broken more windows than any boy has a right. Anna Marie, at age three, is my adventurer, following the neighbour's cat where no child has gone before. And then there's one-year-old Johanna, who keeps her right thumb firmly in mouth—though she pulls it out regularly to tell me what she wants, or more specifically what she *doesn't* want.

Replete with cookies and juice, together we bedeck the kitchen with balloons and streamers. When Daddy finally arrives, the party starts. Only the jangle of the phone intrudes on our fun. It's Nancy, the doctor's receptionist, calling. "Hi, Mary Ann. Dr. MacDonald wonders if you can come see him in the morning?" This is the only blip on the otherwise balloon-filled horizon of birthday bliss. It is, after all, my thirty-first birthday!

Later that night, after wrestling all four kids into their beds, when we are finally nestled into our own, Ken asks if he should come with me to the doctor in the morning. Being the pastor of a church affords him some flexibility in his schedule, but he already plans to visit a widow during the same time slot, so I let him off the hook. Afterwards, snuggling beside my already-snoring husband, I laugh at my own insecurity: okay, so 31 is old, but not *that* old, and I feel fine! I tell myself a happy story and the next time I open my eyes, it's morning.

Mornings at the Benjamins' are designed to afford maximum sleep, and therefore require Swiss-timing to get everyone out the door on time, hopefully clothed and usually fed. Lunches actually in the back-pack are worth extra bonus points! In the middle of the jumble of that morning, I realize I no longer want to go to the doctor by myself.

Ken is quick to acquiesce and after some calls to arrange baby-sitters and switch his schedule, he and I are off to what we both see as a non-event. I feel kind of stupid for even making him come with me, but Ken is the easy-going one in our relationship, so I let it go. It's autumn, my favourite season, and I'm with Ken, my favourite guy. God loves me and all is well with my universe.

The fact that our doctor's office is in a basement should be a clue, right? We're immediately ushered into the doctor's private office… another bad sign. By the time my bottom hits the vinyl of the chair, my heart is pounding. Facing us from behind his paper-strewn desk, Dr. MacDonald, an archetypal Scot, does nothing to sugar-coat the news: there is a large mass in my kidney and things don't look good.

The sounds all run together after that, and I sit stunned. Words such as "appointments," "specialists" and "scans" flow around me for a few minutes. What I see is the worry, the helplessness, in my doctor's eyes. Suddenly, he slams his fist to the desk and swears, "By God, we're going to beat the hell out of this! Don't worry, you're in good hands." Like a child stomping his feet in denial after being caught red-handed, his fierce words, taking God's name in vain, serve to ignite equal parts fear and fury in my heart.

I can't take any more. I jump out of the chair, and run out of his office, up the stairs, and through the front doors.

His words follow me, and I have nowhere to go. The sun is hidden in clouds and the sharp wind slaps my face as the glass doors smack closed behind me. I stand helplessly in the parking lot, searching for somewhere to hide. I see our van, run to its sanctuary and curl up in the front seat, my stomach a solid knot. The words follow me still—the ugliness of the profanity overwhelms me. How dare he use my God's name like that? How dare I have cancer? I feel bile rising in my throat, choking me. At the same time, tumbling thoughts and tears break through. The gloomy cooled sky does nothing to fire up my natural optimism. Reverberating in my brain, the doctor's mantra repeats itself and I rock back and forth hoping for something, *anything* to grasp hold of.

His words reshape themselves. "You're in good hands."

I remember to breathe in and out. Hands. He has no idea whose hands I'm in! I will not, cannot, place my hope for life in his hands, or the hands of a doctor I have yet to meet. Hugging myself, I know, with a certainty I might not always feel, that I am in God's hands. Somehow, even in this, I feel His presence. The knot in my stomach unfurls a little, and with my hand timidly in His, one small hurdle is scaled.

Eventually, Ken and I stumble home. Though I want time to get off the planet and process the information I've been given, having a houseful of children doesn't afford me that time. Babies still want their bottles, toddlers want to play, six-year-olds want Mommy to look at their school papers, and wide-eyed eight-year-olds want to know why Mommy has been crying.

Ken and I gather our little chicks into the now-sunny living-room and try to explain to them what is going on. The idea of explaining cancer to kids seems really difficult, but they make it very simple. Derek asks, "Does this mean you're going to die?"

Glancing at Ken across the room, I draw strength from him and swallow the huge lump in my throat. I explain that God will take care of us either way and yes, I could die, but probably not soon. If and when the time might come, he will know. I promise that they'll never have to guess what's happening.

Derek looks at my tear-stained face and serious expression and quips, "Does that mean you'll look like this, Mommy?" He puts his hands to his throat and throws himself to the ground, gagging and choking, staging a dramatic demonstration of my possible impending death. We all burst into laughter and the pressure seeps away like air out of a balloon. I scoop up my son and with tears and laughter, tumble with him back onto the carpeted floor. Only the living can play dead.

With the setting of the sun, my tenuous hold on peace begins to evaporate. The little ones go to bed early and as stillness settles over the house and darkness falls, fear once again begins to rise in my throat. I simulate watching television, but nothing can stave off the dread of the coming night.

I have to be honest. Up until today, I've had it good. Ken is a saint. *Really.* (Not that I don't want to kill him occasionally, but according to him, that's only because we have occasional "misunderstandings".) We have four healthy, smart, beautiful kids. Ken's job is going great. We love our church and, amazingly, they love us too. They even love me, which I find hard to believe. I am a pastor's wife whose only skill is my ability to carry a conversation. No, I can't carry a tune or sing solos, I can't play the piano, and I hate coffee. But I can talk… and talk. Here I am with a great family in a great community. I have everything. Life is wonderful.

Relentlessly, the dark seeps in the windows and silence steals over the house. Though we go through the motions of readying for bed, my stomach clenches and my mind races and I'm filled with an unending restlessness. I climb into bed beside Ken and we talk and I cry and I cling to him. I can't seem to stop shaking. I'm cold. So cold. Though Ken holds me, he grows sleepy, and when I sense him nodding off, I suddenly feel completely alone and adrift.

Cancer. The word reverberates in my trembling heart. I creep out of bed, out of the room, down the stairs to a couch, and I lie there hugging my arms around myself, desperately seeking peace. If only I could stop shaking. I just want to know everything will be okay.

Ken is a born fixer. Up until that day, Ken fixed everything. Not that I don't pull my load, but he always seems to know what to do. He fixes things and people and problems, and the one thing I so admire about him is that he is always unerringly sure of himself. Or at least he fakes it well—well enough to make *me* feel safe and comfortable.

He notices that I've left our bed, follows me downstairs, sits beside me and hugs me again. But this time there really isn't anything he can do or say to fix my problem. Ken is the minister. He is *my* minister. But he has no magic formula or prayer or anything that can put this right. Faced with the most serious problem I've ever had, he can't fix it. I convince him to go back to bed to get some sleep, but I stay downstairs. I need time to think.

Lying on the couch, I look out the big picture window into the infinite inky sky and realize that somehow I have allowed Ken to become the intermediary between me and God. Ken is a good man and a pastor. I am the random-talking pistol. He has the theological credentials and I am… broken.

I fall to the ground and fold my hands to pray. Hands. I close my eyes and throw myself into God's hands. Again. His words whisper to my spirit, and ever so slowly I remember to breathe in and out. Again.

I'd like to think that after tonight everything will be okay. That my trembling hands will stop shaking and my stomach will be knot-free; that I'll never again have moments of fear where my stomach feels like a washing machine on the spin cycle.

The truth is more complicated, but Jesus helps me keep it very simple. I'm in His hands. Even when I forget or I feel hurled off into space, He's there—pulling me back, shaping me and reshaping me—and I'm always, *always*, in His hands.

So maybe I'm not perfect and maybe my life isn't always just what the doctor ordered either. Maybe I'll still have "misunderstandings" with my husband and maybe Ken can't fix everything. But it doesn't really matter. I've got my hand firmly in the hand of the One who is and was and always will be. And that's enough for today.

As it says in Habakkuk 3:17–19:

> Though the fig tree does not bud
> and there are no grapes on the vines,
> though the olive crop fails
> and the fields produce no food,
> though there are no sheep in the pen
> and no cattle in the stalls,
> yet I will rejoice in the Lord,
> I will be joyful in God my Saviour.
> The Sovereign Lord is my strength;
> he makes my feet like the feet of a deer,
> he enables me to go on the heights.

Chrysalis: Life in the Making

Nonfiction

Ruth Smith Meyer

They say opposites attract and we sure were opposites. Although my husband Norm had a sense of humour that occasionally made his face light up and his clear, blue eyes sparkle with glee, he was so quiet that many people wondered if he ever expressed opinions of his own. I, on the other hand, seemed to have an inner compulsion to explain everything to the last detail. Norm had to figure things out in his mind before he could express himself; I worked out my strategies by talking through them. He loved his privacy and time alone with the family; I was at my best with a whole group of friends around me. I loved writing; Norm did anything to avoid it. I did some of my best work between nine and midnight; Norm wanted to be in bed by 9:30 p.m. at the latest. Neither of us was right or wrong—we were just different.

Funny, those differences had originally drawn us to one another. I was a 14-year-old student when Norm came to do the milking at our farm while my parents went on a three-week trip. Although it was his sense of humour I most enjoyed, I admired his quiet strength and comforting presence. He was almost four years older, but he took note of me, and he admired my ability to put my thoughts into words and the readiness with which I could express my viewpoints. When we started dating a few years later, I learned to love his introspective nature; he was drawn to my outgoing personality.

That changed in a hurry after we were married. Within our first year, I found it maddening when, after an hour of trying to maintain a conversation, I'd ask Norm what he was thinking or feeling and he'd give his answer: "Nothing." He claimed he had no feelings. Now, really!

Where my ability to put my thoughts into words had fascinated and pleased him while we were dating, it soon started to annoy him once we were married. My attempts at conversation apparently taxed his patience and his peace of mind.

After a week of cooking, cleaning and housework, I looked forward to entertaining friends or going visiting. Norm wanted to stay home—just the two of us—alone. When I tried to relieve him of my chatter by going out with my friends, he became suspicious and withdrew all the more. When I got involved in community organizations, exercising my gifts and abilities, he seemed to feel threatened, although he never verbalized it. One look at his tight lips made it clear enough. If I did ask what was the matter, of course his reply was, "Nothing!"

Our son and daughter, born only 14 months apart, brought us joy and helped us work together, but also added a new dimension to our differences because of our varied parenting techniques. By the time our third child arrived, we were under even more stress. We had taken over my father's dairy farm, with twice-a-day milking and an 80-tree orchard to look after, and a mountain of bills to be paid.

At the same time, I was helping look after my grandmother, who displayed signs of dementia and needed to be carefully watched. We had less time for small talk—and because it took a lot of time for Norm to express anything, his verbal contributions were few and far between. The friction between us kept building.

The "quiet strength" I had admired during courtship began to feel more and more like a big club held menacingly over my head. If he wasn't going to tell me what was wrong, how could I change? I tried to guess what displeased him and make changes accordingly, so as not to inflict myself upon him. I entertained much less frequently than I would have liked. I tried to keep my opinions to myself, while at the same time I tried to draw out his opinions as gently as I could. I even attempted to get the children to bed earlier to give us time alone. But the more I tried, the worse the tension became.

Things came to a head soon after our ninth anniversary. Late one stress-filled night when the children had taken too long to settle down to sleep, I was dead-tired. Norm had gone to bed much earlier. I crawled into bed looking forward to finally getting some rest. Just as I was drifting off to sleep, Norm blurted out, "I don't plan to leave you and the kids, but you might as well know I'm finished with our marriage. Don't expect me to put any more effort into our relationship."

I was immediately wide awake. Hurt beyond belief, I was momentarily dumbfounded. *What effort?* I wondered to myself. *I'm the only one trying in this marriage.*

I finally found my voice. "So what are you saying? I'm supposed to just be your housemaid and nanny for our children?"

He turned away to hug the other side of the bed and answered, "Suit yourself!"

I went to sleep with tears running down my cheeks. Norm didn't budge from his side of the bed.

The following days were a deep freeze. We got up in the morning without our customary hug and "Good morning!" Conversation took place at meals, but only about items of daily living that had to be addressed—doctors' appointments, the children's activities, parts Norm wanted me to pick up at farm machinery dealerships. *I'm obviously still useful for these kinds of mundane tasks*, I muttered under my breath whenever he asked me to run errands.

My first dozen attempts to ask if we could talk about our situation got no reply. Finally he answered abruptly, "Nothing to talk about."

After weeks of this treatment, I formulated a plan for the New Year. With a lot of prayer, but without consulting Norm, I arranged for someone to take over milking the cows for a long weekend in January, and for a sister-in-law to stay with the three children, now aged seven, six and two.

I packed our bags and informed him on Thursday night that we were leaving the next morning.

"What for and where to?" he asked in a flat voice.

"To a motel, where we will stay for the weekend and where we will talk," I answered.

No comment.

I wasn't sure Norm was going to co-operate, but the next morning we did leave. I drove.

We rode in silence except for the odd remark about the winter landscape or passing traffic. And then suddenly we drove into a raging blizzard. The car radio informed us that all major roads were closed. Bucking drifts and peering through the blowing snow, we finally reached our exit. We manoeuvred around road closure barricades to reach our motel and adjoining restaurant. The wind kept blowing. It was obvious we weren't going to be leaving any time soon.

There was nothing to do at the motel except to sit staring at one another or talk. To begin, we did more staring than talking, while I silently prayed in desperation.

Finally, Norm's words came spewing out.

I was taken aback by his intensity. Norm never yelled, but the deep anger and frustration were evident in the controlled emphasis of his voice. He made it clear that all the changes I had made over the years had been misguided efforts—the very things that fed his frustration, insecurity and anger.

"You never tell me anything any more." His brows were furrowed with pain. "You're always talking to your women friends on the phone or going to their places. You're telling them things you don't tell me. I don't count any more. I think you'd rather be with other people than me. And whenever I try to tell you how I see it, you argue back and make me feel I'm all wrong."

After another day and a half of finding out all that I was doing wrong, bit by barbed bit, I was decimated. The list of my faults was long. I talked too much. I tried to help him finish his sentences if it took him too long to get the right words. I praised other people for the things they did, but he felt only disapproval from me. I could speak in public, whereas his legs shook at the very thought of it. I could do anything I turned my hand at, but he had only a few strengths he felt were worthwhile.

Since explaining my side came through to him as arguing or telling him he was wrong, I tried to keep silent.

Through the bits of night remaining after his outbursts, he slept. I tossed and turned, trying to think how I could get him to express his needs while still acknowledging my own. I was pleading with God, *Help me out here!* How could it all fit together?

It truly was a very long weekend, made longer by snow-covered roads necessitating that we stay an extra day.

Norm finally *had* shared what was wrong, for which I was thankful, but he hadn't said if there was anything he *did* like about me, nor had he suggested ways I could still be myself while meeting his needs. Furthermore, his dissatisfaction had made every strength I thought I had feel like a weakness. I was so devastated by his revelations that I had no idea of where to go from there.

Finally, the storm let up outside so we could go home, but a new storm raged within me. I've often heard the saying, "What the caterpillar calls the end of the world, the Master calls a butterfly." I was hoping that was true in our marriage. With that weekend, the caterpillar of our marriage had been wrapped up, ready to die. Would something better emerge from the cocoon?

During the next year, it took many agonizing prayers on my behalf and long hours of talking far into the night before Norm could express his desires. His revelations often made me cry, which upset him. I kept telling him, "Even if it makes me cry, I *need* to know what you're feeling." But I didn't know how to hear his thoughts without becoming filled with more guilt.

Through a family life committee on which I served at church, I became aware of the Marriage Encounter movement, a program aimed at revitalizing marriages through weekend retreats that are sponsored by many faith groups in dozens of countries. Norm reluctantly agreed to go, so I immediately signed us up for the next retreat held in Niagara Falls, Ontario.

At Marriage Encounter, we were not only given tools to improve our communication, but time to practice using those tools. We learned to accept responsibility for only our own feelings, receive each other's feelings without viewing them as something we have to fix or change, and respond to each other's sharing with compassion and love. What a treat to have Norm write down some of his innermost thoughts to share with me! Instead of seeing only his own perceptions and needs, he began to hear mine too. I heard and acknowledged his pain, and he did the same for mine. It was exquisite delight.

Finally, we could truly hear each other with our hearts. That's when the butterfly began to break free and stretch its wings to reveal its full beauty.

When we came home, we tried to allow each other our own strengths. Oh, we hit more bumps on the road, but as we learned to share and listen—not only to the words we spoke or wrote, but also to the cries of our hearts—our understanding of each other deepened. As another daughter joined our family, we began to see how our separate and diverse personality traits really were a gift to each other.

I learned that every last detail didn't *have* to be shared; he learned that he didn't need to have everything *totally* and *completely* worked out in his mind before he put it into words. I began to celebrate his ability to see underneath the obvious to the crux of the matter, and often asked his help to clarify my thinking through an issue; he began to fully support me in my more public roles. He even joined me in reading Scripture during the church service or mutually leading a devotional at a meeting.

Because we were so grateful for how the Marriage Encounter movement had changed our lives, we took positions on the board for our Ontario region. Within a few years, we even joined the teams of couples who told their own stories at Marriage Encounter retreats. Norm was amazed at the response he got from the other "quiet" spouses, who appreciated his ability to voice their viewpoints. He soon overcame his reticence and rejoiced to feel that he was finally free to use the talents God had given him.

One by one, over the next decade, we dealt with all the major issues that brought tension. We looked forward to retirement and more time to spend with one another as a complementary team.

However, a year before we planned to give up our daily work and start the next era of our lives, Norm was diagnosed with colon cancer. At first, we thought we could fight it, but three months later, the doctors told us it had spread to his liver. It was terminal.

Typical of the man he had become, when he was told this news Norm said, "Let's accept what we know, go home and take care of business, get you and the family ready for what's coming, then just enjoy to the fullest every day we have left."

The next four months became some of the most precious we spent during our 39 years of marriage. We voiced all our thoughts and withheld nothing. We included our grown children in our openness, helping them deal with grief and grow by the experience. Time and time again, after deeply revealing our inmost thoughts, one or both of us would exclaim, "Thank God for Marriage Encounter!"

Norm wrote love letters to all four of his children, his sons- and daughter-in-law, and his five grandchildren. As death approached, Norman was passionate about wanting all of our married friends and relatives to experience all they could in their relationships.

In the last weeks of his life, many people came to kneel at his bedside, to tell Norm how much they appreciated him and to affirm the gift he had been to them. Each time, he offered them a blessing, reminding them to keep on following the Lord and to be strong in Him.

With the help of home-care nurses and medications to control the pain, Norm was able to stay at home until the end. The night before he died, as we lay side by side in our bed, he held my hand and told me, "You've been a good wife, Ruth—the very best."

Before sunrise the next morning, I was awakened by hearing him joyously exclaiming, "Yes, YES!" As I studied his face, I realized that Norm was seeing something I could not. After a while, he began to whisper "Home!" with each breath.

I laid my head beside him on the pillow and softly sang, "Lead me gently home, Father, Lead me gently home; When life's toils are ended, And parting days have come..."[1] I sensed that I was serenading my beloved into eternity.

With Norm's last breath, the sun broke over the horizon and shone into our bedroom window. Through my tears, I thanked God for His love and grace that had enabled our once troubled marriage to develop into a beautiful butterfly. Lingering in that holy moment, I wondered what would emerge for me from the shadows of this new, dark cocoon.

1. Will L. Thompson, "Lead Me Gently Home, Father." Public Domain.

38

The Forever Kind of Love

 Ruth Smith Meyer

Love...
    not the sweet, gushy, gooey kind
        that spreads sticky sweetness
            over hidden hurts
                and buried resentments.

Love...
    not the fast, thrilling, self-seeking kind
        that fills the present moment,
            and that only,
                then fades away with dawn.

Love...
    not the long-suffering, silent type
        that refuses to ripple still waters,
            but silently bears the martyr's role
                and sits in judgment.

But Love...
    that dares to confront, to confide,
        to suffer turmoil, the stripping of masks:
            to stand naked and vulnerable,
                to reach out and accept.

Love...
    that comes from knowing, truly knowing,
        each revealed strength and weakness
            accepted as a cherished gift,
                handled with loving care.

Love...
>> that draws out hidden strengths,
>>> and gives encouragement
>>>> to each one's personal dreams,
>>>>> then shares in the growing pains.

Love...
>> that offers full respect for what now is,
>>> in anticipation of what is yet to be,
>>>> while ready to move forward,
>>>>> to walk together, with God.

Life with a Capital "L"

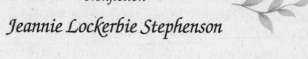

Nonfiction

Jeannie Lockerbie Stephenson

"I just can't see why you won't tell us where you're going," Mom complained. "We won't try to stop you. If you and Kay are old enough to have full-time jobs, I guess at 19 you're old enough to take a trip by yourselves. It's just that your car is so old and unreliable, and neither of you is an experienced driver."

She paused to take a breath, then continued worrying aloud, "And it's November already. The weather is unpredictable. Why, there could be freezing rain or even snow at this time of year."

"And, and, and…" I argued. "Can't you see we just want to go away and be free for a while? We'll stay on safe roads. Maybe we'll go to Washington."

We had no intention of going 200 miles south to Washington, D.C. For three years we had studied hard and worked increasingly long shifts on the wards as student nurses. Since our first paycheques—in fact, since our September graduation from the Methodist Hospital School of Nursing in Brooklyn, New York—my friend Kay and I had been planning a road trip to Québec. We would stay in a ritzy hotel with room service. We would eat dainty *petits fours* and *crêpes suzette* in quaint French restaurants. We would shop and, for once, do whatever we wanted to do with no restrictions from parents or instructors.

The Saturday drive through upstate New York was gorgeous with the leaves on the trees dressed in the reds and golds of fall. Crossing the border into Canada and arriving in Montréal, we were tired, but also exhilarated. The first couple of hotels were too pricey for our budget, but we found a pleasant room in a small hotel.

On Sunday morning we located an English-speaking church. Neither of us heard much of the message. We felt we were doing God a favour just by attending. We declined invitations to spend the rest of the day with the friendly church people. The afternoon slipped by in a round of sightseeing: Saint Joseph's Oratory, McGill University, and the museum with exhibits of life-like historical figures made out of wax.

A light snow was falling by late Sunday afternoon when I got my next inspiration. "Since we've come this far, let's drive on to Québec City. There's a lot to see there."

Twenty miles outside Montréal, we began to hear strange putt-putts from the front of the car. We pulled into a service station.

"I can get you going all right, but you'd better have it checked first thing in the morning," warned the attendant. "Don't go far tonight. There's a storm blowing up. And it's illegal here to drive in the snow without chains," he added, noting our New York State licence plate.

By the time we steered back onto the highway, we could see why he'd told us not to drive far. Our smooth tires scooted the car across the road.

"There's a motel ahead. Let's pull in there," I suggested.

The proprietress was glad to give us a room, confident she wouldn't get any more business from other customers on a night like this.

The next morning, we awoke to find an igloo-shaped mound of freshly fallen snow where we'd parked. We donned our warmest clothes and began to dig out the car. Discovering our hidden treasure, however, brought short-lived joy. No amount of coaxing, fuming, or poking under the hood would make that motor turn over. It wouldn't even give a hopeful sputter. Kay and I walked back to the motel office.

This time, the motel manager hustled us into her sitting room. At least it was warm in there. It became warmer still when the woman, in all kindness, insisted we drink a small glass of whiskey so we wouldn't catch cold. As we forced it down, we realized we hadn't eaten anything since yesterday noon. After being assured that her two sons could get the car going, we had nothing to do but wait.

The sons tried hard, but on late Monday afternoon, they used their farm truck to push us into the same service station as the night before.

"You two again!" exclaimed the attendant. "I thought I told you to get that thing fixed. You've got a leak in the radiator and keep losing antifreeze."

After the mechanic got the car somewhat patched up, we resigned ourselves to turning around and returning to Montréal. Oh, for that comfortable hotel room and some food! Forget the *petits fours*. We were starved, and anything would taste good!

Cautiously, we headed onto the highway, but almost immediately a highway patrolman held up his mittened hand in front of the car and announced that the road was closed. He motioned us to a side road, then hurried on to speak to the people in the car behind us.

The side road consisted of two ruts with snow banks higher than the car on either side. We had no idea where this road was going and it was impossible to turn around. The car's overtaxed heater wasn't working properly and left us in a state of constantly chattering teeth. We had no food, and now it was twilight. A surge of panic nearly made us stop in our tracks, but we saw the headlights of a car following us and had to keep going.

As it got darker, we had more and more difficulty seeing where we were going, and suddenly we plowed right into a snow bank. We felt a jolt and heard scraping as we struck something—maybe a rock—that was buried in the drifted snow. After a few moments, we climbed out of the car. We had no idea what to do next.

We were surprised to see a burly man with a flashlight trudging through the snow from his house about 50 metres back from the road. He came up to us and surveyed the damage, then peeled forth a string of French, not one word of which we understood.

We stammered, "We don't understand."

To which he replied, while motioning with his hands, "Come. My house."

We were too cold, too tired, and too hungry to do anything but follow. As we walked through the deep drifts toward the lights of his house, our feet became blocks of ice and the hair outside our scarves froze solid.

Thawing out in the farm kitchen, we realized that we knew nothing about this man or the situation we were in. Fortunately, there was a wife, a rather dowdy woman of uncertain age. After her husband spoke to her sharply, she produced bread and hot coffee as though she had been through this routine before.

The black-haired, heavy-set man paced the room while we ate, but his eyes never left us. We couldn't understand what he was saying, but his lurid stare and his hands edging ever closer to Kay's shoulder were suggestive in any language.

Suddenly the phone rang. The man answered, then handed the receiver to Kay. Surprised, she listened to a young man say in English, "We were in the car behind you. We saw you were in trouble, but we couldn't help you because we ran into a drift ourselves. We're staying in the house next door. Be careful, won't you? Now let me talk to that man again."

A minute later, the man hung up. Brusquely, he ordered us to sleep in the room with his wife, then slammed the door behind him as he stomped upstairs. Not saying one word, the wife pointed to a room off the kitchen.

Still fully dressed, Kay and I lay on top of the blankets on the double bed, exhausted.

At some point in the night, the wife joined us and spread a dirty duvet over all three of us.

The next thing we knew, the morning sun was shining in through the grimy window. The wife was still snoring as we placed some money on the kitchen table to pay for our accommodations, put on our coats and boots, and hurried out the door. The car wasn't far away, but the deep snow made walking difficult.

As we trudged down the road toward our car, a woman called out in English from the house next door to tell us that the men who'd stayed overnight with her had gone on ahead to a nearby garage. They would arrange for a tow truck to come and get us.

Soon we were riding high in the cab of the truck. With the driver safely manoeuvring the ruts, we had time to see the beauty of the glistening snow.

But all too soon, we were brought back to reality.

"You've cracked your block," the serviceman told us, gesturing upward at our car on the hoist. "It will take the best part of the day to install another."

We had no idea what he was talking about, but "Oh, dear!" seemed an appropriate comment.

We were saying "Oh, dear!" for the third time when two young men who'd been sitting in the waiting room walked over and introduced themselves.

"I'm Pete and this is Joe," the older one said. "Looks like we're all going to be here for a while. We've got car trouble, too. Let's go to the café next door and get some coffee to warm up."

The waitress had just set coffee and rolls on the table when Pete said, "I always pray before I eat. Do you mind?"

Without waiting for an answer, he bowed his head and thanked God for the safety of the night before and for the food. Then he asked the Lord to lead all of us today.

We opened our eyes. Rather sheepishly, Kay said, "We're Christians, too."

"You are?" Pete asked. "Say, that's fine, just fine!"

As we devoured the rolls with butter and jam, we started talking. Since there was nowhere else to go, we just sat and talked until both cars were ready to be driven again. We told them about our families, our churches, and nursing school in Brooklyn.

Pete and Joe explained that they lived in Montréal and were helping to get a new church started there. They had been on their way to visit some relatives of church members when they got caught in the storm.

Late Tuesday afternoon, just before the appointed time to get our now-repaired cars, Pete turned to us and said, "You know, I've been wanting to ask you all day. How did you two land up here like this?"

Then it all came out. I talked, and Kay interrupted as necessary, telling them all about our plans for the holiday—the ritzy hotel, the shopping, and, most of all, the freedom. "We wanted to do something exciting."

"We've just finished the grind of nursing school and now we'll be tied down to full-time jobs," Kay added.

"The truth is," I said, "we're bored with the monotony in our church. And being raised in Christian homes, we've had so many restrictions."

"Oh," Pete interjected, "I see. You wanted to live a bit. You wanted to see some life."

"That's it, Pete," we both answered. "We wanted life with a capital 'L.'"

"You two don't seem to realize the danger you've been in," Pete continued, his voice getting agitated. "That car of yours isn't in very good shape. You could have been killed on the highway. And the house you stayed in last night—why, the neighbour told us that that man has been in jail for molesting young women!"

As Kay and I sank lower and lower into our seats, Pete kept talking, "And even Joe and me, you didn't know us. We were just pickups. I'm not going to preach you a sermon, but when we get you settled somewhere tonight, will you promise to read John 10:10?"

We nodded our heads, promising that we'd do as he asked.

Back at the service station, both cars were tested and pronounced fit to drive. Then the mechanic produced the bill for our repairs. Kay and I went into a huddle and emptied every compartment in both of our purses. After we paid it, we had $2.87 left between us.

Pete and Joe said they'd drive ahead of us to make sure we were all right. Once more, we headed to Montréal. When we got to the outskirts of the city, Pete pulled his car off the highway and walked back to ours. He leaned in the driver's side window and said, "I don't mean to embarrass you, but back there at the garage it looked as if you were a little short of cash. We can take you to the Salvation Army Hostel, if you'd like."

Without looking at each other, we both replied, "Yes, that would be good."

In the lobby of the hostel, we said good-bye to our new friends. Then we took stock of our situation. First, a phone call home—collect of course—asking our parents to wire us money and reassuring them we were fine. Next, one cheese sandwich and one carton of milk to share. Cost? Eighty-five cents.

With $1.01 each left over, we carried our bags to the Charity Room of the hostel. There, for the fee of $1.00 per person, we could have our choice of two in a row of eight army cots, and the use of a bathroom at the end of the hall. Leaving us with precisely one cent each. Where was our swanky hotel with room service? Where were our *petits fours* and *crêpes suzette*?

After we shared our meagre supper, we sat on our adjacent lumpy cots. "We promised Pete we'd read John 10:10, remember?" Thrusting my pocket New Testament toward Kay, I said, "Here, you read it."

"I have come that they might have life, and have it to the full," she read softly.

What fools we had been! Running all over the place, worrying our families, endangering our lives, looking for LIFE, when all along we had within us the source, the *power* for abundant life—the Lord Jesus Christ.

As we flopped down, exhausted, on the hard cots, the announcer on a radio playing in the room next door blared, "Travel advisory... worst blizzard in years... driving is very hazardous... extreme caution is..."

Before he finished, we were asleep.

Four years later, I was overseas in South Asia, working as a missionary in the country that would later come to be known as Bangladesh. For more than three decades, I served as a nurse, teacher, and director of a Christian literature program.

Living through wars, cyclones, and tropical diseases, I had enough excitement to last a lifetime. I also learned that when I do what God wants me to do, in the place where He wants me to be, I can have LIFE with a capital "L."

My Mother's Gift

Nonfiction

Ann Brent

The first day of school was one of my favourite days of the year. I loved orange-yellow HB pencils with soft rose-coloured erasers. I loved the smell that wafted out of a brand new box of crayons with their perfect chiselled tips. And I loved the empty, lined pages of my notebooks that would soon capture my thoughts in writing.

The only thing I dreaded about that day was the first half hour when my new teacher would read the class list aloud and demand information I simply didn't have.

Classes at my elementary school began each day by singing "God Save the Queen." After the teacher read a Bible story, we recited The Lord's Prayer together. Then the roll call began. When "Violet Ann" rang out across the classroom, I acknowledged my presence, and the questions started.

Privacy rules were nonexistent in the 1960s, making each detail of pertinent information public to the whole class. Unusual names brought snickers. One of my answers inspired confused whispers every year.

"Mother's name?" asked the teacher.

"Joyce," I responded.

"Father's name?"

"I don't have one," I answered quietly, providing the answer I dreaded giving. Two-parent families were still the norm in the early sixties, so my response always drew stares from my curious classmates. It was bad enough to say it once, but my grade three teacher persevered, "Violet, what is your father's name?"

Later, I would explain that I preferred Ann to Violet, but first I had to convince her that I really didn't have a father. At least no father I knew anything about.

Those memories raced through my mind on a Saturday morning more than 20 years later as I sipped my tea, waiting for the doorbell to ring. The thought of meeting my father for the first time was bound to stir the emotional pot.

As I waited, I looked over at my grandfather, a surprise visitor, sitting on our brown vinyl sofa in the family room, a storybook in his hand and my two young children cuddled on either side of him. We were all treasuring our few short days together and dreading our impending good-byes.

I had seen my father's father only twice in my 32 years, so I'd been shocked to find this dear man sitting in my yellow kitchen when I arrived home on Wednesday evening. My husband George was busy setting the table and visiting with Gramp when I brought the children home from their piano lessons.

More shocking than his presence was Gramp's news that he had hitched a ride to our house in Ontario from Manitoba with my father, a man I had never met and knew little about, and that my father would be arriving at our house on Saturday morning to pick him up for the return trip.

Now and then while I was growing up, I sometimes asked my mom about my father. On occasion, especially after watching a television family complete with a dad, or seeing my best friend interact with her father, I had pestered my mom for details.

"Where is my dad?"

"What was he like?"

"Why doesn't he live with us?"

I don't remember how my mom responded to any of these questions, but she deftly moved the conversation along or changed the subject without ever conveying the answers I sought.

Now I understand that the deep hurts she'd experienced had forced her to create a wall of protection, but as a child, I couldn't appreciate her situation, and was frustrated at having so many questions and no answers.

By the time I reached high school, the answers weren't as important to me, and I stopped asking questions. Growing up without a father was normal for me. It was the only life I knew, and most of the time I didn't miss having a dad.

All my life, my father's parents had faithfully kept in touch with me, mostly by mail due to the distance that separated us.

Mom and I had travelled by train to Manitoba from our home in Windsor when I was four years old, but I didn't return until I was an adult with my own husband and children. Gram had died shortly before our family's planned visit, so Gramp appreciated even more having us stay at their farm near Riding Mountain National Park.

When I was 25, Mom died at only 53 years of age—from metastasized uterine cancer—having never said one unkind thing to me about the absent man who was my father.

It was only after her death that I learned something about him and the difficult life he had created for Mom and me. He had left not long into their marriage while Mom was pregnant with me—leaving her, I was told, with substantial debts he'd somehow incurred, and no source of income.

Mom had plenty of reasons to become an angry, bitter woman, but she was just the opposite. After I was born, she found a job at a laundry and dry cleaning business, where she worked throughout my childhood to support us. The physically demanding labour left her exhausted at the end of each day, but she persevered for her tiny paycheque, working long and hard to pay off his bills, all the while taking good care of me and providing a happy, though humble, life for the two of us.

I grew up never doubting my mom's love and her support in every part of my life, but my shy, quiet mother found it difficult to share her thoughts and feelings. She didn't talk to me about courage and strength; she portrayed those qualities. And that message spoke to me louder than any words she might have used.

Now, as a young mom myself, I wondered if I could have been as strong as my mother had been. Would I have held my tongue, resisting the urge to assign blame or speak negatively about an absent husband whose actions had caused desperate and long-lasting problems?

I wondered if my mother's faith in her Heavenly Father had given her the strength and courage she needed to carry on. Did she cling to the same words of Scripture that have helped me through difficulties and given me hope? Words like those found in Isaiah 41:10: "So do not fear, for I am with you; do not be dismayed, for I am your God. I will strengthen you and help you; I will uphold you with my righteous right hand."

Giggles and chatter from the family room drew me out of my deep thoughts. I smiled at the sight before me and determined to treasure that picture of Gramp with my children, not knowing when, if ever, we would be together again.

Thursday and Friday had flown by, filled with normal family life made special by Gramp's presence and involvement. We'd driven along the shores of Lake Huron near our home in Brights Grove, pointing out the sandy beaches we enjoy each summer and showing him the original Bluewater Bridge that links Ontario to Michigan.

Friday evening had arrived before Gramp and I were able to visit alone with a cup of tea. He told me how much he missed my Grandma, but assured me he was doing fine. And while the children were quietly watching a *Gilligan's Island* rerun on television with their dad in the family room, I'd turned our conversation to God. I wanted to make sure I shared my story with Gramp before he left for home the next day.

"After Mom died, I wanted to know what happened to her," I said. "I didn't understand if heaven and hell were real places. And if they were real, I wanted to know if she was in heaven."

Gramp remained silent, but leaned slightly toward me.

"I decided to try to get to know God. So I went to a Bible study with ladies from my church and I started reading my Bible. Little by little, I began to understand that God loves me and wants to have a relationship with me."

Gramp appeared to be fully engaged in my story, so I continued. "I believe that God sent His Son Jesus into the world, to show us His love. God promises us that whoever believes in Him will not die, but will have eternal life with Him in heaven."

"Do you think heaven is real?" Gramp asked.

"I do. Absolutely," I continued. "Gramp, knowing Jesus has changed my life. God has forgiven me, I am now His child, and I know without a doubt, I will go to heaven when I die."

As I shared my heart and my faith that evening, Gramp had listened attentively, tears running down his cheeks. Being the reserved man he was, he made few comments, but I could see that my words had touched him deeply.

"I found some papers and keepsakes in my mom's stuff that make me think that she loved Jesus too. And because of that, I hope to see her again in heaven one day." I took a deep breath and grabbed my grandfather's hands before I continued, "Gramp, I'd love to spend eternity in heaven with you, too."

He squeezed my hands and held on, looking straight into my eyes, his face still wet with tears.

At that moment, the children had come bounding up the stairs, ending our quiet conversation. But my last night with Gramp will always remain with me, a cherished memory.

Saturday morning had dawned clear and calm, in contrast to the turbulence I was experiencing in the pit of my stomach while I waited for my father to arrive.

The doorbell rang as I was carrying my empty mug to the kitchen sink. The man who was my biological father stood outside on the sidewalk.

Not knowing what to expect, I walked down the steps to the family room and opened our side door. A slight man, about my height, with a brush cut and wearing glasses, stood on the other side of the screen door. He was dressed in jeans and a plaid flannel shirt. It struck me that I could walk by him on the street and there was absolutely nothing that would make me think I had any connection to him.

He nodded his head slightly. "Hi."

"Hi." I opened the door, inviting him in.

He stepped inside, but never left the entryway.

Looking back, I'm not sure if I invited him any further inside.

He said hello to George, looked briefly at our children, and then said he was ready to go. After hugs and kisses for Gramp all around, both men left. My father had moved in and out of my life in a flash.

My family grasped the significance of the moment they had witnessed and watched quietly for my reaction. George stepped close, his arms enclosing me, to offer the loving support he thought I might need.

"I just met my father," I said aloud, mostly to myself, trying to process my feelings. How was a person supposed to feel after such a meeting? I felt nothing. I was neither disappointed nor sad. I felt no longing for what might have been. It just seemed strange that after so many years of wondering, I had finally laid eyes on my father, and discovered that he was merely a stranger to whom I had no connection—a father in name only.

I had wondered if I would feel deep emotions, but there were none. As I had told my teachers so long ago, I really didn't have a father. And I was okay with that.

I would be forever grateful to him for the brief, but wonderful, time he had given us with Gramp. To have had the opportunity to share my faith in Jesus and words of hope with that dear man was a gift I never expected. And when we received the news only six weeks later that Gramp had passed away, I was even more grateful, and humbled, to realize how God had arranged that visit.

I never saw my father again, but my childhood curiosity had been satisfied. No more questions needed to be asked, or answered.

And I finally understood that my mother's silence, which had so frustrated me as a child, was actually a precious gift. Instead of using words to tear down someone who had hurt her deeply, she left those words unsaid. My mother never spoke unkindly about my father, never instilled anger towards him, never encouraged distrust or hatred towards men.

Whether or not she consciously realized it, my shy, quiet mother was a powerful influence in my life. Through her actions and the way she lived her life, she gave me the opportunity to love and to accept love—not only from my husband, but even more importantly, from my Heavenly Father. And that is truly the most precious gift a parent can give.

Live Life to the Full

Nonfiction

Evangeline Inman

I woke up Tuesday morning after a good night's rest, feeling the familiar warmth of my two children snuggled in close to me. Five-year-old Marquelle and three-year-old Jared always seemed to find their way to our bed at some point during the night. I cuddled them both closer to me, then kissed their foreheads.

Jared's little head felt unusually hot. I quickly got up and took his temperature. I was shocked to see how high it was.

I immediately called our family doctor and then our pediatrician. We had just returned from extensive testing at the children's hospital, where they'd informed us that Jared's health was great. Two years earlier, he'd undergone a bone marrow transplant, and his life expectancy was now considered normal.

The pediatrician reassured me that "a bug" was going around and lots of kids were running unusually high fevers. I took cold wet towels and placed them on Jared's forehead. A short time later, his fever had gone down and seemed to be under control. I was relieved that he appeared to be doing better. *It's probably just the flu*, I thought.

Jared had celebrated his third birthday 11 days before. He'd been most thrilled to receive one gift in particular, a bright red plastic golf set. This little boy thrived on sports. He always seemed to find a way to stay up late to watch a game of some sort with his daddy. I would put him to bed, but he would hear the TV, and out he'd come with his big irresistible smile. He would climb up onto Mark's lap and snuggle into him with a posture that said, *I'm not going anywhere.*

That evening when my husband came home from work, Jared was propped up on pillows watching *Barney* children's videos in the master bedroom. I left to make a quick trip to the store to buy Jared some frozen Popsicles™ and ice cream to help keep his fever down.

As I pulled into the driveway after returning home, even before I had a chance to get out of the van, Marquelle ran up to me, shouting, "Daddy took Jared to the hospital and he said for you to come right away!"

My heart began to pound. *What possibly could have happened that Mark would leave our five-year-old daughter outside playing with her friends? Maybe Jared's temperature has risen?*

I raced across the street and asked our neighbour to watch Marquelle; then I rushed to the hospital, a sick sensation in the pit of my stomach.

When I drove into the hospital parking lot, I saw our car parked in front of the emergency doors where it plainly says, "No Parking." I quickly found a spot for the van and ran up to my husband's car. When I reached it, I realized that the windows were down, the key was in the ignition, and the car was still running. *What's happening?*

Ignoring the front-desk personnel, I ran right through the emergency waiting room into the back where the examining rooms were located. Mark was pacing back and forth in the hallway.

I ran up to him, screaming, "What's going on?"

He turned to me and, in a flat voice, said, "I think he's dead."

"What are you talking about?" I yelled.

"I don't know. He's in there." He pointed to one of the examining rooms.

I ran and opened the door. My precious baby boy was lying on the table with doctors and nurses clustered around him. I cried out, "That's my son!"

All of the medical staff turned and looked at me. I remained in the doorway of the room, just a few feet from where they were working on my son. I was sobbing and screaming, "I'm his mother! He's my baby!"

I heard someone say, "Get her out of here!"

A couple of the hospital staff quickly led me out of the room. Mark was standing nearby in the hallway. They showed us to a small, private waiting room off to the side.

As they went out and closed the door, I said, "Just tell me one thing. Is my son dead or alive?"

The man shook his head and his eyes filled with tears as he replied, "I can't tell you. You'll have to wait to talk to the doctor."

Our son Jared was born on April 23, 1996. Within 24 hours of his birth, two doctors stood at the foot of my bed. They told me that when they had examined Jared, they had noticed little red dots all over his body. The dots, called "petechiae," are the result of blood escaping from blood vessels. The doctors explained that there were several potential causes of the petechiae. Jared could have a virus that would correct itself in several weeks or months. Or he could have a lifelong illness, and need transfusions on a regular basis. They didn't have answers for us, but they knew that something was wrong.

Jared was moved to the neonatal intensive care unit, where they discovered that the platelets in his blood were too low. So began the rollercoaster of good reports followed by bad reports. Every time they checked his platelet count, it had changed significantly. One day it seemed to improve; the next day the results would be worse.

We left the hospital when Jared was just over a week old, but we had to return every day for blood work. The nurses would swipe his tiny baby foot with an alcohol swab and then, using a razor, make a small incision in the sole and squeeze his foot until they obtained enough blood for the test. Each time, he would scream in pain. As I held him close, I could hardly bear it.

When he was about one month old, his head became covered with sores and scabs. The doctors realized his weight was going down and Jared wasn't growing. I began to hear staff use the term "failure to thrive."

At four months, Jared was referred to a specialist at the IWK Children's Hospital in Halifax, Nova Scotia. Our pediatrician had made a potential diagnosis—Wiskott-Aldrich syndrome—but staff at the children's hospital needed to do further testing to confirm it.

A few days after the tests, I was alone at my pediatrician's office, holding Jared in my arms, when she broke the news to me.

"Your son will probably not live to be 50 years old," she began. "He probably won't live to be 30 years old."

I took a deep breath and said, "Okay."

She kept going. "He probably won't live to be 18." After a pause, she said, "He may not live to be 12."

I said a very tentative "Okay."

Then she asked, "Has anyone in your family had boys who died before they were two?"

I was shaken to the core. I could barely comprehend what she was saying. In a matter of seconds the prognosis had gone from a 50-year to a two-year life span. I had never heard of Wiskott-Aldrich syndrome. The genetic disorder is so rare that only four out of one million males have the disease. I was overwhelmed by trying to process all of the information. At the same time, I felt compassion for the doctor. She was a kind, caring person, and I knew it was hard for her to tell me about my son's condition.

The head of the immunology department at the hospital in Halifax met with us shortly after, and confirmed the diagnosis. He explained that one of the disease's symptoms was failure of the immune system to work properly. Jared's tiny body was attacking itself, and that was the reason he had sores all over.

We were referred to one of the world's largest and most respected pediatric health science centres, The Hospital for Sick Children in Toronto, Ontario. SickKids had seen a few similar patients and had had some success treating them with bone marrow transplants.

The 15-hour car trip from our home in New Brunswick to Toronto was made even more stressful by our having to drive it in the middle of a huge snowstorm. I sat in the back of the car next to Jared's car seat, trying to soothe him as I prayed nonstop, asking God to protect us and get us safely to our destination.

I had grown up in a Christian family who believed in miracles. I expected God to heal my son. My constant prayer became, *Please God, heal my son. I will do anything for You. Please just heal him.*

However, when we finally pulled into the hospital's driveway in downtown Toronto, my stomach churned and I felt nauseated. Reading those words on the large sign at the entrance announcing

The Hospital for Sick Children, seeing them in black and white, made it seem so final. *My child is one of those sick children,* I thought. *How can this be happening?*

I battled with my emotions. I didn't want to walk through those doors. That sign was talking about the cute, cuddly, blond-headed, brown-eyed baby I adored. He was my child, and he was sick.

Carrying Jared, I forced my reluctant feet to take us through those doors to the admissions department. A nurse showed us around the sterile hospital. I could spot the parents of sick children in the hallways; they had a haunted look in their eyes. I could sense the fear.

The bone marrow transplant unit was an isolation ward. There was another ominous sign on the door—two words typed on a piece of paper that stated No Admittance. The nurse opened the door and motioned for Mark, Jared and me to follow her into that restricted section. My heart cried out, *No Admittance! The sign says "No Admittance." I don't want to be the one allowed in here. Oh God, why is this door open for me to walk through? Why does my little boy have to stay here?*

Later that week, I was sitting alone in the car. I turned on the cassette player and a song that I had co-written six years before began to play. I was stunned by the words. It was as if they foretold what was happening in my life at that moment.

In You, Oh Lord, there is strength
When it seems all hope is gone
And we're blinded by our pain
In every situation that seems so hard to bear
I will lift my eyes to heaven
And find my comfort there
You can stand on His promises
He is faithful and true
He will never leave you
There's nothing He can't do…[1]

I look back on that song and realize God used it for a greater purpose than what I could have imagined when I wrote it. This song—and others I had recorded—helped my three-year-old daughter Marquelle fall asleep, as she was rocked by her grandparents who were babysitting her back in New Brunswick. It was heartbreaking to leave her so often at such a crucial time in her young age, but though I was hundreds of miles away with Jared, thanks to the original songs I had recorded, God in His kindness allowed me to sing my daughter to sleep every night. I will forever be grateful that God directed me to make that album.

After driving us to Toronto, my husband Mark had to return to his solo optometry practice to continue earning an income for our family. He tried to fly back to Toronto from our home in New Brunswick most weekends to be with Jared and me. During the couple of months that we stayed in Toronto for the transplant, I only saw Marquelle once or twice. Due to isolation ward rules, young siblings were not allowed to visit.

Often I'd sit in the hospital room, far away from my family, and cry out from my heart, *God, I know You can heal. I've seen You heal other people. You've healed me in the past. I don't understand what's going on with Jared, but I will trust and worship You.* The presence of God surrounded us in that hospital room. I held my baby in my arms and prayed and rocked him while the harsh chemotherapy drugs were pumped into his tiny body, destroying his bone marrow before the healthy stem cells could be transplanted.

Finally, at 10 months old, Jared received the bone marrow transplant—and it was successful! After several weeks at SickKids to monitor his progress, we excitedly arrived home in time to celebrate Jared's first birthday.

For most of the next year, we stayed at home because Jared had to be kept in isolation due to his low immune system. Despite being housebound, it was wonderful for us to be together again as a family under the same roof. Our outings consisted of medical appointments with the pediatrician in Fredericton, the family doctor in Sussex, the immunology and hematology doctors at the children's hospital in Halifax, and the specialist at SickKids in Toronto. Eventually, I was able to start working again as the music director for our church. It was exhilarating to be back leading the worship ministry.

Two years passed by quickly, and we were beginning to feel a sense of normalcy again. Jared was a little sweetheart. He would beat on the drums every chance he got. He loved to make funny faces, say something amusing or throw his head back, laughing uproariously while trying to make everyone else in the room laugh with him.

Despite the fact that his short life had been filled with hospitals, doctors, medications, needles and surgeries, he was full of life and fun. Once, when he had to be admitted back into the hospital, I sat down and wept. Jared looked at me, patted his heart and exclaimed, "Joy, joy!"

As we'd been doing every three months, we flew to Toronto again shortly after Jared's third birthday for a couple of days of extensive testing. More than two years had passed since his bone marrow transplant, and all his test results were great. Most of his medications had been discontinued and the doctors were starting to wean him off the few that remained.

We were exhilarated. Jared was doing fabulously. He was looking and acting like an ordinary healthy kid. The reports were brimming with good news. The doctors reassured us that we could relax and treat him like a regular child, and that they expected him to have a normal life expectancy.

We were over the moon with happiness and thankfulness. We spent the weekend with close friends who lived in the Toronto area. Finally, Mark and I could make plans for our future! Now that Jared was healthy, we would travel and go on great vacations, during which I would shop with Marquelle, and Mark would golf with Jared.

We flew home from Toronto on the "red-eye" flight late Sunday night. Monday morning, Jared seemed tired, but I attributed it to the rigours of the trip and all the doctors' appointments. I was still flying high with all the great reports we had just received.

Jared asked me a question that day that seemed insignificant at the time. He looked up at me and said, "Mommy, where is your daddy?" I said, "Grandpa's up in the sky," meaning heaven. Jared threw back his head and laughed. My mother-in-law told me later that Jared had asked her several questions about heaven too, wanting to know where it was.

Tuesday morning, Jared woke up burning with fever and crawled into my bed. Although he seemed to be improving that evening when I left to buy him Popsicles™, none of us realized that his body had been shutting down all day. I had no idea how sick he was. I didn't realize he was dying. I never had a chance to say goodbye.

The doctor finally came to the private room where the hospital staff had told Mark and me to wait. "I'm so sorry," he said quietly. "We did everything we could, but we couldn't save him."

I felt nauseous and I could barely breathe. One of the medical personnel invited us into the examining room where Jared's now-still body lay. We hugged and kissed him goodbye. Mark and I sobbed as we told him over and over how much we loved him and how much we already missed him. We stayed with him until the nurses came in and apologetically informed us that we had to leave. Somehow, Mark and I each managed to drive our vehicles home, where family and friends had started arriving to help and comfort us.

Later that night, when I finally fell asleep, I dreamed that my boy was still alive. The next morning, I woke up in a fog trying to figure out, *Is Jared dead or alive? Did this actually happen, or is it just a horrible nightmare? How could God have allowed this to happen?* When I realized it wasn't a dream, I quickly went outside to the van to remove Jared's car seat. I didn't want my husband or daughter to get in the van and see his empty seat, still buckled in. I sobbed all the way down the stairs to the storeroom.

I don't remember how I made it through the funeral. Afterwards, I cried for months. I felt as if I were in a deep, dark pit, and that even if I strained to look up, I could barely see any light. Other times, I felt empty, as though my chest were caving in. A knife was slowly turning in my heart, making it hurt to breathe. I gasped for air. I thought I would never be able to stop the tears. Marquelle kept asking, "Okay, when is everyone going to stop crying?"

It seemed so cruel, senseless, and unfair. After all that he'd been through, Jared did not die from complications associated with his illness. He'd been given a clean bill of health just a few days before. The most probable cause was that Jared had picked up an unrelated "super bug" (a powerful viral or bacterial infection that is resistant to antibiotics) during his last check-up.

The year following Jared's death was the most painful time in my life. I questioned God—and yet at the same time I clung to Him with every ounce of strength I had. Day after day, I fell on my knees in desperation. As a result, I became aware of God in ways I had never experienced before. Everywhere I went, I could feel angels with me. I sensed the Holy Spirit so thick around me that sometimes it felt as if a warm blanket were wrapped around me.

I came to know God as the One who walks with us through the valley of the shadow of death. I learned to embrace grief, because I could not outrun it. I accepted that mourning is a normal and critical part of recovery, so I grieved—but I did so with the hope that God would work all things together for good as He had promised to those who love Him (Romans 8:28).

I studied the book of Job, where, despite the fact that Job lost all 10 of his children, the Scriptures tell us that "Job lived a long full life" (Job 42:17). I circled that verse in my Bible, and wrote on the side margin, "It *is* possible to have a good life after you have lost a child." That verse brought me comfort and gave me hope that one day, I would begin to smile again—and not just smile, but actually be happy. I, too, could still live a full life.

Gradually, the "Father of compassion and the God of all comfort" (2 Corinthians 1:3–4) restored my joy. I will always miss Jared but I have chosen to be thankful for three beautiful years and the wonderful memories that I cherish. I've learned that no situation is too painful for God to heal. It may seem impossible, but all things really are possible with God. Isaiah 51:11–12 says: "Gladness and joy will overtake them, and sorrow and sighing will flee. I, even I, am He who comforts you."

Not everyone loses a child, but at some point in our lives, most of us face something that devastates us: divorce, sickness, broken relationships, the loss of a loved one, or the death of dreams. We will grieve, but we don't have to endure a life of continuous sorrow. "God is close to the broken-hearted and He rescues those of us who are crushed in spirit" (Psalm 34:18). I don't know how He does it, but I've experienced it for myself. Whatever we're going through, Jesus promised, "I have come that you might have life to the full" (John 10:10).

1. Evangeline Inman and Monica Cota, "You Can Stand" (Langley, B.C.: SOCAN/ MarJar Music Inc./Praise Charts Publishing, 1989). All rights reserved. Used by permission.

Two Men Ahead of Their Time

Nonfiction

Connie Brummel Crook

> I want to leave something behind when I go; some
> small legacy of truth, some word that will shine in
> a dark place. *Nellie McClung.*[1]

Reg Brown asked me to be his wife two years after he'd started work as the founding pastor of the Evangelical Baptist Church in Owen Sound, Ontario. I loved Reg, but I had reservations. I'd observed that most ministers' wives were soloists who could sing like angels. They also led their congregations using their fine musical talents on the piano or organ. And they were warm and outgoing. After many ear infections and a bout with rheumatic fever, I was tone deaf, and had some hearing loss. Furthermore, I was not the extrovert that Reg was.

After accepting his proposal, I wrote to Reg about my concerns. His response came promptly by mail. (Phone calls were expensive in those days, and I was paying back a loan from my preceding year of teacher's training at Ontario College of Education. Reg also had little money, since he was on a low and varying salary from his fledgling congregation.)

> My dearest Constance,
>
> I do not need a Pastor's assistant nor a pianist. We have a pianist and our church is too small for an assistant. If the need arises, God will provide. I do need a helpmate to whom I can go for respite from the cares of my work. It is not good for man to be alone. We will be a great help to each other spiritually and mentally. When I think about our future life together, sometimes the physical aspect of our love and companionship is in the forefront almost bursting into flame, but then sometimes, like last

night and this morning, I just think of how comforting it will be to have you as a very close companion—to talk to, to pray with, to read to, to listen to you read to me. I'm concerned too about the work. Folks have not been coming forward lately for conversion or membership—even though we do have more and more young couples from the new subdivision around our church coming out to services. The Sunday school has grown a lot but I'm still concerned. I did appreciate your encouragement as you reminded me of Jeremiah and how long he waited for results from his ministry.

Darling, when we are married, never let us miss our "quiet time" with the Lord. Nothing is more important— let us put everything else second to it. If we set our hearts to this when we begin, I am confident that He will see us through.

Although I do want you to be a full-time wife at home and with the children I pray we will have, I do agree to your request to teach two years after our marriage in order to make your teaching certificate permanent. As you say, it is not just the certificate itself but the completion of what you began. But after that, I hope you are content to be a stay-at-home wife and mom. As far as ministering to my congregation, I ask only that you don't have fights with anyone. I've known of churches divided by such…"

Although we were very aware of our differences, we married, and it was a very happy marriage. I loved the small city along the shores of Georgian Bay, and the folks I met there. I must admit, however, that I did have a hot dispute with one person in Reg's congregation: Reg's mother, I am embarrassed to say. She lived with us, and I fought with her over who should iron his white shirts. He settled that dispute by taking them to the dry cleaner.

During my first pregnancy, the church women gave me a baby shower and presented me with a brand new baby carriage. At the end of the evening, they sang the little chorus to me, "God Will Take Care of You," mindful of the fact that I was scheduled to go to the hospital the next morning because of my diabetic complications, which were endangering our unborn baby.

Through that difficult time, Reg was most supportive. A couple of weeks later, our first daughter arrived on a Sunday. Reg managed to deliver his radio message, lead his Sunday School Adult Bible Class, and preach a brief sermon at the morning service before arriving at the hospital shortly after noon to wait with me for the arrival of our daughter at 3:33 in the afternoon. Husbands weren't allowed to be in delivery rooms in those days, but Reg somehow caught up with the nurse running with our baby in an incubator towards the elevator. He stared at our daughter for a long minute before the elevator took them away. Then he came to my room and waited with me until I fell asleep. Early the next morning, he wrote a letter that he read the following Sunday to his congregation and his radio audience.

Hi there! My name is Elisabeth Ann Brown. I arrived yesterday, all 6 pounds, 3 ounces of me. Mom told my dad a long time ago that I would come on a Sunday, but he just laughed about it. He was sure I wouldn't do a thing like that to him. He's going to have to pay more attention to the women in this family now, 'cause we have him outnumbered…

Yesterday, I got my first glimpse of my dad shortly after 4 o'clock. It was real funny. (I don't mean my dad.) One of the nurses wheeled me right up to the door of the elevator, and I could see that he was just bursting to shout, "Hey, that's my baby! Let me have a look at her." Believe it or not, he was afraid the nurse wouldn't let him see me. Just then Dr. Quirk came along and that was all he needed. Over he bounded.

It was hard to tell just what he was thinking as he gazed at me. I was afraid for a minute that his eyes would slip their sockets. Personally, I don't think he was overly impressed. After all, I was still kind of new, and Dad just doesn't understand these things yet. Why, Mom looked at me in the delivery room for ten whole minutes and

she thought I was really something! She was pleased as punch with me. Oh well, he was pleased all the same. He was certainly happy to see that Mom was feeling so well after it all...

I would have typed this letter to you folks yesterday, but my dad is a pastor you know, and he wouldn't have been too pleased about it. I didn't want to make things any more difficult between us 'cause I know I'm stuck with him for quite a while now.

One more thing. I just want to say how much I appreciate your interest and prayers on behalf of Mom and me. Especially to the ladies who gave Mom the new carriage. She was really happy about that I know. Hope to see you all sometime soon.

During our years together, Reg, the cheerful, extroverted, passionate church pioneer complemented my more practical, partly introverted, but also devoted self. Unfortunately, in April of 1961, not quite five years into our marriage, leukemia took Reg from me. I left Owen Sound a widow with two daughters, aged 11 months and two years, to support. The permanent teaching certificate Reg had agreed I should obtain was put to full and necessary use as my only source of income that September, and for many years to come.

Seven years after Reg's death, my daughters and I travelled to Manitoba to visit his relatives. My mother-in-law (yes, the one I'd fought with over ironing Reg's shirts) was very happy to see the children, who could not remember her. Not only did she introduce me to her favourite nephew, Albert Crook, a bachelor, but she also arranged for him to drive us about the scenic Red River Valley. A year later, Albert and I married.

Although my second marriage is a very happy one, I am still inspired by the time I spent with Reg, and the joy we took in balancing and strengthening each other. In many ways, Reg was a man ahead of his time.

Perhaps my experience of knowing his support for me as an individual drew me, years later, to write my trilogy of historical fiction books about Canadian heroine Nellie McClung and her husband Wes. Wes, too, was a man who was very much ahead of his time…

It's easy for modern readers to forget what life was like in Canada 100 years ago. Women were not considered "persons" under the law. At that time, Canada was governed by the British North America Act, which had been drawn up in 1867 during Confederation when Canada became a separate country from Great Britain.[2]

Originating in Britain, this legislation declared: "Women are persons in matters of pains and penalties, but are not persons in matters of rights and privileges." Many unfair laws against women had derived from this one; in a number of Canadian provinces (to varying degrees), husbands—but not wives—had complete rights to the children of a marriage. A man also had rights to his wife's property, even property she had owned before the marriage.

In the province of Manitoba, a husband could will his property as he wished. Many a farm wife received nothing from her deceased husband's will and was left destitute, perhaps in the care of a son and daughter-in-law in the very home that had once been hers.

Nellie Mooney McClung grew passionate about righting these wrongs and became the prime force behind the legal reforms and votes-for-women movement in Manitoba. This idealistic and courageous young woman, who had started teaching school at only 16 years old, was motivated by her Christian faith to work for social justice at great personal cost.

Nellie, born in 1873, was in her twenties when she began helping women through the WCTU (Women's Christian Temperance Union). This movement had a much larger mandate than simply working to ban liquor or urging people to abstain from alcohol. At the time, it was one of the few groups to which abused and needy women could turn.

Later, Nellie helped organize the Political Equality League, and these women were known as suffragettes.

Over the years, Nellie became a courageous, compelling public speaker—one of the few women who could fill Massey Hall in Toronto—as well as the author of 16 books (both novels and nonfiction), and the mother of five children.

Nellie faced a good deal of opposition. Male opponents dubbed the WCTU "Women Continually Torment Us," and used unflattering caricatures to harass her, but she was not ruffled by them. Her strength in the face of such ridicule came not only from her own character and deep faith, but also from her husband, who supported her fully. She had been introduced to Wes McClung by his mother, who also was active in the WCTU. Whenever Wes was in the audience listening to Nellie's speeches, he smiled his encouragement. But while their growing children were still young, Wes—who worked first as a druggist, then in the life insurance industry—more often stayed at home in the evenings to care for the family.

At some speaking engagements, Nellie gave readings from her popular novels, such as *Sowing Seeds in Danny*, published in 1908. She would agree to do this without charge if she was allowed to talk about the women's movement afterwards. One such event is depicted in my novel *Nellie's Victory*. It took place at the town hall in Brandon, Manitoba, in 1912.

After her reading and a thunderous applause, Nellie said, "Now, Ladies and Gentlemen, I want to invite you to stay for a discussion of the work of the WCTU and perhaps even some political matters. I will speak only briefly. In fact, I'll give you plenty of time to ask questions. But first, there will be a short intermission, for I must phone home." Nellie left the podium and walked swiftly into an inner office...

The phone rang only twice before Wes's voice came on the line. "Well, how are things at home, Wes?" Nellie asked.

"Everything is fine," Wes said cheerfully. "Jack and Florence are doing their homework on the dining room table. Paul and Horace are in bed, and I'm settling down to read the newspaper."

"And how's Baby Mark? Did he take his feedings all right?"

"Just fine, Nell. Florence was a great help. She's finally forgiven him for being a boy. And you know I'm an experienced father by now. A six-month-old can't get the better of me. He's sound asleep."

"And how are *you*, Wes?" Nellie sounded a little anxious, but she knew she didn't need to be. Wes was enjoying his new job in Winnipeg and the lacrosse league at Manufacturers' Life.

"Couldn't be better."

"I must go, then," Nellie said.

"You tell 'em, Nell. I know you can, and I'm here rootin' for you."

"Thanks, Wes. I'll see you tomorrow. Mrs. Nash and I'll leave early and should be back around noon."

"Goodbye, dear. I love you."

Nellie walked back to the stage with a smile on her face. Wes's support of her work always helped. As she stood at the podium again, Nellie noticed a nasty little man who was glaring at her from the front row. He was red-faced and seemed ready to burst. So Nellie decided to reverse the order of her presentation.

"I wonder if there are some questions before I speak further. Perhaps we could deal with those first."

The man was on his feet in an instant. "I'm going to point out to this fine audience that we should have no respect for any mother who deserts her children." He spoke in a pompous manner with a loud, clear voice, as if he were accustomed to audiences. "For should Mrs. McClung not be at home with her children at this very moment?" He turned to Nellie. "Correct me if I am wrong, Mrs. McClung, but do you not have a six-month-old baby? ... Mrs. McClung would be better employed at home, taking care of her children, for after all, that is a woman's highest duty."

Nellie walked to the edge of the platform and paused long enough to get the strained attention of the audience. She looked down at the man in a kindly way and said, "First of all, you can settle down and not worry about *my* children. I have just phoned home to check. They are well and happy, clothed and fed. The baby is in bed, and all is well. Secondly, you're quite right in saying that our children are our greatest assets. You and I are in agreement there, and while it is true that you cannot do anything for *my* children, there is something you can do for the children of this community. Help the women who are trying to make the school board see that a safe playground is needed.

"I hear that some tight-fisted, short-sighted, mean-souled members of the school board are holding out against it, saying it's a waste of money. Of course, I know such sentiments are foreign to you—for you evidently are a lover of children, even taking thought for mine!"

The audience broke loose with laughter and applause. "He's the chairman of the school board," a woman's voice shouted out from the left side of the hall…

Then Nellie began again, "Some would say that women are the only ones responsible for the education of their children. And if anything goes wrong, they are blamed. But how can mothers be blamed when the communities they live in refuse to help their children become good citizens? How can women take full responsibility if school boards refuse to provide good facilities?"

The chairman of the school board puffed out his cheeks and coughed.

"It is for this reason that women like us at the WCTU have become involved in public affairs…[3] I am a firm believer in women—in their ability to do things and in their influence and power. Women set the standards for the world, and it is for us, the women of Canada, to set the standards high!"[4]

The entire audience erupted into applause—with the noticeable exception of the chairman of the school board. As the audience broke up and he rose to leave, he made a special point of coming up to Nellie.

"I *still* think you should be at home darning your husband's socks," he grumbled.[5]

At another event in Winnipeg, at Grace Church the night of January 23, 1914, Nellie and Wes were greeted outside by young protestors, who shouted, "Well, well, well! It's Calamity Nell, can't you tell!"[6]

Half an hour later, Nellie was standing in the pulpit of the large sanctuary. She took a deep breath and sailed right in.

"Through the ages, people have blamed the Almighty for all sorts of operations they'd botched up themselves. Long ago, people broke every law of sanitation, and when plagues came, they blamed the Almighty and said, 'Thy will be done.' They were submissive when they should have been investigating.

"This is the meaning of the women's movement, and we need not apologize for it. Prevention is the highest form of reform. If we sit passively under unfair and deplorable conditions, we become, in the sight of God, partners with them. Submission to injustice, submission to oppression, is rebellion against God.

"For too long we have believed that it was a woman's duty to sit down and be resigned. Now we know it is her duty to rise up and be indignant.

"So long as women are content to give out blankets and coals and warm woollen mufflers, and provide day nurseries, all is well, but if they dare meddle with causes, they find themselves in politics—that sacred domain, where no woman must enter or she will be defiled.

"Now politics is only public affairs, yours and mine, as well as other people's... If politics are corrupt, it is all the more reason that a new element should be introduced. Women will, I believe, supply that new element. Men and women were intended to work together. Men alone cannot make just laws for men and women, just as any class of people cannot legislate fairly for another class. To deny women the right of law-making is to deny the principle of democracy."[7]

Due to the influence of Nellie's leadership, in 1916 Manitoba became the first province to give women the right to vote and to run for public office. First Canada's federal government, and then the other provinces gradually followed Manitoba's lead over the next 25 years.

Nellie, who moved to Edmonton with her family, went on to become one of the first women in Canada elected to public office and served as a member of the Alberta legislature in the 1920s. Throughout her lifetime, she continued to champion factory safety reforms, dental and medical care for school children, mothers' allowances, property rights for married women, and other causes.

Her work and that of fellow trailblazers Emily Murphy, Henrietta Muir Edwards, Louise McKinney and Irene Parlby, known as "The Famous Five," further strengthened these reforms. The aforementioned five prominent Alberta women signed a petition in 1927 asking for clarification from the Supreme Court of Canada in what became known as "the Persons Case," a landmark Canadian and British constitutional law case that established women did have the same rights as men with respect to positions of political power.

Exactly 80 years after the British Privy Council's 1929 ruling—which had overturned the Canadian Supreme Court's original decision that, according to the law, women were not "persons" eligible to be appointed to the Senate of Canada—in 2009 The Famous Five were given distinct recognition as the only Canadians ever to be appointed honorary senators.[8]

They also have been immortalized on the back of the Canadian $50 bill, and in recently erected bronze statues on Parliament Hill in Ottawa, at Olympic Plaza in Calgary, and at the Manitoba Legislature in Winnipeg.

While the articulate and public-minded Nellie McClung (who died in 1951) was at the epicentre of astounding reforms, surely her husband Wes deserves a share of the credit. She could never have accomplished what she did without his steady, quiet support. Like my own first husband, Reg, Wes was a man well ahead of his time—who had the confidence to allow his wife the freedom to follow her dreams, no matter what anyone else thought.

Author's Note

The Nellie McClung quotations used here were included in my novel *Nellie's Victory* and credited there. Most were taken from the second volume of Nellie's autobiography, *The Stream Runs Fast*, excerpts from which Nellie's grandchildren kindly gave me permission to quote.

1. Nellie L. McClung, *The Stream Runs Fast* (Toronto: Thomas Allen Limited, 1945), 212.

2. "Nellie McClung," *The Canadian Studies Webcentre*, http://www.canadianstudies.ca/NewJapan/mcclungunit.html (accessed December 13, 2010).

3. "Now, Ladies and Gentlemen… in public affairs.": Nellie McClung, *Stream*, 126–31 (quotation and paraphrase).

4. "I am… standards high!": Nellie McClung, 1914 campaign speech, in McClung papers, in Candace Savage, *Our Nell: A Scrapbook Biography of Nellie L. McClung* (Saskatoon: Western Producer Prairie Books, 1979), 74. Permission given by Candace Savage.

5. Based on May L. Armitage, "Mrs. Nellie McClung," *Maclean's* (July 1915), quoted in Savage, *Our Nell*, 98.

6. "Calamity Nell!": McClung, *Stream*, xii.

7. "… people have blamed… principle of democracy.": McClung, "The Social Responsibilities of Women," in McClung papers, quoted in Savage, *Our Nell*, 80.

8. "'Famous Five' Named Honorary Senators, The Famous 5 Foundation, http://www.famous5.ca/news.html (accessed December 13, 2010).

Bibliography

Crook, Connie Brummel. *Nellie's Victory*. Toronto: Stoddart Publishing, 1999 and Markham: Fitzhenry & Whiteside, 2009.

McClung, Nellie L. *The Stream Runs Fast*. Toronto: Thomas Allen Limited, 1945.

Savage, Candace. *Our Nell: A Scrapbook Biography of Nellie L. McClung*. Saskatoon: Western Producer Prairie Books, 1979.

What Is Thy Neighbour's, Do Not Covet

Nonfiction

Paul M. Beckingham

Reflections on The Tenth Commandment:
"You shall not covet" (Exodus 20:17)

I've never understood jealousy. I've considered myself to be immune from it; I've stood above it—almost.

As a child, of course, the green-eyed goddess bit me. In a grasping, jealous moment at school in Glasgow, Scotland, aged about six, I reached out and snatched a pair of cheap plastic sunglasses from a little girl in my class. She cried. And I wore them proudly.

When she loudly accused me of stealing them from her, the other children in the class fell silent in a heavy and accusing stillness. While hearing my carefully carefree utterance to my frosty teacher, they stared me down. They bore witness to my brazen, barefaced lie. "They are mine, Miss," I insisted. Everybody except me, it seemed, knew with unassailable certainty that they were *not* mine.

"Where did you get them from?" My teacher's serious adult voice rang out through the deathly quiet room.

Her fiery look pierced my heart. It evoked a pang of conscience and the shameful admission that I was no longer an innocent six-year-old. I was, in fact, a thief.

I felt doomed. "But I bought them at the wee red shop down the road," I heard myself announce with unnatural confidence in my Glaswegian brogue. In that brief moment, I was convinced that I was convincing. My words sounded believable to *me*.

I was, apparently, the only person in the room that day to be persuaded, and even then, not totally. I knew the awful truth. It lay below the surface of my large and less-than-confident lie.

In the next instant, I felt for the first time that I was standing outside of my own body. It was as if I were trying to gain some distance from the deceiving little being I had so recently become. I stood with the children of the class, looking together in a wonderment of disbelief upon this Young Deceiver. Our fingers all pointed at him in disgust. We all knew that he had convinced none of us. Not one.

Neither had I convinced my teacher. She lifted those plastic glasses firmly from my nose. Slowly, and with a quiet intensity ringing in her voice in a way that truly frightened me, she spoke. "These are not yours, Paul." She said it definitively. She pronounced the truth in her heavy words.

They crushed me, flattening my lies by the weight of their pure authenticity. I felt my cheeks blush in a flush of guilty embarrassment. Stinging tears coursed down my face like slow, white-hot lava. My volcanic shame had, at last, erupted. It burned me inside out. In that moment, I learned that envy always leads, at last, to this.

Having tried jealousy once, I did not like it. I have never wished to try it again. And yet, every time I think of Gerald...

Tonight, I am shocked to realize for the first time that I have a deep-seated jealousy of Gerald. Of course, I have buried it deep where nobody can find it. Jealousy, despite my best efforts to give it no room in my heart, has behaved like rich and deviant compost, feeding manifold weeds of unusual size. Over the years, they've sprouted silently, and now, at last, they've sprung up into the open. How tall they have grown, and how strong!

I haven't seen Gerald with my eyes for more than 30 years. Yet Gerald visits me as frequently as I call to mind my many yesterdays, and that is nearly every day. He pops up unbidden and unwanted; he sours my recollections and tarnishes my fondest memories. I despise his assumed superiority, with its implied criticism of who and what I have become.

Gerald was my senior at high school by just one year. I was in grade 11, so Gerald, of course, was in grade 12. Week after week, my English teacher would read us Gerald's work. He held it up to us as an example, as the work of a man whose reputation made him one who is next to God. His thoughts were perfection squeezed into words upon a page. This was the stuff, we were told, that scholarships to Oxford and Cambridge Universities are made of. At that stage, I had not yet met Gerald face to face, but I was in awe of him. I wanted to hear the pearls of wisdom that must, I was sure, fall daily from his mouth. And then, one day, I bumped into him at school.

I don't remember exactly where or when we met. The picture in my mind is of a corridor in the hallowed halls of learning somewhere deep within the cathedral arches of my school. I see him now. Gerald is standing over me larger than life. I am a diminutive figure retreating from the intense glow of Gerald's haloed bright perfection. Feelings of deep inadequacy overwhelm me in those ghastly moments forever frozen in time.

Gerald's supremacy was daunting. I was hungry for his wisdom. He, alas, returned my simple, honest questions with a look that told me flatly that I knew precisely nothing. His cold and supercilious smile dismissed me. Clearly, I was not good enough for Gerald; he dwelt in a world where only the perfect succeed. It was obvious that I lacked the wherewithal to rise to his gargantuan stature. Even if I stood tall on tippy-toes, I would be lucky to see above the level of his kneecaps. Ah, the anguish of my inadequate soul!

My arrival into grade 12 could hardly come quickly enough. I was utterly relieved to be set free of Gerald. He had finally moved on. He was now shining at some far-off university, probably an Oxbridge College.[1] I imagined him beavering away brilliantly in the bowels of the library, expertly mining its jewels and, doubtless, covering himself in academic gold dust in the process. And I was glad. Until…

Our English teacher kept samples of the collected works of Gerald. Each week, Gerald's ghost gloated over us. His work was read—nay, intoned—to us. We must, we were told, become like Gerald.

It was as if he'd never left us. Worse still, a hagiography quickly grew around his idealized persona. He'd won the reputation of a saint. In his absence, the normal blemishes of a real, flesh-and-blood person were no longer on view. Gerald's reputation stood cloaked in the perfect garments of his well-crafted words. Daily, they were paraded before us. There was no at-a-glance reality here. None of Gerald's embodied faults were present with us in that room. Nothing tangible, muddling or mundane was there to balance his faultless writing. The hopelessness of Gerald's perfection overwhelmed me completely.

A year later, I arrived at university, ready for a brand-new start. I had chosen a place of higher learning a long way from home. I needed to get away from it all.

One evening, I responded to a knock on my dorm-room door. Imagine my horror when I opened it to discover, of all people, the smiling face of Gerald. His superiority, still intact and now somewhat larger, seemed to fill the doorframe. What on earth was he doing here?

He was, he said, knocking at all the doors today to welcome new students. He was doing this, he said, in his role (*important* was assumed) as dorm captain. He had, he said, recognized my name on the list in his office. He wanted to welcome me personally, he said. How perfectly wonderful to see me, he said... especially, he said, as he had thought I was bound never to make it to university.

I thought, by now, that maybe Gerald had said quite enough. I hated him with an exquisite hatred that I could almost taste. I wanted to let my revulsion rise up and bite him. What would Gerald have said then, I wondered? I remained silent—and seething.

Perhaps it lies within the anatomy of jealousy to despise that which we most desire. I wanted so much to be just like Gerald. I wanted his clever confidence; I desperately desired his erudite and casual brilliance. It was as if he had it all, and there was nothing left for me. Rocket-like, Gerald's reputation shot skywards; jealousy sank me deeper into reveries of ire.

After only one year, I fled to find another university in a far-off city, there to continue my studies unbedeviled by Gerald.

Time is warped and shortened when seen through memory's astigmatic lenses. It was certainly longer, but it seems like only months after I arrived in my new home that I rose, one evening, to answer the insistent jangle of the telephone. Like some recurring dream come back to haunt me, it was—of course!—dear Gerald.

He had called, he said, to tell me he'd graduated with honours. And married a girl from one of my former university classes. She had, don't you know, graduated early and with those mandatory honours that now accrued to everything in Gerald's charmed life. And wouldn't I be *surprised* and *delighted* to know, he said, that he had brought his wife to this very city to live. In fact, he told me, they were now my new neighbours. He assumed I'd be so *pleased*.

Gerald was right: *surprised*, I was. Gerald was wrong: for *delighted*, I was not. Whatever my feelings were at that moment, and politeness forbids my sharing them with you, *pleased* was frankly not one of them.

Soon after this brief conversation, I accepted Gerald's invitation to meet him for coffee. How could I refuse? When Gerald called, I answered. At his home, we talked. We caught up on our news. I shared with him some struggles and challenges facing me at that time. I did not, of course, share any of those copious grievances I held against him. My feelings of inferiority persuaded me to tell him nothing—that is, nothing personal, nothing that really mattered. Oddly, Gerald seemed able to elicit from me not only my hidden facts, but also my veiled and dangerous emotions. Smoothly, he pulled them from my grasp, one by one. Despite my best efforts to conceal my feelings beneath our polite handshake and the chink-chink of decorated china coffee cups, my heart escaped full view into the open. For that, I resented him desperately.

Gerald clearly did not approve of the shambles of my life of stumbling studies and student poverty. His career thrived in pristine and polished condition. "My, my…" he said. He chanted those words in trailing downward tonalities. His falling cadences created a dreary, plummeting, droning effect as each vowel sank without trace. A verbal, gravitational pull spun each syllable downward in a spiralling pessimism. I imagined the abyss into which his words, and my life, must inevitably fall. All hope stole quietly away. A ring of sad finality bathed his words. "My, my…" like the echoing peal of funeral bells, "You are just *a person to whom things happen*, Paul. Aren't you, now?" It sounded as if I had contracted a tropical disease of deathly proportions. He intoned his final funeral pronouncement upon me as though my condition were inescapably terminal. I heard the dust hitting the lid of my coffin. It was as if, with disdain, he looked directly into my eyes, to somberly say, "Alas, Paul, I have no medicine for *you*." The interview was clearly over. I was dismissed.

From that day to this, I have never again seen Gerald—except each day that I recall my past, and that is almost every day. Gerald lives rent-free inside my head. Even now, Gerald slowly shakes his head, smiling whimsically at me. He gazes at me. His superiority declares quietly, wordlessly, "My, my…" And that is enough, more than enough. All other words are rendered redundant. Why *would* he waste his perfectly crafted words on this imperfect creature now standing before him?

Isn't it odd how the things we covet, desiring so much to possess, will in the end possess us? Creeping upon us silently, they snatch us suddenly. They will abduct us, for their threat is real. I wanted so much to possess Gerald's success; now Gerald possesses me. It is as if we all become, eventually, *people to whom things happen*. Things we covet trip us and trap us. Eventually, we all trip over Gerald or his myriad clones. Even though we bury our personal Gerald in some dark and secret place, he will jump up like a jack-in-the-box to take us by surprise.

How then to live at peace with Gerald? His power multiplies and grows through all I surrender to him: perfection, power, and popularity. Only lengthening shadows remain, filled with disappointment, shame, and failure. The stronger the light I shine upon Gerald, the darker the shadows that surround me. They form a cold and lonely place to build a home.

To hold Gerald in an even-handed estimation is to lay him to rest. He can relax in my admiration of his achievements and rest in my awareness of his minor imperfections. Thus am I set free to pursue a life that I alone can live. The less I replay Gerald's judging voice chiding me for failing to keep up to the beat of his drum, the more I discover the song that only I can sing. This is not opera; I simply try to improvise. It sounds like jazz to me.

1. Oxbridge refers to the University of Oxford and the University of Cambridge in England. The term implies perceived superior intellectual or social status.

Twenty-five Years Later

Fiction

N. J. Lindquist

"What was I *thinking*?" Since Mariane Klein was alone in the rented Ford Taurus, her words drifted in the air with no hope of response. Alfred and Merlin, the German shepherds she'd adopted from a rescue shelter, were back in Regina being spoiled by her next-door neighbour.

"Lord, I just want to turn around and pretend something came up. Some kind of emergency—maybe one of the dogs could have puppies." She sighed. *Right. Both dogs are male.* Anyway, there was no use trying; she'd never been able to lie with even a modicum of conviction. But now might be a good time to try.

Just the thought of the weekend ahead made her queasy. Four women, all in their late forties, getting together for an entire weekend after 25 years of silence... Why, oh why, had she agreed?

It had been Charlie's idea, of course. Charlie, short for Charlene, the petite blonde sparkplug whose mind had always overflowed with ideas. Tall, mocha-skinned Drew would coolly evaluate Charlie's ideas and choose the best of them. Then pony-tailed Tess, the youngest member of a large Italian family, would put on her brown-rimmed glasses, flesh out the ideas, and see that they were carried out.

And Mariane? The Mariane of old was a dumpy, mousey-haired, tongue-tied nobody who nervously went along with whatever the others decided, grateful to be included, daily expecting the others would suggest she find new friends.

Through four years of Bible college near Winnipeg, Manitoba, the four of them had dissected their classes, their feelings, their dates, and their dreams, barely making any decision without consulting the others. Even Mariane contributed when asked, although she rarely had much information to volunteer since she did well in her classes, had few dates, stayed on an even keel emotionally, and never revealed her true feelings—in case they really did tell her to get lost.

After graduation, all four of them got busy with life, and they lost touch… until a few weeks ago, when Tess had found Mariane on Facebook. Truth be told, when Mariane had seen a "Friend Request" from someone named Tess Stratton, she'd almost ignored it. But something made her take a closer look at the photo, and she'd realized with a start that Tess Stratton was actually Tess Luciani, all grown up and presumably married.

Mariane's heart had sunk to the vicinity of her toes. Those college days were so long ago; she had no desire to remember them, much less to recreate them. But to refuse to acknowledge Tess, who had always been kind to her, would be like slapping Arthur or Merlin for jumping up to greet her when she came home after a trip. There are some things you just can't do.

After a quick prayer (*Oh, Lord, stop me if this is a mistake*), Mariane had closed her eyes and hit "Confirm."

In no time at all, Tess had tracked down Charlie and Drew, and they were all Facebook friends—and Mariane had almost stopped visiting the popular site.

Mariane told herself she was crazy. The four of them had been as close as anyone could be, sharing everything, including their faith in God, after they'd met during their first week of classes. Starting in their second year, they'd roomed together in a fourplex apartment on campus until graduation. Why wouldn't Mariane want to get back in touch? *Let me count the ways*, she thought. Simply put, she was no longer the person she had been 25 years ago, and she had no interest in remembering those painful days of her teenage and early adult years.

The car's GPS device announced that she had arrived at her destination, a Holiday Inn Tess had chosen in the south end of Winnipeg. With a sigh of resignation, Mariane pulled into the parking lot and turned off the ignition. "I've come this far," she muttered, "I may as well face the music. Lord, I think I'm doing what You want me to do. I sure hope so."

The freckle-faced boy at the check-in desk informed her that her friends had arrived and were waiting for her in their suite. Tess had booked their largest executive suite, which had two bedrooms with two queen-sized beds in each, plus a sitting area and tiny kitchenette.

At the door to room #342, she hesitated. *Knock or use the key card?* She knocked.

The door was opened by an attractive blonde in faded blue jeans and a pink T-shirt. She was the twin of the Charlie of old, give or take a few less inches of hair, a few more pounds, and a scattering of laugh lines.

"Mariane?"

"Charlie?"

Charlie pulled her into a bear hug. "Isn't it wonderful? We all made it!"

Mariane was passed from Charlie to a thin woman she barely recognized as elegant Drew—the thick, black curly hair replaced with a blue turban; exotic cheekbones gaunt and sallow; dark chocolate skin hanging in loose wrinkles around her neck. The two of them hugged, but lightly, as if each thought the other might break. Mariane wondered if Drew had any strength left in her body. *Lord, please be with her.*

Tess was next—auburn hair cut in a medium bob, a bright smile on her lips, but with tired green eyes and a faded appearance that made Mariane think of her as a shadow of the old Tess. Her arms wrapped around Mariane with surprising fierceness. Startled, Mariane responded with more enthusiasm than she'd intended.

Charlie retrieved her suitcase from the hallway, and Tess led the way into the bedroom she and Mariane were to share. They left her to unpack a few things and freshen up.

When she couldn't delay any longer, Mariane checked herself in the bathroom mirror. Amazing what a good haircut and a bit of make-up could do. Not to mention knowing which styles and colours suit you. She straightened the collar of her burnt orange blouse, smoothed the skirt of her brown tweed suit, and breathed one final, "Help me, Lord!" Then she walked out to the sitting room.

Tess was sitting next to Charlie on a brown imitation leather chesterfield, with Drew in one of two beige chairs. They were sipping soft drinks and eating food from an assortment of partially-consumed trays of fruit, vegetables with dip, and chocolate chip cookies that had been set out on a coffee table. A couple of open bags of potato chips completed the spread.

"We have a dinner reservation for eight o'clock," Tess said. "But I brought a few nibblies."

Mariane smiled. "A few?" She found a bottle of iced tea in the small refrigerator and poured the contents into a glass before sitting gingerly on the remaining chair.

"It's awesome we could all make this weekend," Drew said. Her large gold hoop earrings swung in time as she turned her head to smile at each of the others in turn. "Like a dream come true."

"I adore Facebook!" Charlie laughed. "The moment I saw Mariane's note about having to come to Winnipeg on business, I yelled, 'Reunion!'"

"It's fabulous," Tess said. "I'm so glad everyone could get away."

Drew sighed. "You don't know how good you all look to me."

"If you ignore the 20 or 30 pounds I've put on," Tess said. She laughed. "Okay, maybe 40."

"I've added a few, too," Charlie said. "In all the wrong places." Grinning, she crossed her stockinged feet on the edge of the coffee table.

Mariane said nothing.

Drew looked at her. "Well, I guess we've made up for them, Mariane. I know I've lost 20 pounds this past year. And you must have lost—well, quite a few?"

"Somewhere around 60," Mariane said. "Years ago, while I was in Japan teaching English."

"You look fabulous. I'd never have recognized you—" Charlie put her hand to her mouth. "I don't mean—"

"I know what you mean," Mariane said. "I wouldn't have recognized me either. And it hasn't been easy keeping it off." She rolled her eyes. "I had to learn to like things like spinach and exercise."

They all laughed.

"How long were you in Japan?" Tess asked.

"Eight years."

"At one place?"

"Yes, I was in Tokyo, teaching English at a Christian academy and helping to plant a church."

Charlie leaned forward. "I know you'd intended to be a life-long missionary, but I guess eight years was enough?"

Mariane cleared her throat. "No, I wanted to stay. I really enjoyed teaching and I felt I was making a difference in people's lives, but I had no choice. My mother died, and someone had to look after my father and help him run the store."

"And you had to be the one?" Drew asked.

Mariane looked down at the glass she was holding in her right hand. "Yes. There was no one else to help with the business. My brothers had their own careers and families, and, well, I always got along with my father better than they did." She smiled ruefully. "You might remember my mentioning that."

The other three nodded.

"But the main thing was that while Dad was a great carpenter, and a first-class furniture designer, it was Mom who looked after all the business issues and the finances, not to mention the house and meals, and he was lost without her. So we decided it was best for me to come home and look after Dad and manage the business."

"So now you build furniture?" Tess raised her brows.

Mariane laughed and shook her head. "Not on your life! I hire people to do that. I just look after the business side."

"It must have been hard for you," Drew said.

"It was a bit of a challenge in the beginning, but the truth is I turned out to be pretty good at it and, honestly, I really enjoy it now. Can't imagine not doing it."

There was no need to mention that under her management, the business had grown to eight stores across the Prairies, and she was currently talking to a major company about carrying their products in eastern Canada.

Mariane added, "I'm on my own now. Dad's happily ensconced in a seniors' home. Every so often he still comes up with an idea for a new product, and we usually end up making it."

"Remember how we were all going to change the world?" Charlie grinned. "I ended up changing diapers."

"Do you really have eight kids?" Tess asked.

"Six of our own, plus two of Brad's nephews. Brad's youngest sister and her husband were killed in a car accident when the boys were small, and they had made us the boys' guardians in their wills. Not that we minded—they're great kids. But it was terrible when it happened, and of course the boys missed their real mom and dad. Still do. But they're part of our family now."

"Eight kids." Tess shook her head. "Wow!"

"Keeps me busy," Charlie said. "And out of trouble. Usually."

"Well, girls, let's do something fun and crazy this weekend!" Drew said with a big grin.

"Well, not *too* crazy," Tess said, looking up. Then she laughed and covered her mouth with her hands. "Don't I sound like the wet blanket!"

Drew sat up straight. "Speaking of wet things, remember the night in first year after the final exam, when we had the water fight, and got water all over the dorm floor?"

Charlie leaned forward, "And remember..."

As the others reminisced about things they'd done and people they'd known, Mariane listened and remembered, but didn't contribute much. Then Drew said, "Remember Todd Pettigrew?"

Tess's face turned beet red and both Drew and Charlie laughed.

"You were nutty about him, Tess," Charlie said. "And you did all sorts of crazy things to get his attention."

"Whatever happened to him? Does anybody know?" Drew asked.

There was another silence.

In a flat voice, Mariane said, "He died suddenly. Five years ago. Heart attack."

No one spoke for a long moment. Then Tess said, "Poor Todd. I hope he had a family."

"He was a widower," Mariane said.

"Well, it's been 25 years since our graduation," Charlie said. "That's a long time. Lots of things have happened, good and bad."

"I hate looking back," Tess said. "I hate hearing about bad things happening to people I knew."

"I do too," Drew said thoughtfully, "but so often it's the bad things that keep us honest."

"When did you find out about the cancer?" Tess asked in her blunt way.

"Almost a year ago," Drew replied. "Been a very strange year. Diagnosed with cancer in the right breast, then a mastectomy, then chemo, and then they found cancer in the other breast, so we went through the whole thing all over again." She paused. "And just after the second round of chemo started, my husband walked out on me. Said he couldn't take all the stress."

The others stared at her.

After a long moment, Mariane mouthed the word, "Jackson?"

Drew had met Jackson in Bible college and married him two weeks after graduation, a few days before Mariane left for Japan. Tall, good-looking, excelling in studies and sports, Jackson had been the student body president as well as the best athlete—not to mention a great singer and a fabulous preacher. In short, he was *the* catch of their graduating class.

"I don't understand," Mariane said. "I thought—we all assumed—you were made for each other."

Drew laughed. "Honey, I'd have said the same thing—right up until this year. We had it all! I don't know if you followed our lives or not, but shortly after graduation, Jackson became assistant pastor of a large church here in Winnipeg, and within a few years, he became senior pastor, and then they started radio and TV ministries. Everything was great. Then Jackson started getting asked to speak all over Canada and the United States at various events.

"As our three kids got older, I began going along and singing with him and doing some speaking, too. I thought we had the perfect combination of marriage and ministry. I was looking forward to working together for the rest of our lives."

Tears welled up in Drew's eyes. "I still have trouble believing this last year actually happened. That's why I was so strong on being here this weekend. I needed to surround myself with people who knew me before I became 'Mrs. Jackson Brooks.'"

Drew laughed. "Listen to me. Talking as if I've had an awful life. I don't regret any of it," she said. "Certainly not my wonderful children. And not even the cancer. But this past year sure has been hard."

"What's the prognosis?" Tess asked. She blushed. "Sorry, I guess that's pretty nosy."

"Not at all. But honestly, no one knows. If the cancer has spread, I might only live another few months; but so far they think it hasn't spread. So I could live another 30 or 40 years." She paused. "Or, of course, I might get hit by a bus tomorrow!"

All four of them—even Mariane—began to giggle. But at the same time, Mariane covertly studied the others. They'd changed physically, of course. But had they changed in other ways? This Drew was different. Much of her beauty was gone, and yet, she had a quiet dignity. Charlie was still gorgeous and vibrant, but exuding a peacefulness rather than the restlessness Mariane remembered. Cute, funny, organized Tess, the one most likely to make her dreams come true, looked 15 years older than the others.

And then there was her—Mariane. *Lord, I had so little to offer back then.* Overweight, not particularly attractive, book-smart but not life-smart, timid… any time she remembered her college days, she wondered anew why the others had included her.

Since the moment Tess had found her on Facebook, all of Marianne's old insecurities had come back. She'd always felt different from the others, wondered why they wanted to be friends with her, felt that nothing she had to say was worth talking about. Who was she, anyway?

You're My child.

Oh, Lord, I know You love me.

Have I ever yet led you wrong?

No, Lord. Never. With Your help, I've learned to be content in whatever situation I find myself.

As the others continued chatting about other people from their classes, Mariane's thoughts drifted off. Sure, she'd loved her time in Japan, but she'd turned out to be a savvy businesswoman and had not only expanded her dad's furniture store, but made a small fortune out of his designs. She'd been a doting aunt to her three brothers' broods, and made sure her brothers and sisters-in-law benefited as the business expanded over the years. She'd led small groups, taught Bible studies, given generously to her local church, and been asked to join the boards of numerous ministries. She'd had moments of romance. One of the other English teachers in Japan. A furniture salesman. But nothing came of them, and afterwards she realized it was for the best. Then, while in Saskatoon on business six years ago, she'd run into Todd Pettigrew, whom she'd known slightly at Bible college. They started seeing each other whenever she was in town, and Todd drove to Regina for a weekend. Then came the shock of seeing his death notice in the newspaper. She'd gone to the funeral and sat in the back row, but spoken to no one; none of Todd's family had known about her.

For a few weeks, she'd grieved, mostly for Todd's family, and a little for herself. But she'd prayed a lot, buried herself in the business and her extended family, adopted the two dogs, and started an outreach group for women who were alone, whether they were single, divorced, or widowed. Not long after that, she'd realized she was sad but not devastated. She had everything she needed; God was still in control and He would take care of her.

But seeing her former friends on Facebook and meeting with them this weekend had sent her reeling back to an uncomfortable past. She was 18 again, embarrassed by who she was and by her immigrant parents, who spoke German instead of English, who were poor, and who owned a little carpentry shop. She'd never told anyone, but she'd chosen to go to the college in Manitoba, a seven-hour drive by car from her home in Regina, Saskatchewan, in order to ensure that her parents would never make the trip—and they hadn't, not even for her graduation. As a teenager, and even into her early twenties, how often had she wished she could be anybody except who she was?

Lord, what was wrong with me? And why on earth do I have that same feeling now?

Drew was saying, "You all know what my life has been like—well, especially this past year. And Charlie and Mariane have told us what they've been up to. How about you, Tess? How have the last 25 years been for you?"

Tess hesitated for a moment; then, as if gathering her strength, looked at each of them in turn. "You may not have realized it—I didn't myself until a few years ago—but I had a huge self-esteem issue. If you want the short version of my story, when I was close to 30, I got kind of desperate. More than anything, I wanted to get married and have a family. So, against my parents' wishes, I married a man I knew wasn't a Christian. I did think he was a good person. I was wrong."

"He always had difficulties at work, and when he drank, he'd get angry and blame me for his problems. At first, he just yelled at me, but then he began hitting me. We had three kids in five years, which made things really difficult." She looked down at her hands, lying clasped on her lap. "One day he hurt me so badly that, after he left, I finally called the police. They took me to a shelter. But I was so depressed, I ended up having to be hospitalized, and my parents got custody of my kids."

Tess paused, still looking down, wrapping her arms around herself as if she were cold. "It's taken me a long time to get myself back on track. But God has forgiven me. And my parents have stuck by me. The kids and I live with them."

She looked up. "I get by, one day at a time. And God helps me."

Mariane brushed away the tears in her eyes. *Oh, Lord, please be with each one of them, especially Drew and Tess.*

"I'm really sorry," Charlie said as she reached over to hug Tess. "I wish we'd kept in touch."

"Me too." Drew echoed.

"No," Tess said, "that's okay. We all had our lives."

She bit her lip. "Part of my problem was that I was so envious of all of you. I wanted to be beautiful and talented like Charlie, and popular and a leader like Drew, and confident and patient like Mariane. When I looked at myself, I just saw a mess."

"Oh, Tess," Charlie moaned. "I always wanted to be organized like you."

"And I always wanted your lovely red hair!" Drew sighed.

Tess laughed.

Her mind whirling, Mariane stared at Tess. She whispered, "*You* wanted to be like *me*?"

Tess leaned toward her. "More than anything. You were always so calm and peaceful, and so sure of yourself."

"Me?"

"And so humble!" Charlie said. "You were so smart, but no matter what you did, you kept it in perspective. You never got excited, but you never got depressed, either."

Mariane frowned. *Lord, are they making fun of me?*

And yet—independent Charlie, whom she'd expected to go out and make waves, was the stay-at-home mother of eight kids; Drew and Jackson, the perfect couple, were no longer together; always-organized Tess had made poor choices…

None of them had become the women Mariane had expected to see this weekend. Could she have been mistaken in other ways as well?

The fears she'd been holding inside made her tremble. *This is ridiculous*, she thought. *I'm 47 years old. I run an expanding chain of furniture stores. I'm on five boards. I'm respected in my church and my community. What am I afraid of?*

Aloud, she said the words she'd never been able to voice, "You know, I never understood why the three of you included me. You were all so beautiful and so strong and so capable—I never felt I belonged."

"Oh, Mariane," Drew said, "you were the one we all wanted to be with! You had so much confidence in God, and so much faith. We all wanted to be like you. We were never as brave or as faithful as when we were with you. You were our heart!"

Tears flowed from Mariane's eyes. *Lord, could I have been wrong about everything?* Looking in amazement at each of the others, the assertive businesswoman Mariane had become recognized the truthfulness in their eyes.

So you did want me here, Lord! Thank you for the gift of this weekend. Help me stay in touch with my friends, so we can support each other. And help me embrace the girl I once was, while I continue my journey to become the woman you want me to be.

Aloud, she said to them all, "I'm so glad—so glad I came."

On Being Still and Knowing

Nonfiction

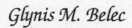

Glynis M. Belec

"The news is not good," Dr. Norman said.

My temples pulsated and I chastised myself for telling my husband Gilles not to bother coming. "I'll be fine," I'd said to my hubby, unaware of the black cloud drifting overhead. "That lumpy area is probably just my uterus doing a flip-flop because this old gray mare ain't what she used to be!" We'd laughed and he'd leaned over to kiss me. I'd clicked my seat belt and headed for the medical centre.

Dr. Norman touched my trembling hand. "It's cancer," she said. "Ovarian cancer."

A kaleidoscope of emotions whirred in my brain. Then a dull thump resonated somewhere deep inside. *Cancer? What do you mean I have cancer? Other people get cancer. Not me. I barely get a cold. I don't even get a headache unless I'm hungry. So this is a joke, right?*

My physician saw the confused look on my face and assured me the tests left no doubt. I had ovarian cancer, and the clock was ticking.

I couldn't make out much of what my sweet doctor said after that. Her lips moved. My ears heard. But my brain didn't register anything except some sporadic words: "CAT scan" … "surgery" … "oncologist" … "cancer clinic" … "bone scan" …

I suddenly felt as if I'd been thrust into the lead role in a play, but no one had given me the script. I'd no opportunity for rehearsal. The spotlight was beaming down on me as I stood centre stage, agape and alone. The audience was staring back at me in anticipation, but I had no idea what my lines should be.

I don't remember driving the short distance home, but I do recall falling into Gilles' arms, tears flowing, and telling my husband of 30 years that our life together was about to change forever.

Be still and know that I am God.

The words jumped into my head as Gilles stroked my hair. It was my favourite scripture verse. Psalm 46:10. I'd had it printed on my business cards for years. But for some reason, I felt a "God nudge."

Don't just repeat the words; think about what they mean.

I kept remembering that verse and what it meant as the days passed and the tests began. My life suddenly filled to the brim with appointments and waiting, waiting, waiting.

The technician at St. Mary's Hospital in Kitchener, Ontario, injected the radioactive tracer in my arm. As it coursed through my body, preparing me for the bone scan, something else started to course through my soul.

I had three hours between the preparation and the test—standard waiting time for a nuclear bone scan. I went to the cafeteria and bought a chai tea and a bran muffin. As I peeled back the paper on my muffin, it occurred to me that I had a choice. I could spend the next three hours in fear, dreading and thinking the worst; or I could focus on the blessings and joys that were beginning to surface as I embarked upon my cancer journey.

Use this moment, God whispered.

When I left the cafeteria, I found myself smiling and saying hello to perfect strangers. I got to the nuclear medicine waiting room and chatted to some others who were patiently waiting for their turn.

I've given you a sense of humour and a desire to laugh. Now do it, God reminded me.

Was I beginning to glow because of the radioactive injection? Or was I glowing because God was massaging my soul?

In between conversations in the waiting room, I closed my eyes and reflected. I remembered how the sun had shone on my face as I woke that morning. As I dressed, I had noticed the framed copy of the Lord's Prayer, lovingly embroidered by my mother, that hung on the wall beside my bed. I took a few minutes to read the words aloud, thinking about the meaning of each line. Then I gave thanks to God for the many friends and family whom I knew would be praying for me.

I'd also looked at my white board on the wall next to the embroidery. Two lines that I had scribbled on it months earlier remained etched in my mind. One was a comment made by Canadian author Phil Callaway at a Christian writers' conference a few years ago: "Courage is fear that has said its prayers." And the other simple sentence said, "Trust God."

As my name was called, I snapped back to reality, at the same time deciding that both those phrases would be my focus for this morning.

I dutifully followed the technician into the examination room. As I lay alone and quiet on the slim, metallic table, I contemplated my destiny. It was a good opportunity to chat with God. *What is it you have planned for me, Lord?*

Fodder, He replied.

Lying supine, the only place I could look was up. I thanked God and decided that from that moment on I would blog and journal and write and speak about my journey. I wasn't to do this with self-serving motivation or to further my career as a writer, but so I could remember and focus on the amazing power of God and the glory He was due.

The bone scan was quite an ordeal. The technician explained in detail how important it was to keep still as the cameras passed over and under my body. At one point I must have nodded off because the technician reported that the scan showed that I had two heads! So they had to redo the scan from the neck up.

"Two heads are better than one," my kindly nuclear guy said with a wink. He patiently repositioned me on the examination table and, once again, stressed stillness.

Throughout the test, he spoke gently and listened intently to my meanderings. By the time my test was over, I had shared my excitement and plans to write a creative nonfiction children's book about cancer.

"Put me on your list and sign me up for a copy!" were his parting words.

My journey continued.

Appointments ruled my days. Countless three-hour round trips to the London Cancer Clinic were bearable only because of family, friends, and the reassuring reminder that God was in control. It turned out my bone scan was negative for metastases, but I needed further investigation into a lung cyst and a breast lump. It seemed never-ending.

Throughout my cancer journey, "God signs" proved that He was orchestrating my days. In one instance, we arrived home after a particularly gruelling appointment in London. Dr. Lanvin, my new oncologist, had checked all the reports, confirmed my diagnosis through examination, and then briefed me about the upcoming surgery. So when we arrived home that day, my emotions were fragile. Although I had never played the "Why Me?" game, blaming God for allowing this to happen to me, I was starting to wonder about God's plan for my life.

As I walked into the kitchen, I noticed my phone flashing red, indicating messages were waiting. A voice I barely recognized said, "Hello, Glynis. It's Sue."

I hadn't heard from Sue for three years or more. We'd been acquaintances through drama ministry and school functions, and when we got together we always had a lovely time, but somehow we'd lost touch.

The recording continued. "So why did God wake me up at three a.m. and tell me that I should be praying for you? How are you doing? We haven't talked for ages. Give me a call when you get a minute."

I was floored. I quickly punched in her number. We chatted for a couple of minutes, chastising each other for not calling sooner.

"Are you okay?" she inquired.

"I have cancer."

Silence.

"I had cancer, too," she replied quietly.

I burst into tears. Sue and I spent the next hour talking and sharing. She encouraged me, promised to pray for me, and assured me I could call her any time. She also reminded me that as a 12-year cancer survivor, she was living proof that cancer can be overcome.

I got off the phone and cried again. This time my tears were not out of self-pity. They were tears of joy and gratitude for God. He had known my needs and was putting people and circumstances in place so that I could see His mighty hand.

I remembered God's nudging to write it all down, so my bedside journal became a therapeutic outlet. Words oozed through ink as I penned my thoughts and my day-to-day struggles with everything from fear, to spiritual questions, to relationships, and more. I started to realize what God had meant by the term "fodder."

If there was any doubt about Who was in control in my life, it was completely obliterated the night before my surgery, May 27, 2008. My journal entry reads:

> This is it. My final sleep before surgery. I am ready. I am Yours. I am prepared to be still and truly know that You are God! I am in awe at the confirmation that You have placed before me (and Gilles) this very night. What was the day's scripture verse in the *Our Daily Bread* devotional for Tuesday, May 27? "Be still and know that I am God" (Psalm 46:10). God—You rock! You know this is my favourite scripture verse. I love the soft, subtle ways You find to communicate with me, Lord—especially tonight. How blessed am I to know You in this heavenly way. How can anyone deny Your existence? You are real. You are living. You are in control...

That night I drifted into the land of slumber and found an amazing peace. The surgery went well, and before I knew it I was preparing myself for six months of intensive chemotherapy at the London Cancer Clinic.

I loved it when my oncologist asked me prior to a chemotherapy session if I was a "religious person." What an opportunity! He heard my heart that day as it lub-dubbed about how I was relying on the Lord for my daily strength and measure of trust. I prayed a seed was planted. Boldness in street corner preaching has never been my forte, but God was preparing me for some "Preach it, Sister!" kinds of opportunities throughout my journey. I decided to heed His nudges and tell my story to whoever was listening.

The next stage involved radical changes in my person. As my hair fell out, my eyebrows disappeared, and I realized I no longer had eyelashes to flutter, I was overcome by angst. When I started to focus more on the travesty of my hair loss than on the seriousness of ovarian cancer, I discovered how vain I was. Then, because I had been shoved into surgical menopause, the hot flashes began. Gilles, bless his heart, bought me an ultra-modern, robot-like, remote-controlled fan. It became my very dear friend. God reminded me how much easier hot flashes are to cope with when you don't have hair!

I remembered my ability to laugh in my midsummer journal entry of July 8, 2008:

> I catch a glimpse in the mirror
> A hairless sight to behold
> I do not like this pathway
> I'm starting to feel very old.
> But then I remember my Jesus
> Who knows every hair on my head
> His counting, of late, has been fruitless
> So He says, "Count blessings, instead!"

No one in his or her right mind would ever hope to receive the diagnosis of cancer. Yet, as I look back on my journey through the valley, I realize that by allowing me to have cancer, God knew what He was doing, and I am grateful. Throughout my journey, I have realized the kindness of friends and the dedication of family, I have experienced marriage vows in action (in sickness and in health), and I have stood in awe, watching the power of Jesus in my life.

Just as He promised, God had not left me comfortless. Never before had I felt so close to Him. Never before had I truly focused on the power of Jesus. Never before had I trusted God so earnestly.

I will continue to print, "Be still and know that I am God. Psalm 46:10," on my business cards, but now I'll do it with purpose and passion. And when someone asks me why those words are there, I'll listen for those angels as they shout in one accord: "Preach it, Sister!"

If Heaven Were Strawberries

Bonnie Beldan-Thomson

If heaven were strawberries
why would I eat turnips?

If heaven is forgiveness
why do I cherish hurts,
build a grudge-wall more sturdy
than the one in Berlin that finally
did topple?

If heaven is praise
why am I so comfortable
in the habit of complaining?

If heaven is bounty
why do I pine for what I don't have?

If heaven is the radiant light of Jesus
why do I scuttle among shadows?

If heaven is the continual presence
of Father, Son and Spirit
why do I not spend more time
getting to know them,
so I will be comfortable with them
forever and ever?

When You're Understood, You Can Put Up with Almost Anything

Nonfiction

Ed Hird

"Inside the heart of each and every one of us, there is a long-ing to be understood by someone who really cares. When a person is understood, he or she can put up with almost anything in the world." I penned those words in 1991 in the column I regularly write for a local newspaper in North Vancouver, British Columbia. As a priest, I've used these columns for 23 years to reach out to the wider community beyond my church doors. However, I had no idea how far outside my local sphere of influence these words had travelled.

My columns are printed in a community newspaper, but I also post them on my blog. When I did a recent Google search of the Internet, I discovered nearly 19,000 links to my column! I was amazed to discover that those words have been posted on thou-sands of strangers' blogs, social networking pages and romance-oriented Web sites. For all I know, they've been quoted in hundreds of essays or sermons too.

I believe that one of our deepest needs is to be truly under-stood. Some of us mistakenly think this is impossible. We're con-vinced that our concerns and problems are so unique that we'll be misunderstood outsiders forever. Yet there are always others who've gone through similar problems and can stand with us, if given a chance.

Many of us hope that if we get married, our partner will auto-matically understand us. When that doesn't happen, we become even more frustrated. Dr. Cecil Osborne, counsellor and author of *The Art of Understanding Your Mate*, once said, "Marriage is the most rewarding and the most difficult relationship known to man."[1]

Before my spiritual breakthrough at age 17 during the 1970s Jesus movement, I viewed marriage as "just a piece of paper." But when I became a believer and started reading the Bible, I discovered that God invented marriage and He believes in it; therefore, marriages are worth fighting for. And couples who believe their marriage is something God desires are more likely to act and think in ways that protect their marriage. "Therefore what God has joined together, let no one separate" (Mark 10:9). In my own life, our family has gone through our share of difficulties, but because my wife and I stand together, our marriage has made it through all the hard times.

Too often, we bring with us into our marriage the disappointments of life and the "baggage" from our families or previous relationships. Clinging to how we were mistreated in the past can steal our possibilities for joy and leave us feeling bitter.

Bitterness is often connected with the death of our dreams. The book of Hebrews in the New Testament says that bitterness will defile and harass our most valuable relationships, and leave our hearts hardened and cold (Hebrews 12:15). Without realizing it, we end up exchanging a heart of love for a heart of stone. Hardening of the arteries can be, not just a physical problem, but also a spiritual and emotional issue.

While one of the most common sources of conflict in marriages is problems with the in-laws, I have been blessed with the gift of the mother-in-law whom God granted me. Actually, Vera found me before my wife did. By God-incidence, we met each other at a 1974 weekend interdenominational conference in Squamish, B.C. Despite my longish hair and embroidered overalls, she was quite impressed with me. Vera really enjoyed a movie that was popular at the time, *Fiddler on the Roof*, and she could sing one of its hit songs by heart: "Matchmaker, Matchmaker, Make me a match, Find me a find, Catch me a catch..."[2]

Unfortunately, when my future mother-in-law/matchmaker commended me to her daughter, the assessment was not mutual. Janice and I had attended the same high school in Grade 12—and we all know what familiarity can breed. She did remember, however, that I had nice eyes.

When I reconnected with Janice at the University of British Columbia in 1975, I also rediscovered my future mother-in-law. I was most impressed by the warm hospitality that I always felt in Vera's home. Some people make you feel stressed by how they fuss over you as a guest. With Vera, it all felt very natural and relaxed. She had that gift of making everyone feel welcome and right at home.

"Like mother, like daughter" goes the familiar saying. Thirty-four years into my marriage, I am now more aware than ever of how much a mother influences her daughter. I give thanks to God that my mother-in-law raised my wife in an atmosphere of love and caring. I know that without that foundational nurturing, my marriage would have been a very different experience. I am grateful to be married to a loving wife and a loving mother to our three sons, James, Mark and Andrew. Janice learned mother-love from someone who really cared.

After Janice agreed to marry me, everything seemed to be falling into place in our lives. By 1980, I was newly ordained as an Anglican priest and had started working as an assistant clergyman at our first church in Vancouver. Janice and I were married and looking forward to the arrival of our first child. Abruptly, due to a rare viral throat infection, I lost my voice for 18 months. The doctors diagnosed it as spasmodic dysphonia, something I had never heard of before getting sick. This voice disorder causes the vocal chords to over-adduct (over-shut) on a spasmodic or intermittent basis, cutting off words or parts of sentences as you're trying to talk.

Ten medical specialists later, I stepped down from my job as an assistant clergyman in order to work on speech therapy. We were shocked to discover that our diocese, at that time, only had three weeks of paid medical leave available. Serious illness of a spouse can be a major source of stress in marriages, as can financial issues. During this difficult time, our marriage vows were sacred as my wife Janice supported me emotionally and spiritually, "in sickness and in health." My mother-in-law Vera, who stood with me in practical and prayerful ways, played a vital role at that time by introducing me to the Order of St. Luke the Physician, where I learned how to combine the dual benefits of medicine and prayer.

And God miraculously met our material needs for a year through the generosity of His people.

In 1982, I was operated on by Dr. Murray Morrison at Vancouver General Hospital. The day of the surgery, our home church held a 24-hour prayer vigil for my healing. When I woke up, I could speak again. I went back to preaching the next Sunday at my home church—and I've continued to preach for 30 years.

Of course, my wife and I don't always agree. No marriages are free from occasional marital conflict. For example, my wife Janice is a very generous person, just like her mom, Vera. Over the years, it has required a lot of give and take for us to learn how to be generous together, while simultaneously managing the resources God has given us.

It also took a while for me to understand that while I may enjoy waking up before 6 a.m., Janice prefers to stay up later at night, and to sleep in when her job allows this.

Because we're unique people with different personalities and backgrounds, some problems never really go away. But wise couples don't get gridlocked on the problems. They refuse to get bitter inside. The Serenity Prayer[3]—which is frequently recited at AA (Alcoholics Anonymous) meetings and other recovery programs—expresses the wisdom of asking for "the serenity to accept the things I cannot change." Excellent advice for all of us.

Problems frequently arise when one's spouse does something hurtful, promises never to do it again, but keeps breaking that promise. As a rector, I've seen much grief among the people to whom I minister when spouses put their work or their children first, merely giving each other the leftovers.

Ministers, too, can easily be overwhelmed by the endless demands on their time and requests for help from other people. I've had to learn to be intentional in making time to be with my wife. We set aside specific appointments in our schedules to reconnect with each other through going for walks or dinner dates.

Often, little things act as irritants when they could be solved easily. Early in our ministry, I stayed out very late one evening to lead a couple to Christ, and Janice was worried that I might have had a car accident. We devised a solution: if I'm going to be coming home from a ministry appointment after 10 p.m., I will phone to let her know.

No one can really change or fix one's spouse. It's always better to work on changing ourselves, which requires, as the Serenity Prayer puts it, having "courage to change the things I can." Or the courage to admit that we have faults, and the strength to try to improve the way we respond to our spouse's needs.

I've found that one of the ways to avoid bitterness is through the use of gentle, self-effacing humour. Aggressive humour, such as sarcasm or mocking, seals the coffin on your marriage. A few years ago, one of my sisters challenged me to give up our family's reliance on sarcasm. This convicted me so deeply that I repented to the Lord, and chose, that day, to swear off sarcasm. It hasn't been easy, because both my and my wife's families traditionally valued sarcasm as a sign of cleverness. I try now to encourage family humour that doesn't put others down.

Another way to support one's marriage is "encouraging behaviours." Marriage researcher Dr. John Gottman has found that successful marriages have, on average, five times more encouraging behaviours than negative behaviours.[4] Encouraging behaviours don't have to be extraordinary events, like taking our spouse on a foreign vacation to Crete (as I did recently when researching a book I'm writing).

Encouraging behaviours can consist of doing simple things, too. A healthy marriage celebrates the ordinary, not just the extraordinary. Janice and I are learning afresh the joy of ordinary pleasures: taking regular time together for peaceful walks, chatting over a cup of tea, listening to each other's daily experiences, watching a video together, going out for dinner, and even reading together. We often read side-by-side on the couch or in bed. When I'm excited about the insights I'm learning from a new book, I love to interrupt my wife and tell her about my new discoveries. Because she's very kind, she puts up with this, before going back to her own mystery novel.

We also enjoy going to the gym and working out, going swimming, and visiting close relatives or friends. Spending time with the one you love doesn't have to cost a lot of money, but the payoff is priceless. When you spend special time together, enjoying each other's company, it's far easier to forgive each other when those difficult situations inevitably come up.

Don't get me wrong; helping one's spouse feel understood takes time and hard work. For those of us who are married or considering marriage, it's our job to study our spouses carefully so that we know them even better than they may know themselves.[5]

A little romance never hurts, too. Alfred Lord Tennyson wrote, "If I had a flower for every time I thought of you, I could walk in my garden forever."[6] If we haven't been romancing our spouse, he or she may be suspicious of our initial efforts, and it may feel as if we're romancing a stony heart. This is where perseverance and gentleness are so vital in the pursuit.

For example, Janice needs to know that, as far as I'm concerned, she's the most beautiful woman on earth, a precious gift from God to me. But she also finds it very romantic when I take out the garbage or do the dishes! As for me, I find it romantic when my wife takes time to edit my articles, and listens to me when I want to bounce around a new idea for a book. Romance is saying, as Robert Browning did, "Grow old along with me! The best is yet to be..."[7]

Marriages suffer when we isolate ourselves from others. Shared spirituality and community help protect our marriages, while simultaneously helping to satisfy our individual needs to feel understood. Gathering together with other believers and building relationships within a community of brothers and sisters in Christ can be a huge source of strength. When you feel that you can't speak to your spouse about a problem, your church friends can prayerfully be there for you. Ordinary practices like attending church, reading the Bible and praying together have been scientifically shown to strengthen marriages.

Praying together softens each one's heart towards the other. Even if your spouse doesn't want to pray with you, your prayers will have an effect. Prayer has an amazing ability to change our stubbornness into openness. I've seen many helpful changes in marriages regarding problems with finances, in-laws and children after couples have started to pray together. It's best to start simply, perhaps beginning with repeating the Lord's Prayer together, and then gradually learn to pray more spontaneously, remembering that the essence of prayer is learning to say to God, "Please," "Thank you," and "Sorry."

Sadly, I've found that many couples view the idea of praying together as too intimate; one or both spouses may feel awkward about showing emotion or vulnerability. If our relationship with God is the most important thing in our lives, sharing that relationship by praying aloud as we each talk to our Heavenly Father reinforces our bond as a couple, and strengthens our faith. Jointly thanking God for the many good things in our lives and seeking His wisdom for the problems we face, makes us closer to each other, and to the Lord.

Thousands of people, through the far-reaching power of the Internet, have identified with something I wrote 20 years ago: the truth that, "Inside the heart of each and every one of us, there is a longing to be understood by someone who really cares. When a person is understood, he or she can put up with almost anything in the world." The truth is, God not only cares about us but He understands us better than anyone else ever will. He is the foundation upon which Janice and I have built our marriage, and the reason that we are even more in love, 34 years later.

1. Cecil G. Osborne, *The Art of Understanding Your Mate* (Grand Rapids: Zondervan, 1988).

2. Jerry Bock (music) and Sheldon Harnick (lyrics), "Matchmaker" (New York: Alfred Music Publishing, 1971).

3. Reinhold Niebuhr, "The Serenity Prayer," as cited in Wikipedia, http://en.wikipedia.org/wiki/Serenity_Prayer (accessed December 10, 2010).

4. Rosanne Farnden Lyster, "Sliding Down a Slippery Slope: Predictors of Divorce," B.C. Council for Families, http://www.bccf.ca/all/resources/sliding-down-slippery-slope-predictors-divorce (accessed December 10, 2010).

5. Gil Stieglitz, *Marital Intelligence: Overcoming The Five Problems Of Marriage,* DVD series (Sacramento, California: Principles To Live By, 2004).

6. Alfred Lord Tennyson, *Becket,* Read Book Online, http://www.readbookonline.net/title/4305/ (accessed December 15, 2010).

7. Robert Browning, "Rabbi Ben Ezra," Bartleby.com Great Books Online, http://www.bartleby.com/236/106.html (accessed December 15, 2010).

True Thanksgiving

Nonfiction

Rosemary Flaaten

On Thanksgiving weekend, the altar at our church was adorned with quirkily-shaped pumpkins and sheaves of golden wheat tied with binder twine. Jars of pickled beans, dill relish, preserved crab apples and Saskatoon berry jam covered the communion table. Bags of potatoes, fresh corn, and luscious red tomatoes gave evidence of this year's bountiful harvest.

As I entered into worship, flanked by my three healthy children, my loving husband of 20 years, and a myriad of friends and family, I felt engulfed in God's goodness, kindness and love. It was easy for me to focus on the blessings that He had provided over the past year: I had no pressing needs; my life was full; I had much for which to be thankful.

However, as my eyes flickered over the congregation, my attention was caught by a woman about my age and her elderly mother, holding each other's hands. I could tell that they were thankful for God's blessings, in particular for each other.

I immediately forgot all about counting my blessings. Where I'd first felt contentment, I now felt envy rearing its ugly head. Where I'd previously been thankful, I now concentrated on my longing, wishing that I could be that daughter. You see, as an adult, I'd never had the chance to lovingly hold my mother's hand, nor to bask in her love reflected back to me.

My thoughts of gratitude for a bountiful life shifted to the one area where I'd always felt a void—having a meaningful relationship with my mother.

My parents had worked hard on their small family farm in southern Saskatchewan, raising four children. Mom was a capable farm wife, registered nurse and active community volunteer. But in her early fifties, changes started to surface that gave way to a niggling sense that something wasn't right. Initially, she forgot where she had stashed Christmas presents, became confused about whether she had added four cups of flour or five to the bread dough, or went downstairs but then had absolutely no idea why she was there. Nothing that others haven't experienced; nothing terribly serious.

But when she couldn't balance her cheque book or use the telephone, we began to wonder if her forgetfulness was more serious than we had originally thought. The clincher came the day she returned home after working a night shift at our small rural hospital, unsure whether or not she'd administered the medications correctly. The next morning, she handed in her resignation and our family began the long journey into the abyss of Alzheimer's disease.

I was the last of four children to live at home. At the age of 12, with Mom slipping away cognitively and emotionally, I became the primary caregiver for our family. If we were to eat, I had to buy the groceries and make the meal. If we entertained visiting relatives, I tidied the house, prepared the food, and then stepped back to make it seem as if Mom were still the functioning matriarch of the family.

At that tender age, I longed to have a mother who would give me loving advice when I needed to make decisions. Instead, I was left to decipher this world alone, all the while pretending that my life was as normal as my friends'.

I grew to resent the amount of work, the lack of direction from either parent, and most of all, the need to present a façade to our friends and family that all was well. Night after night, I cried myself to sleep.

The tears didn't end in my teens; they continued through my twenties after I left home and married. But the night I learned of my mother's death, I lay in bed unable to cry. I was now a 29-year-old woman without a mother, but in reality, I had lived without my mother for most of my life. I had cried so many tears, my well had run dry.

As this array of memories swooped into my mind that Thanksgiving Sunday, self-pity consumed me, with anger crouched on the sidelines.

And then, cutting through the pain, the self-focus, and the resentment that my life should have been better, I heard a question in a crystal clear voice: *Can you be thankful that your Mom had Alzheimer's?*

I knew in my heart that the question came from God, but the magnitude of the question rocked me to the core. *Thankful? You've got to be kidding. Thankful that I lost my mom when I needed her the most? Thankful that our family has never fully recovered from the devastating ripple effects of that ugly disease that affected all of us? Thankful for Alzheimer's?* I knew the answer. *No!* There was nothing to be thankful for within that situation.

There are moments in our lives when we feel frozen in time, even as we see the world continuing around us. This was one of these moments. Although I had quickly answered an emphatic *No*, the question left me paralyzed. I wanted to move on, but the weight of that question pinned me down while the Thanksgiving service continued around me.

While I was lost in my thoughts, my ears abruptly became attuned to the song the praise team was singing. My focus expanded to include the words being sung. Something about the weak being made strong and the poor becoming rich because of God's presence suddenly created a mosaic in my mind's eye.

I saw a line of women, from my childhood to the present, who had poured beauty, love, and affirmation into the life of this relationally poor girl. Their gift of themselves had helped me overcome the deficit of my mother's presence in my life. I had actually become a woman rich with relationships. Not only that, but the hardships I experienced in those formative years had created a strong and capable woman who knew how to care for her family. God had taken a horrific situation and from it had brought forth good.

Tears now streaming down my face, I retracted my forceful *No* and gingerly agreed to continue pondering God's question to me.

Over the next few weeks, God impressed upon my heart that I needed to take seriously the commandment to "always [give] thanks to God the Father for everything" (Ephesians 5:20). Even the ravage of Alzheimer's is included. Either God is always good or He's not good at all.

Once I stopped being horrified that God was asking me to be thankful for my Mom's premature illness and death, I was able to see that the question came out of His desire for me to be grateful for His love and comfort in that situation. He wanted me to get my eyes off the pain and to recognize the incredible ways He had helped me get through my quagmire of loss and hurt. Even in the middle of my pain, He had been at work. Now, He was tenderly calling me to trust Him to take care of me, no matter what.

As I relinquished my need to make sense of the chaos and placed my bitterness in His hands, God enabled me to understand that the loss in my past had indeed become a benefit to me. I was a living example of the promise in Scripture that "every detail in our lives of love for God is worked into something good" (Romans 8:28, *The Message*[1]). I wholeheartedly identify with the Apostle Paul's declaration, "My imprisonment has had the opposite of its intended effect" (Philippians 1:12, *The Message*[1]). God had taken a horrible situation and brought indescribable good out of it.

We live in a world wrought with pain, hardship and injustice. No one is exempt. Every one of us will at some point encounter things that will make us poor or weak. Whether it's the loss of a parent, child, spouse, relationship, job, house, health—or any number of circumstances that cause pain or could be construed as imprisonment—God asks each of us, "Will you be thankful?" When things are tough, will we be grateful for God's presence and love? Will we let go of anger and bitterness, and instead say, "Because of the Lord's great love we are not consumed, for His compassions never fail. They are new every morning; great is Your faithfulness" (Lamentations 3:22–23). The choice is ours.

I no longer wait for Thanksgiving Sunday to reaffirm my commitment to gratitude. Instead, each morning I arise and give thanks for God's deep love for me. Each day, I look for the ways He continues to bring good into my life—not because of my circumstances—but in the midst of them. I can affirm that God is good all the time.

---

1. Eugene Peterson, *The Message: The Bible in Contemporary Language* (Grand Rapids, Michigan: Zondervan, 2002). Used by permission.

Mrs. Onley's Funeral

Fiction

Ron Hughes

It seemed to be taking Florence Onley forever to die. The old woman had kept people waiting all her life, and even though her family was exhausted from trying to look after her, she wasn't about to change any time soon. Nor was she going to fade away quietly. Having enjoyed 87 years without spending a single night in a hospital, Florence, or "Mrs. Onley" as she preferred, deeply resented the broken hip that had felled her. Even more, she resented the ensuing pneumonia that had filled her lungs and was slowly draining the life out of her. But Mrs. Onley was no quitter. Not ever. Not now.

For the last eight weeks, Pastor Paul Chapman had included Florence in his twice-weekly pastoral visitations. Just past 40, with his athletic build abandoning him, Paul was growing comfortable with the knowledge that he'd probably spend the rest of his life needing to lose 30 pounds. But he paid extra attention to personal grooming and attire these days because Mrs. Onley liked her pastor to "look sharp." He also realized his preferred casual approach to details needed to be elevated to meet her expectations. Mrs. Onley was the kind of person for whom spontaneity was a vice. Every aspect of her life was structured as carefully as she could manage. That's why this time in the hospital peeved her so.

During each of Pastor Paul's visits, Mrs. Onley planned and replanned her funeral. Eighty-seven years gives you a long time to firm up your opinions. It also gives you a lot to cram into an hour-long funeral service. She had so many favourite hymns and favourite Bible readings and favourite grandchildren who "might say a nice word" that Paul despaired of getting it pared down to a length even her best friends could tolerate.

Mind you, she didn't have many friends left, and that doesn't simply mean she'd outlived them. Not only did she have firm opinions, but she was convinced hers were the only legitimate ones. Woe betide the person who ventured to hold a different view on anything. You could find yourself summarily excluded from her inner circle for daring to suggest she might be mistaken, or that a reasonable alternative view on the subject at hand might possibly exist somewhere in the universe—perhaps in another galaxy.

Even as a child, growing up in the 1930s when children were expected to be respectful and unassertive, Florence was one of a kind. In school, she would lie in wait for the English teacher to make a tiny grammatical error; then, using only the most polite tones and respectful words, she would draw attention to it. As for her peers, she simply dominated them. No one would even think of making a plan without consulting Florence, knowing it would be overruled if she disagreed.

Her own children's responses to their mother varied according to their personalities. Barbara was publicly compliant and privately resentful. Richard was openly rebellious. Bernice, who was still living with her parents at the time Florence was widowed at age 53, was the most accepting and gracious. She was the only one who had a real sense of the depth of Florence's grief after her husband Wesley died, and that softened Bernice's view. Even after Bernice left home to marry Charles, she continued to be close to her mother.

Bernice's 24-year-old son, Grant, was a different matter. Perhaps it was because he had been exhorted to give in to Grandmother Onley so often that, as soon as he was old enough, he started asserting his independence with her. She liked short hair; he grew his long. She was a stickler for grammar and syntax; his "um, like, you know" speaking style was studiously casual. She had great respect for education; he quit high school halfway through his last year. Grant had the distinction of being her youngest, least understood, and consequently, least favourite, grandchild, which conveniently removed him from the list of those expected to "say a nice word for an old lady" at the funeral. It also removed him from pallbearer duty, ushering, directing traffic… or even showing up at all.

At last, the final revision of the funeral service was done. Pastor Paul recognized it as such when he got the call from Bernice on Thursday that her mother had died early that morning. *Peace at last. Peace at last. Thank God Almighty, we've peace at last.* Paul was too gracious to verbalize his Martin Luther King, Jr. paraphrase, but he thought it.

Bernice sounded tired. "The funeral director said Mom will be ready for the visitation tomorrow afternoon at two o'clock. If you could set the wheels in motion, that'd be great."

She sighed, and Paul wondered if she was just tired—or if she might be feeling a twinge of guilt over the sense of relief that likely accompanied her fresh loss. "Would you like me to meet with you before then?" Paul offered.

"No," she said. "It's not as if this was a big surprise. We're pretty well mentally prepared. I need to get some sleep more than anything. A couple of family members are still on their way. Let's just all meet at Davidson's Funeral Chapel tomorrow around 1:30."

"Your call," he responded. "I'll be there early to go over some of your mom's last wishes with Jim Davidson. I hope you're able to rest."

Just before the visitation on Friday afternoon, Paul met with the family to pray with them. They seemed to be genuinely grateful to him for investing so much of his time in Florence's final days.

He excused himself as soon as he could, and the rest of the day passed in a blur. Paul didn't have much left to do to prepare for the funeral at this point; Mrs. Onley's strict attention to detail had seen to that. Just the same, he had to attend to his hospital visits and put the finishing touches on his Sunday sermon.

At ten o'clock on that Saturday morning in early March, Paul pulled on his long, dark weatherproof overcoat and headed to Davidson's. *Great day for a funeral,* he thought. *Suitably gloomy and unpleasant. At least the graveside service will be quick.*

Paul had always appreciated Jim Davidson's work as a funeral director. He was quiet, calm, and supremely organized. Everything about him, from his dignified grey hair, his perpetually compassionate expression, and his well-tailored suit, down to his shoes with just the right hint of a shine, lent him a calming aura. In Jim's 25 years of experience, he'd confronted every imaginable contingency: missing floral arrangements, hysterical mourners who refused to let go of their loved one's hand, even a flat tire on a hearse. Jim was good at his job, and the service today would be just one more example of his efficiency and unflappable good nature.

Paul, a self-confessed obsessive counter, noted that 57 people were in their places when the service began, and that five more slipped in during the last verse of "What a Friend We Have in Jesus." A few of Florence's old friends, accompanied by adult children who had shepherded them from Wellington Manor to Davidson's Funeral Chapel, occupied the back pews. In front of them were Mrs. Onley's younger sisters, Gladys and Edna, along with a few nieces and nephews. Most of the immediate family sat directly in front of the casket: Barbara, the older of the two daughters, with her husband James and three children; Richard, who enjoyed both "only boy" and "middle child" status, and his wife Grace, with their two sons; Bernice and Charles with their only son, Grant.

Paul was surprised to see Grant at the proceedings. He was uncharacteristically well-groomed, too, with his beard trimmed and his longish hair pulled back. A smart-looking tweed jacket topped a clean pair of Levi's.

Paul guessed that Bernice had orchestrated her son's appearance, both his presence at the funeral and the way he looked. She had a bit of her mother in her, though it would be more than your life was worth to tell her you thought that.

The funeral service went as smoothly as Paul and Jim Davidson could make it. People reached far back into their memories and limited their remarks to the kindest things they could recall. She was "Mother," "Grandmother," and "Mrs. Onley" throughout. No one slipped and called her "Mom," "Granny," or "Florence." Paul expected he'd hear a commotion from inside the casket if anyone referred to her as "Flo." Didn't happen.

At last, Paul stood to give the benediction and invite the mourners to the cemetery and then to lunch afterwards in the church basement. Florence (as he liked to think of her, though he always called her "Mrs. Onley" aloud) had even prescribed that her favourite refreshments be served: tuna on whole-wheat (no onion); ham and cheese (not processed slices) on multigrain; brownies and butter tarts (both made from her recipes).

As Paul concluded the service, a flash of sunlight lit up the Christ The Good Shepherd stained glass window to the congregation's right, lending a mystical atmosphere to the poignant words of the closing hymn, "It Is Well with My Soul."

Nice touch, he chuckled inwardly. I *wonder if she's already running things in heaven?*

Paul said the benediction and asked everyone to rise as Jim Davidson and his staff wheeled the casket through the heavy oak doors, which opened to reveal the hearse waiting by the curb. In accordance with her instructions, a police cruiser with lights flashing ensured Mrs. Onley the right of way on her last trip through town. Paul noted that on this chilly quiet Saturday, even some of the pedestrians stopped in respect as the hearse passed by. Mrs. Onley would have approved.

The hearse carefully proceeded through the open gates of Eternal Hope Cemetery and led the procession up the hill to the Onley plot where a grave was open beside Florence's beloved Wesley. The site, dominated by an ancient oak tree, overlooked much of the town of Wellington. The rest of the cars, still in order, parked behind the hearse.

Because of the heavy rain earlier in the day, the cemetery paths were muddy and the grass was slippery. Jim set his helpers and the pallbearers to the task of moving the casket from the hearse to the grave while he quickly visited each car, cautioning people to be careful where they stepped and to watch out for the puddles.

As he followed the casket to the grave, Paul felt in his pocket for the little notebook in which he had printed out both the standard graveside committal service and a few final exhortations Florence wanted him to leave with her loved ones.

Jim arranged everyone in a horseshoe around the foot of the grave. Since he had a strong singing voice, he led everyone in singing "Shall We Gather at the River?" Then Paul approached the head of the grave where Jim had kept a spot clear for him. The water squished around Paul's muddy shoes as he flipped open the notebook and stepped into his place.

Was it his divided attention? Was it the slippery grass? Was it a slight miscalculation of distance? Paul was never sure, not even after later reflection. What he *was* sure of was that, just as he was about to open his mouth, the wet soil under the little piece of green carpet at the edge of the grave gave way, and his feet slipped under the polished brass cradle holding the casket above ground level. He found himself seated on a patch of wet carpet at the edge of the grave. His hands, still clutching the little black notebook, were resting on the casket, which now looked somewhat like an ornate, oversized lectern.

Rather dazed, Paul tried to take it all in. Someone snorted loudly. That would be Grant. Someone hissed. Likely Bernice.

Lest lightning strike from the clearing sky above, Paul wanted to apologize, but he couldn't think of anything appropriate to say. The words that immediately leapt to mind were unspeakable for a pastor, and "Excuse me" seemed just plain silly coming from someone whose legs were dangling under a casket at the edge of a grave.

Paul put one hand down to push himself up, but his legs were jammed between the edge of the grave and that shiny brass contraption. He set his notebook on the casket so he could use both hands to push. This was beyond embarrassing. Someone—likely Grant—guffawed.

Meanwhile, Jim Davidson rushed up behind Paul. Putting his hands under Paul's armpits, Jim started to lift him out. Alas, rather than bringing a quick end to the horror that was unfolding, Jim made it a good deal worse by slipping in the mud too. As his feet slid sideways, he clutched for some support to save himself—but only Paul was within reach. Jim landed heavily beside his pastor friend, his arms wrapped around him in an awkward embrace.

There was nothing for it now. Giggles began breaking out all over. The sight of these two upstanding gentlemen unceremoniously trying to extricate themselves from a situation that would, no doubt, make a story that would be hard to improve with the telling, was hysterical.

Slipping and sliding, Jim struggled to his feet, his immaculate suit and carefully polished shoes splattered and smeared with mud. By the time he had regained his footing, one of his flustered associates had stepped forward. With Jim on one side and his red-faced associate on the other, they extricated Paul and got him upright.

Paul gave his overcoat a yank to straighten it and, once again, stood at the head of the casket—this time at what he prayed was a safe distance from the edge. He glanced around at the contorted faces, but—afraid he'd lose control—quickly looked down to avoid eye contact. That's when he spied his notebook, still lying on top of the shiny mahogany casket where he'd set it.

When the mourners saw the pastor's stricken look, their pent-up laughter became uncontainable. One by one, people succumbed. Even Paul gave up. Grateful for being unhurt, and well able to put himself in the shoes of these good people who had lived, for years, under the stern domination of the honouree-of-the-day, he allowed himself to join in the laughter. Ever the professional, Jim Davidson managed to suppress everything but a silent smile.

As the weak early-spring sun peeped out from behind a cloud, the group clustered around the grave enjoyed an unexpected celebration of life that the memorial service would otherwise never have included. The frustration and bitterness with which many arrived had dissipated in the mayhem.

Wiping tears of laughter from their eyes, the mourners began sharing stories of Mrs. Onley's exploits, starting with her successful campaign lobbying City Hall to save old trees in a new housing development. Someone recalled her being banned from phoning in to a popular radio talk show because she'd made the host look foolish one too many times. Someone else brought up the time she deliberately arrived one hour late for a doctor's appointment, "Just to show him he's not the only person with important things to do."

Connie Wilson spoke of Mrs. Onley's one-woman crusade to get parent volunteers into the public school to help children struggling with learning, at a time when the principal thought mothers belonged at home. "She was the one who finally taught me to read," Connie recalled.

Old Fred Hollingsworth, one of her few contemporaries, told how Florence kissed him behind the one-room schoolhouse when they were about ten years old. "Never forgot it, but never figured out what it was all about either," he reminisced.

Edna recalled big sister Florence always wanting to organize things. "From childhood to adulthood, everything went her way.

It was annoying having her always telling me what to do," she said, "… until we lost our baby." She struggled to suppress the welling emotion. "I was paralysed with grief, so Florence came and lived with us for three weeks. I credit her 'take charge' ways with getting me back on my feet."

As more stories were shared, it became increasingly clear to everyone that the deceased had been a strong woman at a time when strong women were just beginning to be appreciated. In the end, Florence Onley became an endearing eccentric, which was a more honourable memory than anyone would have anticipated at the beginning of the day.

Paul was glad. He ignored the inconveniently located note-book. He'd repeated all the formal graveside committal lines often enough, he figured he could wing it. And something important he wanted to say to the family had just popped into his head.

"Thank you, everyone, for sharing your memories. Now I have something to tell you about Mrs. Onley which few of you know about. Florence"—he smiled as the word slipped past his filters— "was a fighter. Many of you saw her in action. Some of you knew what it was to be bested by her. She took on causes and fought tire-lessly for them. What you may not know is that she was as quick to take on God as she was to challenge City Hall, or the principal, or anyone else." Paul could see he had everyone's attention, even Grant's.

Glancing around at the mourners, he went on. "I visited your mother, your grandmother, your friend, many times in hospital in the last few weeks as she was fighting for her life. It was perhaps the only fight she ever lost. Several times, I'd think she was sleeping, so I'd jot a note on my card to leave on her bedside table, and be about to slip out quietly. Then her eyes would pop open and she'd fix me with 'the look' we all know so well.

"'I'm not sleeping,' she'd say. 'My eyes are closed because I'm praying, and I want you to help me. The Good Book says, when two agree, God listens extra carefully.'"

The mourners were listening extra carefully too.

Paul continued, "She'd tell me what—or more often, *who*— was on her heart. We'd talk with each other, and with God. In her last days on this earth, Florence prayed for many of you standing in this circle," Paul said, looking directly into Grant's eyes. "Then she'd dismiss me, thanking me for standing with her 'before the throne,' as she used to say."

He added, "You know, whatever old hurts made Florence the forceful woman she was don't matter any more. And I'm sure that in her own way, she's happy you're here today to remember her— and the unique way she loved you all."

Out of the corner of his eye, Paul noticed Bernice and Grant reaching into their pockets for tissues.

Pastor Paul took the little container of ashes from Jim, stepped to the side of the casket where the footing was solid, and made the sign of the cross on the casket with the ashes as he spoke.

"Thus we commit the body of Florence Onley to the ground; earth to earth, ashes to ashes, dust to dust; in the confident hope of resurrection to eternal life in the presence of God."

And everyone said, "Amen."

Life — Interrupted

Nonfiction
Johanne E. Robertson

I never dreamed it was possible to be 36 years old and have a stroke. On Tuesday, July 16, 2002, I woke up humming, rocking in my bed in a fetal position, I felt unusually calm, at peace with myself and with God. I hadn't realized it yet, but my life had radically shifted in a new direction.

The afternoon before, I'd stayed outdoors in the hot sun for at least an hour waiting to meet a client. It was an extremely warm July day, and as I placed my hand on my head, I could feel heat radiating from it. I remember thinking to myself, *I should have worn a hat*. When I returned to my office after my meeting, I was extremely tired. I decided to take a cool shower and call it a day.

I went to bed early, but I was restless. I'm the co-owner and co-publisher of a monthly Canadian Christian newspaper called *Maranatha News*, based in Toronto, Ontario, which is distributed free of charge to churches, Christian retailers and other locations. That night, my mind was filled with questions; I was wondering what changes we needed to make to the newspaper.

Our mandate is publishing news from various church denominations in order to show all the ways that God is at work in Canada, and all the ways that we as Christ-followers are more alike than different. At that time, we'd been publishing for six years, but we had some ongoing challenges to expand our circulation, attract more readers, find long-term advertisers, obtain suitable stories from across Canada, and interest more volunteers in helping in a variety of areas.

So I went to bed early, slept until morning, then got up and got ready for the day as usual. But when Monica, my business partner, walked into the office on Tuesday morning, she noticed that something wasn't right. I seemed a bit confused, and I was struggling to keep up a simple conversation.

Monica asked me if I wanted to go to emergency. I declined. I fought with the idea that I needed to go to the hospital. I kept saying that whatever symptoms I was feeling would pass. Looking back, I realize that it's common for people having a stroke to protest, because denial often goes with it. However, if I'd gone to the hospital as soon as I had some of the warning signs of a stroke (confusion, numbness, headache, dizziness or vision problems), I'd have been able to get drug treatment that could have stopped the stroke in its tracks.

I should have been a lot more proactive and concerned about my situation. But, in many ways, I was living a life of denial. No major health problem had ever happened to me. I was an independent, confident, strong, attractive Black woman, as well as a Christian who loved God.

I knew that my father had had a major stroke when he was 44, but I didn't relate what had happened to him to my condition. His symptoms had been primarily physical. His right arm and leg had become numb and limp, and he ended up paralyzed. I appeared to be fine physically; I had no idea the stroke had affected the cognitive area of my brain, my mental processes and my ability to comprehend.

I told myself that I could sleep it off, that I would feel better the next day. I thought that because I was a Christian who loved God, I was immune from anything bad happening to me.

When I woke up Wednesday morning, I felt worse and my speech was slurred. I asked Monica to take me to the hospital. As I waited to be seen by a doctor, I began to understand that I was really sick. My words were getting all mixed up. I was mumbling. My memory of dates was uncertain. Other people seemed to be moving very quickly around me, and I could only partially understand what they were doing and saying. I felt as though my life, as I had known it just days earlier, was being taken away from me.

The emergency room staff sent me for a CT scan, computerized X-rays showing cross-sectional views of my brain. The technician gave me specific instructions. "Do not move. Stay absolutely still." Questions started bouncing around in my head. *What did he mean by "Don't move"? Did he mean my legs, arms and head only, or did he mean my eyes? Can't I even blink my eyes?* I lay there, confused, tears streaming down each side of my face as my body went into this big CT scanning machine.

Lying alone in that tunnel, I tried to make a deal with God. *Lord, if You help me get back my strength again, I will serve You way better than I've been doing. I promise that I'll opt to do the things that I know You've been asking me to do, but I've been neglecting.*

I'd never had so many tests in my life: MRI, blood tests, cholesterol levels, neurologist's appointments… I quickly became very appreciative of all the people who work in the health care field. I was shocked when the doctors told me that I'd had a stroke.

A few days later, I called my mom, back in my hometown of Montréal, Québec, where she was living with my older sister Debbie. Mom immediately asked me what was wrong: I had only said two words, "Hi, Mom," and she knew something wasn't right! I told her that I'd had a stroke, and I was very confused. Mom told me to stay calm and not to worry, things would work out all right. She soothed me and said I shouldn't panic or get upset.

That was one of the last conversations I had with my mother during which she was coherent and lucid. At the time of my stroke, my Trinidadian-born mother, who had been a strong leader in the Black community in Montréal, was in the first stages of Alzheimer's disease. Although she lived eight more years, Alzheimer's robbed my mother of her vocabulary, her love of language, her ability to think and act on her own—and it robbed me of my mother's support at the time I most needed it.

The worst part of the stroke was the pain of losing control of "me." Not being able to decide what I wanted was awkward. Figuring out the answer to a question—almost any question—was difficult. Having to say to people, "Hold on a minute and let me think," was humiliating.

I often had a hard time just telling others my name. For starters, I couldn't tell if the person wanted my name or was asking me for someone else's name.

Numbers were my undoing. Being asked for my phone number was mortifying: I recognized the word "number" when I heard it, but I never knew if I should give my postal code or my phone number. And writing down someone else's number was equally frustrating; people hurriedly rattled off strings of digits, not taking into account that perhaps the other person couldn't think that fast. If I tried to place a phone call, just getting out "Hello" was an ordeal. It was made worse when some people—not realizing I was sick and assuming I was playing around—would answer back, mimicking me.

When everything that you've relied on in your past has vanished, and you're left to depend solely on God, that's when the questions begin. *Do I really know Him? Can I trust Him? Will He actually do what He said He would do?* I needed the answers to be "Yes."

For a Christian, life means knowing you can depend on God every day, for everything. I had to believe that He was real. So I called out to Him in my distress and asked Him to watch over our business, and all our affairs. And He did.

I later found out that I had undiagnosed hypertension—undiagnosed simply because I hadn't had a family doctor or gone for checkups prior to the stroke. Perhaps it went untreated for years.

I also discovered that I was diabetic. I was really in trouble. I had been ignoring my health, and the need to take care of myself.

My life became focused on weekly hospital visits, medications, specialists and therapists. For someone who had never regularly visited a doctor's office, this was a difficult lesson.

My family had never been the type to go see the doctor about every little thing. No one in my circle of aunts, cousins, grandparents or friends had been on any medications as I was growing up. Maybe it had something to do with our cultural roots in the West Indies, resulting in my family assuming that North American doctors prescribed too much medicine. My discounting of doctors might also be related to some flawed beliefs I absorbed at a church I started attending later in my life. Whether the people intended it or not, I somehow picked up the idea that if I had enough faith in God, nothing bad could happen to me.

Whatever the reasons, I now had to learn how to cope with the after-effects of the stroke. For the first several months, my hand-to-mouth co-ordination was off, making it hard for me to feed myself. I had to learn the meaning of words all over again. For example, I knew what a "table" and "chair" were used for, but couldn't call them by their appropriate names. A speech therapist started coming to my house to help me twice a week, but I was frustrated to have to relearn all the basic things.

Besides affecting my ability to retain information, the stroke left me physically weak, and often wanting to sleep. Although I was still young, my body felt worn out. I loved my job, but I had worked long hours and neglected my health. Too late, I realized that God hadn't intended for us to run our bodies into the ground.

Many nights were spent wiping away tears and asking myself questions. *I'm 36 years old. Is life over for me?*

I tried to explain to others why the tears came so easily. If you sounded angry at me because you raised your voice, I would cry. If I had to use the washroom, I fretted about the 50-step journey, and sometimes I would cry. When I'd get tired suddenly, like a battery that's drained of its power, I would cry. I'd cry because crying was one of the few things I could do. And crying was a portal of release from all the emotional toll that the stress of my situation had taken on me. Crying was my closest friend, but the tears that I cried couldn't console me, and reasoning with me couldn't prevent the tears.

Worry entered my life. I worried about everything. The night. (*Why is it so dark outside?*) Going to bed. (*What if I never wake up?*) Loud sounds. (*Is something wrong?*) Groups of people walking towards me. (*Are they coming to hurt me?*) Mosquitoes. (*What if they bite me and I get West Nile virus?*) As a consequence of my fears, I never wanted to go outdoors.

But being inside wasn't good either. I particularly worried about the telephone. (*Why are the phones ringing so often? Why?*) Every day I had urgent questions for which I needed answers, and I listened for the answers as if they were critical to my very existence.

All that worrying made me so tired that I needed more sleep. If I was away from home and a bed wasn't nearby when I felt I needed to rest, I would start to cry, rock backwards and forwards, rub my legs, and repeat "I'm tired," as many times as needed to comfort myself. When this happened in public, afterwards I would be so embarrassed that I would question whether or not I should continue to be the owner of a business.

Many times I wondered, *When will my normal voice and speech return? Will it be tomorrow? Next week?* My consuming concern became, *Will I ever get back to what I was like before?*

By six months after the stroke, I was weary of trying to cope with my dragging speech and the need to constantly explain myself. I needed a change. As soon as the doctor okayed me to travel, I was keen to head to Montréal to see my family. Since I knew that the bus trip from Toronto would take seven hours, I looked on my bookshelf to find some reading material. A book called *In Time of Trouble* caught my attention because the title matched the way I was feeling.

After I got settled on the bus, I pulled out the book and started reading. It was the first book I'd tried to read since my stroke, and my ability to retain information wasn't good. I had to read the same lines over and over again to try to grasp the true meaning of the story. I discovered that it was a young adult novel, a coming-of-age teen book that fit the type of light reading I needed. It was written by Canadian author N. J. Lindquist.

As I began reading about the main character, Shane Donahue, a misunderstood teenage boy who feels alone and unloved, I found it easy to identify with Shane, and the book gripped my heart. It reminded me not only of my own struggles growing up, but also of all the teen shootings on the streets of Toronto in the last few years.

I wanted so much to be able to keep the facts of the story line in my head. I wanted to understand what was happening to Shane and see how he would respond. I made myself stay calm and just concentrate on the story line.

After about 45 minutes, I was 20 pages into the novel. I turned to ask Monica, who was travelling with me, to give me a bottle of water. But instead of motioning to her with my hand, my new way of coping, I said, "Monica, could you pass me a water bottle? I'm getting thirsty."

It was the biggest miracle that I've ever witnessed! While my mind was focused on reading, God had been at work in me. In that moment, my normal strong speech returned. Monica and

I just smiled, and I kept talking. It was amazing! I hadn't heard myself speak with a regular tone and speed in months. It was a very moving moment for us.

I *so* wanted things to go back to normal right then and there, but within half an hour the slow speech returned. However, Monica encouraged me to keep on reading a little each day.

There was a direct correlation between my reading and my speech getting stronger. A few weeks later, I finished *In Time of Trouble*. The book impacted me so much that—even with everything else that was going on—I was inspired to start a new ministry called Read for Life. It's a program that works to encourage literacy and to get life-changing books into the hands of teenagers who need to read them.

Although we continued to see progress, my speech still was frequently slurred and slow for more than 18 months, and even today it can suddenly become uncertain in moments of stress.

Meanwhile, we had a business to run. My business partner Monica Leis and I have a very good working relationship. I first met Monica while we both were attending a large church in Kitchener, Ontario. We became friends, and we found out that we both had dreams of starting our own businesses. We developed several business ideas together, and in 1996 we launched *Maranatha News*. We shared a vision that the newspaper could be used to link believers all across Canada, from different cultures, ethnic backgrounds and denominations.

To keep our business going after my stroke, Monica had to do both my job and her job. She took over my role as editor and sales person, and did most of my telephone work, calling clients. This was not easy for her, because at the time she was a low-profile kind of person who preferred managing the business from behind the scenes. Monica also handled the newspaper's layout, and worked with our graphic designers and delivery drivers. The year of my stroke, we only missed one edition of *Maranatha News*.

In addition, Monica kept in touch with my family in Montréal, letting them know how I was progressing. She also kept on top of my many appointments with doctors and specialists, my medications, my meals, the banking, the bookkeeping, and paying the bills on time. In each of these areas, God gave extra grace and strength for her to get everything done without my being able to help. I had previously thought of myself as a leader and a visionary; I had never had to surrender control before, so this was a humbling new experience for me.

Once I started recovering from the stroke, I'd have a spurt of energy and be able to work for maybe an hour, but then I'd have to sleep for four hours. Strangely, after those naps, although I would feel guilty that I had slept the day away, I would wake up inspired. I would feel as if I had been attending a motivational workshop where I was being fed new material for the journey. I would awaken very sure of myself, knowing exactly what I wanted to do with *Maranatha News* as its publisher. I'd work for a couple more hours, and then have to rest again.

One of the most wonderful incidents of God's leading during this stressful time was my discovery of The Word Guild. It's a national association whose whole purpose is connecting, developing and promoting Canadian writers and editors who are Christian.

Even before my stroke, we knew we needed to stabilize the newspaper with an array of writers from various denominations and geographic locations, who could supply us with vital information about churches, ministries and Christian businesses from across the country. After a colleague from another publication gave me the number, I called the organization and asked for help.

In a few days, their printed directory of professional members arrived in the mail. I was absolutely amazed that this directory was available to editors and publishers at no charge.

This truly was another answer to prayer for us. I had discovered an army of Christian writers ready to supply exactly what we needed. I soon found a copyeditor, six monthly contributors for the newspaper, a variety of freelance writers and columnists—and people with similar interests and passions who have become my friends and colleagues.

Each year since the stroke, I've become stronger and healthier. My speech, which is connected to the speed of my thought processing, has gradually progressed.

But I still have some triggers I need to watch out for. For example, if I have to meet several deadlines that are too close together, the stress can put me out of commission. Being around too many hyperactive people, who talk too fast and jump from topic to topic, makes me have to work hard to keep things straight. At times, I still have difficulty understanding when people are joking and when they're being serious. Summer heat aggravates my symptoms, and can make me lose focus. Even now, I continue to struggle with depression or sudden outbursts of emotion, which are after-effects of the stroke.

I'm conscious of what a toll the illness took on me psychologically, and on my independence as a person. I'm realizing that since the stroke, I've usually gone along with everyone else's ideas or opinions in order to avoid having further discussions, and I've opted out of tough conversations just to get away.

The most frustrating aspect of my recuperation is feeling good for a week or a month, but then reverting back to the initial symptoms. It's very difficult to remain positive through the tiring process of explaining what's going on to new clients who first meet me when I'm normal, and who later see the second side of me.

In 2008, I was asked to join the board of directors for two national organizations, Women Alive and The Word Guild. I was shocked that they would want me to serve—after all, I was still in recovery—and I knew it wouldn't be fair to accept without telling them about my ongoing struggles. They still wanted me to join, so I agreed, and asked God to lead me and keep me from making a fool of myself in public.

A boardroom is a terrible place to be when you're searching for your words and the people around the table are staring at you, waiting for you to say what's on your mind. I'm thankful to the other members for having so much patience with me. It's been a learning process and, at times, it's taken a lot out of me to keep going and not just quit. But I've tried to do my best, and, over time, I've been able to find my place on the boards, with "both Johannes" feeling comfortable.

I still struggle at times, and I still get embarrassed when my natural strong speech leaves me and the slow speech shows up. That's happened while I've been on stage addressing 300 students, and in church before a Sunday morning crowd. I've lost my thoughts along the way, and had to recover quickly. It's hard for me to do, but I've learned that it's okay to make mistakes in public. You won't die from the experience. And in fact, you'll likely grow stronger and better.

In the nine years since the stroke, I've learned to take improved care of my health. I see the doctor quite regularly now, get annual checkups, and take medication on a daily basis. I've changed my food habits and I mostly cook all my food "from scratch" nowadays, such as making big pots of homemade pea soup. I try to stay away from the salt and sugar as best I can. I'm still working on the keeping fit and exercising part. Most of all, I give praise that I connected even deeper with a God who loves me and cared enough for me to save me from my previous destructive ways.

At the end of the day, I am a child of God and the Lord loves me with all my challenges. He's never stopped loving me. He's watched over me from the beginning of time and He knows my days. I find great comfort in knowing this. I've discovered that, even for those who love God, life is not a promissory note of 100-percent-problem-free living. Life is filled with obstacles and difficulties. When we press on no matter what, that's when we truly grow and begin to evidence His life in us, His characteristics and His love.

More Than One Way

Nonfiction

Ruth Smith Meyer

Quilting has been part of my life since I was very young. The great number and variety of patterns fascinate me. I love the fact that many quilt patterns have scriptural themes, such as "Garden of Eden," "Bethlehem Star," "Joseph's Coat," and "Crown of Thorns." Even more intriguing is the fact that, because the choice of fabrics and colours makes each quilt unique, reflecting the characteristics of its maker, two quilts may be barely recognizable as being made from the same pattern.

Several years ago, I accompanied a group of women on a tour of quilting shows and shops. I came away with the promise of receiving a monthly letter giving me six progressive sets of instructions to make a "Mystery Quilt." I was excited by the idea.

The first letter arrived with instructions to buy varying amounts of fabrics in a dark solid colour, a dark print, a light-coloured print, and a light tone-on-tone design. When I went shopping, however, I became frustrated. How was I supposed to choose good colours and contrasts if I didn't know the pattern of the quilt? Filled with apprehension, I agonized over my choices.

The next letter contained directions to begin cutting the material. I dreaded cutting into good, new fabric without knowing what the finished product was going to look like, but I forced myself to do it, mumbling my discontent the whole time.

My feelings of unease and anxiety grew with the following letter. It required more complex cutting of the different fabrics. I had to commit to the unknown. It didn't feel good.

When the fourth letter advised me to begin sewing the cut pieces together, I balked. I felt like a sheep being herded around without any personal choice. Although I experienced more than a little disgust at my inability to go on step-by-step, I had to know what I was creating. I had to have my goal in sight.

I guiltily stowed the fifth, unopened letter in the box that held all the supplies for my abandoned Mystery Quilt, along with the unused fourth letter.

Finally, the sixth missive arrived. I opened it. The letter contained a photo of the finished product. It wasn't long until I had my quilt done. It was beautiful! But the experience of making the quilt continued to haunt me.

Then one day over coffee, my teacher-daughter started describing to me how the children in her second-grade class worked differently. Some needed to be given small, progressive steps to complete a task. Telling them all the steps in a project overwhelmed them and they froze up, unable to begin.

Others, she said, were just the opposite. Receiving only one instruction at a time made no sense to them. They had to understand what the finished project would look like before they could begin. "It's just the way they're made. Each child functions differently," she commented.

The light went on. I realized that I'm the kind of person who needs to see the whole picture.

That insight gave me a better understanding of myself, and got me thinking about other parts of my life. How does this trait affect the way I communicate with others? What difference does it make in my ability to complete other tasks with which I'm presented? How does it influence my walk with my Lord?

I struggled, feeling inadequate and unfaithful, until one day I read the story of the disciple Thomas in John 20:24-25. His reaction when the other followers of Christ told him that Jesus had appeared to them after His crucifixion has dubbed him "Doubting Thomas." Thomas told the other disciples, "Unless I see the nail marks in his hands and put my finger where the nails were and put my hand into his side, I will not believe it!"

I suddenly saw another side, and I began to have more empathy for one of history's most famous sceptics. Maybe Thomas was simply withholding his opinion because he needed to understand the whole picture. Anything less didn't make sense to him.

Now, how could the "Doubting-Thomas-in-me" reconcile my need to see the whole picture with my need to follow Christ, in

faith, with my whole heart, soul and mind? Do I trust Him with all the unseen parts of the picture, or do I withhold part of my belief and allegiance and try to control what's happening until I can see more?

I struggled several days with my dilemma. What was I missing? God made me the way I am. Why would He ask me to operate differently from what comes naturally to me? Was I somehow defective because I couldn't seem to follow when I knew only one step at a time?

A few mornings later, as I was reading my Bible, I noticed afresh Jesus' words, "I am the way, the truth and the life" (John 14: 6). Another light-bulb moment! Jesus *is* the whole picture! Jesus Christ is *everything*; the Alpha and the Omega, the beginning and the end; the way, the truth, and the life.

Even if I can't see beyond the bend in the road, if I keep my eyes on Him, I *have* the whole picture, everything I need. For all of us, no matter what our personality traits, what could be more complete, more encouraging, more faith-inspiring than that certainty?

Seeing the Heart of God

Nonfiction

Gloria V. Phillips

I set the cardboard box on the table in front of me, then sit down and take a moment to compose myself before opening it. Inside are pictures of my son. I'm fortunate to have these. One day when Elliot[1] was 22, he destroyed every picture he could find of himself. More than two decades of our family photos burned to ashes in only a few hours. I have these few photos of my son only because I had tucked some pictures of my family away in my bedroom several weeks before, planning to get them made into a video.

My hand trembles as I lift the lid.

The photograph on top was taken when Elliot was three months old. It was his first professional portrait. My own eyes fill with tears as I look at his bright blue eyes staring back at me from a tiny oval face. I remember the day this picture was taken. It had not been easy to convince the photographer to do a portrait sitting for a child so young. He preferred to wait until a baby could sit up on its own, and was convinced we wouldn't get a good picture. Somehow, I talked him into trying. Elliot co-operated and the photographer and I both were happy with the results.

I breathe a prayer of thanks that this photo was not destroyed.

I set it down and lift out the next picture. This one was taken on his first birthday. Elliot, dressed in bright red overalls and a white T-shirt, is sitting in his high chair, with his birthday cake on the tray of the chair. His left hand clutches the single candle while his right hand is smeared with chocolate icing.

I move on to a photo taken the day Elliot graduated from kindergarten. He's wearing a red gown and a small black mortarboard cap. The cap's tassel casts a shadow over his face, but it doesn't hide his happy smile.

My hands rifle through the photos. Each one stirs up an almost forgotten memory: his first bike, a camping trip, fishing with his

dad. The situations depicted are common, everyday occurrences, but to me each picture is a treasure that means more than any amount of money.

At the bottom of the box lies a picture of Elliot at his high school graduation. Only a week after he graduated, Elliot moved thousands of miles away. He was independent, he felt ready to begin life on his own, and he wanted to pursue big dreams. Things started out well, but, somewhere along the line, his dreams were crushed.

The sombre 22-year-old who moved back into our house four years later bore little resemblance to the carefree young man who'd left. When he returned, Elliot was in both physical and emotional pain, the result of a number of hardships that he had endured while trying to make it on his own. He was profoundly angry, embittered and depressed, and his method of coping was to lash out.

My husband and I saw the anguish he was going through, and felt his pain, but nothing we did for him seemed to help. When we tried to get other help for him, he left, severing all ties with us.

I pick up the photo and study it. If he walked into the house today, would I recognize him? It's been more than a decade since I last saw or heard from him. Have the years changed him as much as they've changed me?

I think back to the days leading up to his final departure. They were more difficult and stress-filled than anything I had experienced up to that point in my life. But I soon discovered that the emotional upheaval in the two months our son was back home living with us was nothing in comparison to what I felt after we realized he was gone.

At first, the days after Elliot left were filled—though I hate to admit it—with a sense of relief. No more walking on eggshells; no more wondering each time I left the house what I would find when I returned… Would he still be there? Would there be damage to the house? My greatest fear was that in his depression he would do something to himself while I was gone.

After he left, the house was peaceful again, but my heart wasn't. I missed my son more than I'd ever thought possible. Without him in my life, I felt as though the sun had stopped shining and the world was covered in darkness. There was an empty place inside me that nothing could fill.

When I went out, I saw people everywhere who reminded me of him. If I was driving down the street and saw a young man of his age and build walking toward me, I would slow down, wondering if it was Elliot. If I was out walking and saw someone of his stature biking, I would take a second look. Each time I was disappointed, the pain inside me grew.

I couldn't stop looking for him, and I couldn't stop wanting him back in my life. Daily I waited, hoping he would try to contact us, but he never did. Every time I heard the chime of the doorbell or the ringing of the phone, my heart began to race. Was this him? But it never was.

I wondered where he was, how he was doing. I needed to know he was safe, to know he was all right; but I had no idea where to look for him and no way of contacting him.

Weeks passed, then months. As time wore on, hope of ever seeing my son again faded, and darkness settled on my soul the way physical darkness arrives; it crept in slowly, taking its time, with the light gradually fading away and the black of night overtaking it. I didn't see the night coming, nor did I recognize it as depression for a long time. It's puzzling how one can walk in darkness and not realize it.

Life continued. I worked, I ate, I slept, I socialized. As the darkness inside me grew, I ate and slept more and socialized less. I quit going to church and I turned my back on God. He, after all, had given me my son—only to take him away from me. In my pain, I couldn't see that God cared for Elliot as much as I did; that He, too, was hurting.

I felt so alone.

Though the rest of the family shared my grief, it was too painful for us to talk about. Elliot's two older brothers missed him too, but they refused to discuss their feelings. My husband coped by burying himself in his work.

It seemed to me that everyone was uncomfortable if I even so much as mentioned Elliot's name. No one knew how to deal with the loss, and no one knew how to help me.

Not a day went by that I didn't think of Elliot. Rarely did a night pass without my dreaming of him. Sometimes in my dreams he was a baby, sometimes a child, other times a happy, laughing teenager. I began to look forward to sleep, because it was the only time my son was still part of my life. Yet I dreaded sleeping, because the pain each time I woke up and realized he was gone was as fresh as that I'd felt when he first went away.

The dreams I found the hardest to cope with were the ones in which my son was an adult. In one dream, I was sitting in a restaurant. When I looked up, I saw Elliot coming toward me. He was as happy to see me as I was to see him. We hugged. It was such a strong hug that even the memory of it brings back the sensation of holding him and being held by him. Arms clasped around one another, we cried. My own sobbing awakened me.

This dream repeated itself over and over. It varied; sometimes we didn't recognize each other, other times he wouldn't acknowledge me. Although the details changed, the emptiness I felt each time I woke never changed. My body awoke, but my mind held onto the dreams just as I'd held on to Elliot. As we were torn apart when consciousness returned, I ached physically.

These experiences, night after night, were bittersweet—filled with the bitter agony of seeing him only in my dreams and the sweet memory of embracing him again.

Though I missed Elliot every day, birthdays and holidays were the cruellest. Even though I knew better, every year I hoped I would hear from him on my birthday or on Mother's Day. Every Christmas brought a longing that this might be the year he would contact us.

I purchased cards for him for his birthday and Christmas, and wrote long letters to go with the cards. The letters updated him on family happenings and assured him of my love. I had no address to which to send the cards and letters, but it brought me comfort to write them. In one letter, I told Elliot that buying him birthday and Christmas cards was partly my way of coping, but more than that, "It's a statement that I choose to believe you are alive, that I choose to believe you are well, and that I choose to believe that someday you will read the cards and letters I write you, and you will know how much you were and still are loved."

Every card and letter I've written has been tucked away in a drawer, ready to give him should he ever come home.

Although I've heard that time heals all wounds, in my experience time alone does not heal; only God can bring true healing. The change came slowly and gently, and the darkness lifted in the same way it had come—gradually. I can't look back on a particular day and identify it as the turning point. There was no single moment when I suddenly started to believe in God again.

The change that happened within me is as much a mystery to me as is the way a tiny seed planted in the ground can turn into a beautiful plant. I never realized it was happening. I was unaware that God was working in my life, that He had not abandoned me just because I'd abandoned Him.

Gently He called me, whispering words of comfort into my aching heart. In the night when I would wake, troubled by my dreams, the words of old hymns that I had learned in my childhood would play through my mind: "What a friend we have in Jesus, all our sins and griefs to bear,"[2] or "Be not dismayed what e'er betide, God will take care of you."[3] I didn't consciously summon them, they just appeared, comforting me, reassuring me, and reminding me that I wasn't alone.

Several years after Elliot disappeared, I began to attend church again. Although I went regularly, I left the services feeling as empty inside as I'd been when I'd gone in. I was going through the routine, doing the right things and saying the right words, but all the time—though I was unaware of it—I was holding onto my hurt as though it were a prize I'd earned.

People tried to reach out to me, but I was too devastated by hurt to see that they cared.

One day, as I was browsing through a magazine, I came across this statement: "God can mend broken hearts, but you have to give Him all the pieces." In the ensuing days, those words replayed themselves over and over in my mind. I knew I hadn't given God all the pieces. I'd asked Him to take away the pain, but He couldn't take it because I wouldn't let go. I was like a baby crying for milk, but refusing to let go of the bottle so it could be filled.

I told myself that I would give God all the fragments of my broken heart. I was determined not to hold onto the pain any longer. However, the hurt of losing my son had become so much a part of me that I was lost without it. The world was a scary place when I had nothing to hide behind.

It took a long time for me to let go. Oh, how I struggled with giving God all the pieces. Each time I thought I'd done it, something would happen to show me that I was still holding on. I learned that the only way to deal with my pain was to take it to God each time it surfaced. Sometimes that was once a week, sometimes it was once a day, and sometimes it was every hour. I learned that no matter where I was, or what time of day or night it was, God was available to listen to me. Little by little, I handed Him the broken pieces and learned to trust Him with the results.

I reached the point where I could go without thinking of Elliot all day or dreaming of him at night—and not feel guilty. I had neither abandoned him nor stopped loving him when I allowed myself to enjoy life. I learned that when I did think of him, I could take my concern for Elliot to God and trust that He would look after my son. He knows where Elliot is, even though I don't. He's able to care for him and meet his needs, even though I cannot.

One night, lying in bed, I was particularly burdened for Elliot. Though by then it had become my habit to talk to God about my son each time I thought of him—to, as the hymn writer put it, "take it to the Lord in prayer"[4]—on this particular night I couldn't find relief in prayer.

In the darkened room, with tears running down my face, I poured out my heart to God. I told Him how much I hurt, how much I missed my son, how I worried if he were dead or alive, and how much I longed for him to come home. In the stillness of that night, God shared His heart with me.

"I feel your pain," He said. "He's my child too."

"I know, Lord," I told Him, "but it's not quite the same."

"You're right," He answered. "You have one child who has blocked you from his life; I have many."

I had a sudden vision of masses and masses of people, the population of the entire globe, everyone who ever has lived and who ever will live. For the first time, I realized that God loves every single one of them as much as—no, more than—I love my son. I understood that it breaks His heart when His children turn away from Him. The Creator of the universe knows what it's like to wait for children who turn their backs and reject Him, to write love letters that may never be read.

In spite of the pain this experience has brought, I've found that I'm able to thank God for it. I wouldn't say that I've touched the heart of God... but I've glimpsed the love that's in His heart, and I will never be the same.

1. The name of the author's son has been changed to protect privacy.

2. Joseph M. Scriven and Charles C. Converse, "What a Friend We Have in Jesus." Public Domain.

3. Civilla D. Martin and Walter S. Martin, "God Will Take Care of You." Public Domain.

4. Scriven and Converse, "What a Friend We Have in Jesus."

The Road Trip That Wasn't

Nonfiction

Janet Sketchley

You can't give a car more power by gripping the steering wheel and willing it to keep going. Clenching your stomach muscles doesn't help either.

I tried anyway, and tromped the accelerator pedal to the mat. The engine roared and I prayed it wouldn't blow. Our station wagon inched up the hill. At the crest, I eased back on the gas. Going downhill felt relatively normal and we were okay on the flat stretch, but I knew we couldn't make another climb.

Forget reaching our destination; I'd settle for the nearest service station. But we were on a highway 40 minutes south-west of Halifax, Nova Scotia, and I knew we weren't even close to the next community. Ahead loomed a steeper hill than the last, where the two-lane highway widened to make a third lane for overtaking slow-hauling trucks on the incline. A few trucks had passed *us* on the last hill.

I sighed and pulled over onto the gravel shoulder. It was a hot summer day, and the only vehicle in sight was a pickup truck parked on the other side of the road with its hood up. No help there.

My three sons had been quiet until now, playing Game Boys™ and ignoring one another, tuning out the long drive. Now their questions started. "Why'd we stop, Mom? What's wrong?"

I'd promised the boys a day at the South Shore Exhibition, held each July in Bridgewater, a town about an hour outside of Halifax, where we lived. Carnival rides, cotton candy, caramel corn, farm animals on display… a mini-vacation. I hated to disappoint them, but at this point, I was much more worried about how we'd get home. "Sorry, guys. Something's wrong with the car."

At the time, cell phones were new and expensive technology, and I didn't have one. What I did have were three energetic boys, aged 5, 10 and 12, who didn't need much provocation to start quar-relling—especially if they got bored, restless or hungry.

I told Andrew and Matthew to stay put while I popped the engine hood and peered inside. Adam, the eldest, joined me. Every-thing looked suitably greasy and engine-like, with no steam or flames shooting out. I don't know what I'd expected to see, but I fig-ured raising the hood was a good SOS signal to passing motorists.

This car was long past its "best-by" date, and my father had taught us a few tricks to keep it on the road: jiggle *this* wire when it won't start, pull *that* cable if the parking brake's stuck on. I knelt in the gravel, Adam squatting beside me, and we checked under-neath. If a hose or something had let go, I didn't have anything to fix it with, but someone stopping to help might. Nothing was dan-gling, dripping or flopping. No easy repair.

Dread swirled in my stomach. I'd *felt* the engine straining on the last hill, *heard* it howl. We'd had no power. From the Formula One™ auto races I loved to watch on television, I knew what "no power" meant. It meant either engine or transmission failure. We'd just replaced the car's engine, and on this trip I'd had power on the flat sections and going downhill—just not for climbing.

Something inside me whispered *transmission*, and I swal-lowed hard. Another high-priced repair job for an old car we couldn't afford to replace. How were we going to pay the bill? More immediately, how would we get home? As Adam and I stood and brushed our knees clean, a door slammed on the broken-down truck across the road.

A man jogged over to us. "What's the trouble?"

I had assumed the truck was empty, sitting on the opposite shoulder with its hood up to show it was disabled and hadn't been illegally parked. Ordinarily, I'd be nervous about a strange man approaching, but we needed *someone*. I'd been silently firing off those incoherent "Help!" prayers that come so easily when we're in trouble. Maybe they kept me calm now, or maybe the boys' pres-ence was some kind of moral support.

The friendly concern on the stranger's face helped too. Aver-age height, maybe ten years older than me, well-used work shirt and jeans—he looked safe enough, just an ordinary guy. And I didn't think someone hoping to trap a victim would choose a sweltering, sunny day in a high-visibility location.

I shrugged. "We just replaced the engine, so it better not be that. We had no power on the last hill. I think the transmission let go."

Beside me, Adam nodded. "Yeah."

I grinned to myself. *As if you know any more than I do about cars, Adam.*

"This must be the day for it." The man nodded towards his truck. "That's our problem, too. Just waiting for the tow truck to take us into Halifax."

Hope sparked. "Do you think your driver could take us, too?"

"Halifax?" Adam said. "But—"

I pulled my son into a hug. "I know you were looking forward to a day at the Exhibition, but we need to get the car towed back to the city."

The man gave Adam a sympathetic shrug. "No, some of the big outfits can haul one vehicle on the flatbed and roll one behind, but the guy we called runs smaller trucks. He's got better rates."

Stranded on the side of the road with three kids depending on me... *What do I do now, Lord?*

"Could you ask your driver to radio for another truck when he gets here?"

He frowned. "You don't have a cell?"

I shook my head.

"Well, you can use mine if there's any juice left in it. My buddy and I have it sitting in the sun trying to warm the battery, but it's pretty far gone. I'll go check. By the way, my name's Mike."

I smiled. "Janet and Adam, plus two more in the car."

Mike headed back to his vehicle. I opened the driver's door and hit the switch to pop the cargo hatch in the rear. Andrew and Matthew started firing questions from the back seat.

"How much longer?"

"What's going on?"

"Can I have a snack?"

I held up my hands, laughing. "One at a time! We'll be a while yet, guys, but you're being really patient. Do you want to move around a bit?"

As I went around to raise the hatch, my youngest two boys swarmed over the seat into the "very back," as we called it. I folded the seats down to give them more space. "Adam, you climb in too. Just push the cooler to the side and there'll be room for all of you."

The sun shone hot, but with the hatch up and the forward windows open, we had a slight breeze. "Guys, I want you to stay in the car. There isn't a lot of traffic, but when anything goes by it's moving fast. Maybe dig out your books or a snack."

We'd brought plenty of munchies and water bottles for our day at the Exhibition. Andrew opened the supply backpack and they started feasting. I sat sideways on the tailgate, where I could talk with my sons and keep watch for Mike's return.

All three boys were munching granola bars when he came back with his phone. It was at least twice the size of the ones we use now, grimy, and warm from the sun. The low battery warning light flashed.

I keyed in my husband Russell's office number and willed him to pick up, needing a familiar voice as much as a tow truck. One, two, three rings—then it went to voicemail. I spoke as fast as I could, afraid the phone might quit, hoping I was right about which exit we'd passed last.

The phone still had power, so I tried my parents, who lived near us. Dad's friendly "Hello" made me wobbly with relief. I told him the story and asked if he'd arrange the tow through our regular repair shop, in case Russell was in a meeting and couldn't check his messages.

My practical father saw what I'd missed. "I'll come get you. Be there shortly."

"Oh, Dad, that would be great." I hadn't even thought about how we'd get home! The four of us sure wouldn't fit in the cab with the tow truck driver.

Tears of relief stung my eyes as I handed Mike his phone. Help was on the way! He headed back to his buddy, and I wondered how long we'd all be waiting.

The boys had been good, but while I was on the phone they started getting in one another's space. I'd overheard a few quiet insults.

142

"Listen, guys, Grampa's going to come pick us up, but it'll take a while. We're all hot and disappointed, but do *not* start anything. We can't afford to fight."

I dug out a few *Sesame Street* books and snuggled up with Matthew to read. Adam and Andrew swapped *Garfield* books back and forth.

When my voice got scratchy from too many Ernie and Bert impressions, I called another break. Not only had we brought water and snacks, there were hot dogs in the cooler for a barbecue picnic supper.

"Boys, when I was Matthew's age, sometimes Nana would let me eat a raw hot dog. You want to try some now?"

Brown eyes and blue ones widened, and Andrew got that little grin that says, "I'm getting away with something."

They were chomping away on cold hot dogs, not bothering with buns, when Mike came around the end of the car to find me. "You have a phone call. Funny, I was sure this thing was dead."

"Sorry to use your air time." I took the phone and said, "Hello?"

Russell answered, his tone warm and concerned. "This cell number was on my call display so I took a chance the owner was still with you. I know your dad's on his way, but how are you doing? Are the kids behaving?"

I smiled. Russell had seen them—and me—at our worst, but today, in what I'd call a crisis, I was proud of how well we were keeping it together. "We're okay now, but it's so good to hear your voice. We've turned it into a picnic and we're reading stories."

I handed Mike back his phone, and invited him and his friend to share our cold hot dogs and cookies. "Not the most nutritious food on the planet," I said, "but it's better than nothing."

Mike grinned. "Hey, why not?" He hollered across the road to his friend to join us.

By now the sun had moved to the front of the car. The raised cargo hatch made a shady area past the rear bumper on the gravel shoulder. Both men stood in the shade, and I sat on the tailgate near the boys.

The six of us snacked and filled the time with small talk, watching the traffic go past. Every big truck coming from the city caught our attention until we saw it wasn't a tow rig. We were on the last of the cookies when a big blue tow truck slowed, swung a U-turn and rumbled to stop across the road. "Beep-beep-beep" split the air as it reversed towards the men's vehicle.

Mike winked at the boys. "Yours won't be far behind. Thanks for the food!"

"Thank you for the phone," I said. "Good luck with your transmission."

The men jogged over to the waiting tow truck driver. The boys and I watched Mike's truck get hooked up to the tow rig, which then pulled away with a honk and a growl of heavy engine.

I stood and took a few paces at the rear of the car to stretch my legs. As I turned back to the boys, a flicker of motion overhead caught my eye. High in the sky soared an eagle, wings outstretched, white glinting from its head plumage. "Boys, come see this! Be careful to stay off the pavement."

They clambered from the back of the car and looked up where I pointed.

"Cool!"

"Hey, a bald eagle!"

At the time, bald eagles were rare in Nova Scotia, so this was an unexpected treat. And spotting one of the mighty birds in flight held another, more personal meaning for me. This wasn't the first time I'd seen an eagle in connection with this car breaking down.

Four months earlier, when the engine failed a few blocks from home, a bald eagle had circled overhead.

I'd never seen one in the city before, and I haven't seen one there since. The appearance of two eagles in those stress-filled moments felt like a gift from God's heart, speaking peace to my spirit.

I tried to share my feelings with my sons. "Guys, one of God's promises is, 'They that wait on the Lord will renew their strength, and fly like eagles.'[1] Those aren't the exact words, but every time I see an eagle soaring, it's like a special reminder from God that He's with us." They nodded, more interested in watching the majestic bird than listening to another one of "Mom's teaching moments."

Still, they heard. I put my arms around them and pulled them closer and we stood watching together.

Behind us came the crunch of tires slowing on gravel, and we turned to see my father's pickup truck. I held the boys back until it stopped. Then Dad was out of the vehicle with hugs for each of us and with his own calm cheer that always made my world feel more hopeful.

"Sorry about bringing the truck, guys. You'll be a little squished going home, but Nana's out with the car. I didn't want you waiting on the side of the road if your tow got here first."

Retroactive anxiety stirred. I pictured us standing there in the hot sun, forlorn, and dust-blown as cars whipped past. *Thank God that didn't happen!*

I herded the boys back to the car. "Gather your stuff together, and let's move it all over to Grampa's truck."

Adam, Andrew and Matthew shared some surprisingly friendly banter and a few giggles as books and Game Boys™ went into backpacks. I thrust our snack leavings and water bottles into the cooler and snapped it shut.

Dad was tying down our gear in the back of his pickup when our tow arrived. The driver climbed down from the big, red cab and strolled back to meet us. "Everybody good to go?" The boys cheered. While Dad hustled them into his truck, I made arrangements with the driver.

I stayed to watch the hook-up, then headed back to Dad's pickup. Andrew and Matthew, the smaller boys, shared the front seat with him, while Adam and I crammed into centre-facing jump seats behind them.

Once we were headed for home, with the ordeal behind us, my tension started to ease. A shaky feeling took its place.

Dad glanced back at me. "Do you want to stop for anything on the way home? A milkshake for the guys?"

"I need to go home." My voice quivered a bit. For a wonder, the boys didn't argue. Maybe they needed to go home too.

I closed my eyes and leaned my head against the rear window, only half-listening to the boys telling Dad all about their adventure. My thoughts whirled.

Trouble had hit, and God had not disappeared in a puff of confusion. More than that, He'd already planned how to deal with

145

it. How else can I explain the provision of a phone, the peace that kept me sane—and kept my boys from getting on one another's nerves—and my father's showing up just before the tow truck so we weren't left stranded on the side of the highway?

I think most mothers are anxious, especially about caring for their children. Life's "what ifs" had always frightened me, and if I'm not careful they still can. But something inside me changed that day. I realized that if God could meet me on the side of the road, with help already in place, He can handle whatever else is coming.

1. Isaiah 40:31

Active Surrender

Nonfiction

Brian C. Austin

Six years of slow but relentless eyesight loss strips away many of my illusions of being in control. It demands repeated adjustments.

I drive less and less as I realize my eyes adjust more slowly to focusing at different distances. Even after brief periods of driving, visual fatigue slows that adjustment too much for safety. My increasingly rare excursions are reduced to five minutes maximum.

More and more difficulty with my eyesight leads necessarily to my "retiring" before retirement suits me.

Reading, a life-long love, has given me more than 12 years of a marvellous job in a Bible bookstore, and 27 years of involvement in our church library. A growing collection of great old classics lines many shelves in our home. The love of books remains strong. Bookstores still draw me. Yet reading has lost its delight. Those classics cause eye-strain and headaches. The costs prove bigger than the rewards to read them.

The passion for writing, so strong a few years ago, seems to weaken as I read less—no surprise, for great writers almost invariably read voraciously.

Poor me sneaks into my thinking once in a while. Mostly, I respond with what other people call courage. I sometimes suspect it's purely emotional laziness on my part.

As I think about my situation, I realize there are many possible responses to challenges. Three in particular have impacted me. As a Christian, I've tried to convince myself of the authority of *Name-It-Claim-It* faith. At times I've drifted dangerously close to *Passive Fatalism*. And in my better days, I've almost achieved *Active Surrender*.

Name-It-Claim-It teaching points to many Bible verses as a foundation to pray while expecting guaranteed results. But when I read those verses in context, I often see cautions and conditions.

I have also seen too many people tormented by guilt when their "faith" has not been rewarded in the time and way they expect.

Passive Fatalism—whatever will be, will be—tends to empty life of purpose. *If I can't change things, why even keep going?* It's such a small step from there to giving up, accepting defeat, even embracing a suicidal mentality.

Active Surrender asks for and expects healing, but leaves the timing and circumstances in God's hands while living each day in thankfulness for that day's blessings.

Fascinated by paradoxes, I'm gripped by the term active surrender. Surrender itself carries mixed messages. It's usually seen as an act of weakness and failure. Can it ever be positive?

God asks us to intentionally surrender our will to His. For me, this is one of the biggest challenges of Christian living. I want to *commit*; to do the *strong* thing. Somehow that preserves at least the illusion that I'm in charge. However, when I'm in charge, I can easily leave Christ out of the centre of my Christianity. It becomes only a shallow mockery of the promised life. Active surrender, then, is a goal worth pursuing.

I want to claim active surrender as my response. Some days I almost achieve it. Yet I confess the healing recipient I identify with most strongly in the Bible is the one whose response to Jesus was, "I do believe; help me overcome my unbelief!" (Mark 9:24b).

The Bible records an intriguing healing where Jesus asks the strangest question: "What do you want me to do for you?" (Mark 10:51). Duh? A blind man has called for help from the great healer. Why would Jesus ask such a question? But maybe it isn't quite so "Duh." We get comfortable with our excuses. The surrender, even of blindness, costs something. Healed beggars lose their livelihood. They now have to work for a living. Their abilities, unused for years, have atrophied. Who will hire them? What skills do they have? Will there be food for tomorrow? Begging has become a way of life—but who will give to the strong and able-bodied?

Tests finally give my condition a name. Strange the comfort in that. "Damage similar to multiple mini-strokes" fits the symptoms and medical findings. It explains things more clearly than the name itself. I become comfortable with it. Brain damage lends itself as an excuse in so many ways. Yes, I pray for healing, and others pray for my healing. But how much do I really want it? How do you answer such a question? Who but Jesus ever understood people enough to dare ask such a question?

My belief in God has not wavered. My conviction that God is good remains strong. I try to surrender to His will. Most days I live with a positive attitude, but my highest expectations do not include regaining full vision. I've quit looking for improvement, quit believing God's plan for me this side of the grave includes healing. I hope to prevent further loss, but six years of deterioration tempers even that hope.

Fearing that my driving days are over, I go to an appointment with a specialist. I try to give all the essential information for the doctor to evaluate the situation clearly—yet avoid saying more than necessary about my driving challenges. Disclosure and evasion—convinced the time has come, but longing to put it off for even one more day. Still, I almost want the turmoil behind me. *Just take my license and be done with it!* Active surrender? It sounds a bit too passive when I see it in print. In truth, my expectations of that appointment are shamefully low.

But… a new possibility. Braced for one more major loss; instead, almost daring to hope. A chemical imbalance? Could it be something that simple—just lazy muscles distorting the shape of the eye because a chemical is out of balance? Like drilling into an artesian well, this doctor has tapped into a reservoir of hope I didn't know existed. Nothing has changed; yet somehow everything has changed.

My dictionary tells me that "hope" means "to cherish a desire with anticipation." Six years of continuous loss tends to strip one of anticipation. Even desire becomes emotionally draining. The ongoing attempt to make the best of things brings praise from others, but inside, expectation and anticipation shrivel up.

Hope… Three weeks on yet another drug (it seems we could start our own pharmacy) result in maddening changes. Initial effects include greater distortion and cruel headaches, but days later, distance vision and depth perception have improved markedly (although in conflict with my prescription lenses). Headaches subside. Reading is even more difficult, but new glasses just might restore the joy of a good book. Driving remains limited to five-minute excursions. But the artesian well of hope flows ever stronger.

I had accepted my eyesight loss and tried to come to terms with it. I never found a conflict between my condition and my belief that God was good—another paradox, perhaps. I won't pretend I've displayed the strongest or best faith response. The loss over the last six years has been very real. Bridges have burned behind me.

But new hope is a powerful force. Whether partial or even complete healing comes over the next months—or whether this is just a temporary reprieve—God remains worthy of my complete trust. Over the course of my life, He has proven Himself worthy of my full and active surrender. May I find the courage to give it to Him.

Surviving with a Woman of a Certain Age

Nonfiction

Denise Budd Rumble

I don't know what's wrong with my husband Dennis today! He's hardly said two words to me. His answer to all my questions was a grunt. He didn't even kiss me goodbye when he went to work, and he always does that.

Come to think of it, he's been acting strange for the past few weeks. He hasn't tried to steal a kiss when I'm busy working on the computer, and he's been sticking to his side of the bed as if there were an invisible barrier between us. Last night, I tried to snuggle up to him and he actually turned his back on me! What's his problem? I hope he's not having another mid-life crisis. The first one birthed a Harley-Davidson touring bike.

Hmm, I wonder if I've forgotten something important? Could I have said something he didn't like, or not said something I should have, or—? Oh dear, I hate to admit it, but maybe the problem isn't him; maybe it's me. You see, I'm going through "the change."

Do you remember adolescence? For many of us, it's a time we'd rather forget—a sort of metamorphosis with all those hormones going wild, making major changes to our bodies, and causing us embarrassment. Well, it's happening to me again, only this time it's reverse adolescence and it's called "menopause." Yes, my hormones are going wild again! And it isn't much fun.

Doesn't Dennis understand that I need his support to get me through this new stage of life? Over the years, I've always supported *him*. Who encouraged him when he wanted to go back to school, even though it meant he was away from home a lot, so I had to do all the driving around taking the kids to their endless activities? Who jumped in to help when he needed a trainer for his hockey team, sacrificing my own time and comfort? And I could go on. After 31 years of marriage, three children and the umpteen things we've been through together, just when I need him the most, I feel as if he's turning his back on me.

Okay, unless you're also a woman who's reached a certain stage of life, you're probably wondering what I'm talking about. Well, for starters, the hot flashes have been especially plentiful the last few weeks. You'd think that in our minus-10-degree-Celsius Canadian winter weather they'd slow down a *little*! But no.

Even the people at work have asked what's wrong with me. One minute I'm taking my sweater off, rolling my shirt sleeves up, and turning down the heat; the next minute I'm rolling my shirt sleeves down, putting my sweater back on, and turning up the heat.

Every day when I get ready for work I have to pick two outfits—one to put on in the morning and a spare one to change into later, if needed. It's no fun sweating up a shower and then having to stay in clammy, damp clothes 'til the end of the day. Honestly, what can be more mortifying than meeting with a business client, and having him hand you a tissue to mop up the perspiration puddling on your face?

It's a bit easier at home. I can change into a tank top and go sit outside on the porch when it becomes unbearable.

Nights aren't much better. I fall into bed dead tired, but my brain won't turn off. Anxiety and panic chase each other through the cobwebs of my mind—and it takes ages for me to get to sleep. When I finally do drop off into oblivion, the hot flashes rudely awaken me with a blazing inferno—*Marshmallows, anyone*? I often have to get up in the middle of the night to change my PJs because of soaking night sweats.

Dennis is always complaining that he wakes up cold because I'm constantly flinging the covers off, but that's only half true. I only spend *half* the night throwing the covers off; the other half I spend yanking them back on. This cycle repeats itself until my alarm clock goes off and I get up, dog-tired again.

Dennis used to want to cuddle in bed, but as soon as his body heat collides with mine, those hot flashes start again and—*Great balls of fire!*—I think I'm going to burn up. "Hon, could you please *not* put your arm around me?" I ask, as sweetly as I can.

"Hmm, I love you…" he mumbles.

I push his arm off my shoulder. "Please Hon, just please…"

"I like to be close to you…"

"Get away from me! Stay on your own side of the bed!" I screech, kicking off the blankets as frustration and panic gain control.

Many nights, the hot flashes are so bad I simply can't bear to be touched in any way, shape or form. I used to think Dennis is a fast learner, but he always seems to want to cuddle. I really had to get cross with him the last time. I sat up and yelled, "For heaven's sake, just stay away from me!" And he did. As a matter of fact, he still does.

Oh dear, I wonder if I remembered to tell him *why* I wanted him to get away? Did I explain that hot flashes make me crazy and create a fanatical need for me to avoid having anything, or anyone, touch me? Did I make it clear that I still love him and that it wasn't anything personal? Did I go and give him a hug later, when I wasn't having a hot flash?

I guess I've really blown it. He probably feels utterly and completely rejected.

Oh, no! I just realized something else. You see, Dennis expects me to know when he runs out of clean socks, or when he wants supper early because he has to coach a hockey practice. So I tell him, "I'm not a mind reader, you know!" But now, here I am expecting *him* to be one!

Read my mind? Now, that's a frightening thought. A lot of the time, even *I* don't want to read my mind, because lately it's being most disagreeable, or overflowing with irrational fretfulness, superfluous guilt and bogus reality. It's as though my mind has a mind of its own.

There are countless days when it's filled with fog and fuzz. It has trouble focusing, figuring things out, and keeping things filed in the right folders. If I'm in the middle of a conversation, and I have a thought while the other person is talking, I have to interrupt and say it right away, because if I politely wait my turn, that gem of a thought will be gone forever.

Sometimes when I'm grocery shopping, I have to check my list umpteen times. I look at the items on the list, find one, and put it in the cart, but then I can't remember a single one of the other items. Take last week, for instance. The cauliflower display caught my eye as soon as I entered the store. They looked nice so I picked one up. I continued on through the bakery to the meat section. I checked my grocery list. After choosing a package of pork chops, I hustled to the canned goods aisle. I stood looking at all the different sizes and varieties of tinned food, but I had no idea what I was there for. I pulled out my grocery list, and checked it again. Tomato soup was the first item on the list. I grabbed a couple of cans and pushed my cart to the other end of the store for orange juice.

I was sure I had everything now, so I marched over to the checkout and got in line. I started putting my items on the conveyor belt, but I had a niggling feeling that something was missing. I figured I'd better glance at my list one more time. Well, for some reason the three people behind me became very animated when I had to rescue my groceries from the conveyor belt, back up, turn around, and manoeuvre my ornery cart past them. And did you know how easy it is to get the wheels tangled up with another cart? Good job one of the stock boys heard the commotion and came to the rescue.

It took me another 20 minutes to pick up the missing items—mushroom soup, All-Bran, fat-free yogurt, toilet paper, Popsicles™… Not to mention bread and milk, the two things we had run out of. By this time, I needed stress relief, so I threw some chocolate into the cart, then got back in line. The cashier looked at me kind of strangely when she asked "Anything else?" but I guess she must have been having a bad day.

I have a lot of bad days myself, when I'm so tired I can't even think. Sure, I can put one foot in front of the other, but I tend to forget where I was going or why I wanted to get there. And some days the best thing I can say for my mind is that it's frenzied—and at least that's better than futile.

When I was in my twenties, one of my co-workers was an older lady whom I supposed must be near retirement age. She went around making weird pronouncements and proclamations, such as, "I had it all together, but I set it down somewhere and now I can't find it!" One day, I offered to help her find what she'd lost, but she just gave me a funny look. Sometimes she confided to me, "Of all the things I've lost, I miss my mind the most." Other days she'd walk through the office warning us, "I have one nerve left and you'd better not get on it!"

I stayed clear of her at the time, thinking, *Jeepers, what's her problem?* She retired a couple of decades later, so I guess I was a little off in my estimation of her age.

Now, I understand exactly what her problem was because I have days just like hers. And I've borrowed her sayings, because now I, too, am a woman in mid-life, or, as I prefer to say, "a woman of a certain age."

I love that expression, "a woman of a certain age." The Oxford English Dictionary says it means "no longer young but not yet old."

The men I know aren't quite sure what to make of this phrase, so they become a little wary. That's a good thing, because I often only have one nerve left, and I'm just waiting for that one final comment, look or attitude to make me nerve-less—and then you'd better watch out!

My husband isn't the only one who's been getting on my nerves lately. Our son Michael is home from university for a few days, and between him and his younger brother Josh… well, let's just say I have half a nerve left.

Take this morning, for instance. Their words, punctuated by laughter and little choking sounds, accosted me as I dragged myself into the kitchen.

"Does she look awake to you?"

"Hmm, it's hard to tell, Josh, but she is vertical."

"Yeah, but she hasn't yelled at us yet."

The teasing continued as I transmitted the best glare I could conjure up at that time of day. So what was their response? In unison, they rolled their eyes at me, "Ooo, scary, Mum!"

Where have my children been all their lives? They know that mornings aren't my strong suit; they never have been. They also know I'm going through "the change." So where is their sympathy, and why didn't they have the coffee ready? They know I need a large mug of coffee with milk and sugar to perk me up and kick-start the day. And later in the day, lots of chamomile tea to calm me down.

It's all right for them to laugh. Just wait 'til it's their turn. Okay, yeah, I know, boys don't go through menopause—but their wives will. I just hope I'm still around to help it along, you know, the way that only a mother-in-law can...

My sons love to tease, but I have my own way of getting back at them. Whenever we're driving together, I take control of the car's air conditioner. Doesn't matter to me whether it's summer, winter, spring or fall, if a hot flash attacks, the air conditioner goes on. It's great in the winter because I can open up the windows too—nothing like a snowstorm taking a detour through the car to chase a hot flash away. Naturally, the boys complain about it, and even try to roll their windows up, but I've got child locks for their windows, so I just tell them to think warm thoughts! Not much they can do. I'm pretty adept at blocking out their whining; I've had years of practice.

Hot flashes seem to be the symptom that gets all the attention, but they're only one of the strange things happening to me. A few weeks ago I treated my sister to a movie. We both thought the leading man was gorgeous (and single again, if the tabloids are to be believed). Anyway, there we were sitting in the theatre, totally enthralled, when my heart went into palpitations. I've never had a racing heart quite like that before. I just figured it was because of the hunky leading man. For a second, I thought I might swoon!

But then I had palpitations a second time, when we stopped for gas. The service station attendant's greasy coat didn't quite cover up his stained T-shirt, which was stretched to the max across his bulky belly and gaped above his belt. Right away, I knew for certain that neither he nor the good-looking actor had caused those heart flutters.

Plus there's the whole redistribution thing. The scales claim I haven't gained weight, but I can tell you for sure my clothes don't fit the way they used to. Some things are definitely rearranging. Of course, all that bloating doesn't help either.

Talking about weird physical manifestations, the other day, I noticed new hairs growing on my chin. Long black ones. Another one on my upper lip. One in the middle of my neck, too. I knew that menopause had something to do with changing levels of estrogen or testosterone, but I didn't know it was going to make me turn into my father! Next thing you know, I'll be getting a shaving mug for Christmas.

I suppose, when it comes right down to it, I have two choices: laugh or cry. The reality is that menopause isn't easy. It's not a joke, but neither is it a disease. It's a stage of life that all women go through. Most of us even live through it. In fact, an older friend told me that after menopause I'll have more energy than I know what to do with! And that's good news.

By the time I'm on the other side of menopause, my children will, hopefully, be independent, and I'll have more free time. Come to think of it, I'll have about a third of my life left. I could go back to university and get a degree, or teach a night course on writing or bookkeeping at the local college. I love to draw and to paint with oils and acrylics, but there's never been enough time to pursue my art in a serious way. Speaking of painting, there are a couple of rooms in the house that could use some fresh paint and loving care.

I might even enjoy feeling cold for a change. I could go shopping for sweaters! Then again, some silence, a good book and a mug of hot chocolate sound like a perfect day. Maybe there'll even be time for Dennis and me to go for rides on the Harley, with no particular destination in mind, and stop at all the interesting places that catch our interest "just because."

There seemed to be more than enough time when I was a kid. I remember lying in the grass and looking at the clouds. I'd watch the elephants chasing lions across the endless sky, pixies and fairies playing hide and seek, and lambs sleeping around the throne of God. God—the Creator, the mighty King, the One who made me.

Psalm 139 says, in part, "O Lord, you have searched me and you know me… you are familiar with all my ways… For you created my inmost being; you knit me together in my mother's womb… All the days ordained for me were written in your book before one of them came to be."

God knew me before my parents had any inkling I was there. All of the days of my life were written before I was born. God knows me inside and out—all facets of me: mental, emotional, spiritual, and physical. Now, *there's* Someone who understands!

God knows everything about menopause. He knows why women go through it and all about the struggles each of us has. He won't roll His eyes or look at me in that "condescending tone of voice," as my family puts it. I'm His child. He loves me just the way I am. It doesn't matter if my brain is fuzzy, or if my anxiety is at panic level, or if I can barely drag myself through my days. He loves me when I'm having hot flashes or night sweats, when I'm dead tired, even when I feel like a creation gone amuck. He's always there for me, ready to listen to my ranting and raving, my fears and irrational thoughts—ready and able to help me through this frenzied storm called "menopause."

But my family members and friends aren't all-knowing, as God is. And since I want my relationships to be intact when I get to the other side of this storm, I'd better make an improved effort to keep my family and friends in the loop. If I don't start the conversations, how will they know I'm willing to talk about it? Besides, they have their own lives to live, decisions to make and issues to solve; I can't expect them to focus on me and my struggles all the time.

I want my family to know they're the most important people in my life, and if they'll just hang in there, things *will* get better. After all, menopause is a stage of life, not a life sentence. So if I can tell them when I'm having a bad day, or when I need a hug, that will help them understand how I'm doing. Then we'll *all* feel better.

The good news is that the day is coming when I will once more have enough energy to go to work, make a decent meal *with* dessert, and do a load of laundry—all on the same day—without whining. Someday soon we'll drive down a snowy road in January and I will turn the heater *on*. Until then, I'll keep control of the car windows.

Most important, I'll keep the communication going with my husband. After all, when I'm on the other side of menopause, and the hot flashes have burned themselves out, I'll need him to cuddle with so I can get warm!

Careful What You Whisper

Nonfiction

T. L. Wiens

The icy blast of winter had bullied spring back into submission and it was too cold for the season; that time of year when farmers get cranky with the seeding itch they can't scratch. Their mood rubs off onto the children trapped between the cold and dampness that imprisons them indoors. On one of these days, my frustration overruled my common sense.

If I'd asked Matthew, my ten-year-old son, to wash the car, he would have smiled and gone to do it. But the car didn't need washing—the dishes did. So instead of a smile, Matthew gave me a look of disgust followed by the argument that his sisters needed to take a turn at this chore. Kendra, my eight-year-old daughter, busied herself fighting with Katelyn, her five-year-old sister, over which video they should watch. The arguing made Jenna, my one-year-old daughter, start to cry. In that moment, those fateful words slipped from my mouth in a desperately whispered plea, "Lord, give me patience!"

Two days later, not much had changed. The wrestling match between rain and snow persisted, but I couldn't take another day in the house with my grumpy, not-used-to-being-housebound kids. When my husband Allan announced he had to get us a new tank of water, I decided to bundle up the whole family to go with him on the 10-kilometre trip in our pickup truck.

Hauling water for drinking and household use was a necessary chore in our area, nestled in the Coteau Hills beside the South Saskatchewan River. The many attempts by locals to drill wells had resulted in poor-quality water, if they were lucky enough to find water at all. Hauling water is a cold, wet job that never goes away, summer or winter. But today, I looked at the task as an opportunity to escape.

Allan filled the tank while I left baby Jenna sleeping in her car seat and took the other three children a short distance away to explore. Rural wells aren't designed to offer entertainment. Some have a small building to house the pump, but this well didn't even have that feature. We had to get creative to entertain ourselves. Browned-off grass covered with ice had become works of art, but it was too cold to stand around staring at grass sculptures. So I suggested that we play a game of tag.

Matthew was "It" and was determined to catch me.

I took off at full speed to avoid getting tagged. Stepping on a patch of black ice caused me to catch air instead of ground. As I watched my feet flying above my head, my brain formulated the thought that somewhere in this would come a landing. As I hit the hard ground, pain exploded inside my chest and I crumpled. When I tried to breathe, I couldn't draw air in or push it out.

I heard one of the kids scream, "Dad!"

While I hoped being winded was the extent of the damage, I really didn't believe I'd be that fortunate.

My family gathered around me and Allan knelt down to help me into a sitting position. As he began to raise me up, I cried out for him to stop; even though I had always taken pride in my high pain tolerance, this hurt too much.

We didn't have a cell phone, so Allan had no choice but to drive to the nearest farm to use their phone. Leaving Matthew to watch over me, he bundled the girls into the truck with Jenna, and quickly took off.

As I lay on the hard, frozen grass, the cold began to seep through my jacket and jeans, and I started to shiver. Then I felt Matthew's hand on my head and I heard him pray, "Dear God, please help Mom to be okay."

In the midst of my pain and fear, I felt a jolt of joy as I witnessed my ten-year-old son's reaction to the crisis.

It felt like forever before Allan returned from making the 911 call. Then a second eternity passed before I heard the ambulance arriving. When it stopped, I stared at the back doors and wondered how the paramedics would get me off the ground onto the stretcher. I knew there would be no avoiding pain for this journey.

I'd been curled up, but the move from the ground to the backboard necessitated straightening my body. I clenched my teeth to stop from crying out as I was loaded onto the stretcher and into the back of the ambulance. Allan and the kids followed in the pickup truck.

The ambulance lurched as we began to move. Knowing I was finally on my way to get help should have brought relief, but instead, it brought more pain. I hadn't realized it, but the cold that made me shiver had been a hidden blessing, numbing my body. Now, the warmth from the ambulance's heater hit me, erasing the cold's numbing effect. My pain intensified. Every stone bigger than a marble felt like a boulder beneath the ambulance tires—and Saskatchewan gravel roads have lots and lots of small rocks.

But that was the luxury cruise part of this trip. I knew the exact moment we hit the pavement, because this Saskatchewan highway lived up to its reputation of being littered with broken pavement and potholes. Good thing being strapped down onto the backboard made it hard for me to breathe; struggling for each breath diverted my attention from the throbbing caused by the bouncing ride.

Rural areas in Saskatchewan don't enjoy access to local hospitals. Instead, buildings that once served as hospitals have been converted into medical clinics, which have to make do with old equipment. Most days, only a nurse practitioner is on duty. A doctor or laboratory staff are only available part-time. I could hear the ambulance attendants debating whether the nearest clinic had what was needed to treat my situation. I prayed it did—I didn't want to ride one extra metre in the ambulance.

They decided to go to our local clinic. Fortunately, the doctor was present. He'd been filling his car with gas when the call came in, so he decided to stick around instead of heading to the next community, where he was expected for appointments.

The X-ray machine couldn't take the images the doctor needed with me lying down. By the time the lab technician managed to sit me in place, I was shaking with intense pain and shock. Not wanting to risk a call for a second photo shoot, I forced myself to remain still.

The technician and the doctor made their way into a little side room where they read the X-rays. I could hear hushed whispers. The doctor emerged and made his way towards me.

"Your back is broken." The doctor didn't blink as he told me.

I've never broken a bone in my life, I thought. *Looks like I've decided to start in a big way.*

"I'll give you some painkillers. Call me if you need anything." The doctor handed me a bottle of Tylenol™.

"What? I'm being sent home?" I said incredulously. *Does this guy not understand that I can't even sit up?*

"There's nothing they can do for you in the city, and the ride to the hospital would cause you more discomfort," he said as he exited the room.

And with that, I was left on my own. I had no idea how I would even get back into the truck to get home, much less care for my family.

With help from Allan and Matthew, I managed to slowly walk to the truck and manoeuvre myself into the passenger seat.

Once home, I had to make another painful journey from the truck to the house, then face climbing two sets of stairs to get to my third floor bedroom. A few minutes later, I had to make another trip back down to the second floor, where the only bathroom in the house was located. Allan and the children helped as much as they could, but they couldn't take away the pain. I shivered as the shock wore off and pain became my master.

Over the next few days, my new reality became clear. I couldn't dress or undress myself and my right hand didn't listen when I asked it to do things. My life consisted of moving from bed to bathroom and back.

Extra Strength Tylenol™ was the only painkiller I could use; because of my many drug allergies I didn't want to risk taking anything stronger. Breathing hurt. Everything hurt.

The call I received from the doctor a week after my injury didn't lift my spirits. The clinic had sent the X-ray to a better facility to be read, and the "official" results were back. My back was broken in two places. The area that was most affected supported my shoulders. That explained why it felt as though my whole body was going to cave in when I tried to sit up.

But that was just the opener. Some muscles had torn away from my spine. I had nerve damage. My right hand might never be fully functional again. To cap it off, with a broken back, you often get broken ribs. I had two.

When I asked how long it would take me to recover, the doctor wouldn't give me an answer.

Family and friends urged me to go back and demand more treatment, but I couldn't face the painful truck ride that would require.

The next few weeks were intolerable. I had been a very independent person. It was hard for me to accept being dressed by my five-year-old. From my third floor bedroom, I couldn't see the goings-on in the rest of the house. Katelyn became my personal nurse while the older kids, Kendra and Matthew, took over many of the household duties, such as cleaning and cooking.

Family and friends came and went, bringing food and practical help. My mother in-law provided many meals that the children could warm up in the microwave. My mother did our laundry and filled our freezer with homemade buns.

Allan decided to take some time off from his full-time job driving a semi-trailer so he could be at home to take care of baby Jenna and the household duties the children couldn't manage. But this added financial stress; our durum wheat and canola crops had been poor the year before, and we needed the extra income. When his regular paycheque didn't arrive two weeks later, I convinced Allan that I could handle things—but in truth, I couldn't deal with being a burden on my family.

To keep depression at bay, I convinced myself that I would recover from this injury in six to eight weeks, because that's how long it had taken my brother to heal from a broken arm. I was wrong.

And with absolutely no guidance or instructions on what I needed to do to recover, I failed to keep those muscles that weren't injured working.

One year after the accident, I was still pushing myself to get back to normal. My neck was so stiff I couldn't turn my head more than an inch either way. I couldn't bend over to reach the floor. Everything I tried came with my new friend, pain.

I had wanted to avoid another round of making the effort to endure the 30-minute trip to town to see the doctor, but I gave up that fight. Because he was the only physician in the area, I went to the same doctor I had visited after the accident, and demanded that he do something.

So a year later, after much unnecessary damage, he sent me to a physiotherapist in a clinic two hours away.

As the therapist examined my back, he began to look upset. Then came the questions:

"When did this happen?"

"Have you been to another therapist?"

"Didn't you get a list of exercises to do to keep you limber?"

On and on it went.

As he told me all the things that should have been done, I was consumed with anger. The truth was, I'd been abandoned, and now I would pay.

The therapist answered my single most pressing question. "How long will I be in pain?"

"Another year, and that's a promise," he said.

He also told me there was one huge hurdle I needed to overcome: my high pain tolerance would hinder therapy and the healing process.

The one thing I had seen as a positive had actually been a negative from the beginning.

My level of uselessness hit a new low. My entire upbringing of pushing through pain had to be ignored. I wasn't allowed to do anything that caused as much as a twinge of discomfort. In fact, I wasn't allowed to do anything except the exercises given to me by the therapist.

My children had to go back to carrying out my household duties. I had to watch while they did the cooking and cleaning, and accept the reality that I couldn't even hold my now two-year-old youngest child on my lap.

Depression took over. I didn't see how I could survive another year of agony. The question that doesn't have easy answers slipped from my lips in prayer, "Why, God?"

To my surprise, I got an answer. God showed me that my prayer for patience more than a year before had come from a deep place within me. It had been much more than a few exasperated words spoken in an overwhelming moment.

But knowing this answer didn't take away my physical pain.

Once again, my family helped me rally. Where once I had begged for help, the children now offered. Allan never complained about the messy house, the simple meals of eggs or macaroni and cheese, or, at times, the total lack of meals. The kisses they all planted on my cheeks—with careful manoeuvring to avoid hurting me—were treasures that kept me going. Love became an action, instead of an expression of affection.

Eighteen months after the accident, I could finally turn my neck. I walked out of the therapist's office on cloud nine, so thankful for this small miracle.

I'd never been one to see the little things—which often left me depressed when the big picture didn't turn out the way I wanted. Now, I celebrated everything! I praised my children for trying even when they didn't succeed. My old competitive nature, which had demanded perfection, melted away.

The pain left almost to the day of the two-year anniversary of my injury. What a strange feeling to be able to get out of bed without constant pain.

But there was still a lot of work to do to get my body functioning normally again. My right side continued to suffer from the effects of nerve damage, and my ribs would occasionally "catch" and send a surge of pain though my chest.

All my life I'd been a loner. That's why I chose long distance running as my sport, and kept at it even after racing for ribbons and trophies were no longer part of my life. Now, I had to shift to being a team player. When Allan needed someone to drive the tractor, I offered, but I took Matthew along to be my eyes behind me. He'd watch the cultivator we were pulling at the back of the tractor while I looked ahead for rocks and washouts in the field. I couldn't do the baking alone, because even punching down bread dough proved to be too much for me. So my children lent a hand, and in the process learned to bake.

Each day brought a bit more healing. Soon, I could stand by the stove and cook meals for my family. I can't describe my joy the day I was able to hold Jenna on my lap and read her a story. With each step towards a mostly pain-free existence, I rejoiced.

Ten years have passed since the accident. My right hand still can't grip small objects, so it's hard to turn smaller lids like those on jars of relish. Even now, muscle spasms strike if I work too many hours in a day. But all of these annoyances seem small compared to what I endured for those two years.

I'll never forget what I went through. It changed me. I have a deeper love and appreciation for my family. But even better, my injury made me a more patient, kinder person who can accept others' efforts instead of demanding perfection. If my children make a meal, I'm thankful—even if the egg yolks are too hard and the bacon is more burned than crispy.

I thank God that He answers prayers, though not always as we expect. And I thank Him that He gives us the strength to endure the lessons that may come after careless words whispered in moments of desperation.

A Personal Makeover — Inside and Out

Nonfiction

 ### Kimberley Payne

With three older brothers, you'd expect I'd have more of an aptitude for sports. But while each of my brothers enjoyed playing all kinds of sports, and seemed to have been gifted with strong athletic genes, I lacked co-ordination and felt awkward. What predominant gene did I get? The anti-athlete gene.

I wasn't a horrible athlete, but I never felt the euphoria of being picked first for any team. Ever. I never hit a home run, never scored the winning goal, and never made a touchdown. I couldn't run 10 metres without my calf muscles cramping into what looked like tennis balls. In grade eight, I signed up for shot put just so I could say—for once in my life—that I was part of the track and field team. Don't even get me started on how badly I threw a Frisbee!

Consequently, after I left grade school, I stayed clear of anything that had to do with sports or unnecessary athletic activity.

It wasn't until I discovered that I was three weeks pregnant with my first child at age 27 that I began to think about changing my anti-athletic ways. I wanted to set an example for my baby—something more positive than being a stay-in-bed mom.

I figured that since I had already mastered walking from my kitchen to my parked car in the driveway, it couldn't be that hard to start a "program" of walking. I began with walking around my neighbourhood. Then I graduated to doing errands on foot: walking six blocks to the grocery store, the bank and the video store.

However, after only eight weeks, nasty Canadian winter weather interrupted my newly-adopted outdoor walking regime. To keep going, I joined the local YMCA in Waterloo, Ontario. I went from walking on my street to walking on a track in a gym.

But I soon got bored with walking in circles.

I heard about people using funky machines in the Y's "Life-style Room." Apparently these machines told you how far you walked, how many calories you burned, and even what you ate for breakfast. So I dared myself to venture into this room so I could go further on my journey into the world of fitness. However, my initial expedition didn't last long. After five minutes on the Stair-Master, with my lungs burning and my face plum-purple, other patrons begged me to step off for fear the pregnant lady might just give in to morning sickness right then and there.

But I was hooked. I snuck back in every day to try, not only the StairMaster, but the treadmill and the elliptical-thingy too. I learned that elliptical trainers provide a low-impact way to simulate walking while also working your upper body. You grip the handles of the levers in front of you, and push or pull them while your legs stride back and forth on moving foot pedals. I could not only vary the resistance but even walk in a reverse direction. How cool is that? I was exploring completely new territory, and loving it.

In a few weeks, I was able to walk a mile in under 20 minutes on the treadmill. Soon after, I found I could let go of the handles for seconds at a time; then I realized I could lift my head so that instead of watching my feet I could look forward and see what was going on around me.

I then noticed other, more perplexing, equipment at the far end of the room. People were doing what was called "strength training." This concept intrigued me.

I asked a young man wearing a "Volunteer" T-shirt if he'd teach me how to use one of the machines, and he signed me up for the weight room training. I wondered if he thought my four-month-baby-bump grew out of a three-doughnuts-a-day diet, but decided to go for it anyway.

I started taking group courses and learned all about strength training (and what I could and could not do while pregnant). I became well-versed on all the contraptions available to tone this part of the body, shape this part, and send that part to another province. By spring, I had enough training to take the exam and certify as a weight-training instructor. With my impressive new title, I began to volunteer in the weight room—right up until the day before my water broke and I had to head for the hospital. My daughter's birth went off without a hitch. I was in and out of the hospital within two days, and the doctors credited my exercise regime to my quick four-hour labour.

Six weeks later, I began a brisk outdoor walking routine. I was excited to walk again to lose my "baby fat," but I had an ulterior motive—my daughter loved the rocking motion of the stroller, so it was an effective way to get her to fall asleep and give me some quiet time.

One day, I tried walking with another new mom. She preferred "power walking" and had one of those baby strollers with the mag-wheel on the front. I tried to keep up by riding my stroller the way I ride the back of the cart in the grocery store, but it didn't work so well. So I feigned a sore ankle and returned to my own solo leisurely walks.

Another baby mama invited me to her post-natal exercise class. I thought, *Why not?* At that point, my baby only weighed four kilograms—I imagined I could bench press that much! I especially liked the idea that if I felt tired, I could pretend that my daughter needed to eat and head to the sidelines, throw a towel over half my body, and nod off for a nap… all under the guise of breastfeeding my newborn.

I loved the class. I wanted to learn more. I asked the young instructor if she'd teach me how to lead a class, and she signed me up for the fitness class training. A year later, I was leading my own pre- and post-natal exercise class with other new moms.

As I approached the ripe old age of 30, my interest in the health field continued to grow—in vivid contrast to my growing-up years when I'd believed I had no athletic ability.

While pregnant with my second child, I faced my life-long awkwardness and lack of co-ordination by taking more fitness training courses. I learned about "exercise physiology," "anatomy," and "kinesiology." Not only did I learn how to spell these fancy words, but I learned what they meant, too!

In a completely unforeseen and astonishing twist of fate, I became certified as a personal trainer, an accomplishment I'd never have dreamed possible when I was younger. I had become the "three-more; two-more; now-take-it-to-the-left" lady at the front of the room leading the class!

Imagine me, the anti-athlete, now helping others make permanent lifestyle changes—and teaching them about healthy eating and balance (both how to balance on one foot, and how to balance one's life expectations).

But I still had something to learn. Although I'd been born and raised within the church, it wasn't until I attended a Christian women's retreat that I realized how much I had compartmentalized my life: family in one corner, work in another; finances here, health there; faith in one box, doughnuts in the other box. I began to see that my faith shouldn't be kept partitioned off from the rest of my life in a storage trunk, just pulled out for Christmas and Easter, or even for every Sunday morning. Instead, it needed to be intertwined with all the parts of my life. If I was going to follow Him as my Lord, God wanted me to include Him in everything.

I began a partnership with God. Each morning, I started my day with a prayer. "Dear Lord, I pray that You'll remind me every day that You're at work within me and around me." Or, "Dear God, I pray that You'll instill in me a sense of responsibility to care for my body—to both nourish and sustain it."

I added prayer to my regular walks. I opened with praise to God and thanked Him for the good in my life. Every day, I purposely identified five new things for which I was grateful. My neighbours thought I had finally gone crazy when they saw my lips moving as I talked to the air, but I just waved and smiled and continued on my prayer walk.

At the end of the day, I would write in my diary about my new faith and fitness journey. One of my entries reads:

> I am feeling good about myself since I started this partnership with God. I have more control over my eating, as I am mindful of what I put in my mouth. I call on God's strength every day. I feel energized to work in my gardens, continue my daily walks, and strength train at least once a week. My clothes feel looser around the waist, so I know I'm losing inches.

I also spent time reading my Bible and seeking out scriptural truths about God's character. I started to memorize favourite verses such as, "It is God who arms me with strength and makes my way perfect" (2 Samuel 22:33) and "I can do everything through Him who gives me strength" (Philippians 4:13).

Then I felt a God-nudge that this type of program would also help others. So I used what I had learned to create a workbook, which I published as an e-book. *Fit for Faith: 7 Weeks to Improved Spiritual and Physical Health* offers scriptural principles and practical tips to help readers develop a healthier lifestyle and a deeper relationship with God. It's a straightforward reference on cardiovascular exercise, strength training, healthy eating, flexibility exercise, prayer, Bible study, and journal writing.

Now that I'm in my forties, I'm committed to trying new things. My kids are teenagers and they encourage me to "play" with them. In the last year, I've tried golf, rollerblading, ice skating, and even ball hockey. Since I'm the oldest woman on my ball hockey team, it's easy to spot me on the rink—I'm the only one who wears a helmet, protective gloves and shin pads.

These days, when we have family reunions, I'm no longer the last one picked for a team. My three brothers actually argue over whose team I get to play on!

I'm living proof that it's never too late to start getting fit. I love to encourage others who have always considered themselves unathletic or anti-athletic. And I also love to challenge those whose walk with God is getting flabby. I may set myself goals for losing pounds, lifting weights, or running marathons, but I know that my most important goal is getting to know God more closely, serving Him, and seeking to be more like Him each day.

What Do I Want to Be When I Grow Up?

Nonfiction

Les Lindquist

"What do you want to be when you grow up?" For generations, adults have asked kids that question. But these days, as more and more people change jobs frequently or retire in their fifties, adults are now asking themselves the same question. In the two years since I retired from a 35-year career with multinational corporation IBM, I've frequently asked myself, "So what *do* I want to be when I grow up?"

The truth is, before leaving my job, I hadn't been happy for a couple of years. I struggled with the purpose behind what I was doing. My own specialty was change management, but I found that I was becoming the establishment that I had set out to transform. I knew it was time I made a change, but I was comfortable. I liked the people I worked with, I enjoyed some of the work, and I was well-paid. However, I knew the company was downsizing its workforce all over the world and that anyone in a high-paying staff job was a prime target. I even mentioned to a colleague that the writing was on the wall for me.

So when I got the call that Tuesday morning, I was somewhat prepared. "Your department is being cut in half. You'll need to find another position in the company... or we can offer you an early retirement package."

To my surprise, my primary reaction to the phone call was a huge sense of relief. I was free from the long boring meetings that went nowhere; from back-to-back-to-back conference calls all day long; from training people who didn't want to be trained—all of the things that I'd begun to find frustrating and meaningless.

My immediate decision was easy; I had no desire to look for another job within the company, and I knew in my heart it was

time to leave. At the same time, I was only 57 years old, and while I might be retiring from IBM, I had no intention of actually retiring.

What I loved most was the idea of a fresh beginning, but I found myself struggling with where to start. It was as if my brain wasn't ready to shift gears. I'd still wake up in the middle of the night with an idea about something I could do in my old job.

Eventually, I heard an experienced politician who'd gone down to electoral defeat refer to his time of transition into a new job as "decompressing." That resonated with me. I realized I, too, needed time to decompress and to reorient my thinking.

Even though I'd been happy to leave, I found myself going through a grieving process. Something that had been a huge part of my life for nearly 35 years was gone. Even though I'd worked from home for years and most of my connections with colleagues all over the world had been made through phone calls and e-mail, I still missed the people, I missed the daily structure, and I even missed having deadlines.

In the end, months passed before I was ready to start trying to find the answer to the question, "What next?"

At that point, when I was all set to focus on finding a new career, it occurred to me that I had no idea what I wanted to do next, and that, in fact, I'd never really picked my job with IBM as my ideal career in the first place. Like many people, I kind of "happened" into the job.

My original goal, back when I was 17, was to become a mathematics professor in a university and to work with youth as a camp director during the summer. When I was beginning the fourth year of my Honours Bachelor of Arts degree at the University of Regina, my older brother, who worked for IBM, convinced me that going though the job interview process on campus would be a useful experience for me.

So, that November, I signed up to talk to several large companies, including IBM—an American computer, technology and consulting corporation nicknamed "Big Blue."

I felt no pressure during the IBM interview, and enjoyed "playing the game" by asking insightful questions, rather than trying to impress them with my accomplishments. In retrospect, I unintentionally did all the things a good recruiter looks for. I also found the aptitude test really easy.

The recruiter told me there would be two further interviews before I might be offered a position. When I heard nothing more from them for several months, I wasn't at all disappointed; I planned to stay in school to get a PhD so I could become a professor.

However, over the next few months, my thinking began to change. Because I had wide-ranging interests, I'd taken so many English, philosophy and other humanities classes during my first three years of undergraduate studies that I had to take all math classes in my fourth year in order to graduate with my planned mathematics major. I realized that I wasn't all that interested in math. While I found the subject easy, and I liked problem solving, I began to question whether I'd be happy teaching equations and proving theorems on imaginary numbers for the rest of my life.

In February, while I was beginning to wonder what to do, I spoke to a friend who was a regional representative for Christian Service Brigade Ministries, an international organization that mentors groups of boys and disciples them in the Christian faith. I'd been involved in the ministry for many years, first as a participant and then, from the age of 17, as a local leader. It occurred to me that I might like to work in regional leadership in the organization. However, my friend strongly recommended that I get a couple of years of business experience first. He said the business experience would help me relate better to the people with whom I'd be working. I thought about my interview with IBM, but since I'd heard nothing more from them, I assumed they had no interest in me.

By March, I was beginning to get concerned. My wife Nancy and I had been married for a year and a half. She was taking a writing course and only working part-time, so we were starting to feel the pinch financially.

Then, out of the blue (pun intended), a letter arrived from "Big Blue." IBM was not requesting another interview; IBM was offering me a full-time job after I graduated the next month. Apparently I had impressed them, not to mention acing the aptitude test.

Accepting the job was a no-brainer. I assumed God must be opening the door and leading me in that direction.

Well, my planned two years somehow turned into 35. I worked on many different teams in various departments and found the challenges engaging; there were always new problems needing to be solved, and it turned out I loved solving all kinds of problems, not just mathematical ones.

In hindsight, I find it strange that I could have spent that much time working in a career I hadn't expressly chosen. On the other hand, a very successful businessman once told me that, in his experience, most people are in their current jobs "because they walked down the left side of the street." In other words, because they were in a certain place at a certain time, they saw a "Help Wanted" notice, and stumbled into a job that started them on a particular path. If they'd strolled down the other side of the street, they might have ended up doing something entirely different.

Now, here I was, at 57 years old, for the first time since I was a teenager, pointedly asking myself what I wanted to be when I grew up. I knew that the most prudent thing to do, from a financial stand-point, would be to leverage my years of consulting experience into a similar job in the information technology industry. But my gut told me that I had "Been there, done that." And, while I wasn't wealthy, my retirement package allowed me to put other consider-ations ahead of exclusively material needs.

So what *did* I want to do? I knew that, whatever it was going to be, it had to be something meaningful. I was struck by watch-ing a videotaped lecture on time management by Carnegie Mellon University professor of computer science Randy Pausch, who had been given six months to live due to pancreatic cancer. In 2008, his book, *The Last Lecture*, became a *New York Times* bestseller just before he passed away at age 47. While I didn't have quite the same sense of immediacy, I could relate to what Pausch said: "Every hour you spend on something unimportant is one that you can't spend on something important."[1]

Although I've invested 35 years at IBM, God willing, I still have significant time left. Three decades ago, when I looked at death notices for former employees in our company newsletters, I was amazed by how many people died less than two years after they retired. I got a similar newsletter last week, and noticed that the gap between retirement and death now is frequently more than 20 years.

At the same time, I realize that time is short. Barring something unexpected, I'm in the last half of my life. (Yes, I do plan to live into the triple digits!) I want to use my time wisely and have no regrets. I'm truly grateful for my corporate career. God placed me in an excellent company, where I not only got vital business experience, but was paid well. We were able to raise our family, purchase a home, help our four sons get university educations, and give to charities. My job also allowed me to be very active in church leadership. I'd been a deacon from the age of 22, worked with boys in Christian Service Brigade, led small groups, served on several boards, been a charter member of two church plants, and more. I'd even ended up directing some church summer camps for kids, as I'd hoped to do when I was a teenager.

My job also made it possible for my wife Nancy to home-school our four sons, take an active role in church and small-group leadership, pursue her writing career, and devote full-time volunteer work to co-founding The Word Guild.

But at this point, I'm still thankful to have a second opportunity to choose what I want to be when I grow up. I just wish I had some idea of what I *do* want to be.

Some people have a dream—perhaps deeply hidden—but a dream that they've always wanted to fulfill. For them, the challenge is getting started on the path toward making their dream a reality.

However, my problem, and that of many other people, is the inability to name a particular ambition. Often, an inspirational speaker, trying to help the audience members articulate their dreams, will say, "Picture yourself in 10 years having a perfect day. What are you doing?" For years, I'd say, "Beats me. All I know is that it's not what I'm doing now!"

I decided that I needed to look at what motivates me.

Popular wisdom says that people are motivated by money. Many companies set up financial incentive programs to get employees to change behaviour and to achieve certain objectives. A number of years ago, however, I studied reward systems for a project at work. We were trying to figure out how to prompt managers and employees to make a major shift in their behaviour. We were surprised to learn that, once a person's basic needs are met, money actually is *not* a practical source of motivation. *Lack* of money can be a *de*motivator, and people need to be paid fairly in order to stay in a job, but once our basic needs are met, the promise of more money doesn't effectively motivate us.

As a matter of fact, current research is revealing that, except for relatively mindless tasks such as assembly-line work, monetary incentives actually *inhibit* performance. Daniel H. Pink, in the bestselling book *Drive: The Surprising Truth About What Motivates Us*, calls this the "mismatch between what science knows and what business does."[2] If money doesn't work, what does?[3]

I strongly related to the three things Pink says do effectively inspire people. The first is the ability to choose what we work on and how—what Pink calls *autonomy*.[4]

As an employee, being able to make simple choices, such as working flex hours or working at home one day a week, gave me a sense of having some control of my work environment. Some companies have had great success giving their staff one day a month to work on any idea they like, as long as it *isn't* part of their normal job. Many of us believe that the ultimate in autonomy is working for ourselves, so we're attracted to starting a small business. But autonomy doesn't necessarily mean working alone; in fact, I've found that working on a team can actually increase my flexibility.

The second thing that motivates us is the opportunity to use our skills and strengths to our full potential—what Pink calls *mastery*.[5] However, many of us don't have a good sense of what our own strengths are. Perhaps that's because we tend to take for granted anything we find easy to do, and fail to recognize this as a strength.

I've recently become conscious of the reality that over the years, I've spent a lot of time and energy trying to improve in the areas where I had weaknesses. In fact, at IBM, we had formal programs to identify weaknesses and implement plans to address them. But lately, I've learned that I might have been much better off focusing on the areas where I was strong and developing those— and compensating for areas where I'm weak by partnering with others whose strengths complement my weaknesses. A trilogy of books by Marcus Buckingham and Donald Clifton (*First, Break all the Rules*; *Discover your Strengths*; and *Go Put Your Strengths to Work*) have helped me understand that it would not only be in my *own* best interest to focus on my strengths, but would also benefit any organization I work for.

A few years ago, I took an online test to identify where I stood on the Kolbe Assessment A™ Index,[6] a test that measures innate abilities and instinctive methods of operating. Understanding how I naturally do things has been instrumental in allowing me to accept myself, and to understand which activities I should choose to do, and which undertakings I should leave alone. I discovered that I have great strengths in some areas, but great deficiencies in others. Teaming with other people whose strengths complement mine is crucial.

Of course, I wouldn't have progressed in my career if I hadn't been using at least some of my strengths, especially the problem-solving that I love to do. But going forward, I want to focus on making the best use of my strengths.

The third thing that motivates us is the sense that we're contributing to society through what we're doing—what Pink calls *purpose*.[7]

As I identify a path to which I want to devote myself, I know that working for any business whose only focus is quarterly profits won't motivate me. I could choose to work in public service, or for a charity or a not-for-profit organization, but I'm intrigued by an emerging option—businesses that are "not *only* for profit." This growing trend has been dubbed "social entrepreneurship," combining business with charity.

As opposed to not-for-profits, these companies operate with the intention of making money for the owners, but with an additional, deeper purpose that allows the companies to contribute to society, even if that means sacrificing some earnings. In one example, a shoe company donates one pair of shoes to a needy child in the developing world for every pair sold to a paying customer.

While I was pursuing my corporate career, I realized that, from the time I was a teenager, I'd found purpose through volunteer work in churches and other ministry organizations. In fact, an IBM personal development coach I consulted many years ago encouraged me to keep the balance between business and service, suggesting I needed both to feel fulfilled.

In my experience, the sanity of working for volunteer organizations helped balance the insanity of my work environment. Conversely, at times, the sanity of my business world helped me deal with the insanity of the volunteer organizations. Unfortunately, volunteers often are not appreciated because they are "free." People tend to value what they pay for much more than what they receive at no cost.

Now, I'm trusting God to lead me into a new place where I'll still be able to use the abilities he's given me to provide for the needs of my family while exercising my freedom to contribute to society.

I recently taught a college continuing education course on implementing change in our personal lives. I was surprised to find that nearly three-quarters of the men and women in my class were seeking ideas about what they should do next. Some had retired and were looking for something meaningful to do; others were unhappy in their current jobs and wanted to make a change.

The truth is, many people these days are deciding that they don't want to retire quietly. Nor do they want to work hard with the sole objective of earning cash or making money for stockholders. They're looking for meaningful jobs that will provide income, but will also give them opportunities to use their strengths, to have freedom to choose, and to contribute to a greater purpose.

As for me, a dream is slowly emerging, and the challenge of making it work excites me. Fulfilling a dream always involves believing that we can do it—but I've learned that merely believing will soon let us down if we don't learn some tools and techniques to keep us on track to accomplish the required steps.

I've always enjoyed working with teams, so I appreciated what Barbara Sher, author of *I Could Do Anything If I Only Knew What It Was*, suggested: find a group of other people who are also seeking to fulfill their dreams. As she points out, "We have better ideas for each other than we do for ourselves" and "We have more courage for each other than we do for ourselves."[8] Sher suggests that being part of a "success team" will encourage us to articulate our dreams, give us new, creative ideas (along with contacts with people who can help us implement our ideas), and keep us focused on the dream, and the hard—but exciting—work of making it happen.

So what have I learned?

I need to work with a team. My role will include using my strengths, while the other members of the team will have complementary strengths.

I need to be solving problems of some kind. Actually, in the last couple of years, I've been learning a lot about the publishing industry, which is currently going through major change. As chair of the board for The Word Guild, an organization of Canadian writers and editors who are Christian, I've been able to focus on some interesting projects that involve changing the way we equip writers and creating new models for publishing.

I want to help other people who want to make a difference. A few years ago, God helped me see a need to "release stifled Christians to serve Him joyfully and effectively." For now, that involves writers, but in the future I see myself speaking to other people and doing what I can to help them figure out where God wants them.

The bottom line is that I firmly believe God directed my first career choice, and I can't wait to tackle whatever problem He has for me next.

1. Randy Pausch, "Lecture on Time Management," Carnegie Mellon University: Randy Pausch's Web Site, http://www.cs.cmu.edu/~pausch/ (accessed December 17, 2010).

2. Daniel H. Pink, *Drive: The Surprising Truth About What Motivates Us* (New York: Riverhead Hardcover, 2009), 9–10.

3. Surprisingly, one of the top morale-boosters is seeing a poorly performing peer get fired. Not because it scares employees into performing, but because it gives confidence that management will deal with tough issues.

4. Pink, *Drive,* 84–108.

5. *Ibid.,* 109–130.

6. See http://leslindquist.com/kolbe.

7. Pink, *Drive,* 131–146.

8. Barbara Sher and Annie Gottlieb, *Teamworks!* (New York: Warner Books, 1991), 7.

Visual Gymnastics

Nonfiction

Ann Brent

Until a few short years ago, my eyes were finely-tuned instruments of precision. No matter how tiny the print on the back of the cake mix box, I could read each ingredient down to the final scary chemical. Regardless of how minuscule the directions for use printed on the cough syrup bottle, each and every letter and symbol was clearly visible to me and my accurate eyes.

I vividly remember the rainy day, soon after my fiftieth birthday, when I zipped into Shoppers Drug Mart to pick up a few lunchbox snacks. I grabbed a box of granola bars, located the ingredients list, and searched for any mention of nuts, no matter what kind. You can imagine my surprise when I discovered that the manufacturer had changed the print on its packaging, shrinking the words to such a minute size as to make them unreadable.

I was slightly relieved to find that by simply extending my arm 12 to 15 inches, the words could still be deciphered. *Good, no nuts!* I popped the package into my shopping cart.

Before long, though, my arms wouldn't extend far enough to allow me to bring tiny package information into focus. And to make matters worse, I discovered that more and more companies were shrinking, not only their ingredient lists, but also the recipes on the back of their packages. I began to have difficulty determining whether to add one tablespoon or two of baking powder to the new dessert squares I was making. Or was that teaspoon?

So, the day came when I buckled and admitted I had to buy my first pair of glasses.

On my next visit to Walmart, I checked out their assortment of ready-made reading glasses. I tried on various pairs to figure out what prescription strength I needed, and ultimately chose the least horrible-looking pair.

And just like that, I could read the fine print again!

However, after decades of living glasses-free, I didn't adapt to this new stage of life very easily. The glasses irritated my nose when I wore them too much, and because I only needed them for reading, I was always leaving them somewhere. When I wanted to follow a recipe in the kitchen, my glasses might be in the bedroom. Invariably, when I headed to my office to balance the cheque book, I first had to track down my eyewear on the kitchen table or in the family room.

I tried the jewellery-type metallic chains that hold a pair of glasses around the neck for easy access, but found them uncomfortable, difficult to get on and off, and potentially hazardous. If I used my glasses during a phone call, getting tangled and strangled in the telephone cord was a very real threat.

Eventually, I discovered that the handiest place to keep my glasses, when not in use, was perched on top of my head, making them easy to reach and always accessible.

This solution worked well until the right arm of my glasses snapped off while I was at work. No doubt the head-to-nose-to-head action, repeated multiple times daily, was too much for them. By this point, my glasses had become indispensable, so I made a quick trip to the optical department at Walmart, where the original arm and hinge, and the teeny-tiny screw holding them in place, were replaced for free with what the optician called a "similar" version.

Although the new arm was slightly different in shape and colour, this repair did the trick—but the new hardware has created another challenge. Now and then, when I lift my glasses off the top of my head too quickly, the new hinge grabs onto one of my brown, straight hairs and yanks it out. Ouch!

But, the good news is that, with my repaired glasses, I can read the tiny directions on my new bottle of extra-volumizing, restorative, thickening mousse for fine and limp hair, and I'm pretty sure I'll be able to fluff up my layers enough to hide the thinning patch of hair just above my right temple.

My Parents, My Friends

Nonfiction

A. A. Adourian

I sit in the early morning hours, resting my left cheek in the palm of my hand, reflecting on my parents, thinking back to those quiet moments in life where silence speaks so loudly. For as long as I can remember, I've loved my mother. She was my best friend, always ready to understand what was on my mind. But it wasn't until my first year of university that my father became my friend. And it wasn't until I risked my job to be at the hospital with him every day, that he understood—or that I began to grasp—my capacity to love him.

My parents, Nerses and Marie-Jeanne, met, married, and started their lives together in Beirut, Lebanon. Five years later, I was born; two years after that, my brother received a joyous welcome. My parents often wistfully described how much they loved their lives in the "Paris of the Middle East" until the Lebanese civil war erupted in the 1970s.

As the war continued, the roof of our Beirut apartment complex was often used as a base from which to discharge gunfire. Recognizing that it was dangerous to remain in our home, my parents moved us from one aunt's house to another, returning to the apartment to pick up items we needed whenever there was a temporary ceasefire.

During one of these brief trips home, as my mother stood in front of her bedroom mirror quickly assessing the white sweater she had just put on, a bullet flew past the side of her head and embedded itself firmly in the wall. Mom immediately determined there had to be more to life for her young family, but the decision to leave Lebanon was very hard because she was the youngest of seven close-knit siblings.

We joined the mass exodus from Lebanon early in the conflict, when I was four and a half years old. We were among the

183

nearly one million people, mainly of Christian descent, who fled the country. The civil war would rage on for 15 years in total, leaving tens of thousands dead and a million or more wounded.

My father would often recount, as we were growing up, how we left Lebanon for Canada, and how he fought for his family to have a better life. The story never failed to stir our hearts. My mother hastily packed the essentials—clothing, photos, some cherished heirlooms including the Bible from her wedding day. Despite my parents' fears about what would happen if we were caught, we took a very expensive taxi ride from Beirut to Aleppo, the largest city in the neighbouring country of Syria (where the driver, who was related to us by marriage, was himself planning a fresh start).

It took about five months for Dad to guide the four of us from Damascus, Syria (where we stayed with my father's cousins) and then, when we heard our immigration papers were ready, on to Athens, Greece. My father's siblings had already emigrated from Lebanon and Syria to Canada and the United States; they had been doing their part to speed up the paperwork. My parents fondly described how kind the staff of British Airways were to us as we flew from Athens to Toronto, Ontario.

When we first arrived in Canada, I would come home crying because I didn't understand English and couldn't follow what was going on in kindergarten. Fortunately, since she had been an English teacher back home, Mom was able to teach my brother and me English—with the help of the television programs *Sesame Street* and *The Electric Company*. I thought that my mother was so smart because she knew French, too. And she was the first person to teach me how to subtract 389 from 1,000 by telling me what to do with the zeros. I still remember feeling victorious the next day in grade three when I knew the answer and no one else did.

My mother dearly missed her loved ones every day, and spoke of them so often that it was as though the family members she'd left behind were with us on a daily basis.

She was a very private person, always smiling, despite what was going on around her and inside her. Mom frequently repeated verses from 1 Corinthians 13 to help her endure the hard times. The one I remember most is 1 Corinthians 13:1, "If I speak in the tongues of men or of angels but do not have love, I am only a resounding gong or a clanging cymbal."

Although we had not fully adjusted to this new country (and its cold winters), we soon became Canadian citizens. My father easily conversed with the judge presiding over the citizenship interview about how much he admired then-Prime Minister Pierre Trudeau for having had the good sense to let us into the country three years earlier. Dad likes to say that the judge admired his knowledge of Canadian politics and quickly approved our citizenship.

For a while, we were the only Armenians on our west-end Toronto street. We often had to explain that we were not Romanian, and that Romania was actually a different country altogether.

"But Romania is close to Armenia, right?"

"No," we would reply patiently, "not really."

"But if you are Armenian," they would ask, "why were you born in Lebanon?"

We would then provide a crash course in Armenian history, an area of interest for me that carried right through to university as I became fascinated with Russian, European and British history as well. We would explain that Armenians had scattered because of the massacres and forced deportations carried out by the Ottoman Empire (now known as the Republic of Turkey) around the time of World War I (1915–1923). Although Turkey still denies that the events were genocide[1], Armenians believe that one and a half million people were martyred. Our ancestors fled from death, and my father's mother survived. We would conclude our account by explaining that, except for a few distant relatives by marriage, as a result of the Armenian diaspora created by the Genocide, we didn't know *anyone* who lived in Armenia.

The more we spoke, the more fascinating we became to our neighbours and classmates. At times, my brother and I wished we had "normal" names like Jill and Jack, instead of Armig and Sevag, so that we could blend in. But we knew our ancestors had not died so we could forget who we were or the God we believed in.

Although we came from a long line of Christian believers—Armenia was the first nation to declare itself Christian in 301 AD—neither of my parents lived out their faith until later in their married life. Their commitment to serving Jesus as their Lord and Saviour became stronger once our family began to attend an Armenian church each week in Toronto. Dad worked behind the scenes, usually taking care of the church's kitchen appliances or driving youth group kids to our weekly meetings. Mom served for many years in the Ladies Group and taught during the inaugural years of Daily Vacation Bible School in the summer months.

Mom also helped us with our homework and, when she realized we were forgetting our Armenian, sent us to Armenian School on Saturdays to learn about our language and culture. Looking back, we are so thankful that Canada let us be Christian Armenians in an atmosphere of religious and cultural freedom.

Our Canadian public schools also opened our horizons to worlds beyond our immediate family life; our teachers encouraged us to be and do whatever we wanted. My grade six teacher, in particular, was very encouraging. When Mr. Sleightholm read *The Hobbit* and *Watership Down* aloud to us, he could see my creative response and the potential in my writing, and shared that with my mom. He also complimented her for her by-the-book-no-slang English.

Mom reciprocated his kindness by occasionally sending him freshly made Armenian pizza or *baklava* (delicate phyllo pastries filled with crushed walnuts and soaked in sugar-laden syrup). Mom created the best Armenian pizza, or *lahmajoun*. It's the size of a personal pan pizza, topped with minced lean ground beef (we used lamb back in Beirut), tomato, onion and parsley, along with herbs and spices such as cumin, fresh mint and basil. Mom had special techniques for flavouring the *lahmajoun* topping (this remains a family secret) and rolling out her homemade dough to a specific level of thinness before baking the pizza. I still remember thinking how invincible she was, standing in front of a hot oven, toiling away, her hands busily preparing delicious food for her family to enjoy, showing us that we were loved. I thought my mother was capable of doing anything.

When one of us had had a long, tiring day, Mom and I often quoted verses to each other from a well-loved Armenian poem, "A Mother's Hands." The heart of the poem, and pretty much our classic refrain, went something like this: "What can be asked that can't be done by a mother's hands?" Many were the works of my mother's hands—soothing my cuts, mending my aches, helping me with anything that required help, at any time. She was always kind and smart, a friend through all my mistakes. Her words were as soft as the palms of her hands, building me up, giving me love, encouraging my ideas, no matter how small or grand. My mother's hands were frequently clasped in prayer, as she daily read her Bible in conjunction with the latest devotional from *Our Daily Bread*. Hers was a love that could only come from God above.

We both shared an odd habit of putting our hands in front of our mouths when something was really funny, so that our laughs tickled our palms. Mom's smiles, her laughter, her sound, were her brand. When I was growing up, I cherished the reaction of Mom's friends mistakenly presuming she had answered the phone when it really was me. "But you sound just like your mother!" they would exclaim. And when Mom held my face between her beautiful, warm hands, it made me proud to be called her daughter. She had my loyalty forever.

The story of my relationship with my father is in many ways the complete opposite of my close bond with my mother. Dad had been strict with me and my younger brother as we were growing up. He always wanted us to look him in the eye when he was speaking to us. For him, this was how we displayed respect and showed him that we understood the point he was trying to make. It was all right for him to joke around with us (nothing worth repeating here, for each corny joke elicited successively louder groans from us), but it was not all right for me to be silly. When I questioned his objection to a comment I had made, and ended my self-defence with the phrase, "But I do that with my friends," he would reply with an offended, "I'm not your friend. I am your father. Don't treat me like a friend."

Looking back, my father and I began to become friends during my first year at the University of Toronto. He was excited and proud that I was the first member of my family to go to university. By the end of my first year of classes, we'd moved from the west end of Toronto to the east, to be closer to Dad's job in Scarborough. Much to my surprise, if I was willing to wake up early enough and stay late enough to commute with him, he never objected to saving me an hour's bus ride by dropping me off and picking me up in front of the library at U of T's Scarborough campus. I think he actually enjoyed the company. So much so that he continued to give me a ride to wherever—subway station, school, work, youth group, or to a friend's house—no matter what time of day.

I always felt safe with Dad driving because it seemed so effortless for him. His left hand—calloused and often grease-stained—resting on the steering wheel, would adroitly guide us home. Those car rides made us friends. Sometimes Dad would treat me to a classic Armenian ballad, and at other times he would recall childhood stories of his life back home in Beirut. He was a great storyteller, explaining past events with such detail that you could picture the hue of the light emanating from the lamp post on the southwest corner of the street intersection in question. He talked; I listened. We talked. We joked. I tried to accept advice from him; well, at least he tried to give me advice.

I hadn't realized how much he loved to talk about his workday. As he described each of his co-workers, I smiled to myself that the cast of characters was like an extension of my university English courses—though Shakespearean they were not. He got such joy out of telling me (and anyone else who would listen) the specifics of his specialty of refrigerator repair, all the while weaving in tales of how he had demonstrated his wit using wordplay at work, and how he had outsmarted a co-worker with this or that clever retort. I soon had all of his witty remarks memorized.

In addition to his knack for acting as our personal Household Handyman, Dad was particularly good at making up new words to familiar Armenian folksongs. His voice, untrained but full of raw talent, always sounded a tad too "soprano" for a teen who was more into Canadian rock star Bryan Adams than what I then considered old, depressing songs. But when he would make up new lyrics, his creativity and inventiveness were the source of many household laugh-out-loud moments, because he purposely chose to mispronounce the correct words by substituting other words (from another language) that sounded the same, yet had a different meaning. Armenian, Arabic, Turkish, French, English— all were fair game. Even though we had decoded his tactics, the unexpected way he would make the words "fit" had us in stitches, marvelling at the inner workings of his mind.

After six years of university, I graduated with a Masters degree in Information Studies and took a job in the library field. My younger brother had moved out on his own, but I stayed at home, as is commonplace for women in my culture. My parents continued to uphold the importance of taking care of us both, making regular phone calls to check in on us. If they perceived that either my brother or I had a need, having fully weighed the matter at hand, they presented the "just-in-time solution"—before we had even articulated our issue. Most of our concerns, whether at school, at work, or with friends, were covered by their wisdom. We always had what we most needed: our parents' unconditional love and support.

Mom and I were close as I was growing up. The older I became and the more time we spent together, the more time we wanted to spend together. As an adult, I valued my mother's advice, especially as I shared with her the complexities of workplace dynamics (okay, office politics). Meanwhile, to me Dad was just Dad, the guy who had brought us to Canada and provided for us. And yes, we were now friends. What more was there?

"You went to U of T, right?" the nurse asked as I reluctantly removed my hand from the top of Dad's and slowly backed away from his hospital bed in the critical care unit.

"Yes, I went to the University of Toronto," I replied slowly. "But how would you know that?"

"Your dad told me," she responded.

My dad? I had just witnessed an army of doctors and attendants rush down to the emergency room to begin to aggressively treat Dad's septic shock—a type of massive infection that has a 50 percent mortality rate. I looked at him lying on his hospital bed, and I was amazed. My dad, who was now in a perilous situation that required overnight monitoring to make sure his kidneys and other organs didn't fail; my dad, who was heavily drugged and hooked up to hospital tubes and machines, had told the nurse about me! How could he even speak? I realized that Dad needed me, and I still needed him—in a different way.

At first, I went to the hospital every day so that I could be at Mom's side, but later I stuck around because I wanted to make sure Dad was taken care of properly. When he became more lucid, I'll never forget the look of recognition and gratitude on his face as he realized that I had not only taken care of Mom, but I had cared about him enough to stay by his side continually—no matter the cost to me, even risking my job to miss so much time from work. And I remember squeezing his hand while thanking God for how understanding the people at my workplace were—after I was done praising Him for bringing Dad back to us.

Looking back, I realized that as we had grown into adulthood, Dad had become more vocal about extolling his children for their unique talents. While my brother was lauded for the way his hands could work magic with anything electronic, Dad could recount with absolute precision all of the volunteer work I had done in church over the years, even when I had forgotten. He often surprises me even today with all that he remembers as he proudly talks about both of his kids.

Nowadays, our memories of Mom are often the focus of our conversations. My mother went to be with God in November 2008. Dad and I trust each other all the more now that Mom is gone. All three of us—my father, my brother, and I—honour Mom's memory through our friendship and closeness. In some ways, we have come full circle: now Dad has added the devotional in *Our Daily Bread* to his own nightly Bible reading routine, and now I see his hands clasped in prayer before he sleeps.

I so wish that I could once again hold the palms of my mother's hands in a gesture of calm, quiet, unending friendship. I long to show her anew how much more I now understand the meaning of love and of the hereafter, the destination of our soul-trip.

As the Holy Spirit continues to comfort us, God continues to teach me. When Dad told me the other day that all he wants is for me to "Do a good job," I thought of my Heavenly Father's words in Matthew 25:23 urging us to strive to hear His praise, "Well done, good and faithful servant."

When Dad periodically advises me to "Do good to others by treating them well," I'm reminded of "Do to others as you would have them do to you" in Luke 6:31.

By comparing my dad with my Heavenly Father, I don't pretend that my father is perfect. But just as I am learning to be His child, I am thankful to God for giving me a father who cared enough about me to serve me sacrificially, and provide whatever he had for my comfort.

My dad has always shown love by his actions. He would often tell Mom, "What's the point of me saying 'I love you' if my actions don't show it? Anyone can use words, but real love is action." Mom would agree, but she had her own twist.

From Mom, I learned an equally valuable lesson: Don't love people because of what they do, but simply for who they are. Whenever Mom would give me something I wanted, I would excitedly exclaim, "I love you, Mom!"—only to be met with a piercing, "Oh, is *that* why you love me? Because I gave you what you wanted?"

My mother made me realize that, just as she loved me for who I was, I needed to love her and my father and brother, no matter what.

And isn't that exactly what God does? He reaches out to us because He loves us no matter what (as 1 John 4:19 tells us, "We love because He first loved us"). His actions showed His love through the Cross.

When I became a teenager and was beginning to understand the God I thought I knew in my childhood, God drew me to Him because of the promise that He would be my Friend, and never leave me or forsake me (Joshua 1:9).

As I grew older, the words of Psalm 73:23–26 (which were an enormous comfort to both Mom and me) have deepened my love for, and my friendship with, God. They assure me:

> Yet I am always with You; You hold me by my right hand. You guide me with Your counsel, and afterward You will take me into glory. Whom have I in Heaven but You? And earth has nothing I desire besides You. My flesh and my heart may fail, but God is the strength of my heart and my portion forever.

Once God draws me to Him, He holds my right hand—a simple gesture assuring me that I am always with Him, no matter the circumstances. He becomes everything that I desire, to the point where I echo what Psalm 73:28 affirms: "But as for me, it is good to be near God. I have made the Sovereign Lord my refuge: I will tell of all Your deeds."

In my life, it has become impossible *not* to tell of His deeds and marvel at how He reveals Himself through them. I now understand that if we only love God because of what He has done or can do for us, if we don't realize who He is when we see the works of His hands, our love will remain shallow—and our belief in God will constantly be confused with that of Santa Claus. We'll never get beyond the superficial to the depths of knowing God, and loving Him simply for who He is.

My parents may not have realized it, but not only were they giving me a taste of God's love; they were teaching me how to love God, our greatest Friend.

1. Although the Armenian Genocide is controversial and the facts continue to be disputed by Turkey, on April 21, 2004, Canada's House of Commons voted to adopt a motion that recognized the mass killings of Armenians as purposeful extermination and stated, "This House acknowledges the Armenian genocide of 1915 and condemns this act as a crime against humanity." Reference: "Canada Recognizes the Armenian Genocide," Embassy of the Republic of Armenia, http://www.armembassycanada.ca/News/genocide_recognition.html (accessed December 14, 2010).

My Love Ladder

Nonfiction

Heidi McLaughlin

She was battered, dented and old; yet she looked curiously beautiful as I pulled her off the back of the pickup truck and propped her up in the corner of the garage. She wasn't ready to be discarded just yet. I stared fondly at this old stepladder—spattered with paint and gobs of glue, with bits of leftover wallpaper still sticking to her steps. Over the years, she had been invaluable to us during our home renovations, for putting up birthday balloons, and for placing the angel toppers on our Christmas trees. No, I wasn't done with her yet.

I cleaned off all the glue and wallpaper and bought a can of semi-gloss spray paint. Setting the ladder on newspapers spread in the middle of the garage floor, I gave her two coats of transforming, dazzling white. When I was done, I stood back and smiled in amazement at the glorious, restored beauty.

She was too unique and beautiful to be left sitting in some dark corner. I decided to get creative and use her in our home as a focal point whenever decorating for upcoming baby showers and wedding celebrations.

For each event, I pulled her out of the storage area in the basement, draped her with tulle and organza fabrics, strung white mini-lights, and set flower pots and gift bags on her rungs. I was able to make this distinctive stepladder so attractive that everyone stood back and remarked at her intriguing beauty.

When Christmas came around, I placed the ladder in our home's foyer, draped artificial evergreen garlands along the sides, wound mini-lights through the greenery, and positioned red and gold angels, snowflakes, and decorative musical instruments on her steps. Visitors were curious and mesmerized. Year after year, people eagerly asked, "Heidi, when can I come over to see what delightful treasures you've added to your ladder this year?"

December, 1994, was filled with excitement and anticipation as my husband Dick and I decorated and baked in preparation for the holiday season. This would be our first Christmas in our new home in Kelowna, British Columbia since our move from Lethbridge, Alberta. We could hardly wait for our daughter Michelle and our son Donovan to arrive so that we could begin the Christmas celebrations. I hummed Christmas carols as I placed my stepladder in her new place of honour, in the foyer beside the circular staircase. I stood back and smiled at her "makeover." Dressed in gold netting, strings of pearls, and angel figurines, she was stunning.

I wonder what memories and treasures we will add this year? I thought. *Life just doesn't get any better than this.* My reverie was interrupted by the doorbell, and my world was forever changed. A policeman informed me that Dick had just died of heart failure while playing a game of basketball at the local high school gym.

Time stopped. It felt as if someone had thrust a sharp knife into my heart. Throughout that Christmas season, my body was in shock and I found it difficult to breathe. I was continually gulping and gasping for air. *One breath, one hour, one day at a time.*

On Boxing Day, December 26, I could no longer tolerate the Christmas decorations. They were a mocking reminder of everything that had gone wrong. My children and I started ripping the decorations from the Christmas tree and the fireplace mantel.

Then I saw her. My Love Ladder. Friends and family who had looked after me during the past two weeks had covered every rung of the ladder with funeral plants and flowers. I was horrified at how my world had been violated and turned upside-down. Angry and sobbing, I pulled both the flowers and my Christmas treasures from the steps, folded the ladder up, took her to the basement, and hid her in a corner. I thought, *I never want to set eyes on you again.*

As the winter of the New Year passed into spring, healing began. Gradually, I was able to see the beauty in the stars and raindrops and the brilliant colours of the summer flowers. I realized that God's blessings had never left my life—I had simply been in too much pain to be aware of them.

I met a tall, handsome and kind man named Jack whose wife had died from cancer. As we began to take long walks, we discovered mutual family and spiritual values, and a desire to live life to the fullest. We dared to share our hopes and dreams for the future, and eventually, friendship evolved into love. With the blessings of our combined five children, our immediate families, and our closest friends, we were married on a glorious, sunny June day.

One autumn, a couple of years later, I was rummaging through our basement looking for an empty cardboard box to ship a Christmas present when I saw her. I gasped and held my breath as I stared at my discarded, barren ladder. Memories burned through my mind and once again I felt the horrific pain of my loss. The reminders were an intrusion and collided with my present life and my new, bigger, blended family. I took two steps forward, determinedly picked up the ladder, and carried her upstairs and out into the garage. I laid newspapers on the middle of the garage floor, found a can of leftover spray paint... and gave my forgotten Love Ladder two coats of dazzling gold paint.

That Christmas, I boldly positioned my golden ladder in the middle of our living area. With renewed energy and joy, I added angels, mini-lights, and evergreen garlands. I wove tiny music scrolls of Christmas carols throughout the garlands. On each step, I placed my new treasures: framed photos of my blended family, consisting of my two children, three new stepchildren, their spouses, and seven darling grandchildren.

Stepping back in awe, I grasped how God had restored my life in a magnificent way, making it more fulfilling, more gorgeous, than anything I could have imagined.

The first time my stepchildren Janice, Jennifer and David saw the ladder, they were amazed at her beauty but puzzled about her significance. I said to them, "Let me tell you a story about a battered old ladder that evidenced the transforming power and beauty of God's love in an extraordinary way..."

Since that Christmas, I've frequently folded up my Love Ladder and travelled all around the interior of British Columbia with her in the back seat of my car. God has given me opportunities to tell my story to hundreds of women—a story of how God used an old rickety stepladder to bring new hope and transform a broken heart.

Befriending the Beast:
A Parable of Perception

Fiction

Heather McGillivray

A Maritime minnow, living on the outskirts of her school, was enticed and mesmerized by the murky dark waters of the Atlantic. Though she'd been warned in school never to go beyond the safety of her shallow borders, she longed to slip into the forbidden stream, experience its embrace, and know what it was like to feel the ocean press its icy squeeze against her scales. One day, she plunged headlong into the inky depths.

A shark, on the edge of anxiety, was beside himself with despondency—he could not control his insatiable hunger for prey, had devoured many a good soul, and yet remained hopelessly empty within. This day, he made an oath to himself to leave the smallest and most helpless of creatures alone.

As if by providence, the minnow, wearied by the dizzying undercurrents, stopped to rest in the crevice of a towering shoal of rocks.

Frightened by all the strange sights and sounds, and longing to find her way back home to the quiet waters of the bay, there, beneath the rocky fortress, she sought succour from above.

The shark came near to pray. He was nervous, having never prayed before, yet driven by extreme desperation. Ever since his vow, he could think of nothing else but soft, succulent minnow scales slipping between his teeth.

He wondered how to go about it—this praying—and, fearing another shark or huge beast of the sea might see him and ostracize him, he mumbled silently toward the Unknown. *O, Thou Divine Deity of the depths below and heights above, grant that I might be released from these relentless cravings for Thy creations.*

As the minnow also supplicated, for protection and guidance, she felt a salty gush rush over her body, enveloping her in a momentary warm embrace. Surely, this was the hug of God. She looked up to see the most handsome creature she had ever set eyes on.

His smooth, majestic body was girded with sinewy strength, and his anguished smile gleamed with the myriad of shiny jewels encased within. And, though his expression was impossible to read, tears escaped the hollow depths of his eyes where no emotion could be seen. This must be the creature she was supposed to be afraid of; the beast she had heard so much about in school. Perhaps no one had ever taken the time and courage to really understand what caused his pain.

As the shark continued to petition the Unknown, a most amazing thought occurred to him. Maybe he was cold and callous because he had never taken the time to get properly acquainted with the poor creatures he devoured. Surely, if he could see beneath the savoury surface, he would learn to treat each one with respect and love.

This was it—the answer to his prayers. He would try to befriend one of the least of the least of his appetizers.

As the minnow gazed into the hollow depths of the beautiful creature's eyes, a longing stirred deep within her. Somehow she knew she could bring joy to the sadness. Surely, this was the answer to her prayers. Befriending the troubled beast would lead her home again.

When the shark had finished praying, he looked down and saw the tiny minnow staring up into his eyes. A strange emotion lassoed his heart and yanked it into his stomach. Panic jittered into his cartilage, and the sensation left him paralyzed. Surely this was fear.

The minnow stared up in amazement at the overwhelming sentiment of the moment. She, too, was afraid, and did the only thing she knew to do. "Hi," she braved.

The shark did not respond.

"I'd like to be your friend," she continued.

As the shark coolly studied her eager face, the minnow realized that a creature of such magnificence probably found her all too insignificant and repulsive. Befriending him would prove to be very difficult and perhaps even painful.

But when he nodded clumsily, she was caught up in the cross current and she whirled around his huge body several times with great glee.

The bubbly initiation sent swirling shivers through the shark's connective tissues, and he found it strange that this small creature might actually be enjoyable—apart from lunch. And so, he followed her flitting escapade through the deep, the two awkwardly getting used to the other's lead. She circled and he was drawn in by the ripples. He lunged and she descended into the whirlpool. Late into the night they cavorted, until they found themselves back at the rocky shoal, where the shark waited until the exhausted little minnow had fallen into a deep sleep before he left to indulge his insatiable appetite.

All night long he glutted and gorged himself with bloodlust. Then he returned to sleep beside his new friend.

All night long the minnow slumbered, dreaming of the enthralling encounters they'd had, and feeling safe beneath the shark's canopy of protection. When morning came, the two swam off on another exhilarating exploit.

Every day, they revelled in one another's company, never tiring of the adventure. Not only did they share exciting experiences, but there were moments where the thrill would so overtake them that all sense of time and place would be completely lost in the sheer joy of living. They grew comfortable with each other's gestures, and the silence no longer made them nervous—rather, it was swollen with unspoken verbosity.

Each night, the shark would wait until the minnow was soundly sleeping before withdrawing for his feeding frenzy.

But one evening, shortly after the shark had left, the minnow was awakened by a sea storm. The murky and muddy waters pummeled her tiny body, and, in the chaos, she couldn't see the shark anywhere. She cried out to him, but no response came.

Long into the evening she was tossed and carried about by the currents. Torrents of water lunged in and out of her gills and tore at them as she cried out for help. At last, exhausted from the struggle, she gave in to the current's strong desire and let herself be carried wherever the deep sea would take her.

After what seemed like an eternity of drifting, she found herself in quieter waters. In great pain, she surveyed her surroundings, and rejoiced to see the shark in the distance. She swam toward him as quickly as her broken body was capable of moving, expecting to find solace in his presence.

But when she was almost close enough to rest her weary self upon his tail, he lunged at a family of sleepy turtles swooping into the cool waters after sunning themselves on a sandbar. Ferociously the shark ripped apart the helpless animals until the water grew red with blood and the dismayed little minnow could no longer see the shark in the massacre. Stricken with panic, she forced herself through the horrifying haze.

The school had been right all along. Surely this was the beast they'd warned her of. How had he so deceived her? Was he playing a horrible game, trying to entice her into his company so that he could devour them all?

The only thing that mattered now was getting back to the stream; to the safety of the school. She would swim back from where she came, until she was out of danger; and pray she might find her way back home. How foolish to think befriending that hideous beast would somehow bring her home. Bring her to utter ruin was more like it. How foolish to think God had actually spoken to one so minuscule and insignificant as she.

As the shark, full and contented from his evening buffet, was leaving to return to the shoal, he felt a slight swoosh against his skin. In great surprise, he turned to see his tiny friend furiously swimming away from him, blood trailing from a torn gill. *How could this be?* he wondered. And he followed after her.

When the minnow saw the shark chasing her, she became even more afraid and, in spite of her pain, swam faster than she ever had in her life.

The shark saw that the minnow was afraid of him and realized that she had seen his attack on the turtles. His heart plummeted to the depths, as it so often had on their breathtaking journeys—only this time without the ensuing thrill of the rise. Instead, it collapsed, and there it stayed, and he knew this feeling to be remorse. Not just for what he had done, but for who he was, and what he simply could not change about himself.

The heaviness clung to him, and he understood that, once you share in someone else's joy, you cannot escape being slain, yourself, by the grief you bring them. Letting someone get close was, indeed, a very painful cure.

Faster and further the little minnow swam, intent on only one thing—getting home to safety.

The shark followed, wondering if he would ever be able to regain the friendship that made him feel as though he'd only ever been sleeping a long, dreary life away. How stupid to think a shark could have befriended a minnow. What a fool he was for believing that the Deity of the Depths would give kind and aspiring ideas to such a wicked creature as he.

As the weightiness dragged him down, he saw in the distance the gaping orifice of his enemy, the Giant Devourer. The minnow was swimming unwittingly into its deadly entrapment! He called out loudly, to no avail, until he ached from the effort. He would never get her attention in time to stop the inevitable slaughter.

With no time for formalities, he spewed out a desperate prayer. "Help!"

A sudden rush of adrenaline propelled the shark along.

In great panic and dread, the minnow glanced behind and saw the brutally fierce look on the face of the shark as he gained on her, and, still swimming her fastest, she closed her eyes tightly, not bearing to see his cold expression as he swallowed her whole. She only hoped it would be quick and painless. Then she felt the waters swirling around, impeding her escape. Had she made it into the shark's belly and survived? Courageously, she opened her eyes—perhaps there would be a way out.

What she saw, though, was not the ceiling of the shark's gullet, but rows and rows of razor sharp teeth encircling an enormous, unimaginable deathtrap. As she swirled helplessly towards the ravenous cavern, the shark surged from beneath her and plunged himself against the underside of the enormous killer whale's mouth, slicing a huge tear.

The Giant Devourer shifted slightly, and the minnow escaped capture.

Again, the shark plummeted toward the colossal beast, this time from above, and he tore another rend close to the killer whale's eye.

The huge creature pulled away with such force that the shark was hauled into its undertow. The creature heaved suddenly toward the shark with tremendous repercussion.

When the minnow realized that the shark was saving her, that he had been a true friend all along, and that, somehow, this magnificent creature had made an exception for her, a deep sorrow engulfed her, and she, too, tasted the grave sadness that is remorse. She understood that, not only had she doubted her new friend's intentions, but she was, at the very core, mistrusting of others; incapable of accepting anything but perfection in them; fearful of what she didn't understand.

The shark's body split apart from the impact, lacerating what remained of her faint hopes, and the Giant Devourer plowed into him once more before stealing off into the darkness.

Down, down into the depths, the mangled shark swirled. He felt weightless and giddy. *So this is caring for someone more than yourself; seeking another's safety at the expense of your own. This is love.* He had been right all along. Seeing below the surface was a far more fulfilling reward than even the most delicious and savoury delicacy. Feeling true love had been the greatest and most precious experience of his life. Surely the Deity of the Depths had heard the cries of his heart and released him from its chains.

Down, down into the swirling trail of blood, the minnow followed her faithful friend. *Please, please don't let him die*—her silent plea willed away desperation.

But, as he landed on the sandy bottom, she saw the shark look up at her and smile. A peaceful gleam replaced the hollowness in his eyes, and she knew that he understood, and that what they had shared would always live on.

The gleam in his eyes flickered for the final time and ascended through crystal waters until it was enveloped in a whirling display of colourful light that swirled with dazzling shades of radiance. It

glistened off the school of minnows swishing by overhead until it all became a blissful glimmer in a magnificent procession of familiar faces.

God *had* spoken to her, after all. Befriending the beast had brought her safely back home.

But even more than that, she had learned to trust: she had recklessly abandoned her heart in the pursuit of helping someone else find his, and in the end it had been returned to her, restored.

The Best Recipe Around

Nonfiction

Rosemary Flaaten

My son makes the best chocolate chip cookies you will ever taste. The recipe is fairly basic, not very different from what you'd find in a standard cookbook. He combines the usual ingredients—butter, sugar, eggs, and vanilla. Then he follows the standard method of scooping the flour and levelling it with a knife, adding baking soda and mixing everything together thoroughly.

Graham follows the recipe precisely until he gets to the last ingredient. Then he puts away the measuring cup, throws all caution to the wind, grabs the bag—the giant size you buy at Costco—and dumps it into the mixing bowl. Yes, what makes Graham's cookies so extraordinary is the extravagant amount of chocolate chips he uses. His motto: use just enough dough to hold the chips together.

Graham's cookies taste terrific, but the enjoyment I receive from eating them is accompanied by some inner angst. In my search for the recipe for success in life, I've discovered that "extravagance" is a word that causes me some discomfort. I grew up on a farm in southern Saskatchewan with parents who had lived through the Dirty Thirties, and Mom and Dad taught me that extravagance was something to be avoided. Prudence, simplicity, and thriftiness were valued next to godliness. Extravagance—described as lavish, unreasonable, and costly—brushed dangerously close to sinfulness.

My values didn't change when I left home. If anything, my beliefs became stronger, fuelled by numerous short-term missions trips I made to the developing world where I witnessed people's daily struggle to feed their children or put a roof over their heads. Each time I returned home from these trips, my Western lifestyle conflicted with my experiences abroad. As a result, the value of avoiding extravagance took an even deeper hold in the broader spectrum of my life.

But a while ago, I realized that I had a dilemma. I was reading the Bible passage often called The Love Chapter (1 Corinthians 13), where the Apostle Paul lays out a variety of examples of how we are to love others. The last verse summarizes Paul's instruction by saying, "And now these three remain: faith, hope and love. But the greatest of these is love" (1 Corinthians 13:13). *The Message* version of the Bible adds the adjective "extravagant" to describe the measure of love we are to show others.

I was initially tempted to disregard the word "extravagant." Frugality and stinginess, even in relationships, are certainly easier and safer. But then I recalled the extravagance I had been shown while in an African village. As a means of welcoming me to his village, a pastor who struggled to feed his own six children presented me with a live chicken. This outpouring of love was extravagant, not just in the valuable item with which he had gifted me, but in his love, acceptance and esteem. I realized that his liberal generosity exemplified how Jesus related to the people with whom he came in contact.

Consequently, I put aside my aversion to the notion of extravagance and sought to discover for myself what it would look like to love extravagantly. I decided to look at Jesus, who so perfectly modelled it for us.

I began by looking at the verse, "Greater love has no one than this: to lay down one's life for one's friends" (John 15:13). Now, I don't have many opportunities to end my life so that someone else can live, but laying down my desire to promote myself and instead looking for ways to help others to succeed is loving extravagantly. In my workplace, being diligent to give credit where credit is due, rather than grabbing as much of the attention as possible, is loving extravagantly. Choosing to go along with my husband's desire to repair the refrigerator rather than insisting that we replace it with a new one is giving up my preference to allow for his. Looking for the strength of character in my mother-in-law rather than focusing on her idiosyncrasies allows God's love to pour through me to her. In short, loving extravagantly involves taking the high path of humility rather than the well-travelled freeway of pride and self-promotion.

My goal of loving extravagantly also forced me to look at one of my ugly little secrets that has for years bubbled just below the surface and only erupts occasionally: anger. The things I should be angry about—human sex trafficking, hungry children, and godlessness—cause little more than a brief and half-hearted flare of anger. But others' insinuations about me, backstabbing, or repetitive emotional bruising all cling to me, fostering a sense of personal hardship that fuels anger. These roaring fires are not justifiable anger, but sinful anger that mutates my soul and impedes my relationships.

Loving extravagantly means choosing to follow God's directive to go way beyond dutiful forgiveness and to instead be lavish with our forgiveness. By the standards of Jewish law, it was considered presumptuous and unnecessary to forgive more than three times. When Peter asked Jesus if he needed to forgive more than seven times, Peter no doubt thought he was already going over the top—*he* wasn't going to be accused of frugality of forgiveness. But Jesus' response was lavish and unreasonable when he said that we are to forgive "seventy times seven" (Matthew 18:22). Jesus' words remind me that, all too often, I'm stingy with my forgiveness. But, as long as I am in need of God's extravagant forgiveness, then I am called to love extravagantly by continuing to forgive those around me. God didn't promise that extravagant love would be easy, but it is the way He has asked us to relate to each other. "A new command I give you: Love one another. As I have loved you, so you must love one another. By this everyone will know that you are my disciples, if you love one another" (John 13:34–35).

Since we're looking at ugly little secrets, I have another one that looms dark and rampant in my inner being: comparisons. If I'm really honest, I must confess that I devote a huge amount of brain space to comparing myself to others. *Are my hips really as big as hers? Did he get the same percentage of pay raise as me? How come they get to go on their third cruise and I've never even been on one?* After allowing myself to indulge in such comparisons, I either come out feeling less significant than the people I'm comparing myself to, which causes a chasm in our relationships—or else I come out feeling superior to them, and that, too, erodes my ability to love. How can I love like Jesus when I'm feeling either envious of or superior to those I should be loving unconditionally?

A heart filled with love doesn't make idle comparisons. Extravagant love occurs when we put down the yardstick we use to evaluate ourselves against others, and instead celebrate the uniqueness of the individuals God has made. Extravagant love produces unmeasured celebration.

Just as my son's delectable cookies include an extravagant amount of chocolate chips, so the recipe for success laid out in 1 Corinthians creates a desirable life. Extravagant love—whether it comes in the form of humility, forgiveness, or celebration—will build relationships that are robust. Prudence will stifle; thriftiness will erode; but extravagance will strengthen.

From now on, I want to incorporate an extravagant amount of love in all my recipes for relationships. I'm going to put aside the measuring cup, throw caution to the wind, and simply dump on the love.

Bannock and Sweet Tea

Fiction

M. D. Meyer

1957

The dough is soft and pliable, absorbing warmth from my hands as I gently mold and shape it. It is my work but my pleasure, too, anticipating the smiles of my children, knowing their tummies will be full and their hearts satisfied.

The door opens and they burst in, laughing, scolding and teasing, each wanting to tell me a bit of what they have discovered about the world, themselves or each other. I listen to each one as I serve bannock[1] and sweet tea.

Mary, my firstborn, says the others wouldn't listen when called. Jessie ran to pick flowers; Tommy climbed up a big rock and fell. Jessie smiles as she hands me buttercups, honeysuckle and daisies; Tommy manfully frowns as I bandage his knees.

My husband, John, stomps in with a grin, a string of fish held proudly in his hand. Saying, "I'll clean them later," he lays them on a newspaper and sits with our children to listen to their chatter. Then he winks at me and suggests it is our turn to go for a walk in the cool, fall air, my favourite time of the year.

John's mom, who lives next door, watches over our little ones. We know they are safe and content and will be spoiled just a bit, so we walk and talk and dream with each other, of our future together; of the new little one in my womb, and our young family growing day by day.

A plane flies low overhead and we look up in awe. It's still a strange sight for us when they pass by, and this one looks as if it will land quite near! We idly wonder what it's all about. Some visiting missionary perhaps, or a tourist wanting a guide to the best fishing spots. We clasp hands and run back to join in the excitement.

As we come in view of our house and our neighbours', the plane roars again overhead as the crowd below gazes skyward.

People are crying and clutching each other. I don't see my children and I run inside. My mother-in-law lies on the floor, wailing in grief. Tommy hides in a corner, trembling with fear. Mary and Jessie are gone. [2]

1962

I gasp at the sound of a plane flying low overhead and the babe in my arms begins to cry. My anxious eyes seek for my son and I call him to come near. With disdain in his voice and in his eyes, he reminds me it is spring, not fall, and he is going to meet the ones who are returning. Perhaps his sisters will come home this time.

Tommy's words thrust like a knife through my soul and I struggle to my feet, knowing I cannot—and must—bear it again, and alone. John is away in a sanatorium, sick with tuberculosis.

I fear that he too may never come home. I must—I must—be strong for those who remain. I cannot see, through the tears in my eyes, the faces of three little girls and four boys, their hair cut short. Wearing strange uniforms, they huddle together, hesitantly looking about, family trying to find family that has changed over time. I am too weary to hope, and I turn away to comfort and console the child in my arms.

Tommy gives a shout: "Mary is here!" My heart races and my knees grow weak; a neighbour takes my baby and another takes my arm as I stumble half-laughing and half-crying toward the group of waiting strangers. I feel ashamed that I would not know my daughter's face if Tommy hadn't been holding onto her.

I feel her stiffness as we embrace, and I sense her fear. She whispers, "I'm sorry," and pulls away. It's like a strange dream where nothing is real.

But one thing I need to know. I ask everyone around me, one by one, "Where is Jessie?" "Where is Jessie?" "Where is she?"

The truth comes slowly, or maybe it's just that I can't take it in no matter how many times the priest explains to me. "It was late in January when flu hit the school. Everyone got sick and some died. Your family was at your winter camp hunting, and there was no way to get you the news."

They'd buried her, of course, in a graveyard close to the school. The priest said he had wanted to deliver the news in person but had been delayed and thought it best to just wait and tell us on the same day that Mary returned. Wasn't it good she could come? They made an exception for her—let her fly for free.

1967

The tears come often and always in the fall. It is no longer my favourite time of the year. I miss Jessie, her eyes sparkling with joy, her cheeks pink with excitement, her hair tousled by the wind as she hands me a bright bouquet of buttercups, honeysuckle and daisies. If I could just see her once more—to say goodbye.

Mary has come home for good now, but she has changed so much that I don't know her. I cannot even understand a lot of what she says, and she gets angry at me for not knowing English and the white man's ways. She spends most of her time with a boy who also went to a residential school.

And I know she still feels guilty for not protecting her sister.

One day, she told me that it wasn't just the flu, that Jessie had been beaten for wetting her bed. She'd heard it second-hand from someone in Jessie's building. I didn't want it to be true and I said she must be wrong. It was hard enough to bear the memories as they were.

Tommy tries hard to take his father's place, but he is too young to hunt and fish. Our neighbours give us food when they have extra. I do sewing and cooking in exchange. Tommy chops the wood and stokes the fire. I'm thankful that the priest has settled here, and has classes for the children so they don't have to leave.

My family is so small now, nothing like what we dreamed. There's only Mary, Tommy, and six-year-old John, named after his father who passed away the winter after little Jessie died. They said it was the tuberculosis, but I think that he died of a broken heart. I wish God had taken me too.

When I look back, it seems as if there are so many who have died and so few of us who remain. John's mother died the winter the girls were taken. I lost my baby then, too. It seems that death is always around me. I live in the past and cannot see a future.

But Mary has told me that she is pregnant, and it is as if a part of me has been reborn. I whisper in the still night air, "A grandchild, John! A part of me and a part of you." Mary is so young, too young—but I will help her.

1972

I am making bannock and sweet tea for my three grand-children as they laugh and chatter. It is so much like the old days that I find myself glancing towards the door, expecting John to come bounding in with a string of fish for our supper.

Mary is off drinking again. It is almost a relief to have her gone, though I wish she could find another way to cope with the pain in her life. At least the children are here with me, and I can protect and care for them, make sure they have lots of love.

Tommy is nothing like his father. He seems to be angry all the time. He refuses to go down south to high school and he sleeps a lot during the day. He goes out hunting with the men, and regularly brings home fish for the family. But sometimes I think his anger will consume him.

Little John is the one I worry about the most. He used to be such a cheerful little boy, but for the past year or so, he's been so quiet and withdrawn. He doesn't ever want to go to school and he ended up failing grade five for the second time. At least at this rate, he won't be flying down to high school either.

The sound of an airplane fills my heart with dread, but I try to shake it off. Gone are the old days when the young children were taken away to residential school; my grandchildren are safe. A knock comes on my door and I walk slowly to open it. A white woman stands there asking for my daughter. I tell her that she is not in but will be back soon. She tells me that I need to get the children ready to go; they are being apprehended by social services. I ask her why and she says their mother is unfit. I try to tell her that I can look after them—I am their grandmother. My English is bad; she doesn't seem to understand. The woman takes away my grandchildren.[3]

It is many months before they come home again. The priest helps me get them back. They are not the cheerful, carefree children that they were. Those people even took their deer-hide moccasins with the beautiful beadwork and thick rabbit fur lining.

Their little feet are so cold in those hard rubber boots. It will take much time to warm them.

1977

My precious baby boy has taken his own life, and I no longer want to live either. It is too much. I cannot go on, even to care for those who remain. It is too much. I cannot go on.

He was only sixteen. My baby. So young. Too young to die.

Everyone is trying to help. They bring food and never leave me alone. The priest has been so kind. He came right over as soon as he heard the news. He is very understanding and seems to be as upset about little John's death as the rest of us are.

Tommy has been away, but I know the moment he returns. The door slams and I hear him shouting. I don't understand why he is yelling at the priest, ordering him out of our house. This is *my* house and we are grieving. For once, can't Tommy think about how *I* feel? But no, he is telling everyone from the church to leave.

After they are gone, Tommy starts yelling at me, saying that it is all my fault that little John died. He says that it is because the priest was abusing him, that he did that to a lot of the little boys at the church school, that he did it to him. Tommy is angry at me for not sending him away to the residential school his sisters went to.

Mary sent her kids outside to play as soon as the yelling began. She tells Tommy that it wasn't so great for her either. Did he think he was the only one who suffered abuse? Did he think Jessie was better off than him?

As the sound of Jessie's name rings in my ears, I know I can take no more. I leave the house, determined to go far away. This time, I will be the one who does not return. But, of course, I do. I think about the little ones and wonder if Mary will feed them. I know they will wonder where I am, and I don't want to cause any more pain for them. They've suffered enough already, and maybe everything that's happened really is my fault...[4]

1982

Mary's moved down south with her kids. She started AA[5] there and has been sober now for three years. Tommy finally got married to Julie, the mother of his kids. They've moved in with me; I help take care of Sarah and Jim.

Tommy still has a temper, but he's kept it in control—until yesterday when a police officer stopped by. Some minor infraction of the law. Before we knew it, Tommy was fighting and wouldn't stop. It was as if all the pent-up rage of years was released in that one moment of time.

There is no way to describe the pain in a mother's heart as she sees her son being led off in handcuffs. I wish things could have been different for him. Maybe if his father had lived; maybe if the priest had not lived.

Months pass before I am allowed to see my son. I travel down south with the children. Julie meets me at the hotel, and after the children are asleep she tells me what has been happening "inside." The stories of what Tommy has endured make me ill. Julie is angry and at the edge of despair; she needs to blame someone and I am here.

Visiting him in prison, I barely recognize my son. He's lost so much weight; his eyes are feverish; his skin pale. I long for the days when he was young, and a bandage and hug could make everything better. I cannot stop weeping no matter how hard I try. Tommy tells me I need to get a grip; he's the one who's in jail. He's angry and needs someone to blame and I am here.

Back at the hotel, Julie is anxious to go visit friends. She's bought the children some treats and they're outside. She points out the window to where they sit on the grass. The oldest is eight and has a room key, so they could get back in by themselves.

Julie leaves and I go to find something to drink. I need something to ease the pain in my throat; it is so raw and sore from crying.

A man smiles at me and I smile back. It's been such a long time since anyone smiled at me. He seems to care as he listens to my story. He says the chairs are more comfortable up in his room. I haven't eaten all day and the alcohol goes straight to my head. One thing leads to another and before I know it I'm waking up in the dead of night in bed with a stranger.

I cry out in panic and he yells, "What's the matter with you?"

"My gran-babies!" I sob. "My gran-babies!" I rush back to my hotel room where Julie sits alone.

With a cry of rage, she comes at me, fists flying as she curses and yells. "What's wrong with you? How could you leave them? Do you know what you've done? Someone reported them. Didn't you know they'd get picked up by social services if you left them alone?"

2002

I've been an alcoholic for almost 20 years. I don't have a home or family. The house that John and I built with love was taken over by others long ago. I left the community and headed south to the city, ashamed to live among those I had once called friends.

I sleep outside most nights, except in the winter when I stay at a shelter; or if I get picked up by the police and put in a jail cell; or occasionally at the hospital. They've dried me out a few times, but I can never stay away from the booze for long.

Recently, there's been this woman, pesky as a horsefly... noisy... buzzing around my head, talking, talking, talking. But she listens too, and she brings me hot coffee and sandwiches and cookies. I don't like to talk much to anyone, but she listens good.

I've never been back to church, not since Tommy told me what the priest did. Tommy's gone now too—died in a prison fight. Only Mary is left, but I never see her. Someone told me she was a grandmother now. They told me she got religion. I say, "Good for her," but I'll never go back.

They're doing church in the park, and that woman asks me to join her. Sitting far away from the crowd, I listen, and drink her hot coffee and eat her warm cookies. They sing of love and talk of love, but I know that if I open my heart, it will break. Even a tiny spark of hope could roar into flame and consume me.

Every Sunday afternoon, I come back and listen to the preaching, the songs and the prayers. Funny, it doesn't feel like church out here with the blue sky overhead and the soft, green grass beneath us. It's more like a gathering of friends—and I am invited to be one of them.

The preacher's words are filled with kindness. He speaks of forgiveness and love. The little children sing "Jesus loves me," and I wonder, can it be true?

The preacher always ends with "an invitation" and on the last night of the summer, I can resist no longer. Though I still don't fully understand, I know I want what is being offered. I step to the front of the crowd and kneel to pray. Someone's arm goes around me and I flinch. But others lay their hands on me also, and their gentle touch reminds me of love.

One by one, they pray for me, and the iron walls of protection fall away. I have no booze to numb the pain that claws up from my throat and spills out in wild sobs. They keep praying and their voices fall like summer rain. I have no words to speak, but none are required.

"Come home with me, Gracie," she says, and I have no idea what she means. "There's an extra room that we keep for guests." But I still can't take it in. Why would she want someone as dirty and dishevelled as me in her pure white home? But still she says, "Come, you are welcome here."

2011

Tamara is her name, and we've become friends, though not without pain and much sorrow along the way. Moments of laughter, also, and some joy, but anger and jealousy and mistrust, too. It took me some time to come to terms with the fact that she had everything I once had—and now I have nothing.

Living without alcohol is like being in a boxing ring with someone bigger and stronger who is hitting you all the time, knocking you down. It's unrelenting, and there is nothing to do except keep on taking it, over and over. Eventually, you learn to walk through the pain, though you long for escape, and you take those brief moments of comfort in the corner with your Coach.

Tamara is a widow like me, but she has children and grandchildren who visit often. Eventually, we warm to each other and they say that I am part of the family too—though I long for Jessie's twinkling eyes, Mary's comforting words, Tommy's strong arms, little John's smile and my own grandchildren, my own, my own.

I'm learning more every day about how to lean on my Coach in the corner. He's there for me when I need a healing touch, an encouraging hug, a shout of encouragement, "Go champ, go!"

Recently, I've helped others too, find their path towards the God of all comfort.

One day, Tamara has a surprise for me. She has found my daughter, Mary, and perhaps we can meet. I am filled with dread, and wonder, is it wrong to try to intermingle the old with the new? There is still too much blame. I know she will be ashamed of me. I am ashamed of myself.

But Mary brings her youngest granddaughter for me to see, and the ice between us melts as my great-grandchild takes my gnarled old hand in hers. My tentative smile is rewarded with a bright grin and a gurgle of delight as this tiny child reaches for me with two chubby arms and says, "Hug." My heart feels at peace as I hold her close.

Tonight, Mary and I go to see her oldest grandson graduating from university. Up on the stage, I see many others with faces the same colour as mine, and I wonder at the changes that have taken place, the healing over time for some of us.

It gives me hope that in generations to come, there will once again be children's laughter, fresh bannock and sweet tea.

1. Bannock, also known as "frybread," is a traditional Aboriginal quick bread that is made from flour, lard, baking powder, salt and water, usually cooked on a griddle. "Sweet tea" is not a traditional Aboriginal term but is used in the above writing to depict a hot tea sweetened with sugar and cooled with canned evaporated milk, a drink that was common to many Canadian Aboriginal people, especially in the days before refrigeration.

2. On June 11, 2008, Prime Minister Stephen Harper made an historic apology to the Aboriginal people of Canada on behalf of the Government of Canada for their 100-year-long act of cultural genocide—their stated policy to "kill the Indian in the child." This apology was in reference to the residential school system where children were forcibly removed from their homes, some as young as age four. They were separated from their siblings and beaten if caught speaking their indigenous language. Many were physically and sexually abused. When the children were returned to their homes, usually at age 16, they no longer understood the language of their family; since they had been raised in a different culture, they did not have the intuitive knowledge of how to live in the community; they were unable to live off the land as their ancestors had done for centuries, yet they also didn't fit into the (white) mainstream culture. The repercussions of the residential school system on successive generations continue to be felt to this day.

3. "The Sixties Scoop" is a term describing the removal of thousands of Aboriginal children from their homes and communities—and the placement of these children into non-Aboriginal foster homes. It began in the 1960s and continued into the 1980s.

4. On April 29, 2009, the Vatican made this statement: "Given the sufferings that some indigenous children experienced in the Canadian residential school system, the Holy Father expressed his sorrow at the anguish caused by the deplorable conduct of some members of the Church and he offered his sympathy and prayerful solidarity."

5. AA (Alcoholics Anonymous)

Dancing in the Kitchen

Nonfiction

Marcia Lee Laycock

"What's Grandma like, Mom?"

My daughter's question caught at my heart. I hadn't seen my mother since before she suffered a stroke.

Until a short time ago, we had been living in Canada's far north, too many miles away for visits, and now I was fearful. Had the effects of the debilitation changed her more than just physically? We would soon know. She and my father would arrive any day at our new home in central Alberta.

I swallowed my apprehensions and answered the question. "You'll love her, girls. She loves you both very much."

I could see my response wasn't quite satisfactory. My daughters needed something more.

I watched nine-year-old Katie do a pirouette. Her sister Laura, seven, did an attempt at a tap step.

A friend had given us an old pair of shiny black tap shoes and both girls had laid claim to them.

I smiled. "Grandma was a dancer, you know."

Two little faces lit up. "She was? Did she tap dance?"

"Oh yes. She won prizes for dancing when she was young. I think I have some pictures. Let's see what we can find."

For my daughters, the old black and white photos that spilled out across my bed were an introduction to extended family. They pointed, and giggled. Katie peered at a photo of three young girls, about 11 or 12 years old.

My mother, the girl in the middle, wore a polka-dot blouse, short flared skirt and tap shoes adorned with big bows. Her short dark hair was gelled into kiss-curls on her forehead and cheeks.

I didn't disturb Katie as she studied the picture.

When she looked up, her eyes were hopeful. "Do you think she could teach us to dance?"

217

A memory flooded back—a slight, trim woman, holding the edges of her apron, her eyes twinkling as she did the "soft shoe" on black and white kitchen tile.

"I'm sure Grandma will—" I started to say.

The realization hit again. After two years of fighting the paralysing effects of the stroke, Mom now wore a heavy brace on one leg and walked with a cane.

"Well," I faltered, "Grandma's legs don't work the way they used to, but we'll see…"

When Mom arrived, she had barely sat down in the kitchen for a cup of tea when Katie blurted the question that had stayed on her heart. "Grandma, will you please show us how to tap dance? We have these shoes…" She plopped the shoes into her grandmother's lap.

Mom beamed. "Oh, what wonderful taps, Kate!"

Mom grasped the edge of the table and struggled out of her chair. With all of us holding our breath, my mother planted her cane firmly and gave my daughters their first tap lesson, shuffling her feet to demonstrate.

"Step, touch, click, step touch click. Oh, this brace is so clumsy! But it's easy, girls. Come stand beside me and try it."

As I watched them, the taps on Katie's tiny feet clicking on the hard linoleum, giggles coming from all three, I suddenly knew that, though the fortress that was my mother might slowly crumble, her indomitable spirit would never die.

Later, I thought of Jeremiah, a prophet who often had to speak words of doom and destruction to the people of Israel. In the midst of pain, he was given words of hope and a promise: "Then the maidens will dance and be glad, young men and old as well. I will turn their mourning into gladness; I will give them comfort and joy instead of sorrow" (Jeremiah 31:13).

I realized I had seen the embodiment of that promise before me. My fear turned to joy and thankfulness for that moment, a moment that was so much more than just a dance lesson in the kitchen.

O Canada

Nonfiction[1]

Marguerite Cummings

Kindergarten. First child, first day, first week—and so many things to learn and understand! Recently settled in Canada from Europe, I was the "at-home mom" of two young children. With the eldest just entering this brand-new world of school in Toronto, my whole life was changing fast and my mind was full of questions. So when Maria, an old hand at kindergarten since she had an older son, handed me a little note inviting me and other interested parents to meet for coffee for one hour every month just before pickup time from school, I knew I had to go.

And that is how our little group started. The coffee shop was warm, cozy, and welcoming, and in this relaxed atmosphere, our friendships blossomed as we shared our worries, our joys, and our daily problems. We laughed, we almost cried, and we slowly learned about each other. And then we ran like crazy to be on time for the bell!

It didn't take long to realize that almost every single child in my son's class was using a language other than English at home: Russian, Farsi, Cantonese, Mandarin, Japanese, Arabic… and in our case, French! What took a little longer was the conviction that this school, this class, these children, these parents, all desperately needed prayer. Every day. Every moment.

By the time my son started grade one, we'd moved into a house right next to the school. The neighbourhood had captured our hearts, and so had the school. Every day on my short walk to drop off or pick up my son, I would embrace the view of the neat little building surrounded by trees—and sigh, with a mixture of anxiety and praise, murmuring a short prayer. *Thank you for this*

neighbourhood, Lord. Thank you for this school. Please watch over these children!

Every morning, while clearing breakfast, I would glance at the school from my kitchen window, and my heart would fill with emotion. *O Lord, be with my son. Protect him. Encourage and guide his teacher. Help us to be lights in this school.*

That year, Joyce and her children arrived—and everything changed. At her previous school, Joyce had been part of a small, organized prayer group, dedicated to praying for the school community. The idea hit home immediately. With two other firm friends from the original coffee group, our prayer group was born.

We met at our house since it was so close to the school, and we had plenty of toys to keep toddlers occupied. Just like the kindergarten coffee meetings, our prayer meetings were usually one hour before pickup time, and running for the bell continued to be a fixture of my life! We found it so hard to stop our meetings on time. True, we spent a great deal of time talking rather than praying, and thoroughly enjoying each other's company—but pray we did.

We prayed for everything and anything related to the school. We prayed for each of our children, by name. We prayed for the teachers, the principal, the school secretary, the caretaker, the parent volunteers (and the shortage of such volunteers)… We prayed fervently through difficult times at school, especially when hard decisions had to be made regarding cutbacks, student placements, and reorganizations. With several of us also involved in the parent council, we tried to cover special events in prayer: parent meetings, fundraisers, fun fairs. The list was long! And of course, we also prayed for our husbands, our extended families, and our friends.

Joyce tried her best to give some structure to our ramblings. Adoration. Confession. Thanksgiving. Supplication. It hardly ever worked. Our hearts and tongues kept racing ahead to the next request, the next urgent need.

Despite our inadequacies, we soon found ourselves amazed at the answers that came.

Kay had come to our neighbourhood from mainland China the previous year. She'd had a child in the same kindergarten class as my son, and we'd struck up a friendship right away. Her smile was contagious, her courage obvious.

One Sunday at church, a guest speaker from China urged the congregation to pray for one, just one person. Immediately Kay's name flashed into my mind. *Kay. Pray for Kay.* It was so clear: *Pray for Kay.*

All right, Lord, I thought. *I will pray for Kay.* However, since our schedules were now different, I rarely saw her at school. Yet the next day, as I was driving past the local library on my way back home, there was Kay, walking along! My heart jumped. *Pray for Kay,* I heard in my heart again. *Pray for Kay.*

Tuesday came. I went to school to pick up my son from his after-school program. Very few parents were around at that time. However, my expectations were rising! Surely God was preparing something.

So when I saw Kay arrive, I became very agitated. I was listening intently. *There she is again, Lord! What next? What do I say?*

I was stunned when the still, small voice inside came, loud and clear: *Ask her about church.*

Ask her about church? When I hadn't spoken to her in weeks? Was that a way to start a conversation? *Lord, I can't.*

But the feeling was insistent. *Church.* I had to ask her about church.

And so, mustering all my courage, I greeted her.

"Hi, Kay!" Pause. "Have you… ever thought about coming to church?" I trembled as I said the words. Surely she would think I was mad!

I was overwhelmed when her answer came: "Church? I'm so glad you asked!"

She went on to explain that she had been very interested in trying to go to church for quite a while. Her grandmother was a believer, and her Christian faith had been a strong influence on the family, despite many restrictions imposed in China at the time.

Now Kay really wanted to know more. And so her journey of faith was strengthened—and so was mine!

Month after month, year after year, our little group prayed. We prayed for Kay, for other parents, and for our children's friends. We prayed to be useful to God, each of us in our different ways. Each year we were amazed at the way God used our everyday conversations and our friendships to work in our school community.

One particular incident encouraged us all. It started with YoungHee, a lively Korean woman who had joined our prayer group a short time before. YoungHee sparkled with enthusiasm, and, although new to the school, quickly made a number of friends among the parents. One such friend was Sandra. Sandra and YoungHee each had a daughter in kindergarten, and when the two little girls became friends, so did their mothers.

One day, Sandra's daughter developed some tooth problems. As soon as she heard about this, YoungHee offered to pray for the child. Touched by this offer, Sandra started asking YoungHee questions about her faith. What was it all about? And what was it like to attend church? Sandra—a recent immigrant to Canada—had never been to church before.

But since YoungHee attended a Korean-speaking congregation, Sandra couldn't accompany her new friend to services. Still, her interest was genuine. So one Sunday, with YoungHee's encouragement, Sandra bravely decided to try an English-speaking church all by herself. Unfortunately, the church building was large and complex... Sandra got lost inside the maze of hallways and meeting rooms, and ended up even more perplexed!

When our prayer group heard about this, we were all moved, and we started praying earnestly for Sandra. We longed to help her, but there was one problem: only YoungHee knew Sandra personally—nobody else was able to put a face to her name. Still, we prayed for Sandra, asking God to help her find a suitable church.

The morning after our prayer meeting, as I stood holding the kindergarten door open to let children in from the rain, I noticed one woman waiting. We exchanged a few casual words... and my heart missed a beat. I asked for her name: could it be...? Yes, it was Sandra! From the brief description I'd been given, and with the eyes of faith, God had allowed me to recognize her. With a huge smile, I told her we had been praying for her the previous evening. We immediately arranged for her to visit my own English-speaking home church with me. Moreover, I found out that Sandra lived just across the street from Joyce, our prayer group leader!

In all these ways, God truly surrounded Sandra with His care, and used our group and its friendships to communicate His love.

Three years passed. Joyce's family, as well as several other families from our prayer group, had sadly moved away from our neighbourhood. So when September came along once again, our depleted prayer group was clearly faltering. Would we meet again this year? We were all so busy. Who would take charge?

On the Friday just before Labour Day and the end of summer vacation, I stood in deep thought in front of the school. My daughter, now eight, was with me, and we were studying the new class lists that had just been posted on the school doors. We were eager to see who would be teaching my children's classes this year, and who their new classmates would be.

I suddenly noticed another family standing next to us: a father with his young daughter, both looking bemused, pointing to the notices and debating in Mandarin. Brand-new to Canada, brand-new to our school, they were trying to make sense of the bus schedule—and with the school office already closed for the day, this was no easy task!

As I did my best to help them and explain how things worked, we slowly warmed to each other. Originally from China, the family had lived in England for a while, but their hearts were set on Canada, and they had come with high hopes. By the end of the conversation, we had exchanged e-mail addresses and telephone numbers. Their smiles had returned, and we had discovered possible new friends.

That Sunday, my family went to church as usual. The hallways were packed with hundreds of worshippers. Suddenly, my daughter pulled my sleeve: "Mommy, look!" And yes, here they were again, the same father and kindergarten daughter, together with the mother and grade four sister! As it dawned on us all how God had arranged for us to meet at school just two days before, everyone was smiling from ear to ear, praising God for His sense of timing and for using us in this small way to encourage one another.

After that incident, I knew for sure—our prayer group had to continue. We were there for a reason, and God wanted us to pray, and to be there, right there, in the school community. Just as our children in all their diversity were learning the Canadian national anthem by singing it every day in their classrooms, we—their parents from far and wide—had to "stand on guard," united in our prayer for them and for the entire school community.

> O Canada![2]
> Our home and native land!
> True patriot love in all thy sons command.
>
> With glowing hearts we see thee rise,
> The True North strong and free!
>
> From far and wide,
> O Canada, we stand on guard for thee.
>
> God keep our land glorious and free!
> O Canada, we stand on guard for thee.
>
> O Canada, we stand on guard for thee.

1. Based on a true story. All names and some details have been changed to protect the privacy of the people described.

2. Adolphe-Basile Routhier (words in French), Robert Stanley Weir (words in English), and Calixa Lavallée (music), "O Canada/*Hymne National O Canada*" (Québec: 1880). Public Domain.

Cries for Keyon

Spoken Word Drama

Vilma Blenman

Author's Prologue:

My plea for peace is inspired by Keyon Campbell, a 16-year-old Black teenage boy who was gunned down in the middle of a snowstorm on December 2, 2007, outside his Scarborough, Ontario townhouse. He had simply gone outside to warm up the car before his mom drove his friends home after a Saturday evening playing video games. He managed to stumble back into the front hallway of their home, where his mother discovered Keyon bleeding to death, the car keys still gripped in his hands. Keyon was Toronto's eightieth murder victim of the year.

Style:

Read the poem aloud to absorb the rap-style cadences and hear the many voices crying in the urban wilderness. Each character's monologue contributes to the many dialogues, the many perspectives on violence in Toronto's Black community.

Setting:

A well-worn meeting room in a community centre in Scarborough, where a citizens' forum is about to take place. Dozens of people of all ages from the neighbourhood—virtually all Black—fill rows of stacking chairs, and more are standing against the back wall. Various speakers go to the microphones to voice their concerns.

The chorus enters. It consists of 10 women dressed in black, each holding a framed photograph of her deceased son, all of them murder victims. The women sit in a circle rocking rhythmically back and forth as they chant:

225

Cry,
Don't Cry!
Cry! We Must Cry
Why Cry?

A Black teenage boy, looking back over his shoulder as he walks to the front, goes to the microphone to speak:

Yo, guy, you know we're gonna die.
Die if we don't fly outta here!
'Cause, like, everybody 'round here know not to name names,
'Cause nobody know nottin'; nobody see nottin'.
But the cops coming an' knocking an' coming
An' asking again and again and again…

A mother of a teenage boy comes up to speak:

So where we must fly, when rent sky high
And the mailman brings bills every other day,
And the school calls me twice a day
Calling to say, he's in trouble again, today
Suspended, 'cause he won't stop fighting? Well, *I* stop fighting!

A social worker speaks:

Cry, mothers and grandmothers who raise sons to die.
Cry, fathers who flee from mothers' cries,
Fathers who break ties before sons wear bowties, or learn to tie ties,
Mothers who let fathers leave without an address or redress, if you
   please,
Leave before saying "I do" or "I will, so help me God."

The chorus chants:

Cry,
Don't Cry!
Cry! We Must Cry
Why Cry?

An elderly man speaks:

Fie for shame! Where did they learn to play that game?
So many voices calling in the wilderness; too many forms and
     forums.
While the Summer of the Gun[1] fades into the Fall of a Few
More, and the Winter of our Despair springs no hope eternal,
While Keyon dies with keys still in his hands,
And a mother cries for the child carried from womb to tomb.

*A female university student, carrying a history textbook and
wearing a T-shirt that says, "I survived the Middle Passage," goes
to the microphone to speak:*

Cry, cruel history, recalled in the sound of every shot,
Middle Passage[2] madness making mayhem again.
Son of a drum becomes son of a gun;
History becoming her story and my story and our story,
But no true story ever told of how and why,
So now they live and die and all we say is, "Oh my."

*An activist carrying a placard that says "Save Endangered Sons"
speaks:*

Pick up the pen; raise the lament;
Cry till your cries echo on Parliament Hill and Queen's Park,[3]
Till mountains move and money well-spent
Saves sons from certain sudden death by systems unintended,
Till solutions surface, in families and in faith communities,
In classrooms, and in cloistered boardrooms and in the comfort of
     each other's cries.

The chorus chants a final time:

Cry,
Don't Cry!
Cry! We Must Cry!

Author's Postscript:

This poem grew out of my sorrow for Keyon's mom; I didn't know her, but I cried for her when I heard the news, haunted by the image of how she had found her son. I had met Keyon one year earlier, when he was invited to the Scarborough high school where I work as a teacher and counsellor. He attended a student showing of the documentary *EMPz 4 Life* (EMPz is slang for Empringham, the street on which the public housing townhouse complex is located). Keyon was one of the at-risk young men from the Toronto suburbs profiled by award-winning Canadian filmmaker Allan King, in the documentary shown at the Toronto International Film Festival.

Keyon's death was all the more a tragic irony because he was one of the Black youths whom this film showed as being on the right path, likely to beat the dreadful cycle of violence and incarceration. All showings of *EMPz 4 Life* now include this caption: "Screenings of this film are dedicated to the memory of Keyon Campbell (1991–2007)."

1. "Summer of the Gun" was a name given to a particularly violent period of deaths by gunshot in Toronto during the summer of 2005.
2. "Middle Passage" refers to the horrific middle or second leg of the Triangular Trade in which slaves were transported from Africa to the Caribbean and Americas. It is estimated that 10 to 20 percent of those herded into the cramped quarters of the slave ships died in the trans-Atlantic crossing.
3. "Parliament Hill" in Ottawa and "Queen's Park" in Toronto are the locations of, respectively, the federal and provincial seats of government.

Love in the Ice and Snow

Fiction

Bonnie Beldan-Thomson

Wind, laden with the stench of jet exhaust, screamed between pillars of the parking garage beside Terminal 1 at Toronto Pearson International Airport. Karen shivered in the raw, damp cold, thinking with longing of her home in Alberta, covered with snow and encompassed in a cold that made face, fingers and toes tingle, but didn't settle deep into her bones the way Ontario's late autumn chill did.

Jim was loading luggage into the trunk of their rental Hyundai while Karen knelt in the back seat trying to find the other half of a seatbelt for Rachel. The nine-year-old was heavy-eyed after the 7 a.m. flight from Calgary and delayed landing in Toronto because of a freak thunderstorm, but she was absorbed in watching the explorations of a tiny sweater-clad Chihuahua on a rhinestone leash.

While her husband extricated them from the maze of airport roads and joined midday traffic, Karen mentally reviewed her brother's e-mail.

> Dad's failing, and it's not safe to leave him alone anymore while Jan's at work and the kids are in school. He wandered off today. It was a good thing I had to go to the shed for a wrench and I saw him. He was halfway to the bush—in his slippers, no coat. Who knows what could happen next time?

"I think you would want to come," John had said on the phone. "I know you can't be away over Christmas, but could you make it sometime in November or early December? You know we always have room for you here. Check out the nursing home. See if you're happy having him there. See for yourself how he is."

So here they were two weeks later, driving north on Highway 10 through a desultory drizzle, while patches of fog clung to streams in the valleys. Later, when they turned west, they ran into snow flurries and Jim turned the heater up a notch.

Karen listened to Rachel singing to herself in the back seat and wondered again how her father would be when she saw him at the end of this journey. It had been over a year. Too long.

She shifted in her seat, closed her eyes, and took comfort in silently reciting The Prayer of the Heart.[1] *Lord Jesus Christ, Son of God, have mercy on me, a sinner.* Then she began her practice of breath prayer. Inhale, *Lord have mercy.* Exhale, *Christ have mercy.* Inhale, *Lord…* Exhale, *Christ…*

Suddenly, the car lurched. Rachel abruptly went silent and Karen's eyes shot open to see the world revolving crazily around her. Instinctively, she braced herself against the dashboard, saw Jim's knuckles white on the steering wheel, heard Rachel's sudden intake of breath.

Then it was over. The car had settled on the other side of the road, facing the way they had come, the driver's back wheel on the gravel shoulder, the other three wheels headed into the shallow grassy ditch.

"That was scary!" Rachel gasped. "What happened? I felt like I was in the middle of a giant snow globe that somebody was shaking."

Karen quickly undid her seatbelt and reached back to touch her daughter. "It's okay, sweetie. The car had a spin, but everything is okay."

"It was black ice," Jim added. "When it's wet and cold like this, water freezes clear so the black of the wet road shows through it. I didn't know it was there."

Jim was able to back the car onto the road and cautiously turn around, thankful for the absence of other traffic. They slowly drove on, alone in a world of icy snow that seemed to pelt the car from all sides.

When they reached the nursing home in Elmwood, Karen opted to see her dad by herself for a few minutes while Jim and Rachel headed to a coffee shop across the street in search of hot chocolate and a snack.

"It's not a good day for travelling," the slim, grey-haired woman at the reception desk observed, "Our first big snow of the season. Have you been on the road long?"

"About three hours," Karen replied, removing her gloves and stamping snow off her boots, "and we flew in from Calgary before that. We're just fifteen minutes from my brother's place. Maybe you know him—John Meyer? But I wanted to see my dad first."

"Yes, I know John," the receptionist responded. "You must be Karen. They've been looking forward to your coming. Carl's room is up on the third floor. You'll find the elevator around the corner on the left."

He was alone in the lounge, sitting at one end of a blue vinyl couch, looking at the whirling snow through a large window. He watched impassively as an ambulance screamed by and disappeared down the street.

Karen hesitated behind the half-opened door, searching for signs of his well-being. His frame, though shrunken, was still substantial. The grey hair had become both sparse and thin, almost baby-fine. His face had the ruddy hue of a man whose work had often kept him outdoors; red veins showed on his nose. The hands that had built fences and fed cattle were smooth now, palms free from calluses, nails trimmed and clean, skin pale and waxy, almost as if the hands had predeceased the rest of his body.

With a deep breath, Karen pushed back the door and advanced across the plant-filled room. Forcing a smile, she greeted him. "Hi, Dad."

As his gaze shifted to her, he spoke slowly. "I don't see the cattle. They're likely in the barn when the weather's like this. They're a nice bunch. All white faces, mostly polled, a couple have horns but nothing to speak of… That was quite a loud horn just now. A siren, I guess it was. Some poor beggar in trouble." He paused in his ruminations; his eyes strayed to the window again.

She felt the smile lines around her eyes tighten. She asked brightly, "How are you feeling, Dad?"

He focused on her with difficulty. "Do I know you?"

"You used to." She hesitated. "I've been living in Alberta so you haven't seen me for a while. I'm Karen."

"No!" His pale eyes widened in astonishment. "Karen," he repeated. "You were just a little girl with pigtails, shining brown hair in pigtails. 'Puppy tails' you used to call them."

"I have a little girl of my own now, Dad. Her name is Rachel. She's not so little anymore. She just turned nine."

But he went on as if she hadn't spoken. "I remember the day I took Karen and young John with me to Alvin Weber's. I left them in the car—it was the old '50 Chev—while I went into the barn to talk to Alvin about some calves. When I came out, why, the car had rolled halfway down to the manure pile. And there was little Karen stretched out, half lying on the driver's seat, pushing her feet against the brake for all she was worth! That little girl held the car until I got there."

"I remember that, Dad," Karen said. "I was so proud. When we went home, you told Mom I'd saved you half a day's work, from having to pull the car out and clean it up. We had chocolate cake for a celebration supper that night."

She sat down beside him and took his hand.

He looked at her sharply, then said with astonishment, "Why, you *are* Karen. I didn't know you at first. You have your mother's eyes. Sweet, loving eyes. Honest eyes, too…" He hugged her awkwardly. "It's good to see you, girlie." They sat quietly for a moment; then he rose abruptly and moved toward the door.

"I have to walk a bit. My hip gets sore if I sit too long."

"Do you mind if I walk along with you?"

"You're welcome to come, though the scenery's nothing to brag about."

"You liked the scenery where we lived near Calgary, Dad. Do you remember visiting us in Canmore with the mountains all around? You enjoyed the day we drove up that narrow, twisty road to the Spray Lakes. You and Jim went out in the rubber dinghy."

They circled the corner of the nurses' station.

"I believe I do remember that. Martha was still with me then. It was the last good trip we had. The last time we went west. Beautiful cattle there, all feeding so peaceful, with the mountains behind." His breath came in uneven gasps from the double exertions of walking and talking. He coughed.

"Are you okay, Dad?"

"You had a little girl. She had a big smile. I used to hold her on my knee. She liked to sing."

"You're right, Dad. That's Rachel, and she's downstairs with Jim. They'd like to come up to see you."

He paused, smiled, and said warmly, "Why, that would be just fine. I'll be here checking the fence." He pointed vaguely at the handrail that ran the length of the hall. "You bring her along whenever you can."

During the elevator ride down to the main floor, Karen's feelings were a painfully whirling kaleidoscope. Confusion, grief and fear tumbled madly. Had the ravages of time destroyed the person who had been her father? Was he gone forever, leaving only what seemed to be a caricature of the man he'd been? Surely some essentials of her dad remained intact, despite humilities of body and mind.

When Karen found her husband and daughter waiting downstairs, she felt a surge of possessive love for these two people who were whole, and who were still hers. She brushed Rachel's bangs off her forehead and dropped a kiss there before they went upstairs.

Jim and Karen left the elevator with Rachel between them, as if to protect her. Karen was pleased that Rachel didn't cringe when a large woman, clutching a rag doll, rushed up and asked if she had seen Allistair since school let out. The little girl blushed, mutely shook her head, and watched the woman stride down the hall, robe flapping behind her.

Karen's dad was sitting in a straight chair beside his bed. He looked vacantly at them as they approached.

Jim reached to shake his hand and said, "Hello, Carl, I haven't seen you in a while. You look pretty good."

"Oh, yes, I feel pretty good. This one hip and leg bother me sometimes, but I can still get around." He looked at Rachel and then at Karen. "Are they with you?" he asked.

"Yes, Dad. You remember Jim?" She smiled reassuringly at her husband. Then she put her arm around her daughter and said, "This is Rachel. Do you remember when she was little and you held her on your knee? You enjoyed her smile so much."

"Yes, I remember her. And now she's grown up big." He leaned toward the girl and winked. "Do you see that cupboard over there?" he asked, pointing to the bedside table.

"Yes, Grandpa," Rachel said.

"Look in the top drawer and you'll find something you like."

The girl squeezed past the chair. She opened the drawer and stared in bewilderment at paper scraps, bits of string, elastics and paper clips.

"There's a box," he prompted. "It has peanut brittle in it."

Rachel handed it to him.

"I'm not supposed to have much of this," he said as he lifted the lid. "It makes sugar diabetes. My mother had that, you know, so I have to be careful. But sometimes a person likes a treat."

He carefully smoothed back the liner and, with a courtly gesture, offered it to Rachel.

Recognizing the courtesy, she made a little bow, flashed her dimple, and said, "Thank you, Grandpa."

He passed the candy to Karen and then Jim before taking a piece himself.

As they ate, Karen felt the tension drain out of her. This scene was like home. Dad had always wanted to feed people. When she was first dating Jim, her dad had almost driven him out of the house with his insistence on second and third helpings at mealtime. She chuckled to herself. Yes, this was her dad.

Jim brought two chairs and they sat around the end of the bed. Rachel also seemed at ease, perched on her mother's lap.

Karen chatted about their home and family activities. Her father munched on peanut brittle and seemed content to listen to stories of hikes into Johnston Canyon, wildlife sightings, Rachel's gymnastics and school concerts. When she mentioned singing lessons, he became more alert.

"Is that girl a singer?"

"Yes, Dad. She sometimes sings solos at church."

"Good for her!" he said heartily.

Rachel stirred. She slid to the floor and went to stand by her grandfather. "Would you like to hear my song, Grandpa? The one I sang at Thanksgiving? It's called 'This Is My Father's World.'"

Her grandfather smiled. "I'd like that just fine."

She moved back, by the window, and began to sing in a clear voice:

> This is my Father's world: He shines in all that's fair;
> In the rustling grass I hear Him pass;
> God speaks to me everywhere.[2]

As he listened intently, his hand began to move in time with the music. When Rachel sang the second verse, he hummed along, then started to sing in harmony with a surprisingly tuneful tenor.

Startled, Karen glanced at Jim. He smiled at her, reached for her hand, and began singing too. After a moment Karen joined them.

When they finished, the old man sat motionless, staring out the window. Then he spoke in a detached way. "Jesus... He holds everything together, you know. Sustains it." His hand was trembling as he raised his sleeve to his face.

Pellets of snow beat against the window.

Suddenly Carl's face took on a crafty expression. He turned hooded eyes to Jim and said, "Of course, I have it insured."

He went on irritably, "Those insurance men—they'd stay all day and talk your leg off. Out to make a sale. Always somebody after your money. We never had a lot, but we got by. And we had some good trips too, Martha and me."

He sighed. "I hope John can make a go of it on the farm. It's hard for young ones starting up. I should be there to help him, but I just don't seem able to do much any more."

The old man raised his hands wearily, then said with quiet dignity, "It was good of you to come. I'd like to visit longer, but I have to sleep now."

He carefully closed the candy box and handed it to Karen. Using the arms of his chair to push himself up, he stood, walked a couple of steps to the side of the bed, and climbed unsteadily onto it.

Karen put the peanut brittle back in the drawer and gently removed his slippers from his feet.

By the time she had covered him with the green thermal blanket from the end of the bed, he was breathing sonorously, oblivious to her kiss and her whispered promise to come back soon.

Once downstairs, Karen and Rachel waited inside the glass door of the lobby while Jim started up the car and cleared the snow off the windows.

Rachel spoke first. "Grandpa liked my singing, didn't he?"

"Yes, dear, he did," Karen said. "Very much."

"Does he really know Jesus?"

"Oh yes. He decided to follow Jesus when he was younger than you are now. All his life Jesus has been his Saviour and friend. It showed in everything he did." She smiled at Jim as he came in, quickly closing the door against the wind.

"I liked it when Grandpa sang along with me. But why did he start talking about insurance salesmen right after that?"

"It's hard to explain," Karen said.

She reached for her daughter's hand as they all went out to the car, though she could not have said with certainty whether it was to give or to receive comfort.

Once they were driving, Jim reopened the subject. He turned slightly toward the back seat. "Rachel, do you remember why we went spinning around on the road when we were coming here from the airport?"

"Yes, Dad. You said it was because of black ice. The black road showed through the clear ice, so you couldn't tell it was there."

"That's right."

"I was afraid when it happened. It was scary when the car spun around and we were pointing backwards."

"That's exactly like what happens in your grandpa's mind, Rachel," Jim explained. "It's as if his thoughts are slipping on black ice. Before he knows what's happened, he's flipped around and changed directions."

"Is it scary for him?"

"I don't know." Jim thought a moment. "When we skidded, there was so much snow falling that we didn't realize right away we were pointing in the opposite direction. It might be like that for Grandpa. He has so many years of memories in his mind, maybe he doesn't realize when he switches from one to another."

"So after he sang with me, a patch of ice surprised him into thinking about insurance?"

"That's it, sweetheart. I think singing with you reminded him of God's love and care." Jim paused. "I guess you could say that his mind jumped to thinking about how valuable God's love is. People buy insurance to protect valuable things."

They drove in silence for a while.

"I like Grandpa," Rachel announced. "He shared his candy with us, and when the ice and snow weren't getting in the way, he was very polite and nice."

Karen let out a big breath. She felt as if she had been holding it for a long time. Her voice shook as she said, "You're right, Rachel. He is a kind man. He was a good farmer. He loved his family and he did everything he could to help them. And we love him very much whether or not his ideas get mixed up.

"I love both of you very much too," she went on, in spite of tears and a painful tightness in her throat. "I want you to know that I will still love you even when I'm a tottery old lady carrying a doll everywhere I go."

Jim took his right hand off the steering wheel to reach over and rest it on Karen's knee as he kept his eyes on the road ahead.

"And," Karen took a trembling breath, "even when my thinking slips on ice, or I get lost because it's snowy, I'll try to remember to keep a jar of jelly beans in my drawer for when you come to sing for me."

"It's a deal, Mom," replied Rachel, as she reached between the two front seats to solemnly shake hands with Karen.

"And, Mom?" Rachel added, "If you don't remember about the jelly beans, it's okay. I could always bring some with me."

1. The Prayer of the Heart, also known as The Jesus Prayer, has been used throughout the history of the Christian church. It is revered in both Eastern and Western traditions because it focuses wholly on Jesus.

2. Maltbie D. Babcock (lyrics), *Terra Beata* (traditional English melody), "This is My Father's World." Public Domain.

The Wheels On the Bus Go 'Round

Angelina Fast-Vlaar

Perched on the edge of a chair
my husband anxiously waits
for the coming of the little yellow bus.
It will take him to his Day Program.
"You'll need your boots, Hon, it's cold outside."
"Where is your warm hat?"
"Yes, dear, you need to wear your gloves."
A lump forms in my throat as I hear
the echo of words spoken long ago.
"Is the zipper stuck again?"
"Do you need help with your gloves?"
The little yellow bus rolls to a stop
and I support him up the steps.
"I'm going to school," he quips
to the driver, who helps him find a seat.
The doors click shut, I wave good-bye
and the huge lump in my throat
bursts into a thousand tears
coursing down my cheeks.

Late in the afternoon I'm the one
sitting on the edge of the chair
waiting for the little yellow bus,
waiting for my husband-child.
I steady him down the steps.
"Did you have fun at 'school' today?"
"What games did you play?"
"Did you have a nap?"
I know the questions well because
the wheels on the bus go 'round and 'round.

Margie and Me

Nonfiction

Judi Peers

I do a lot of brainstorming while standing at the kitchen sink up to my elbows in soapy water: problem solving, organizing material for various projects, and planning upcoming events. Is there something about sudsy, watery warmth that helps my brain function more clearly? Often, when confronted with a problem in my fiction writing, I'll fill up the bathtub and sink into the hot, luxuriant bubbles, hoping to pamper listless brain cells back into front-line action. Strangely enough, the answer often comes—slowly… seeping… into my mind. Perhaps the kitchen sink has the same effect. What a shame we've come to rely so heavily on dishwashers!

While scrubbing pots and pans one afternoon a few years ago, I planned out the logistics of an upcoming spring event for the ladies of my church, an event to which they would readily invite friends. Down the Garden Path would be a major production—informative, yet fun—but, most importantly, like yellow-cupped crocuses poking through lingering patches of snow in early spring, energizing and uplifting, restoring hearts, souls and minds.

We would offer educational workshops, a perennial plant exchange, and a brief talk using garden analogies to illustrate spiritual truths. *Now let's see,* I thought. *Maybe we could entitle the devotional part "The Flowering of the Soul."*

While I reached for a fresh blue scouring pad, my mind raced on. *Fruit, perhaps, to serve while the women gather. And later, a fancy tea—downstairs—with clotted cream, scones, and interesting jams and jellies. I have a couple of jars of strawberry/lavender freezer jam left. And Calvin and Nancy Stillman probably have a few exciting creations in their pantry cupboard. They've produced many exotic varieties over the years: prickly pear, sumac, dandelion, quince…*

Hmmm… the entire church will need to be transformed in order to give the proper ambience.

The sanctuary will need to become just that—a haven of serenity in the midst of busy, stressful lives.

Pot scrubber lying at ease in my hand, I stood gazing out of the kitchen window, seeing in my mind's eye the progression of the upcoming evening, moving from bud to blossom, as if captured on film in time-lapse photography; the church beautiful, the décor natural, yet sophisticated—a stark contrast to the grease and grime that lingered in my frying pan, calling for my immediate attention.

Who should I ask to help decorate? I wondered, busying my hands once more as I pondered the possibilities... Liz Telford? Shari Auger? Pauline?

Margie Oswald, God interjected.

Margie Oswald? I was somewhat startled, not only confused and surprised by the answer, but also by the fact that God Himself would want input into the décor at our ladies' night out.

Margie Oswald, He repeated. His gentle whisper was as soft as sheep's wool, yet His voice was crystal-clear.

Margie Oswald was the middle-aged woman I gave a ride to church every Sunday morning. Her mother had contracted German measles while she was pregnant, and Margie had been left with a number of health problems, including some physical and mental limitations. I had to help her up into the seat, then bully her wheelchair into the back of my van. Surely God wasn't serious about her being part of the decorating committee.

Foam flowers, He added.

I squeezed more liquid soap into the now tepid water. *Foamflowers?* I questioned, even more confused, but at the same time fascinated and intrigued. Being a gardener, I knew about foamflowers. Tiarella. A shade plant with heart-shaped leaves and dainty, enduring, pinkish-white flowers. A modest specimen plant, but an impressive ground cover in rich, moist soil. I had seen a massive drift of them several years ago in a large woodland garden near Port Perry, Ontario.

I finished scrubbing the last pot and placed it on the drying tray. *Margie Oswald? Foamflowers? What is God talking about?*

The next time I was in Margie's apartment, she directed me to her bedroom. "I want to show you something," she said.

Plastic bins crammed with craft supplies lined one side of the wall. Sprawled over the top of a small desk in the far corner of the room were numerous sheets of soft foam, cardboard tracing patterns and several foam cut-outs. In the midst of this colourful field of foam lay a single, white and yellow daisy-like flower she had recently assembled.

"You do a lot of crafts," I said. "You make flowers out of foam."

"Yes," Margie answered, her countenance brightening.

In my initial vision of the Down the Garden Path event, there had been nothing remotely akin to Margie's foam flowers. "Tacky" would have been my normal reaction to such a display, but I knew, then and there, that God wanted Margie's flowers included.

I had already decided on a pansy theme. "Could you make pansies out of foam?" I asked.

"Sure," Margie said. Her eyes danced with delight when I asked her to be on our decorating committee. "Really? Me?"

For the next month, Margie came to our Tuesday morning Bible study, then remained afterward, crafting dozens of pansies out of purple and yellow foam. I could see that the project was giving her an incredible sense of purpose and accomplishment, causing her to blossom as well.

And the pansies? Well… they turned out even better than I could have imagined. In the back of my mind, however, the question lingered: *What am I going to do with all this floriferous foam?*

The program was planned, four wonderful workshops were set to go, and a few of us spent a couple of days decorating the church for the big day. Twig chairs and pansy-filled planters flanked the church entrance. Rhubarb punch and colourful fruit-laden trays were prepared to serve the ladies as they gathered upstairs.

Decorated for a formal tea, the church basement no longer resembled the basement. The table centrepieces (petite Johnny-jump-ups planted in beautiful antique tea cups) were inspired by the same design on the serviettes. Amazingly, and unplanned by those involved, even the pansy sculptures made of icing on top of the sugar cubes matched perfectly. Everything had come together in a marvellous way. And the décor was both natural and sophisticated, just as I had envisioned.

As I stood back, surveying the scene one last time before the crowd was about to arrive, I felt satisfied with everything—everything, that is, except the tables that would hold the pots for the perennial plant exchange. That particular area looked a little dark, a little drab. *Oh well,* I figured, *there's nothing we can do about it now.*

Margie was the first to arrive, with a big plastic grocery bag full of foam flowers. A friend had kindly offered to pick her up knowing I would be extremely busy.

The truth was, I was so busy that I hadn't yet figured out what to do with Margie's flowers. Suddenly, it hit me—one last moment of inspiration.

I propped a few of the foam flowers against both the dark green and the black pots that a few of us had already placed on the plant exchange tables. They looked fine. They looked better than fine. They looked fabulous—multi-coloured purple petals and yellow centers brightening up that dark corner with their perky pansy faces.

Margie grinned from ear to ear as we showed the women where to place their plants and then scattered the foam flowers around the base of the pots. I had never seen her as happy as she was that night.

Margie continued making crafts for our church: animal foam figures for every child in the Sunday school; floral arrangements as gifts for each lady attending Bible study; yarn-and-plastic-canvas hot plates in colourful quilt-block patterns for a special quilt-themed event. It gave her such joy to generously give away her handiwork.

Initially, I had befriended Margie thinking I was doing her a favour. But through my relationship with her, I was able to experience first-hand the wonderful, glorious, incomprehensible nature of our God. By allowing me to see exactly what she needed during a particularly low time in her life, He proved to me that Margie was, indeed, precious in His sight, and He also showed me that Margie was an important member of the body of Christ.

Despite her disability, despite her weaknesses, she too, had great strengths—a wonderful sense of humour, a generous, giving spirit, and many other abilities that were unique to her.

When Margie died a few years later, I shared the foam flower story with the small group of family, friends and church members who attended her funeral. Soon after, I received a note from Debbie Fraser, a kind and godly woman who had befriended Margie many years before, and the person who had organized the funeral:

> It was so nice of you to share with us how Margie touched your life. She spoke to me especially of the flowers you had her make. She was so excited and pleased to do it. It was a turning point for her. She desired to share her gift of crafts with everyone...

How fitting that this familiar verse from Matthew 25:40 was penned inside Debbie's card:

> I tell you the truth, whatever you did
> for one of the least of these...
> you did for Me.

When Grown Men Cry

Nonfiction

Brian C. Austin

Wonderful news reaches me this morning—something to celebrate. A close friend who has worked so hard has achieved a high goal, winning a national contest to get her book published. It's a dream come true and the joy of the moment grips me.

Members of the same writers' group, we've shared challenges, glimmers of hope, and painful disappointments. We've encouraged and spurred each other to higher levels of excellence. I catch myself choking on the words as I share this joy with my wife.

Yet brief moments later, after the phone rings and I speak with my daughter, I find myself sobbing—a startling response, unexpected, unprepared for.

The man was an acquaintance, never part of my circle, not of my generation. I chatted with him briefly from time to time, but I wouldn't have called him a close friend. I'm quite sure he would have said something similar about me.

Yet the tears sneak up on me—take me by surprise. For his death impacts my daughter and her husband intensely. A member of their wedding party, he was full of life and a little bit crazy. He was husband to a young wife and dad to an 11-month-old daughter. His death directly wounds those I love.

Grief is such a strange experience. The emotional turmoil seems to ignore the norms of everyday life. Like most men, I've grown up with the cultural lie that "men don't cry." I've internalized that lie to a great extent. Tears rend something deep inside me. My whole being fights them. The rational reasons for letting them flow never totally overcome the fear of the male ego, which has been conditioned to think tears childish and weak. But moving beyond that lie demands a costly battle every time.

It's not the pain I fight. Somehow, I almost welcome it, dare to hope with a strange illogic that someone else's pain is lessened as I feel more. It's the sobbing I fight, the tears, the response that comes without warning and is beyond my control.

Grief never used to impact me this way. I used to have answers. Not platitudes such as, "God needed another angel," or even, "He's in a better place." My answers came directly from the Bible: "We do not grieve like those who have no hope," paraphrased from 1 Thessalonians 4:13; or the words of Jesus after Lazarus' death that ring with triumph, "I am the resurrection and the life. He who believes in me will live, and whoever lives and believes in me will never die" (John 11:25). They're wonderful words, rich with hope.

But then Dylan, an infant grandson, died. I'd seen pictures. I'd heard a baby's cry in the background over the phone. But I never got to hold our second grandchild.

Biblical answers didn't lose their truth at the time of Dylan's death. I still retained hope and trust. But I felt a depth of pain and loss beyond anything I had ever imagined. I clung to my wife, and we wept together. The answers, in which I wholeheartedly believed then and now, did not lessen the pain.

Ah, but years have passed since that loss. My arms often hold a little one. Other grandchildren bring delight and joy. I can gaze on a picture of Dylan with warmth and little pain, most of the time. Yet something in me changed when Dylan died.

These days, even when I'm celebrating a triumph, tears sometimes intrude. Grief and joy come together—such a strange blend. Triumph and tragedy. They so often seem to overlap.

But tears torment foolish male ego. With joy and celebration added to the mix, they become even more unpredictable. They overflow and spill, somehow always a surprise, somehow always a mingling of vulnerable ego and shared pain. My ego cringes; my heart surrenders—hopefully with grace. And instead of offering answers, however true they might be, I cry—grown man that I am.

The Bathroom and the Neighbours' Cat

Nonfiction

Bill Bonikowsky

It began as an innocent project. Well-meaning. Possibly heroic. My wife Joy was out of town and I thought I'd have a little Mother's Day surprise waiting when she returned. Our bathroom floor was in a state of worsening decay, getting spongier by the week.

I've got five days before Joy returns, I calculated. *I'm going to redo the bathroom!*

We lived in what some refer to as a "Delta Box"—a term of affection for those who live in one, and a bit of a slur for those who don't. Our "Delta Box" (named for the Vancouver suburb where we lived), was a raised bungalow. The main floor, accessible up a few steps from the front door, featured the usual kitchen, living and dining rooms, along with three bedrooms and the main bathroom. A short flight of steps down from the front door led to the basement, half-way below ground level, which contained a family room, a small fourth bedroom inhabited by our nineteen-year-old son Mark, and a laundry room that led to the garage. The basement also included a very small washroom, also claimed by Mark, with a sink and a toilet featuring a headshot of extreme free-style skier Glen Plake, sporting his distinctive mohawk haircut, taped to the fixture's lid.

Two other boys rounded out our family of five: seventeen-year-old Tim, and twelve-year-old Jonathan, who had accompanied Joy on her trip to Florida to vacation with her mother and sister.

Our home was 25 years old. The upstairs bathroom contained the only tub and shower in the house. During years of enthusiastic showering, bathing and splashing by three growing boys and their parents, water had surreptitiously leaked through a crack in the caulking where the linoleum met the base of the tub, causing the sub floor to rot. It was becoming harder to ignore that sinking feeling when you stepped from the tub onto the disintegrating floor. With two of our home's five inhabitants out of town, I decided to seize the day.

At first, all went well. Ripping things apart gives a man a sense of accomplishment. But even *that* wasn't peaches and cream. To fix the floor properly, the tub had to be removed. But in order to access the tub, I had to rip out the wall tiles and underlying drywall.

While I was at it, I noticed the wall opposite the vanity, to which the previous owner had nailed tongue-and-groove cedar strips. Few things can match the warmth of Western red cedar, but through the years it had accumulated enough coats of paint to disguise its original identity. In short, it was ugly, and my wife had often wished out loud that we could get rid of it.

Aha! The time is now, I thought as I grabbed the wrecking bar.

Removing the cedar resulted in the annihilation of the drywall beneath it, and more hauling of rubble down the stairs and out of the house.

Behind the drywall, a rotten stud needed to be replaced.

And so on.

In the deep recesses of my mind lurked the realization that this bathroom project was somehow becoming more than I had anticipated. But my unfailing optimism, coupled with the satisfaction of daily adding to the growing pile of debris beside the house, lulled me into a sense of complacency.

Abruptly, without warning, it was the day before my wife's return. I became desperate.

A friend joined me. We worked feverishly past midnight cutting out the old flooring, treating our neighbours to a bedtime cacophony of the grating rasp of a reciprocating saw, the tortured shriek of nails being wrenched from floor joists, and the thump of pieces of plywood being tossed out of the bathroom window and crashing onto the ground below.

Morning dawned. The nightmare was real. The hours before Joy's arrival were a kaleidoscope of activity. Removing the latest bathroom debris. A bit of laundry. Dishes. Vacuuming. And the clock—that relentless clock—each tick kicking the pieces of my shattered dream, and reminding me that all too soon I would be bringing my wife into the middle of it.

Suddenly it was time to leave for the airport. And my Mother's Day gift? A bathroom with bare studs for walls. No floor—just the supporting beams. No tub or shower. No sink or toilet. Somehow, the knowledge that we did have a toilet and a sink in the basement did little to console me. It wasn't the sort of place where you'd want to spend quality time.

We had a pleasant trip from the airport. I really was glad to see my wife; why spoil the moment by telling her what I was up to?

My pulse quickened as we pulled into the driveway. Bravely, I swung open our front door. Hmm—not bad. Fairly clean, considering what had transpired, added to the fact that the place had been deprived of any feminine influence for a week. As we climbed the stairs to the main floor, I positioned myself in such a way as to shield Joy's eyes from the hulking new tub and shower enclosure sitting in the middle of the living room.

Summoning up any courage still remaining in my battered ego, I led my good wife down the hall to the bathroom doorway— the door itself lay on its side in Jonathan's bedroom—and uttered the rehearsed words, "Happy Mother's Day!"

It's hard for a spouse, even a kind, loving one like Joy, to act grateful when part of her world has been destroyed. Phrases like, "I know you meant well," were mixed with sentiments such as, "I don't want you to *ever* do anything around the house again!" (Some husbands might welcome the latter declaration.)

Things got worse. I tried to gently break the news that I was scheduled to leave the next morning for a three-day staff retreat. I quickly added, "But I'll be off work for two days after that."

It didn't take me long to figure out that my marriage was more important than going on a staff retreat. I hoped my boss would agree.

I awakened him with a phone call around 11 p.m. to plead my case. Fortunately, he too is committed to the biblical concept of marriage, and we agreed that it would probably be prudent for me to stay home and finish what I'd started.

I took Joy out for breakfast the next morning. The food was good—and it was a pleasure to use the restaurant's sparkling facilities. Then we looked at new bathroom vanities. I believed it would help re-orient our thoughts, creating a vision of things as they would be. Neither of us realized how *long* that would be. I was about to learn the terrible truth that *de*struction is much quicker than *con*struction.

The adventures continued. There was the night I took a misstep and put a foot through the basement ceiling. I was kept from falling completely through by a floor joist conveniently positioned between my legs.

Then there was the cat episode. I had almost finished laying the new plywood flooring in the bathroom when I discovered our neighbours' cat checking out our kitchen. I must have left the front door open while I was sawing plywood on the driveway. When the cat saw me, it took off like a shot down the hall and through the open bathroom door.

Ordinarily a cat in a bathroom would be easy to spot, but it was nowhere to be seen. There was, however, a three foot by four foot opening in the floor where I had yet to fasten the last piece of plywood to the floor joists. It didn't take much figuring to guess where the cat had gone.

I went outside and left the front and back doors of the house open, assuming the misdirected feline would be sufficiently motivated to find its way out. I returned—after what seemed a reasonable length of time—with the carefully cut final piece of plywood flooring under my arm. No sign of the cat, so I triumphantly fastened the last piece of the floor in place.

At 5:00 a.m. the next morning, my wife and I were awakened by a horrific racket. I sprang from my bed thinking an intruder was in the garage stumbling over the garbage cans. I bounded down the stairs to the basement.

By the time I reached the laundry room that led to the garage, the truth stabbed through the fog in my brain like a bolt of lightning—*That cat is trapped under the bathroom floor!*

It was true. Having passed the dark hours of the night in silent despair, the neighbours' cat had reached a state of panic and, in a frenzied scramble for freedom, had begun to flail around amidst the metal ductwork beneath the floor.

The boys—living proof of the propensity of the typical adolescent to sleep through anything—were blissfully unaware of the pandemonium.

Fortunately, the basement had a suspended ceiling, so I didn't have to face the unthinkable prospect of tearing up my precious new floor. Perched on my old aluminum painter's ladder, I gently lifted one ceiling panel in the laundry room, which is directly underneath the bathroom. The panel seemed heavy... about the weight of a scared cat. I carefully set it back down and removed the panel next to it. Slowly, slowly, I raised myself until I could peer through the opening into the blackness.

As my eyes adjusted to the dark, I saw the cat... crouched, and glaring at me with a wide-eyed stare that gave me the impression it was blaming me for its predicament.

The cat wouldn't budge. I couldn't quite reach it, and wasn't sure I wanted to. I tried coaxing. "Here, kitty kitty! Nice kitty. Poor kitty. It's all right. You can trust me." The cat remained unconvinced that it was safe—or prudent—to do *anything* I wanted it to do. I suppose I could have offered a saucer of cream, but I doubted it would trust me after what had passed between us.

I resorted to the same tactic that should have prevented the cat's dilemma in the first place—leaving the panel out, I walked away, giving it time to make its escape. Actually, I went back to bed for an hour or so to contemplate, while my wife twitched and turned beside me. Joy doesn't like cats at the best of times, and knowing there was an emotionally distraught one sitting in our basement ceiling had altered her state of mind. I did make sure our bedroom door was firmly closed, in case the cat carried a grudge.

As morning dawned, the solution arrived in the form of our white short-tailed cat Bonkers. Unsure of what might transpire, but wanting to create options, I opened the front door, then retreated a safe distance. Bonkers must have talked the traumatized fellow feline down, because a short time later, the two of them strolled sedately out of the laundry room, up the stairs and out the door.

At breakfast, the boys enjoyed a good laugh as I regaled them with the tale of what had transpired while they were sleeping. By the end of the day Joy was even speaking to me again.

At last, three weeks after the adventure began, it was time to install the shiny new acrylic tub and shower enclosure. I couldn't wait! But first I had to re-configure the plumbing.

Mark and Tim began showering at their girlfriends' parents' homes. And my wife, in desperation edged with vague anger-like emotions, began to shower at the local swimming pool.

The plumbing went quite well, considering I had to cut out the side of my bedroom closet so I could lean the whole network of copper tubing away from the bathroom side of the wall to allow me to slide the new unit into place. Fortunately the debris field was confined to my closet alone, as Joy's closet was located on the other side of the room.

It is with particular sadness that I recall the Saturday evening I proudly announced to my family that they could shower in their own home before church the next morning. I tried so hard to fulfill that promise. Working into the wee hours of the night, I finally surrendered to reality, crawling wearily and humbly into bed, only to arise a few hours later to break the news to my family that they had better secure alternate arrangements for washing.

By Sunday night, the plumbing was done (I'm sure that God has forgiven me for working on the Sabbath). I wish I could describe in triumphant tones the moment I turned on the water supply valve for that first shower. But even that moment was tarnished by one tiny jet of water that squirted from a single flaw in all those carefully soldered joints. When I discovered that the jet was reduced to a drip when the shower was turned on, the solution seemed obvious—simply turn off the supply valve when no one was showering, and turn it on when someone was. That idea grew old very quickly, and I repaired the offending joint.

Finally, we could all shower with a joyful abandonment known only to those who have been deprived for so long.

I have to admit that everyone's joy was somewhat tempered by the long list of other things I still had to install, including drywall, a light in the shower, and a switch on the wall, not to mention a toilet, a sink and a faucet.

Yes, I had completely underestimated the scope of the project. My proposed five-day job cost me two weeks' vacation and the investment of every spare minute after work and on weekends—usually at the expense of sleep—for two additional weeks.

But I learned a lot. Among various lessons in marital harmony, I learned that a fully functioning bathroom is an integral part of everyday family life. And I learned that cats hate small spaces.

How do you put such memories behind you? You start another project. That fall, I cut a large hole in our dining room wall to build an extension to hold our china cabinet. It took only a week of fresh autumn breezes blowing through our house to redirect our focus. I haven't heard a word about the bathroom since.

Thou Shalt Have No Gods But Me

Nonfiction

Paul M. Beckingham

Reflections on The First Commandment:
"You shall have no other gods before me" (Exodus 20:3)

In a dyslexic systematic theology, "God" is spelled "Dog." And, like all false gods, Dog is so close to the real thing that it becomes quite easy to confuse the two. And people regularly do. I know, because I did.

Dog first came into my life when I was about five years old. The reality of his presence overwhelmed me. I experienced an in-your-face confrontation with his unconditional love. He licked me until I thought that I would melt in the pleasure of those carefree moments of abandon. True, he was really Puppy, but in my child's imagination, he represented all the power of Dog.

Dog spoke to me in ways that transcended human language. He was responsive to my requests and attentive to all my needs. Even when the world turned its back on me, he always welcomed, always affirmed, and always loved me. He knew all about me because I would tell him all I knew about the person that I was. I held nothing back. I spoke to him often. Throughout each day I would call to him. And in the cool of the evening we walked together in the garden. I would run and hide from him. Quietly, he would come after me, ears cocked and head inclined, to find me. It was as if he called to me, "Paul, Paul... Where are you?" And I could not resist. I walked towards the warmth of his presence and embraced him, ready to receive fresh evidences of his love for me.

In the garden, in those days, there was but one rule, one pro-hibition, one thing that was forbidden that I should do. My mother brought me the edict, but I knew it was from Dog. "Puppy," she told me, "doesn't like it when you mess with his leash. When his leash is tied to the rail in the garden, you must leave it. Do not release it."

I heard. I understood. I did not believe. The one thing I could not do, I wanted now so much to do. This terrible restriction cut right across my relationship of trust with Dog. And so, one day…

I could wait no longer. I walked over to that rail, where the leash and the collar met in a loop of steel, and I began to pull. I pulled and pulled with all my might. The loop was a single curved piece of metal pushed tightly together at either end. Heaving at it, I managed to pry it open at the join—just enough to release the leash and let Dog roam free with me in the garden.

When we were done, full of joy and happy fatigue, I walked with him back to that place where the leash hung limp and loose from the rail. I pushed the clip through the open join and squeezed… and squeezed. Oh, how I squeezed—with little or no result. The ring remained twisted and ajar. Even had I been able to close it, and I was a long way from doing so, the ends would not have met squarely. At best, they would overlap. But maybe Mom would never notice.

Dog looked at me softly and loved me hugely. His heart was to forgive all my crimes and misdemeanours. So, off I wandered, happy in that moment, running into the house as my Mom hollered out the supper call.

How long does it take for a world to fall apart? For me, it was the briefest of moments. A screech of brakes; a yelp; adults knocking at our door. A shovel; a trashcan; a tragedy. Dog left my life in an instant. Pain overwhelmed me: shock… despair… guilt… I ran upstairs and hid beneath my bed for what seemed like forever. Mom came to coax me out from that cool, gloomy place of quiet solitude. I refused her entreaties. Life after Dog was a dark and lonely existence. Guilt weighed heavier than a bed upon my shoulders.

It was almost 40 years before Dog came back into my life again. In the high tea country of Tigoni, just north of Nairobi, Kenya, I toiled and sweated, learning to speak Swahili. I laboured long and hard in that high-pressure zone called Language School. One day, a playful German shepherd bounced into the compound and into our lives. He seemed to make a beeline for our home. Handsome and young, he played and scampered with our children. His winsome beauty and sharp intelligence captivated all our hearts. But I shunned him lest I love him, only to have him snatched away again by his rightful owner. And sure enough, after a couple of days, he was gone.

A week later he was back, but oh, how different he looked this time. He was fearful and reticent, starved and half-dead. One of my kids found him cowering in a corner of an empty building. I talked to him as I carefully approached and placed a dish of milk before him. He refused it and shied away from me. Talking low and slow, I calmed him with my voice and stroked his dank coat. I reached for his collar fur and he did not pull away or attempt to bite.

As I walked him to our cottage I noticed two gaping wounds, about four inches high. They formed a ring of torment around each rear leg. The skin and fur were completely gone. The flesh was infected and turning green. This poor animal stank like rotten meat as his suppurating wounds freely oozed their pus. Steel wire, it seemed, had been used to tie him to the fence of someone wanting to take ownership of this stray dog. Had he been cruelly wired down for the past few days? In his fight for freedom from the wire, he likely had bitten into his own flesh.

The vet declared the dog to be an inpatient for at least a week. Releasing him back to us, she gave us pills and strict instructions. We must, she instructed gravely, bathe his wounds three times a day and walk him constantly.

The wounds of Dog, at last, broke my heart wide open. I finally made him my own. It was not that I had looked for him; he had sought and found me, and made my heart his home.

In those days of desperate loneliness, I was cast adrift in a strange land, languishing in a language I knew not of. In those dark days, I began to love Dog deeply. He understood my pain; he, too, had suffered much. I walked with him and I talked with him and I told him he was my own. Daily, we sauntered through the high tea fields of Tigoni.

As Dog grew stronger, he chased after monkeys. I watched them fleeing before us. I felt the monkeys on my back, those worries, fears and care, begin to lighten, too. I spoke to him in deep ways, pouring out to Dog my anxieties and my concerns. He always listened; he never broke trust. I could tell him anything, and I frequently did. He heard the confessions of a broken heart, yet still he loved me. He accepted me for the person that I truly was, not for some other persona that I assumed when trying to impress. Oh, what joy Dog brought me in those tea fields!

But Dogs don't live forever. Things happen, and life moves on. One day, he too was gone.

My days of African adventure seem distant now, and long ago. Sitting in rain-drizzled Vancouver, British Columbia, I am a world away from safaris, droughts and malaria. Yet some days, my thoughts are as vivid as the red embers of the setting African sun—and just as spirit-boosting—as I ponder quietly the wisdom Dog once taught me.

My Dogs filled my life for a short time only; yet they left me lonely, desolate and dejected.

There's a stretch of choppy water lapping the Pacific coast. The locals call it *Desolation Sound*. Too often, the gods I've relied upon have, in the end, discarded me, and I've found myself, derelict and desperate, washed up on the desert shores of *Isolation Island*.

Oddly, *desolation* and *isolation* form fruitful places; there, fresh discoveries can be made. In lonely places and empty spaces, I discover a God who refuses to abandon the people He loves. While pain is the cruellest teacher, and her lessons are well taught, I learn that God never runs away from me.

As my Dogs trusted me, I will trust Him, but while I was never fully worthy of my Dogs' trust, He is more than worthy of mine.

I find His love to be unconditional and forever.

In the garden, that place of deepest being, I daily walk with Him, and talk with Him, and tell Him I am His own.[1] There, I discover that His love is warm and always present to me. He extends a love that demands no preconditions.

Resting in His care, relaxing in His love, I become no longer a stranger to myself. I grow comfortable, at last, within my own skin, recognizing myself to be not only forgiven, but accepted as I truly am, accurately known and fully loved.

That's the kind of love that I long for—that we all long for. Love that bears our woundedness and carries scars for us.[2]

Love that enables us to trust God's gift completely. Love that shares the weight of our pain, so that we never again face it alone. And love that whispers grace to us beyond life's deepest challenges.

1. Reference to "In the Garden," hymn written by Charles A. Miles. Public Domain.

2. See Isaiah 53:5: "But He was pierced for our transgressions, He was crushed for our iniquities; the punishment that brought us peace was upon Him, and by His wounds we are healed."

What's Next?

Fiction

Jayne E. Self

"What am I going to do?" I asked the cat.

It had been two days since my husband and I had pulled away from the campus parking lot, our youngest daughter, Lucy, growing smaller and smaller in the car's rear view mirror. Last of three kids to leave the nest, she'd been eagerly anticipating this day for months. I, however, had been dreading it.

Dave reached across and squeezed my hand. "She's going to be fine."

I leaned my face against the cool car window. "But will I?"

"Are you crazy?" Dave's gaze flashed towards me. "This is going to be great." He pulled our car onto the expressway, quiet for a moment as he concentrated on merging with the traffic. "The house to ourselves. The fridge to ourselves. No late night phone calls from her friends. Lower hydro bills without all her computer time." His eyebrows arched rakishly. "Clothes optional any time we want."

Great. In one fell swoop I'd gone from full time parent, with its endless demands, to full-time Bunny. I glanced down at myself; I supposed I should have felt thankful he still found me enticing.

For a long time, I said nothing. "I guess I've been hoping for more."

Dave, no doubt lost in his own imaginings of overflowing fridges and frisky romps through the house, had lost track of the conversation. "More what?"

"I don't know. More purpose. More meaning. More—"

"Your life's been meaningless?"

"I'm not saying that. I *had* a purpose. I loved being home with the kids. But I'm not a full time Mom any more. The kids are gone and I don't know what I'm supposed to do." To my horror, scalding tears slid down my cheeks. I swiped them away before Dave noticed.

"Well, what are you good at?" he asked.

Great question. I thought for a moment. "Laundry?"

"You want to open a Laundromat?"

I snorted, grateful for an idea stupid enough to stop my tears.

"Then what do you want to do?"

"That's the problem. I'm half-way through my life and I still don't know what I want to be when I grow up."

Dave hummed thoughtfully, the way he did when he was mulling over an idea. "Well, my love," he said finally, "Don't you think it's time you found out?"

The problem was I'd been trying to do just that. For the last few months, I'd been devouring every empty-nester book I could find. I'd prayed myself silly. I'd quizzed the older women from our church who'd survived their own empty-nest transitions. Why did I still feel so unprepared? What was wrong with me?

Two days after Lucy's departure, I was none the wiser and Sam the cat had offered me no comfort. I crossed the hall to Lucy's room, curled up on her bed, and had myself a good cry.

Dave would expect supper when he got home from work. I peered into the freezer, searching for inspiration. All I saw were the mounds of pizza pockets and bagel bites the kids hadn't consumed over the summer. I could cook the six-pound pot roast I discovered beneath the pizza pockets. Or make a stew. A stew would feed Dave and me for the week. BBQ chicken legs? I pulled out a rock-hard lump of chicken parts—twelve, I counted. Another week's worth of dinners.

Diving deeper into the freezer's murky depths, I scavenged for anything in a portion small enough for two. Nada. I grabbed my purse and car keys, and headed to the grocery store.

I met depressingly gorgeous Marnie Penswitch in the pre-pared food aisle. Marnie runs an interior decorating business and always looks as if she's stepped out of a magazine layout. Her oldest daughter had headed to university with Lucy, but Marnie still had kids at home.

Dressed in jeans and an over-sized hoodie, I angled myself behind my cart and asked, "How have you been managing the last couple of days?"

She pushed at her perfect hair in obvious distress. "I'm going crazy. I can't believe how much I depended on Tiffany's help. I had no idea how much she did to help keep the house running smoothly. I'm up to my ears in dirty laundry. I have no idea how to help Pete with his calculus homework. Erica's six o'clock hockey practices are insane. Tiff actually enjoyed driving her to the arena—you know kids and cars. And now George has invited his biggest clients for dinner tonight."

This wasn't the first time her husband had invited company on a school night. Lucy'd often told me how Tiffany and her younger siblings would eat take-out pizza in the rec room while their parents entertained upstairs.

I studied Marnie's grocery cart. "So what are you serving?"

"I've got these cute little frozen hors d'oeuvres." She showed me a combo-pack of mini quiches, cheese-stuffed puff pastries, and triangular veggie turnovers. "Pop them into the oven for ten minutes and they're done. Ready-cooked stuffed chicken breasts—just heat and serve. Wild rice pilaf, pre-cut veggies and—" she held up a jar of *dulce le leche* caramel sauce, "—this to drizzle over the Dutch apple cake I ordered from the bakery."

Brilliant, I thought, mentally adapting her menu to fit our tastes. *Tonight we will dine Penswitch-style.*

As Marnie hurried away, I scoured the store, grabbing frozen Chicken Kiev, bagged salad, shamefully expensive imported strawberries (better than Dutch apple cake any day), and a jar of 10,000 calorie chocolate sauce to dip them in. Dave wasn't a big strawberries and chocolate fan, but Lucy and I loved them.

I stalled in the middle of the produce section, remembering the way Lucy would even devour strawberries and chocolate for breakfast if, by some fluke, there were leftovers. I felt my lower lip tremble. I missed Lucy so much. And not because the laundry was piling up.

"Wow," said Dave, a week later, when he'd gathered his wits enough to speak.

I spun in a slow circle so he could get the full effect.

I'd spent days thinking about it before I'd called Marnie's hair stylist and made my appointment for a makeover. I'd mentioned nothing to Dave in case I chickened out.

That morning, I'd gotten a stylish new cut, highlights, and makeup.

Then I'd splurged on four new outfits from Winners, my favourite discount fashion outlet.

At the moment, I wore a bright green scooped-neck sweater—a new colour for me—wide-legged jeans, high-heeled boots, and big earrings. Although I was neither, I looked long and lean, if I did say so myself.

"So, what do you think?"

"You look amazing!" Dave swept me into his arms, dancing me around the living room. "What brought this on?"

"Just figured it was time for a change."

"Well, it certainly is that. Wow!" he repeated. "I think we should go out for dinner to celebrate."

I tried not to frown. Was my looking attractive so unusual he felt the need to reward me for good behaviour?

He caught the sudden temperature change. Dave is quick that way. "What's wrong? Did I say something I shouldn't have?"

"Of course not," I lied. "You know you're always free to speak your mind. That's what marriage is supposed to be about. A safe place where you can say what you think."

"Then why do I feel like I just said the wrong thing? Don't you want me to tell you that you look amazing?"

"Yes. No. I—"

His eyebrows inched up. "You... what?"

I flopped inelegantly onto the couch. "I feel like a fraud dressing like this."

His eyes widened, the way they always do when he's totally bamboozled. "Why?"

"Because these are just trappings. I don't feel any different inside. If anything, I'm more confused than ever about what I want to be."

"Can't whatever it is look like this?"

I folded my arms across my chest. "I thought we believed that God cares more about our insides. What if I've missed His mark by spending all this money on my outside?"

He scratched his head. "The hairdresser can't glue your hair back, but I suppose, if you really feel that way, you could return the clothes." He sounded doubtful.

"You want me to return these?" I hiked up my pant leg to reveal one of my snazzy little ankle boots.

"No. I don't mind you jazzing up your outside. But I'm just your husband: what do I know? If you really do believe God disapproves…" Dave sank down beside me, slid his arm around my shoulder and hugged me close. "This no-kids thing is hard for you, isn't it?" he said.

I chewed my lip and nodded.

"Look, I don't want you to bite my head off, because I mean this in love, but do you think maybe something is wrong?"

I started to sniffle. "Wrong?"

"You know—hormones and all that. Maybe you should see your doctor. Maybe she can help."

I agreed without a fight.

Thanks to an unexpected cancellation, my doctor was able to see me within days. She put me through a battery of unpleasantries, from Pap test and mammogram to blood work and hormone levels.

Her conclusion, when I went back to discuss the results: I was as healthy as the proverbial pre-menopausal horse.

"But I feel like I'm floundering in soft cement," I told her. "Sometimes I skim right over the surface and other times I'm being sucked so deep I think I'm going to drown."

"What do you do then?" she asked.

"Hide in Lucy's room and cry."

"Does that happen often?"

"What's often?" I watched her closely, afraid what she'd say.

"Well, several times a day."

I almost laughed with relief. "The first week after Lucy left was bad, but not so much now."

She nodded. "What's your normal schedule like?"

"Too much spare time and not enough chocolate."

She smiled, another good sign. I mean, surely she wouldn't see the humour in my remark if I was approaching terminal meltdown. "What you need," she said, "is a health and fitness regime you can stick to. Could you join a fitness club? Pick up some new hobbies. Maybe look for a job?"

I squelched the mental image of me chained to a Bowflex™ exercise machine and said, "It's been years since I worked. I'm too old for the job market and hobbies seem so—" I searched for the right word, "—insipid. I don't want to be one of those women who while away their golden years with bridge and free bus trips to the casino. I want to contribute. I want to make the world better."

I was so startled by my unexpectedly insightful answer, I almost missed her assurance that I was decades from my golden years. *I want to make the world better!*

It seemed so obvious I was shocked by how long it had taken me to figure this out. And I felt ashamed of myself. While I had polled Dave, my friends, and even my doctor for advice on what to do next, I had been avoiding the One who was best equipped to help me.

My doctor and I talked a little longer; I'm not sure how much I took in. We shook hands and I headed for the Dollar Store, my mind in a whirl. Why the Dollar Store? To buy a journal.

As soon as I got home, I ran upstairs and knelt beside Lucy's bed. Quietly, but out loud, I began to pray. I prayed for a clear head, self-understanding, wisdom and guidance. I prayed out loud so I could hear myself—somehow it made my prayer feel more intentional and harder for God to ignore.

Contrary to what Dave, or everyone else, for that matter, might have thought, I *had* been listening to the piles of advice doled out over the past few months.

Now, I cracked open my new journal and labelled each page with their various suggestions: See the Doctor, Join a Health Club, Take Up a Hobby, Get a Job... Under each heading, I wrote, in point form, any insights, thoughts or pertinent information I might have on the subject.

On my See the Doctor page, I wrote what she'd told me about my health, including my weight (ugh) and my blood pressure (acceptable). For the Fitness Club page, I called every club in town, then wrote down their rates and any unique selling features the club offered, such as: women only, unlimited classes, tanning rooms, whirlpool tub…

Hobbies? What did I like to do? Read, garden, knit… What had I always wanted to learn? Calligraphy.

Job—now that was a toughie. I'd been a grocery store clerk, a telephone operator and a waitress back in my college days—none of which I wanted to repeat. What else could I do?

Dave had once (or maybe twice) suggested I make a list of all the things I'd done over the years we'd been married. He said this would help me identify what I enjoyed and/or excelled at, which brought to mind my quip about laundry. Some might consider me warped, but I actually enjoy organizing and putting away fresh-smelling clean clothes. I wrote Laundry at the top of my list with a caveat in block letters, NO LAUNDROMAT!

Although I had no teaching degree, I'd home-schooled Jeff and Lucy until they turned thirteen, so I put that next.

I'd taught Sunday School and led Bible studies. I'd even taught the kids in our church youth group to knit. It had been a project they adopted—knitting bright-coloured vests for babies in India— and I still chuckled when I remembered Jeff awkwardly wielding his knitting needles with as much finesse as a hockey player might show while trying to dance in ballet toe shoes.

I'd helped organize a couple of fundraisers for the local library and volunteered at their after-school reading program. I wrote that down next.

I'd driven people to doctor's appointments in the city. Hated that sooo much—not the helping people part, but the driving into the city part—that I'd only done it twice. HATED, I scribbled beside Driving.

I'd helped Jazz, a school chum of Lucy's who'd gotten pregnant at 15 years old, prepare for her new baby. Jazz's own mom, also a single parent, had admitted she'd neither the time or patience to help Jazz herself. So I taught Jazz how to bath the baby, what to feed her, how to decide which baby doodads were essential and what were luxuries, even how to manage her limited budget.

As I studied my notes, I started to notice a pattern. I liked helping and I liked teaching. Was there any way I could combine these two activities to create a meaningful future for myself? The possibilities seemed limitless. Like Lucy when she'd been choosing courses for her first year at university, I felt overwhelmed with the number of options available these days. My nebulous goal, teaching/helping, was too vague. I needed a way to narrow down the field.

When I told Dave, he was immediately onboard, eager to help me with the next phase—research. We brainstormed, clipped newspaper and magazine ads, hunted ideas online, and imagined the impossible. I even tried filling in one of those personality inventories. But perhaps more important than all those—though I don't negate their value—were the hours Dave and I spent talking and praying. Whenever I got discouraged, Dave reminded me that God had a purpose for this second half of my life. Even though my child-centred years were over, my Christ-centred years were not. God had created me for the future and had created a future for me.

It sounded great; I ached for it to be true.

I'm not sure when, amidst this process, the idea first emerged in my head—just a niggling, shapeless little quiver at the periphery of my imagination. Molecule by molecule, inch by inch, it grew, until one day I was at the grocery store. I kept running into this lady wearing a glorious turquoise sari under her overcoat, and her young, teen-aged son as they combed the aisles, hunting for the items on her grocery list.

She had apparently written her list in her mother tongue. I couldn't even guess what she was saying, but she'd read a few phrases aloud, and her son would scoot off and collect a half-dozen different cans of chickpeas or curry sauces. He'd then translate the English labels so she could understand the difference between each, and after she made her selection, he'd return the unwanted cans to their shelves.

The whole affair was taking ages, and her son kept trying to rush her, which only seemed to frustrate her and delay the process further.

It's too bad she can't read the labels herself, I thought. *Her son, if he had any imagination, would teach her. It would save him a lot of time and trouble in the long run.*

Boom! There it was, an idea in living colour. I could teach women like this lady to read English. In our small town, there weren't many services for recent immigrants to Canada. It must be frightening, I reasoned, to be thousands of miles away from anything familiar, unable to speak or read the language around you, suddenly, totally dependant on another to translate everything you see or hear.

I kept the idea to myself for a day, praying, imagining the possible obstacles, mulling them over, considering solutions, watching the idea take shape and solidify.

Dave loved it and helped me formulate a plan. We approached our pastor with it, and he agreed to bring our project proposal before the church board.

The Tuesday evening meeting I'd been invited to address had my knees knocking. Not that our church board was an archaic group of *Never-Been-Done-Befores.* They'd always been pleasant at congregational suppers and Christmas Cantatas—smiling, shaking hands, welcoming visitors. But chatting with them over coffee in the church hall was a far cry from standing before a room full of their dead-pan faces, and explaining why my new idea was worth their time.

By the time I was introduced, their meeting had been underway for over an hour. It was dark outside, and the windows in the board room acted like mirrors, reflecting back my image—hair smooth, neat grey suit, sensible pink nail polish on nervously fisted fingertips.

"We've been praying for ways to meet needs in our community," Pastor Smith said to the dozen men and women seated

266

around the long table. "This is a great opportunity for us to reach out and ask nothing in return."

I passed around a handout that Dave had helped design—I'd wanted it to look unquestionably professional—and described what I planned to do.

"How much will you charge?" asked one especially stern-faced man. He was the church treasurer.

"Nothing, if I have the use of a rent-free facility," I said, holding my breath.

A few board members nodded. The treasurer's frown intensified. They asked a few more questions that I did my best to answer, and then I was dismissed.

"How did it go?" Dave asked as I stepped into the hallway.

"Honestly? It was hard to gauge their response. I'd hoped for more enthusiasm. On the other hand, they didn't turf me out on my ear." I tried to sound positive.

Dave hugged me close. "If they don't want to help we'll go somewhere else. I know God is in this, and He'll find you the perfect location—one that's warm and inviting and unintimidating. Who knows, maybe a church isn't the right venue."

"Do you think we should wait to hear what they decide, or just go home?" I asked.

Pastor Smith stuck his head out of the boardroom door. He'd heard what I'd just said. "Why not go for coffee and celebrate? It may be your last quiet evening for a while." His encouraging nod kick-started my heart into overdrive.

I grabbed Dave's arm to keep myself from bouncing to the ceiling. "You mean they're giving us a room?"

"Giving *you* a room." Dave kissed me soundly. "This is all *your* doing."

Pastor Smith grinned, apparently enjoying our reaction to his news. "You have a room *and* their blessing."

I squeezed my hands over my heart, afraid it might burst from my chest. "Thank you so much for your support." Until that moment I hadn't realized how much hope I'd invested in the project. Truly God was good.

"It's us who should be thanking you," Pastor Smith answered.

With a wink and a wave, he sent us on our way.

Dave and I shared celebratory coffee and double-glazed doughnuts at Tim Hortons. Sitting at a table-for-two overlooking the drive-thru, Dave reached across and squeezed my hand. "This has been an amazing few months," he said. "There were times, watching you struggle with what to do next, I thought my heart would break. I *so* wanted to fix it for you, make it so you wouldn't hurt so much. But I watched you hang in there, seeking God's direction, and now He's opened this door. I'm in awe."

"We still have to see if it works," I said, trying to keep my feet on the ground.

Dave's smile made my heart skip a beat. "My love, it already has."

Forgiven

Nonfiction[1]

Angelina Fast-Vlaar

Susan struggled against the heavy black blanket that was smothering her. Frantically, she tried to bring her hands up, but someone was pinning them down. She groaned and gulped for air, but the blanket was covering her nose and mouth. Then, curiously, she saw a faint outline of Ken's face floating in the room above the bed. Ken, trying to smother her! She fought back harder, knowing she had to find a way to keep breathing.

Susan woke from her nightmare with a start and sat on the edge of the bed, shaking. The disturbing dreams she'd been having off and on for the last several months all had the same theme—Ken, a church committee chairman, was smothering her with a thick black blanket while Susan desperately fought to keep breathing. Fully awake now, she cradled her face in her hands and moaned, *No, not another nightmare— not here, not while we're on holidays.*

Susan slipped out of the bedroom without waking her husband Rob, and tip-toed onto their tiny deck. It overlooked the inner courtyard of a condominium complex on the beach in Gulf Shores, Alabama, where they'd rented a unit for two months to escape the Canadian winter. It was still dark, but the courtyard was lit by a tall, shaded lamp with a fat, round bulb, whose reflection in the swimming pool looked like a yellow harvest moon. Susan inhaled the night's silent peace. The rhythmic sound of the Gulf's waves lapping the beach calmed her rattled nerves.

Her mind wandered back to last spring when the nightmares had begun—after that infamous Sunday School committee meeting—the meeting where she'd suggested she teach a course on communications to the adult class. She'd gotten carried away with enthusiasm because she'd designed the course and taught it successfully at another church. After the meeting, Ken, the chairman, had cornered her in the church parking lot and spewed out a tirade of angry words. "Who do you think you are, suggesting some fancy course outside our curriculum?" he'd barked. His eyes had flashed, his voice risen to a high pitch. "I *hate* your uppity attitude. You're selfish, unrealistic, unreliable, irresponsible…"

Backed against her car, Susan had covered her cheeks with her hands as if to protect them from the sting of his words. Too shocked to speak, all she had managed to say in her defence was, "You are *so* wrong." Then—as Ken's tirade continued—"I'm resigning from the committee."

"Fine!" Ken had spat out the word, turned on his heels, and marched away.

The pain of that incident and the nightmares it had triggered still resonated as Susan leaned against the deck railing and took a deep breath. Puzzled and exhausted, she crawled back into bed.

Rob's cheerful voice woke her in the morning, "Ready for our walk on the beach?"

"Be right down," she replied.

They walked hand in hand in silence on the cool sugary sand, the water sparkling in the morning sun. Finally, Rob said, "Why so quiet?"

"It happened again—the nightmare."

Rob stopped walking and faced her. "Sue, I thought you were over that, had left it all behind."

"It followed me," she said simply.

"Sue, you're a strong person. You teach. You help others. You do *not* have to let Ken's anger influence you. You *can* let it go."

"Hon, you know how I've prayed, tried to forgive him the best I know how."

"Yes, I know." He took her hand and they continued walking.

"I thought I was over it, but the nightmare brought it all back, and now it feels as if there's a big black blob in my heart."

"But you know who you are, Sue. Let it be."

Tears welled up in Susan's eyes and she blurted out, "The nerve of him—screaming those insults at me! And no other committee members around to hear him." She stopped walking. "I wish I had confronted him afterwards. It upsets me that I seemed so weak; it was as if his shouting paralyzed me."

"But I called him that very night, remember?" Rob said, trying to soothe the situation. "And his story was very different. He basically denied it, said it was all 'a misunderstanding.'"

She backed away from Rob and glared at him. "So it's a case of 'he said/she said,' isn't it?" Susan replied with a bite in her voice. "And the 'he said' always wins, doesn't it?"

Rob reached for her.

Pent–up tears spilled from her eyes. She fished a tissue from her pocket, hoping the other morning strollers wouldn't notice.

"I know he hurt you," Rob whispered, pulling her close. "But Ken is a relative and I don't want a family squabble on my hands."

"I know."

Rob lifted her chin to face him. "Enough for now, okay? Let's enjoy the day. Look, we're almost at the Best Western Restaurant— our favourite breakfast place."

"All right," she sighed, blotting her eyes.

Over bacon and eggs, Rob said, "Let's drive into Foley, visit the library, and have coffee and ice cream at Stacey's."

"You're on," she replied.

At the library, Susan jotted down her name on the computer waiting list in order to check their e-mail. While Rob found a magazine and an easy chair, Susan wandered aimlessly among the stacks. In one of the aisles, she noticed the word "God" on a book's spine.

Curious, she backtracked, removed the book, opened it at random and read, "From time to time an angel of the Lord would come down and stir up the waters. The first one into the pool after each such disturbance would be cured of whatever disease he had" (John 5:4).

Susan recognized the passage—the pool of Bethesda was one of several purification pools at the Jewish temple in Jerusalem in Jesus' time. Those who needed healing sat around this pool. Once in a while, as the story goes, an angel would come to stir the water, and whoever was the first to enter was healed.

The book's author suggested that the mystery of the Bethesda pool may also happen within us. Sometimes an angel may come to stir up what's hidden in the recesses of our lives—pain or grief we've pushed away. If we're willing to enter into our "troubling event" and address it, we may find healing.

The desk clerk announced, "Susan, a computer is available for you," so she replaced the book on the shelf, and went to check their e-mail.

Afterwards, they drove to Stacey's Olde Tyme Soda Fountain. It was an historic, happy place, a favourite with locals as well as with vacationing "snowbirds." Rob poured them each a cup of coffee and dropped two dimes in the jar beside the pot—probably the price a half century ago.

They sat by a window to sip the delicious brew and watch the shop's miniature train make its rounds on an elevated track, then they browsed for gifts and ordered an ice cream sundae at the store's antique soda fountain.

But no matter how Susan busied herself, the passage she had read at the library kept interrupting her thoughts. *My nightmare— is an angel coming to stir up what I still haven't laid to rest?*

She struggled with it all day. That evening, as she was updating her journal, in an attempt to face the issue once more, she found a loose page and wrote down each of the hurtful statements Ken had made, then tucked the page in the back of her journal.

The next morning, Susan felt compelled to find that book, so she returned to the library and wandered the aisles, unsure where she had seen it or what the title was. At last, she found it: *God's Joyful Surprise: Finding Yourself Loved* by Sue Monk Kidd.[2]

After lunch, Susan and Rob took lounge chairs and books to the beach. She was anxious to read the whole of Kidd's spiritual journey, but she found herself leafing back again and again to chapter one to reread the author's comments about having the courage to confront the painful experiences from our past, and the "empty, broken places" in our lives, in order to find healing.

At mid-afternoon, Susan got up to stretch. "I need a break," she said. "See you later."

"Sure, Hon," Rob answered.

Susan took the car for a leisurely drive along the beach. The Gulf water glistened on her right; brightly painted houses, nestled among trees, lined the left side of the road. A majestic church built of pink and cream brick came into view, towering above the trees. A cross on the steeple shone like a beacon. She hadn't planned to stop, but at the last moment she veered her car into the parking lot. A few cars were parked there, but no one was in sight.

Susan approached the small chapel adjacent to the main sanctuary and pulled on an oversized handle. The tall, heavy wooden door slowly opened. She stepped inside and breathed in the soft-scented silence. Filtered light streamed in from stained glass windows: deep blue, scarlet, green, gold—royal colours. Sculptured plaques, painted in soft pastels, hung on the walls. A single candle glowed in the hushed stillness beside a life-sized statue of Jesus.

As Susan sank into a pew at the back, a fountain of tears seemed to gush open inside her. All the hurt, the anger, and the confusion about the recurring nightmares poured out. For more than an hour, she cried and questioned. *Why can't I let it go? Why did I just stand there and let Ken say all those nasty things? Why didn't I at least explain, have a conversation, come to an understanding? Why did I let Rob make that phone call that nullified it all? Why am I behaving like a victim? And why do I keep having the recurring nightmare about the black blanket smothering me?*

Black blanket... Susan had a sudden recollection...

She is three. She is in their house in Northern Holland. Mother blankets all the windows with ugly, dark brown material.

Susan hates those curtains. They make her feel closed in, trapped. She wants to look out into the yard, see the barn and the chicken-run, even if it is dusk.

But Mother is adamant. "The curtains need to be tightly shut," she says. "This is ' blackout' so planes can't see the lights in our house."

Susan curls up her nose. The curtains make her feel unsafe, as if something ominous is lurking outside.

The black curtains; a black blanket... Was there a connection?

A black blanket to hide our light; a black blanket to silence my "voice."

More memories tumbled into her mind about World War II and the great devastation it brought to her country, as well as the rest of Europe, during 1940–1945. She remembered the burning planes, the bombs, the explosions, the city gone up in flames. The deaths: the lady in the houseboat killed by a bomb, the boy down the street blown to pieces by a land mine.

Susan pondered, *How did I, as a young child, process it all—the oppression, the five years of continual danger? Did I internalize the powerlessness of the adults, let alone the children? What did I do with the constant fear I felt?* Her heart began to race as her thoughts returned to her childhood...

Four Nazi soldiers march down the driveway as if they're on parade. Guns slung over their shoulders, boots clicking. The sight of the soldiers terrifies Susan and she runs to hide behind the hedge surrounding the sandbox.

The soldiers approach her dad and shout, "*Wo sind Ihre Fahrräder?*" ("Where are your bicycles?")

Dad points to the bicycle shed, and opens the sliding door. Susan, peering through the hedge, sees only two bikes in the shed. And they have no tires!

The soldier angrily raises his voice, raises his gun and repeats his question. Dad says these are the only bikes he has.

Susan wonders, *Has Dad hidden the bikes? Have other soldiers stolen them?*

The soldier jabs Dad with his gun, spits at him and yells "*Schweinhundmensch!*"

Susan knows the word is a degrading slur and literally means "swine-dog-person." She watches as Dad silently takes the insult. *Will they shoot him?* She hides her face in her hands and trembles.

Shaking, reliving the fear, Susan vividly recalled another scene.

Susan is playing in the schoolyard with some friends. The Nazis have occupied the school, so there are no classes, but children are allowed to play on the playground. She needs to use the washroom and, carefree, skips to the back of the building to the row of outside toilets.

As she opens the first door, an ear-splitting blast of angry foreign words hits her like a wave, almost knocking her over. She struggles to stay on her feet and bangs the door shut.

Terrified, she runs home as fast as her wobbly legs can carry her, looking over her shoulder to see if the soldier is following. She plops down behind the sandbox hedge. She trembles a long time but doesn't tell anyone she angered a Nazi soldier and he yelled "*Schweinhund-mensch*" at her.

Sitting on a pew in a peaceful chapel so many miles and years removed from that scene, a shiver ran up Susan's spine. *Are these memories, and all that happened so long ago during the War, my "troubling event," the "broken, empty places" I need to confront?*

She thought further. *Did Ken's loud, derogatory name-calling somehow tap into my past? Do I automatically behave like a helpless child when confronted with cruel, angry insults?*

Susan got up and walked to the front of the chapel and stood beside the glowing candle.

How much influence do years of childhood trauma have in later life? she asked herself. *Is a "victim mentality" born during those years? Is it true that "we are our memories"?*

After turning it all over in her mind, Susan walked around the perimeter of the chapel to view the series of 14 plaques that depicted Christ's walk to Calvary. She knew the story well. Jesus condemned to death, berated, ridiculed, insulted, whipped. Tears welled up as she lingered at an image of Jesus bent over, arms and hands raised in an attempt to protect His face from a beating. She remembered how she had covered her face as if to protect herself from Ken's angry words. Yet what were the few "lashes" she had received compared to all that Jesus had endured—for her?

She crossed to the other side of the chapel to ponder the remaining plaques: Jesus nailed to the cross, more insults, more pain, and then the famous words, "Father, forgive them, for they do not know what they are doing" (Luke 23:34).

Ken doesn't know me, Susan reasoned. *He doesn't know the work I've done; my enthusiasm to try something new. But then, do I really know him?* As she tried to analyze the issue from his perspective, she abruptly realized, *To feel secure, Ken probably needs to have a plan in place and work that plan. And maybe the loud name-calling, the expression of anger was part of his past!*

Father, help me forgive, she prayed.

And then something else broke through and she asked herself, *What about me? What about all the things I've said about Ken as I related the story to family and friends? What about all the imaginary conversations I've had with Ken, telling him exactly what I thought of him, calling him names, being angry, hateful, unforgiving...*

Tears of remorse spilled as she confessed, *Lord, I see now that I'm just as guilty. I've said more than Ken ever said. I need Your forgiveness. Please forgive the anger and ill will I've harboured against one of Your children. Help me to forgive Ken as You've forgiven me.*

Quieted, and with new perspective, Susan walked out of the dim chapel into the soft light of a late afternoon. As she drove back along the beach, the sinking sun was now directly ahead, casting a shimmering path on the water. When she arrived at their condo, Rob had supper almost ready.

"Where did you go?" he asked with concern.

"I sat in a church. I think I made some connections."

"Oh?"

"Memories of being a small child in the War."

Having experienced the same war, Rob looked at her with compassion. "You're so brave, Sue."

"I don't feel brave at all. I feel rather messed up."

Something was still troubling her. She couldn't put her finger on it, so after their meal she mumbled, "I'm going out for a walk."

"It's almost dark," Rob said, but she had shut the door before he finished the sentence.

She took off her flip-flops and walked barefoot along the water, now black and heaving in the wind. Foam swirled around her ankles. She observed the wild water and thought, *It looks like an angel has "stirred up" the water! I must jump in!* Defying the waves, she waded in.

It felt eerie, yet exhilarating, to have her jeans and T-shirt soak up the cool water. While she told herself, *This is not a good idea. It's dark; there are currents,* she didn't climb back on shore. Instead, something inside her goaded her deeper into the ocean.

She tried to swim, battling the waves. The physical fight seemed to mirror her inner battle. Gradually, she began to understand what she was struggling with. *If I truly forgive Ken, that means I have to let go of my anger and stop talking about him. Can I do that?*

She stood up and, with her feet firmly planted on the sandy bottom, let the waist-high waves crash against her. She shouted into the wind, "Go ahead waves, crash all you want! I am strong. I can withstand your force. I am not a small helpless child. I am not a victim. Ken is not a Nazi soldier. He has no power over me. He cannot silence me. What he says has nothing to do with who I am."

After hesitating a moment, she looked up and said determinedly, "With God's help I *can* forgive, I *will* forgive. I *will* let go."

Susan turned and realized how far she had come from shore, and how cold she felt. At that moment, she detected the faint outline of a person standing at the edge of the beach in the dark, watching her. Susan moved to her right; the figure followed. Trying to stifle growing fear, she pushed through the waves in the opposite direction, but again the figure tracked her. For an instant she panicked, feeling trapped. Then she heard Rob's anxious, yet comforting, call drift faintly over the waves. "Susan, come home! Susan, come home!"

Rob, dear faithful Rob, she thought, her eyes filling with tears.

Slowly, laboriously, straining now against the tug of the undertow, Susan hauled her weighted self to shore.

Rob reached out his hand and helped her onto the beach.

"What's this all about?" he asked.

"Well, the angel stirred the water, so I jumped in," she quipped, trying to inject a touch of humour.

"This is not funny," Rob replied. She heard desperation in his voice. Rob started for home and she walked behind him, like a scolded child, her sagging wet jeans slurping the boardwalk with each step she took.

Back at the condo, she had a hot shower, dressed, and came back down into the kitchen. "I need to be finished with this," she said, her eyes red and swollen.

"Yes, you do," he answered.

The concern she heard in his voice touched her deeply and she said, "I don't know what else to do."

"Well, what did you do with that special group of students at school?"

"What do you mean?"

"How did you teach them that forgiving means letting go?"

She stared at him for a long moment before answering. "You mean when I had them write their pain on pieces of paper and then burned them in a pie plate?"

"Yes." And after a moment, "Well?" His deep blue eyes held hers.

"That's for twelve-year-olds."

"Is it?"

Still resisting, Susan countered, "We don't have a pie plate."

"We'll use a pot lid."

"We don't have any matches."

Rob still held her eyes. "I'll roll up some newsprint, light it on the stove element."

It took a long moment before Susan turned, went upstairs and opened her journal to fetch the sheet of paper that contained her pain. She unfolded the sheet and added one more sentence.

Back in the kitchen, she cut each sentence on the paper into a strip.

She looked at Rob and said, "You need to tell me what you think of each statement." She read the first one. "You are selfish."

"That's the last thing you are," Rob replied.

She put the strip of paper in the pot lid.

"You are unreliable."

"Completely false," Rob said, anger rising in his voice.

Susan went through the whole list and Rob refuted each statement. Her last slip read, "You are a *Schweinhundmensch*."

"Where does this come from?" Rob asked, surprised.

"The Nazis."

Horrified, Rob exclaimed, "I know they labelled us all with that derogatory term, but they even said it to *you*, a young innocent girl?"

"Yes. And maybe that's what's at the bottom of all this upset."

Rob nodded slowly.

Susan added the last strip to the pile in the pot lid. Rob lit the roll of newsprint on one end and held it to the strips of paper in the upturned lid above the sink. The fire curled each strip, then devoured them. Tendrils of ash floated up.

"It has to be completely gone," Rob said. He turned on the faucet, filled the lid with water, held the pool of ashen pain for a moment, and then poured it down the drain.

"It's gone," Susan murmured, peering down the drain hole.

"Yes, Susan, it's gone." Rob held her close.

She lingered long and then said, "Thanks, Hon."

"I love you too," he whispered. "Go out on the deck; I'll bring you some tea."

Susan stepped outside into the soft glow of the courtyard lamp. The light danced on the wind-ruffled water in the pool. The enclosed space provided some shelter from the wind but Susan could hear the roar of waves crashing on the beach behind the condo.

Rob came out, placed two steaming cups on the table, and joined her at the railing.

"How are you?" he asked ever so gently.

"So much happened today that I feel overwhelmed. But I feel so free."

"I'm glad."

After a long silence, Susan said, "I'm listening to the thunder of the waves rolling on the beach. Do you know what the sound reminds me of?"

"No, what?"

"The rumble of Canadian tanks rolling into our village in Holland in '45 to liberate us. We cheered and waved and the Canadian soldiers waved back and smiled and tossed us chocolate bars."

"I have similar memories," Rob whispered, choking back tears. "What a day that was!"

"The oppression was over, we were free. And even though there's no comparison as to the scale of events, that's how I feel now—free."

"And you were brave enough to do the work, Sue. Come on, let's sit down and have our tea."

"No, Hon, one more thing. Look at the pool. See how the light reflected in the water from the lamp seems to shine all the way to the bottom?"

"Yes?"

"It reminds me of my journey today."

"How so?"

"Well, once I found the courage to enter into my 'pool,' into my 'broken, empty places,' as Kidd put it in her book, there was light to show me what lay buried, what I needed to face, what I needed to do."

"Yeah, I see," Rob said, squeezing her shoulders.

"I'll always treasure the image of this pool—the healing it represents. Healing, like those people so long ago who found God's healing at the Bethesda pool."

Rob's squeeze on her shoulders tightened. "I'm so glad God led you to some answers," he whispered. "This may be our best holiday yet!"

1. Names and some incidents have been changed to protect identities.

2. Sue Monk Kidd, *God's Joyful Surprise: Finding Yourself Loved* (San Francisco: HarperOne, 1989).

Praise from a Cantankerous Soul

Nonfiction

David Kitz

Anticipation has a way of heightening our expectations. The long wait was finally over. It was a beautiful day, and it all started so well.

For many years my wife had told me she wanted her own desk and her own bookcase. It would help her be more organized; every woman needs her own space. I couldn't agree more. The only problem was money—there was never enough of it. My income from supply teaching was very unpredictable. With a young family and a mortgage to pay, there always seemed to be more month left than money. These extras were always put on hold.

Then one spring day our income tax refund cheque arrived and Karen renewed her perennial plea. This year the roof didn't need shingles, the driveway didn't need paving, but Karen did need that long-delayed desk and bookcase. At long last, the time had come to answer her request and this time a shortage of funds was not standing in the way.

After some judicious shopping, she narrowed the range of furniture choices, and then brought me in to help in the final selection process. Together we chose a compact and versatile three-drawer desk with a fold-down top that acted as the writing surface. She loved the little compartments that could be used to store papers and valuables. A matching three-shelf bookcase completed our order. Both selections were unfinished furniture made of solid maple.

We both love solid wood because of its grain and texture. Of course, solid hardwood furniture is supremely durable as well. I gave some consideration to finishing the furniture myself, but a glance at my work schedule led us to decide it would be easier to have the furniture company apply the wood stain of our choice, and then we would pick up the finished product upon completion. We paid our hard-earned money and waited.

About a week later, the call came. The desk and bookcase were ready for pickup. But our car was too small for the job. No problem. Our neighbour kindly lent us his pickup truck. Now this old Ford had seen better days. When Rick briefly introduced me to Old Betsy, he mentioned that her rear tailgate was a bit cantankerous. I practiced closing it. Then Rick handed me the keys and watched as I drove off with my wife by my side. We headed off like two giddy kids on a Christmas morning race to the tree.

At the furniture warehouse, the bookcase and desk were packed in corrugated cardboard boxes. We did a quick inspection to confirm they were the right pieces, finished with the right stain, and then we loaded them onto Old Betsy. I slammed the tailgate shut and we set out on the twenty-minute return trip to our home.

Moments later, as we drove down the four-lane expressway at 100 kilometres per hour, Old Betsy's tailgate popped open and the bookcase toppled out onto the hard black asphalt.

I slammed on the brakes and pulled off to the shoulder. My wife was frantic; okay, we were both frantic. Even at a distance, I could tell the bookcase was probably still intact inside the corrugated cardboard box. Perhaps the damage was minor, or so I hoped.

I jumped out of the truck and began running back to this hapless box. Three quarters of it lay on the paved shoulder—only one corner protruded onto the far right lane of the busy four-lane expressway. As I ran toward it on the shoulder, several cars zoomed right by. They didn't even need to swerve to avoid it.

I thought it was safe. But…

The next vehicle was a twenty-ton cement truck. It did not swerve. It bore down relentlessly on that cardboard box. What I saw next was an explosion. On impact, the bookcase exploded out of its cardboard box. Shelves and splintered pieces of wood went flying through the air and into the ditch.

It all happened so fast. In just an instant our long-awaited treasure was turned into a mangled, splintered mess.

While Karen cautiously backed the truck toward the scene of this explosion, I made my final approach on foot. I gathered the debris out of the ditch, put it back in Old Betsy, and slammed the cantankerous tailgate shut. I gave my wife a hug, hopped back in the truck and again started the drive toward home.

This should never have happened! A thousand regrets flooded my mind. Why? Why this disaster? What did we do to deserve this mess?

Karen was in tears.

Strangely, on another level, a different set of thoughts was welling up from within me. They went something like this: *"Give thanks in all circumstances, for this is God's will for you in Christ Jesus."*[1]

And then, from the distant recesses of my spirit, I heard, *"Praise the Lord, O my soul; all my inmost being, praise His holy name. Praise the Lord, O my soul, and forget not all His benefits."*[2]

What lunacy was this? Why should I give thanks to God in the middle of this disaster? If God cared one whit about me—about us—why hadn't He prevented this fiasco? My God is bigger than a cement truck. He could have steered that twenty-ton behemoth around our bookcase. Better still, the Lord Almighty could have kept that tailgate from popping open. And now, at this moment, I'm supposed to praise Him? What insanity is this?

Again, I heard the Spirit's prompting, *"Praise the Lord, O my soul; all my inmost being, praise His holy name. Praise the Lord, O my soul, and forget not all His benefits."*[3]

There are bigger things in life than a broken bookcase, I conceded. Under my breath I began to mumble, "Bless the Lord, O my soul and all that is within me, bless His holy name."[4]

Those were tough words to whisper at that moment. You see, my soul doesn't always want to bless the Lord. If I'm going to praise Him, shouldn't it be in church while the choir sings softly in the background? Why praise Him on an expressway, with my wife sobbing at my side, while I have fresh images of a splintered bookcase lodged in my brain? There are times when cursing the Lord would seem to be a far more appropriate response than praising Him. Surely this was one such time.

The reminders in my mind continued, *"Be joyful always; pray continually; give thanks in all circumstances, for this is God's will for you in Christ Jesus."*[5]

I wondered why God was bringing these Scriptures to my mind now. I would much rather blame Him and feel totally miserable, than give thanks in these wretched circumstances.

But God's Spirit would not relent. I can't say I heard this audibly. But if I were to translate what I felt God was saying to me at that moment, it would go something like this: *"Just shut up. Quit your bellyaching, Mr. Know-it-all."* (God sometimes needs to be blunt with me.) *"All I'm asking you to do is praise Me. Praise Me, whether you feel like it or not. You don't know the beginning from the end, Mr. Wise Guy. Don't you think I'm bigger than a few pieces of shattered wood?"*

In sullen reluctance, I agreed. And I obeyed. In my thoughts, I began to praise God. That's right. I began to praise the Lord God Almighty who let my wife's long-awaited, brand-new, not-even-out-of-the-box bookcase get hit by a twenty-ton cement truck.

Praising the Lord?

Yes, praise the Lord!

Now which Lord was that again?

The Lord, "who forgives all your sins and heals all your diseases."[6]

Ah, yes, *that* Lord. He really is quite wonderful. Imagine forgiving all my sins, every last one of them. That's a lot of sins. That's a lot of forgiving.

Praise the Lord. He's quite some God.

Which God was that again?

The Lord who "heals all your diseases."

Ah yes, *that* Lord. He really is quite fantastic. Imagine healing all my sicknesses and all my injuries too, from my childhood to this very moment. Now that's a whole lot of pain and woe. Gone. It's all gone. I don't feel any of it now. Praise the Lord. No aches or pains—that's amazing. He's an awesome God.

Now tell me again, which Lord is this?

The Lord, "who redeems your life from the pit and crowns you with love and compassion."[7]

Oh yes, *that* Lord. He redeemed me—redeemed me with His blood. He went to the whipping post, was stripped naked, and nailed through hands and feet to a cross. The Lord who was despised and rejected.[8] The Lord who came to His own, but His own would not receive Him[9]. That forsaken Lord who loved me to death. The Lord my Redeemer, that's the Lord I praise.

I praised the One who pulled me out of the pit—the pit of self-pity, the pit of despair, the sucking pit of self-indulgence that spirals only downwards. He redeemed me from that sinking pit. And now He is the One I praise.

As I continued to drive, I reached over to give Karen's hand a quick squeeze and then returned to my inner dialogue.

Jesus doesn't just redeem. He crowns me with love and compassion. Now that is beyond amazing. Though I don't deserve it, He puts a crown of love on my head. He wore a crown of thorns, but on *my* head He puts a crown of love and compassion. He encircles my head—my stubborn, sin-drenched head—with love and compassion. Awesome. What an awesome God!

Praise the Lord!

I'm a bit slow today, God. Remember? I've got a splintered bookcase on my brain. Could You just remind me—remind me one more time? Which Lord are You?

The Lord "who satisfies your desires with good things, so that your youth is renewed like the eagle's."[10]

Oh yes, Lord, You do satisfy me. You satisfy me with a thousand good things. I live like a king. My every need is met; every comfort is mine. I have abundance. Compared to billions on this planet today, and compared to billions going back through the ages, I am blessed—blessed beyond measure.

You renew my strength. You put a glint in my eye, a spring in my step, and a well of hope in my heart. My youth is renewed like the eagle's. Now I'm soaring. "Praise the Lord!" I said. "Praise the Lord! Praise the Lord, O my soul!"

By the time we got home I was feeling much better and so was my wife. I believe Karen had been having her own conversation with God.

As for that bookcase, I'm glancing at it even as I write this. It looks great!

Some carpentry clamps and a little wood glue can work wonders. Despite being hit by a twenty-ton cement truck, only one shelf was broken beyond repair.

While I was replacing that shelf at a woodworking shop at a middle school nearby, a friend encouraged me to take a university course in design and technology. That course led to a permanent teaching contract; it rerouted my whole career and brought me into a line of work I simply love.

And I started on that new route because of a broken bookcase.

Praise the Lord!

I said, "Praise the Lord, O my soul!"

Yes, praise the Lord! In any situation, it's one of the best things a cantankerous soul can do.

1. 1 Thessalonians 5:18

2. Psalm 103:1–2

3. *Ibid.*

4. Psalm 103:1–2 NKJV

5. 1 Thessalonians 5:16–18

6. Psalm 103:3

7. Psalm 103:4

8. Isaiah 53:3

9. John 1:11

10. Psalm 103:5

Charlie

 Nonfiction

Adele Simmons

"Could you do us a favour?" The nurse tipped her head and studied me.

"What's that?" I had learned not to say yes on impulse.

"Charlie's not feeling great today. He missed your chapel service. Would you bring your guitar down the hall and give him a song or two?"

An easy decision. "You bet. I'll tidy up my equipment later. Lead the way."

The other patients waved good-bye as we left the common room where we had chapel on Friday afternoons. The chaplain took up his post by the door to shake hands with them and promise to pray for the concerns they had shared. There's a lot to be concerned about in a hospital.

This group of patients consisted of about 25 adults, ages 35 to 82. Some had been in the hospital weeks, others in long-term care for years. Most shuffled along in their slippers, leaning on the walls for support. Others used walkers or wheelchairs. Some pulled IV carts or oxygen tanks.

The nurse led me into Charlie's room. His lip curled when he saw me and he turned away to look out the window. He was 79, grey-haired, grey-faced, wrinkled and sick. Papery skin hung over the bones of his hands. White sheets hung over the bones of his legs. With swollen arthritic knuckles, Charlie tugged at the sheet and pulled it up to his armpits. I knew the nurses tried to cheer him up, tried to make him attend activities and chapel. He set his jaw.

The nurse smiled. "Hi, Charlie. I don't have to introduce you. I'm sure you two know each other. I'll leave you to chat for a few minutes." And she quickly made her exit.

Charlie eyed me as I squeezed past the end of the bed and eased onto the chair crammed between the bed and the window.

His stare was daunting. This man was a sour pickle. No way would he smile back at me.

It's hard to balance a guitar in a chair that has arms, so I perched on the edge of the seat with my knees wedged against the bed.

Whitby General Hospital in Whitby, Ontario, is a friendly place. For years I had supported the ministry of various chaplains. I found out what patients liked, learned new songs, chose hymns, led the singing, and sang solos for special events, such as memorial services. The hospital's social director even asked me to sing for their pub nights, although she stammered through her request, trying not to offend me, a blatant Christian. I chuckled. I know 2,000 songs, old and new, gospel, contemporary, rock and roll, big band, and war songs. I was glad to oblige. A tender melody can ease pain for a moment and refresh a cherished memory.

I felt appreciated by the staff. And I felt God smile on me. But now, Charlie's leer dared me to just try to sing some sappy gospel song. Would I sing "Jesus Loves Me" and risk a tirade of curses?

"Hi, Charlie. The nurse said you're feeling really sick today. She asked me to sing for you."

Charlie clenched his fists and his teeth.

This was bigger than irritation. This was a battle. I needed a plan.

Interesting how the Holy Spirit helps just when you need an idea. Immediately, I was reminded that God uses everything, both noble and ignoble.

Although I now worked in business management, for years I had ministered and entertained through music. Thanks to my entertainer mom, I was raised on three generations of music—her own World War II, her mom's Great War, and her grandmother's ballads from the 1800s. I learned all those songs plus my own baby boomer tunes. And thanks to the bar scene of my mother's entertainment act and the military life of our soldier father, I also learned a few songs that weren't exactly appropriate for polite company.

I was struck with inspiration.

"Charlie, I've got just the song for you," I said. I smacked a loud chord on the guitar, inhaled, threw back my head and let go with a raunchy voice and my best country twang.

"Cigareetes and whuskey and wild, wild women; They'll drive you crazy, they'll drive you insane."[1]

I whooped and drove the bass strings of my guitar in a typical country walk-up to the next chord and continued the chorus, "Cigareetes and whuskey and wild, wild women; They'll drive you crazy, they'll drive you insane."

One corner of Charlie's mouth twitched.

"Ah, you know that one, eh, Charlie?"

Charlie looked at me, but his gaze was less provoked and more interested.

"Know any war songs?" I asked while I strummed.

His scratchy voice was muffled but proud. "I'm Navy. Spent three years on a Corvette."

I smiled and wailed into another song, "All the nice girls love a sailor; All the nice girls love a tar…"[2]

Now the other side of Charlie's mouth turned up and he actually smirked. "What would you know about it?" he challenged. "You're too young."

"Not too young to know that a tar is a sailor."

My sparring seemed to impress him. But we were headed somewhere more meaningful.

I got serious. "Great old songs, aren't they? Bring back any memories for you?"

Charlie sobered. "Met my wife in England. London, 1942. Got married in two weeks and left for France the next day. She stood by me. Died last year."

Fingering a softer melody, I crooned, "There'll be bluebirds over the white cliffs of Dover, tomorrow, just you wait and see…"[3]

As I sang out the ballad, Charlie whispered the words with me, but I could scarcely hear him. We sang the ending together, "… when the world is free."

He took a deep breath. "Vera Lynn," he said. "That was her song through the war. She made it famous. We all sang it. Heard it everywhere."

I nodded and plucked a gentle rhythm on guitar. "If you know that, I bet you know this one." I rolled into "Oh Danny boy, the pipes, the pipes are calling…"[4]

Charlie let me hear his voice this time. His steely blue eyes were moist and he gazed into mine as we sang, "Oh Danny boy, Oh Danny boy, I love… you… so." His breath ran out on the last note and I sang alone.

Charlie closed his eyes and swallowed. Then he looked out the window.

"I have two sons," he said. "They live ten minutes away with the grandkids. Haven't seen any of them for six months."

I touched his hand. My heart heard. "That stinks."

He shared with passion just what it stank like. I agreed.

"Hey, Charlie, do you know this one?" I changed key and strummed a new rhythm. "It is no secret what God can do; What He's done for others, He'll do for you. With arms wide open, He'll pardon you…"[5]

Charlie knew it. Four tears ran down his cheeks and caught together in the creases around his mouth as he sang with me. His voice cracked. He wiped his chin.

"She sang that to me. All the time. I was pretty grumpy when I first got sick. She'd sing and pray. I didn't appreciate it. What I'd give now…" His voice trailed off.

"You're still pretty grumpy, Charlie."

He chuckled. "I suppose I am." He was quiet, gentle, vulnerable. "Pain does that. Pain all day, pain all night. Pain so bad, my head is full of curses."

"God knows," I said. "He's on your side."

It was the right time now. No risk of a cursing tirade. He was open. I tiptoed into the song, "Jesus loves me, this I know…"[6]

Charlie was right with me. He sang the next words and his tears flowed freely. "For the Bible tells me so…"

He tugged a tissue out of the box on his night table and brought it to his eyes. His gnarly knuckles scrubbed the tissue hard into his face.

"Yes, Jesus loves me…" My own tears were close. When the song ended, it grew quiet. I stood and touched his hand.

Charlie let me hug him. His bony arms and hands hurt my back with his pressure.

"Come back," he said as he waved good-bye.

I felt God smile on our bawdy ministry time together.

We never spoke again. Charlie died six days later. Seems God can use the strangest things to show His love.

1. Tim Spencer, "Cigareetes, Whuskey and Wild, Wild Women" (Louisville, Ky.: Tim Spencer Music Inc., 1947; copyright renewed, assigned to Unichappell Music Inc.; Rightsong Music, Publisher).

2. Likely Fred Godfrey; public credit given to his colleagues A. J. Mills and Bennett Scott, "Ship Ahoy, All the Nice Girls Love a Sailor" (London: The Star Music Publishing Co. Ltd.; B. Feldman & Co., 1909).

3. Nat Burton (words) and Walter Kent (music), "White Cliffs of Dover"(New York: Shapiro Bernstein & Co. Inc., 1941).

4. Frederic Weatherly (words, 1910), traditional melody ("Londonderry Air," added 1912), "Danny Boy" (England). Public Domain.

5. Stuart Hamblen, "It Is No Secret (What God Can Do)" (New York: Duchess Music Corporation, 1950; renewed, Miami, Fla.: Songs of Universal Inc.; Warner Bros. Publications U.S. Inc.).

6. Anna Bartlett Warner (words) and William Bradbury (music), "Jesus Loves Me" (New York: 1860). Public Domain.

Soulmates

Nonfiction

Wendy Elaine Nelles

Attracted by the big city's culture and sophistication, Nancy Pressutti, a 24-year-old nurse from Des Moines, Iowa, moved to Manhattan. One day she met Don Krain in the elevator of their apartment building. He was a 29-year-old lawyer, a graduate of Columbia University who'd grown up in The Bronx. Don invited Nancy to go with him to one of New York's most famous street festivals, the Feast of San Gennaro.

As they joined the crowds strolling through Little Italy, Nancy fell in love with Don's enthusiastic outlook on life—and she knew by the end of their first date that she wanted to marry him. When Don proposed to Nancy six months later, their only question was, where would they be married?

Nancy had been raised Roman Catholic by her Italian-American family. Baptized and confirmed as a child, she had little interest in the church by the time she was an adult. Don had been brought up within Conservative Judaism, learned Hebrew and had his bar mitzvah at age 13, but he was used to treating Jewish holidays as cultural celebrations, highlighted more by the cuisine than the religious significance.

In 1967, neither a priest nor a rabbi would consent to marry the mixed-faith couple.

Don and Nancy discussed the problem and decided that religion was irrelevant to the successful lives they planned to lead. Despite their families' misgivings, they got married in a civil ceremony at New York City Hall.

For the next 37 years, God had no place in their lives.

Don concentrated on building his career, switching from corporate law to the burgeoning field of computer hardware and software. Nancy focused on raising their family: daughter Honey Jill and sons Ed and David. Don had been transferred to Toronto, Ontario as a consultant soon after they'd married. When his contract ended three years later, the Krains had to make an important choice.

"We liked Canada so much, we decided that I would look for another job and we would stay and become Canadian citizens," Don explains, vestiges of his Bronx accent still perceptible. "We liked the people, we liked the school system for our children, and we felt very comfortable here."

So they settled happily into life in Toronto. Once the children were older, Nancy used her nurse's training to work as a pharmaceutical sales representative.

The years passed. With Don getting near 65 and Nancy close to 60, the Krains decided to retire so they could spend more time with their grandchildren, and pursue their great loves of travel and learning. Because they lived within walking distance of the University of Toronto's downtown campus, they started taking as many courses as they could cram in, on any subject that struck their fancy.

"We were free lecture junkies," Nancy laughs. "We went to everything, post-World War II history, influence of the media, quantum physics, you name it."

A friend who had recently moved to British Columbia phoned to tell them about a lecture she thought they might enjoy. The topic was the history of the Bible and the authorship of several Old Testament books.

Although the Krains had never expressed any interest in the subject, it was a beautiful spring evening in 2004 and they figured they'd enjoy the after-dinner stroll, if nothing else.

Nancy says, "Something happened to us as we left that lecture. We were absolutely struck by the fact that there was a part of us—related to our relationship with God—which we had left dormant for nearly 40 years. We had forgotten about the most important part of ourselves!

"We'd both had some religious training as children but we really knew nothing about the Bible at all," she adds. "We believed in God—but we'd never discussed this aspect of our lives, never acknowledged it. We kept asking each other, 'Why have we never looked into this before?'"

A couple they met at the first lecture invited the Krains to attend a multi-faith discussion group that studied historical aspects of the Bible.

"We were so inspired by this couple, both of whom were interested in biblical scholarship, that we decided that we wanted to understand how the Bible was assembled," Don explains.

While the discussion group considered the historical authenticity of Jesus to be an open question, it encouraged each attendee to explore a wide range of religious traditions and to develop his or her own unique spirituality. Don and Nancy inexplicably found themselves drawn to New Testament writings. "For some reason," Don says, "we began to really love this stuff."

Eager to find out more, they tracked down Crux Theological Bookstore, hidden in the lower level of Wycliffe College on the U of T campus, nearly invisible to passersby. Peppering the staff with questions, the couple found them a tremendous resource to recommend books to get them started. In fact, Don and Nancy became regular customers, and Don developed a close friendship with storeowner Pat Paas (who sadly died at age 55 in 2009).

The Krains first devoured *Who Wrote the Bible?* by Richard Friedman, followed by the 560-page tome *The New Testament: A Historical Introduction to the Early Christian Writings* by Bart Ehrman. Because they had no background in the subject matter, they read aloud in tandem—one reading the textbook, the other looking up the relevant passages in the Bible and in commentaries.

"We were brand new at this, so we had to create our own vocabulary list," Don says. "We developed a three-page, single-spaced list that defined words we'd never heard of before, like 'exegesis' and 'eschatological.'"

Don and Nancy found themselves falling in love with the parables, the simple yet profound stories Jesus told to illustrate spiritual truths to His listeners 2,000 years ago.

But something else was happening. "The more we got into it, the more we realized these weren't just interesting stories," Don says. "We began to feel that Jesus was a messenger sent by God. Without really planning it, we started trying to live by who Jesus was and what He did."

One cold day, Nancy noticed a garbage collector heaving trash into the back of the garbage truck. Walking closer, she said, "You've got a rough job. We're very appreciative of what you do for us."

The worker dropped the garbage can, stared at her and demanded, "What did you say, lady? What did you say?"

Nancy stepped back, "Ah, I just wanted to tell you how much we appreciate the service you do."

He answered, "Lady, I've been doing this for seven years, and *nobody* has ever talked to me before like a human being!"

Waving her hand a few inches from the floor, Nancy recalls, "I felt 'this high' because I was one of the people who used to walk right by people like him. It was a wake-up call."

The Krains started volunteering every Tuesday night at the Out of the Cold program run by an inner city mission that serves homeless and marginalized people. Despite the fact that their vision of retirement hadn't included peeling potatoes, making soup, washing dishes, and standing at streetcar stops on wintry nights, waiting to get home and collapse exhausted into bed, they loved it!

"The turning point happened when we read what Jesus said when He was asked, 'What is the most important commandment?'" Nancy says. "He replied, 'Love the Lord your God with all your heart, soul and mind *and* love your neighbour as yourself.'¹ We decided that if we were going to walk Jesus' path, love and compassion had to become the most important things in our lives."

Because of Don's Jewish background, the couple grew fascinated with studying first-century Judaism in Palestine—and they began to realize how radical Jesus' message was in that context.

"We put ourselves more and more into the place of these early Christians," Don says. "We kept asking, 'What was it in Jesus that made these Jewish believers look to Him as their Saviour and Lord, and be so changed? What made them willing to lay down their lives because of Him?'"

Wanting to learn more, the Krains persuaded professors at the Toronto School of Theology to permit them to audit PhD-level seminar courses on New Testament topics. Although they stopped short of teaching themselves Greek or Aramaic, they did all the other required reading, which amounted to 30-plus hours a week.

Feeling the need for a more hands-on type of learning, they decided to look for a modern Christian community. As Nancy explains, "We don't live in first-century Palestine anymore, so who could tell us, 'This is what it looks like to follow in Jesus' path today'? Who could we emulate?"

Every Sunday morning, they headed off to church, visiting various congregations and denominations, asking for referrals from friends or people they met in class. But most Sundays they came home discouraged, puzzled because the word "Jesus" had never been mentioned during the service, and no passages from the Bible had been quoted during the sermon.

They continued reading voraciously, including books written by a British theologian, N. T. Wright, the Anglican Bishop of Durham. In May 2006, the Krains were thrilled to discover that the bishop was coming to lecture at Wycliffe College. And they were delighted when Crux bookstore staff offered them the last two tickets to a party in Wright's honour.

Nancy and Don arrived at the crowded Revival Club on College Street to discover they were the oldest ones there; even worse, all the tables looked full. As they hesitated in the doorway, a young man got up and asked, "Would you like to join our table?"

"Those young people were absolutely wonderful to us," says Don. "We had a fantastic evening. They were friendly, they included us in the conversation, they were interested in us and we were interested in them."

"They radiated a kind of goodness," Nancy interjects. "How do you put your finger on that when you see it? There was something unusual about them."

Their tablemates told the Krains they came from a large church called The Meeting House in Oakville, Ontario, which had a contemporary style but was part of an Anabaptist denomination with a Mennonite heritage. The church recently had started a satellite site in downtown Toronto.

"We left there just shocked by their warmth and enthusiasm," Don's voice grows more excited. "So the next Sunday, we show up bright and early for church at the address they told us. We have no idea what it will be like.

"First of all, we're meeting in a movie theatre. We're surrounded by students and young people, all talking and drinking coffee. Then we see [teaching pastor] Bruxy Cavey on the big screen. Look at him!" Don laughs. "He's got long hair and a beard; he's wearing blue jeans and a baggy sweatshirt! He's not like any minister we've ever seen before.

"Then he starts talking about what it means to be a 'Christ-follower.' Now you can imagine, after all that we had gone through, it was as if he were talking directly to us! *Finally*—someone was talking our language!"

Although the Krains were unsure what to expect, the next Wednesday evening they arrived at one of the home churches sponsored by The Meeting House. Over coffee and snacks, a dozen or more people met in a host's living room to get to know one another, pray for each other's needs, discuss how to apply the previous Sunday's teaching to their everyday lives, and work together on volunteer projects to show Christ's love to the community.

"We were so blown away!" Don says. "We started to meet young kids who were 30, 40, even 50 years younger than us. They were true Jesus people, Christ-followers in the best sense of the word. Almost everyone we met was doing something to serve God, along with his or her schooling or job. Some of them were putting their careers on hold to go overseas on mission trips to help others.

"Do you know how exciting it was, for new people like us, to see the Kingdom of God in action? We had started by learning about the historical Jesus, and now we were learning how to live in Christ from these dedicated young people. Nancy and I said to each other, 'We've been trying to find examples of Christianity in the twenty-first century—it's here!'"

Discovering others who were on the same spiritual pilgrimage confirmed the Krains' own mustard-seed-sized faith. The more they learned, the more their belief strengthened that Jesus was the Messiah, the One sent by God to reveal His heart and His desire that we live in relationship with Him. While they didn't have a "Saul-on-the-road-to-Damascus"[2] moment of sudden conversion, their choice to make Christ the cornerstone of their lives gradually crystallized.

They were startled to discover they were looking forward to attending worship services. Nancy observes, "It changed 180 degrees. As children, we both felt it was a duty to go. Now it's a gift. We go to be filled up with knowledge and ideas and encouragement and motivation. Then we go home to turn that into action, helping the community and sharing the excitement of God's love."

Despite the fact that they were "starting from zero," prayer became a major part of their lives. "We've never read books or taken courses on how to pray, and I'm not sure we're interested in 'improving' in this area," Nancy says. "Our words are very simple but we feel close to God when we pray. We just talk to Him."

Their lifestyle also altered dramatically. Nancy reveals, "I used to really be into shopping, home décor, art galleries. I'd spend days looking for the perfect doorknob!" Now, signing up for cruises, seeing the latest plays or operas, going out for gourmet dinners, shopping for a replacement for their 1992 Buick Park Avenue— none of them were priorities anymore.

Instead, they started having naps on Monday afternoons— because Sunday nights they'd joined their home church members chopping vegetables and cooking dinner for 120 people at a Christian outreach centre for the homeless. They scoured the aisles of Costco looking for bargains on soap, toothpaste and towels— because they were collecting supplies to make AIDS care kits for patients in Africa being helped by the MCC (Mennonite Central Committee) relief and development organization. They walked briskly through Toronto's streets for daily exercise, listening to their iPods™— filled with downloaded sermons from The Meeting House.

The Krains began to carefully allocate their budget to support a number of charities close to their heart.

Their biggest extravagance has been buying books. They've built up a library exceeding 260 catalogued volumes on faith-related topics, and keep reading widely and avidly, finding C. S. Lewis, Dallas Willard and N. T. Wright to be their "holy trinity" of the most life-changing authors.

"Our children were pretty startled, and they worried about us for a while," Nancy admits, smiling. "They thought their parents had joined some kind of cult in their old age! But they've seen the dramatic change in us. Now our expectations of what life should be like are so different, and our kids—as well as our five grandsons—are very supportive."

Wanting to make a public declaration of their new life in Christ, the Krains invited a diverse group of friends and family to witness their baptism. On a hot Sunday afternoon, August 19, 2007, a standing-room-only crowd of several hundred gathered in an old church to see the Krains and a half-dozen other people, dressed in shorts and T-shirts, get baptized by immersion.

Paul Morris, the then-lead pastor of the downtown Toronto Meeting House, baptized Don; then Don baptized Nancy. As a symbol of their submission to Christ, they each knelt and bowed forward into the water one, two, three times, in the name of the Father, the Son, and the Holy Spirit. The audience sang worship songs, applauded and brushed away tears.

Afterwards, the Krains threw a party at a nearby restaurant. Their 75 guests included some street people from the homeless shelter where they volunteered.

The Krains have affectionately nicknamed the pastor who officiated at their baptism "Paul Junior" (after the Apostle Paul), in tribute to this "really special young man's" ability to explain difficult theological concepts, and his crucial role in helping them "uncover the path God had designed for us." In turn, Paul calls Don and Nancy "… simply the most encouraging people I've ever met. I consider them to be my secret weapons… if I ever want someone to feel cared for and loved in our community."

Don and Nancy found more ways to lend a hand. They started setting the alarm before dawn every Thursday morning, putting on the coffee and getting ready to greet, with warm smiles and hugs, 10 or 20 people who crowd around their condominium's dining room table for breakfast. This way, busy professionals who work long hours in downtown Toronto can be part of a home church that meets at the only time convenient for them.

And the Krains got involved in mentoring young couples from the church during their marriage preparation courses.

One of the unexpected benefits of their new faith is realizing their own marriage is much stronger today, 44 years after they wed.

"We had a fairly good marriage; we never had any major problems," Don says. "But we never understood what Jesus says about marriage bringing two people together to become one. We've shared this faith journey together, and it has enhanced our marriage tremendously. If you're giving love to others as well as to each other, you have much more understanding of what love is."

Nancy adds, "When you share a spiritual, God-filled life, when you pray together, it adds a whole other layer of meaning and love. It's been easier to downplay our weaknesses and encourage the positive aspects of our personalities."

"We're much happier today," Don says, "because we've learned to be more thankful, and because we have a capacity we didn't have before—of being able to understand other people, to share in their joy or their problems."

As for their backgrounds, Don feels no disconnect between being raised a Jew and becoming a committed Christ-follower. Instead, it's the reverse: his Jewish upbringing has enabled him to better understand and appreciate the historic Jesus.

"Here's the beauty of it: I see it as seamless," Don says. "Jesus said that He didn't come to abolish the Law or the Prophets, but to fulfill them, and I believe that."[3]

Ever since the Krains decided to follow Jesus, they have reserved Friday evenings to celebrate a Sabbath Eve supper, often inviting family and friends to join them.

The Krains realized that many of their Christian friends know little about the Jewish roots of the Christian faith—while many of their Jewish friends know little about what Jesus taught, and may be hazy about *Shabbat's* significance because they no longer commemorate it themselves.

So they created a unique Sabbath observance that fuses both Jewish and Christian elements, focusing on common beliefs that underpin both faiths.

As Don describes it, "*Shabbat* is a precious gift from God, a time when we can set aside all of our weekday concerns and devote ourselves to reaffirming our relationship with God. It's also an opportunity for togetherness, joining with family and friends, taking time to appreciate each other."

The couple view their respective religious heritages as treasures, unique blessings that have enriched their spiritual pilgrimage.

Commenting on some Christian believers who fear that taking scholarly courses in religious studies will cause people to lose their faith, Nancy says, "We find that attitude astounding, because that's how we *found* faith. We see intellectual pursuit as God's gift, something that opened so many doors for us, helping us discover how we could connect with God."

Don adds, "What makes Christianity so great is its freedom; we all can come at it from different directions and perspectives, and the Holy Spirit can open our eyes to spiritual truth."

"Once you seriously start analyzing what was happening in first-century Palestine, you realize that Jesus' message was extraordinarily powerful," Nancy says. "How can that *not* change your life? How can you then continue on the same path you've been on for 65 years?"

Both echo the same thoughts: "Everything that happened was God-driven. God brought us to think about the Bible. God brought us to recognize Christ and what it meant to be a Christ-follower. He put people in our path, and at every single point He directed us. You're looking at two very blessed people."

1. Matthew 22:36–40.

2. Acts 9:1–8.

3. Matthew 5:17.

A Glimpse of Heaven

Nonfiction

Donna Fawcett

We never knew that our mother was dying. She hadn't told us—not with any conviction anyway—that she had been diagnosed with cancer 15 years earlier. I do remember a casual comment: "The doctor says I've got cancer, but I think he's nuts." And when nothing changed in her health or her lifestyle, the statement faded into the obscure corners of my mind. It was yanked out of hibernation in the last week of July of 2006, when my father pounded at my patio door and shouted for help to get her to the hospital. I followed him into the bedroom of their attached apartment to discover Mom, on her bed, weak and moaning.

As we settled into the emergency ward for a ten-hour wait, Mom lay on the raised hospital bed like a monarch who had just been dethroned—dignified yet resigned—and listened to the doctor on duty throw out words that landed like mortar shells on my heart. "The cancer's finally got the best of you." Cancer—several kinds of cancer, in fact—all brought on from working as an X-ray technician in the '40s, when training didn't include the effects of radiation. The emergency room physician had checked the electronic medical records and quickly grasped Mom's prognosis.

So her family doctor hadn't been nuts after all. We sat silent, listening to the death knell, waiting for its harbinger to leave so we could say—what? The emergency room doctor patted Mom's hand, offered us a pale smile, and left us to absorb the shock.

"I never made a big deal of it because I didn't want you to worry. And I didn't want you to coddle me." She tossed her words at us like a dropped gauntlet. Nothing more needed to be said. She had given us 15 years of burden-free relationship. In her mind, it was a gift. In ours, it was a loss. Although 79 years of age, she came from a long line of near-centenarians and we expected at least another decade of treasured time together.

Because of a shortage of beds, it took hours before Mom could be admitted into the critical care unit.

With her hospital bed came her first morphine shot. "Oh my!" she said. "If I'd known it felt this good, I'd have been on the stuff long ago."

We laughed and the tension eased. And then came the time for the phone calls. Six of them—stretching across the map like the Trans-Canada Highway. I phoned my siblings in order of age, as though birth-rank somehow made it okay to be the last one called. "Mom's in the hospital. Cancer everywhere—lungs, liver, pancreas, gallbladder—you name it. They give her two weeks to live." Two weeks. The words tasted like plaster dust and I struggled to chew around them.

Lives were dropped and family members came from far and wide. Sombre faces. Well-chosen words. Stiff gestures. And then Mom had had enough. She began to tell jokes. To banter with those with whom she had always bantered. She wrote love notes to each of us. She called her children and grandchildren into the room one at a time and poured out stern admonitions.

"I'm going to heaven. I know it. The Bible tells me so. I want you there when your turn comes. Read the Book and do what it says." No one argued.

Jaundice invaded her skin like an all-consuming tobacco stain, yet she refused to let it dampen her spirit of optimism. "Bring me sunflowers. I want to match the décor."

I brought her handfuls of huge sunflowers from my garden and we laughed again as she placed them against her arm to make sure they were just the right shade.

She good-naturedly scolded the pastor, reminding him to behave himself when she was gone, and she applauded the hospital staff for their tender care. "Don't fuss over me. You have people who need you more than me."

She conspired with her fellow quilting group members to finish the quilts I had hired them to make for our daughters' weddings—when each one's time came—and then presented the completed works of art to me one morning when I arrived to visit. Her eyes danced with her feat and her discoloured lips wore a smug grin.

She had us sing old gospel songs for her and revelled in the sounds of her children's voices bouncing off concrete walls. We were cajoled into taking her for wheelchair rides out into the sunshine. She raved over the August display as I showed her, on my laptop computer, a slide presentation of her gardens. Through each moment—each moment of suffering in joy-filled silence—she reminded us of her Lord's love.

And as I sat helpless by her bed, I watched her glory fade and God's glory shine brighter. In her eyes. On her face. Then one afternoon, she had a dream. In that dream, a girl stood at her bed beckoning her. A girl in a flowing gown.

Watching, I could see Mom's face glowing with the flame of a spiritual fire. As her dream faded, I thought that she had never looked so beautiful.

"Did you see her? Did you see the girl?" She looked from my sister's baffled face to mine. We shook our heads and watched her expression deflate as though she was disappointed that we couldn't share the experience.

"Do you think it was an angel?" My sister and I asked each other the question when we were away from Mom's hearing. Neither of us gave an answer.

As the ninth day of her hospital stay passed, Mom slipped into a dying slumber, a small smile on her face. My siblings and I began to take turns sleeping on the cot by her bed. When my turn came, she was restless through the night—as though fighting to draw breath—fighting the pull heavenward.

"It's okay, Mom," I whispered to her in the wee hours of the morning. "I'll look after Dad." She settled and the laboured breathing continued.

Morning came and I watched the clock tick toward 9 a.m., when it would be Dad's turn to sit by her side. Right on time, he slipped into the room with quiet steps and approached the bed. He spoke to her in a soft voice. "Hi honey. I'm here."

I was watching Mom. She suddenly pursed her parched, yellowed lips. Her eyes stayed closed. Nothing else moved—nothing but her heart. She had waited for him.

"Do you know who it is?" Dad asked.

A small nod answered his question.

He leaned forward and kissed her.

I looked away, giving them that brief moment of privacy. Dad settled into the chair by her bed and took Mom's hand. 9:05 a.m. One breath. Two breaths. A deep sigh. She was gone. She had kissed Dad goodbye and left us.

It was all strange and alien and abrupt after that. So much organizing of things. Mom had always been the family organizer, and we were at a loss. Friends stepped in and carried the burden for us as we prepared to honour a life well-lived.

The funeral marched its way through the day, leaving us with gaping holes in our hearts. I pondered the truth of eternity. Was it real? Was she really in heaven? I craved assurance. *God, I just need to know.*

I didn't really expect an answer, but it came. That night at home, I slept deeply, and then awoke—but not here. I stood on the edge of a road in a land filled with colours I had never known. The sky had no end, no stars beyond it, but it was a kaleidoscope of hues that are too perfect for an earthly eye. The road was full of travellers milling about, going to and fro along the steady incline, chattering amongst themselves. I stood at the side as though viewing a cosmic television screen, watching, but not part of it.

Out of the millions came a familiar figure and my heart jumped. I knew those square shoulders, that broad ribcage, the soldier's march for which my mother was known. Her hair, now blinding white, shone in a thick halo around her face. The jaundice was gone, replaced by a rich bronze that glowed with robust health. Her eyes. Oh, her eyes! Living fire. Burning life burst from them.

My mother approached me and stood for an eternity—yet only a second in time. Her hand, no longer gnarled with arthritis, reached out and touched my face, and I felt the fire of life pulsing through her.

"Heaven's beautiful." She breathed the words and my heart jumped again with the certainty of her statement. She turned and began to walk along the road's edge, beckoning me to join her. I walked beside the road, she on it, and we talked. She described heaven to me—and she told me of other things that later I wouldn't bring back to my waking world. My soul soared, not because I was in her presence but because of the Presence that was in her. We walked for hours. Days. Years. And we talked. Her face continued to shine with contentment as she turned to me one last time.

"I have to go now." That was all she said, but the love shining through her eyes filled me with a love that words could never speak. And then she turned, walked into the milling masses, and disappeared from my sight.

I awoke and cried in profound loss. I had come back. I had come away from a place I had no desire to leave. I had seen, if not heaven, then heaven's foyer. I had seen my mother—true—but it wasn't leaving her that ripped me asunder. That Presence, that love that He poured through her, that perfection was all, once more, behind the veil—not clearly visible as it had been while I was there in my dream. I longed to have that clarity back. I ached with that longing.

Yet God had answered my cry and I knew—I knew it's there for me some day. I had hope again. And faith that I'll see that hope fulfilled.

The days since my mother's leaving march on, one by one. I grow older. I see my children become parents. I see the world through my mother's eyes as I age. And I draw closer to that time when I will pass through that veil again. I feel the surge of true life, bask in the flame of unearthly love, and, like my mother, I am not afraid.

Morning Glory

Judi Peers

I am like the morning glory,
Unfurling in the light of the sun.
I will seek Your face each morning,
For I desire to become—
One who reflects
The beauty,
The fragrance,
The glory of Your Son.

Editors and Contributors

N. J. Lindquist

www.njlindquist.com

Photo by Daniel Lindquist, DVM

N. J. Lindquist is driven by a desire to see people become everything they were created to be. An award-winning author, an inspiring speaker, and an empowering teacher, N. J. has 12 published books, including the award-winning Manziuk and Ryan mystery series and the coming-of-age Circle of Friends series. N. J.'s vision led to the founding of The Word Guild in 2001. She served as executive director for seven years, and continues as director of Write! Canada. Among her many awards, N. J. received the Leading Women Award for distinctive achievement in Communications and Media in 2006, and a Deeds Speak Award from the York Regional Police for her book, *In Time of Trouble*. Originally from the Canadian Prairies, N. J. now lives in Markham, Ontario.

Hot Apple Cider (That's Life! Communications)
Glitter of Diamonds (MurderWillOut Mysteries)

Wendy Elaine Nelles

www.wendynelles.com

Photo by Sue Careless

Wendy Elaine Nelles is an award-winning journalist, writer, editor and speaker with wide-ranging experience in the corporate, not-for-profit and publishing sectors. She co-founded The Word Guild in 2001, and has played a key role in equipping Canadian writers who are Christian to achieve increased professionalism and greater influence. Wendy directed the Write! Canada conference from 2002 to 2010, served on its leadership team for 22 years, and oversaw writing contests and literary awards. Wendy was honoured with the Leading Women Award for distinctive achievement in Communications and Media in 2006. She holds an MA in Communications with high honour from Wheaton College. Based in Toronto and Norfolk County, Ontario, Wendy was one of 45 inductees selected from her secondary school's 118-year history for its inaugural Wall of Distinction in 2010.

Hot Apple Cider (That's Life! Communications)

A. A. Adourian

www.aaadourian.com

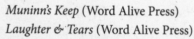

A. A. Adourian is a writer—creative, focused, ready. A librarian by profession with more than a decade of experience in the field, A. A. is a skilled researcher and author of numerous business-related reports in a corporate environment. A. A. is in awe of how God brought this, her first published work, to pass. While A. A. recently completed a half-marathon, she is daily challenged to run after God, serve Him, and make Him known.

Photo by Darcie Sutherland Photography

Brian C. Austin

www.undiscoveredtreasures.org

Brian C. Austin is a writer and speaker. His work includes print and audio poetry, nonfiction articles, historical fiction and dramatic monologue. Brian is an active member of The Word Guild and contributed several poems to *Hot Apple Cider: Words to Stir the Heart and Warm the Soul*. He lives near Durham, Ontario.

Muninn's Keep (Word Alive Press)
Laughter & Tears (Word Alive Press)

Paul M. Beckingham

http://walkingtowardshope.blogspot.com

For Paul M. Beckingham, writing became a life-saver. In Kenya, a car wreck threatened three family members' lives, and left him for dead at the road-side. Writing builds new meaning into his life. Paul's first book—and many of his richly woven shorter articles—earned literary awards. Contributing to both *Hot Apple Cider* volumes (2008 and 2011) and to *The Cradle and the Crown* (2006), Paul wrote the memoir *Walking Towards Hope* in 2005. He calls Vancouver, B.C. home.

Walking Towards Hope: Experiencing Grace in a Time of Brokenness (Castle Quay Books)

Bonnie Beldan-Thomson

http://bonniebeldanthomson.wordpress.com

Bonnie Beldan-Thomson's writing is informed and enriched by the diversity of her life experience. She is an award-winning poet and journalist who has been published in Canada and internationally since 1987. Her writing often revolves around themes of mercy, grace and redemption. She is a retired elementary school teacher, a music teacher and a director of music ministries. Now living in Pickering, Ontario, Bonnie has also lived in Alberta and, for shorter periods, in the Middle East and Scotland.

Glynis M. Belec

www.glynisbelec.com

Glynis Belec is a freelance writer, children's author, and private tutor in Drayton, Ontario. She loves mentoring beginning writers, speaking at schools, and leading writing workshops. Glynis particularly enjoys being published in the children's market. Her work includes newspaper editorial columns, devotionals, stage plays, short stories, Sunday school take-home papers, and nonfiction articles for children's and adult magazines.

Jailhouse Rock (Concordia Publishing)
Jesus Washes Peter's Feet (Concordia Publishing)

Mary Ann Benjamins

http://maryannbenjamins.wordpress.com

Photo by Scott Reynolds
www.memorylanestudio.ca

Mary Ann Benjamins, an elementary school supply teacher, writes from her home base in Brantford, Ontario. Born and raised in Pembroke in the heart of the Ottawa Valley, Mary Ann has lived all over Ontario and the United States. She is a member of The World Guild and this is her second published work. An earlier essay in the "My Hometown" contest was published in *The Observer* newspaper in Sarnia, Ontario. Mary Ann writes and speaks for area churches and schools.

Vilma Blenman

http://writerteacher.wordpress.com

Vilma Blenman is a teacher and counsellor with the Toronto District School Board. She holds a Master of Education degree in Counselling Psychology. Vilma writes sporadically between counselling at-risk teens, facilitating personal growth groups, and managing a private practice. "Lost: One Green Scarf" and "Cries for Keyon" are her first published pieces. Originally from Jamaica, she brings the voices of the Caribbean-Canadian community to her writing. Vilma lives in Pickering, Ontario.

Photo by Kristy Wills

Bill Bonikowsky

www.billbonikowsky.com

Bill Bonikowsky is a writer, editor and photographer based in Surrey, British Columbia. His work includes editing *Alpha News* for Alpha Ministries Canada, and editing *Report to the People* for Greater Vancouver Youth for Christ, where he served for 27 years. Bill was a contributing writer for the *NIV Life Application Study Bible* while serving as pastor of Grove Community Church in Arlington Heights, Illinois. Born in Niagara-on-the-Lake, Ontario, Bill was raised in Guelph before moving to B.C. in 1974.

Ann Brent

http://writerbrent.wordpress.com

Ann Brent is passionate about getting God's Word and His message of salvation through Jesus to as many people as possible. As director of national ministries for Empower Ministries, she produces publications that inform, challenge and inspire people with the news of how God is working around the world today. A lover of words, she fully understood the meaning of "overjoyed" when she held her first grandchild, Jacob. Ann is determined to face life's changes and challenges through the filters of laughter, optimism and faith. She lives in Brights Grove near Sarnia, Ontario.

Photo by Kelly Brent

Connie Brummel Crook

www.conniebrummelcrook.ca

Connie Brummel Crook, a retired teacher from Peterborough, Ontario, is the author of 11 historical fiction novels, and two picture books. Her novels include the Nellie McClung trilogy, the Meyers saga, and other pioneer stories, such as *The Hungry Year*. Her books have won numerous awards. *Meyers' Rebellion* was a 2007 finalist for the Geoffrey Bilson Award for Historical Fiction for Young People. In 2008, Connie received the Leslie K. Tarr Award for a major career contribution to Christian writing in Canada.

Meyers' Rebellion (Fitzhenry & Whiteside)

Marguerite Cummings

http://margueritec.wordpress.com

Marguerite Cummings has a distinctively international background. Born in Belgium into a French-speaking family with roots in Austria, Belgium, Poland, and Romania, she moved to England in her late teens. There she completed an Oxford degree, attended Bible college, trained as a technical writer and editor, and worked in computing, until her move to Canada in 1998. Marguerite now feels completely at home in Toronto, the multicultural capital of Ontario. "O Canada" is her first article as a freelance writer.

Kevin J. Dautremont

http://thestethoscopeandpen.com

Kevin J. Dautremont, MD, is a family physician in Moose Jaw, Saskatchewan and an associate clinical professor with the University of Saskatchewan College of Medicine. His writing focuses on mysteries and historical fiction. In 2008, Kevin won the Best New Canadian Christian Author Award for *The Golden Conquest*. This alternative history novel is a story of adventure and faith set during the Spanish Conquest of Mexico in the 1500s.

Photo by Dawnelle Brown
brown-eyedgirlphotography.ca

The Golden Conquest (Castle Quay Books, 2011)

313

Donna Fawcett (Donna Dawson)

www.donnafawcett.com

Donna Fawcett (pen name Donna Dawson) is a speaker, singer, novelist, news columnist, magazine writer, and creative writing instructor for Fanshawe College in London, Ontario. Her novel *Vengeance* won two categories in The Word Guild Canadian Christian Writing Awards in 2009. Her newest novel *Rescued* offers a potential solution to the abortion issue. Donna lives in southwestern Ontario.

Vengeance (Word Alive Press)

Rescued (Word Alive Press)

Angelina Fast-Vlaar

www.angelinafastvlaar.com

Award-winning author Angelina Fast-Vlaar was born in Holland and resides in St. Catharines, Ontario. Her writing includes nonfiction books, articles and poetry. As an inspirational speaker, Angelina draws on her wealth of experience to captivate and motivate audiences. As a cancer survivor, she offers hope and encouragement. She won the Best New Canadian Christian Author Award in 2004.

Seven Angels for Seven Days (Castle Quay Books)

The Valley of Cancer: A Journey of Comfort and Hope (Word Alive Press)

Rosemary Flaaten

www.rosemaryflaaten.com

Rosemary Flaaten, MA, is a sought-after speaker for professional and women's groups, retreats and corporate training. She is also one of the speakers with Girls Night Out. Her writing, which focuses on relationships, encompasses study curricula, books, devotionals and articles. Rosemary leads the Professional Women's Network in Calgary, Alberta, where she resides. She was raised on a farm in southern Saskatchewan.

A Woman and Her Relationships (Beacon Hill Press)

A Woman and Her Workplace (Beacon Hill Press)

Ed Hird

http://edhird.wordpress.com

Ed Hird, MDiv, BSW, DMin candidate, has served as the rector of St. Simon's Church North Vancouver since 1987. Ordained in 1980, he also served at St. Philip's Vancouver and St. Matthew's Abbotsford, all located in British Columbia. Ed is past president of Alpha Canada, and former national chair for Anglican Renewal Ministries of Canada. Over the past 23 years, Ed has written two books and more than 300 articles for local North Vancouver newspapers.

Battle for the Soul of Canada (independently published)

Ron Hughes

www.peopleplacesandplots.com

Ron Hughes is a producer, writer and presenter, both on radio and in person. A missionary in Ecuador from 1983 to 1993, he now lives in Ontario's Niagara Peninsula. Most of Ron's recent work has been inspirational and devotional in character, produced in conjunction with FBH International, a multi-language media ministry based in St. Catharines, Ontario. While most of Ron's output is available in text and audio format through the Internet, some is also in print.

Evangeline Inman

www.evangelineinman.com

Evangeline Inman is a speaker, writer, and multiple award-winning recording artist. Her work includes a Bible study, radio devotionals, a large catalogue of songwriting credits, and recording projects. She travels internationally singing and speaking, and is the founder and president of Women Who Worship Conferences. Evangeline makes her home in Fredericton, New Brunswick.

Photo by Mary Ellen Nealis

Bible study by Evangeline Inman for the book *Shine On* by Sharon Hamilton (Life Vest Publishing)

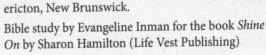

315

David Kitz
www.davidkitz.ca

David Kitz is an actor, award-winning author, and teacher. He served as an ordained pastor for 12 years. His love for drama is evident to all who have seen his Bible-based performances. He has toured across Canada and the United States with a variety of one-man plays for children and adults. Raised in Saskatchewan, David now lives in Ottawa, Ontario.

Psalms Alive! (Forever Books)

Little Froggy Explores the BIG World (Essence Publishing)

Marcia Lee Laycock
www.vinemarc.com

Marcia Lee Laycock is a writer, speaker and teacher from central Alberta. She won the Best New Canadian Christian Author Award in 2006 for her novel *One Smooth Stone*. Her devotional book *Spur of the Moment* has been endorsed by Mark Buchanan and Phil Callaway. The sequel to *One Smooth Stone* will be released in 2011.

One Smooth Stone (Castle Quay Books)

Spur of the Moment (VineMarc Communications)

Les Lindquist
www.leslindquist.com

Photo by Rebecca Baxter

Les Lindquist is an experienced change consultant with a passion for helping organizations and people embrace change in a positive way so they can go forward in difficult situations. He specializes in intuitive, visionary and cost-effective approaches to address complex problems. He has a knack for finding alternatives and discovering unique ways to get things done. Les is currently chair of the board for Christian Info Canada, the ministry that includes The Word Guild.

Heather McGillivray

http://rapturedheart.wordpress.com

Heather McGillivray lives in Greater Sudbury, Ontario, blocks from where she grew up. Since God has changed the direction of her life, she's rekindled an old flame—writing. She lives with a chronic illness and the grace to carry her through. Stories, poems, blog posts, and songs are some of her best company. She's written regularly for a local newspaper, had a smattering of articles and poetry published, is trying her hand at editing, and is currently working on two book projects.

Heidi McLaughlin

www.heartconnection.ca

For more than two decades, international speaker, author and columnist Heidi McLaughlin has been inspiring women to discover and unleash their most valuable, unexpected, God-given gift: the endowment of their genuine, beautiful selves. Her *Beauty Unleashed Study Guide* is being studied by hundreds of women across Canada. Heidi lives amongst the beautiful vineyards of West Kelowna, British Columbia.

Photo by Michelle
Wilson-Penninga

Beauty Unleashed: Transforming a Woman's Soul (VMI Publishing)
Sand to Pearls: Making Bold Choices to Enrich Your Life (Deep River Books)

Ruth Smith Meyer

www.ruthsmithmeyer.com

Ruth Smith Meyer, a writer and speaker raised in the Stouffville area, now alternates living between Ailsa Craig and Listowel, Ontario. She has published two well-received adult novels and a children's book. As an inspirational speaker, she addresses a wide variety of topics. Ruth also teaches how to positively face death, dying, and the grief journey.

Not Easily Broken (Word Alive Press)
Not Far from the Tree (Word Alive Press)

M. D. Meyer
www.dorenemeyer.com

M. D. Meyer is the award-winning author of five novels and two children's books set in the fictional First Nations community of Rabbit Lake in Canada's North. She is also the editor of 10 anthologies, many featuring the works of Aboriginal authors. Dorene currently resides in Norway House, Manitoba, where she is a part-time instructor at University College of the North.

Photo by jaygaune.ca

Jasmine (Word Alive Press)

The Little Ones (Word Alive Press)

Kimberley Payne
www.kimberleypayne.com

Kimberley Payne is a motivational speaker and writer. Her writing relates raising a family, pursuing a healthy lifestyle, and everyday experiences to building a relationship with God. Kimberley, who lives near Peterborough, Ontario, offers practical, guilt-free tips on improving spiritual and physical health. Her energetic and enthusiastic workshop presentations have encouraged listeners at churches, women's retreats and conferences.

Fit for Faith (Within Reach)

Where Family Meets Faith (byDesign Media)

Judi Peers
http://judipeers.wordpress.com

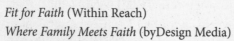

Judi Peers is an author, speaker, publisher and Bible study leader. She has produced children's books for many publishers: Scholastic, General, Stoddart, and James Lorimer. A passion for Old Testament history is reflected in her recent allegorical adventure and its companion adult Bible study. Currently, Judi is at work in Peterborough, Ontario, where she is beginning a study of Isaiah and compiling an anthology entitled *Shekinah: God's Glory Revealed in Unexpected Places.*

Guardian of the Lamp, novel and Bible study (Jacorn Press)

Gloria V. Phillips

www.rogdah.com

Born in northern Alberta, Gloria V. Phillips lived in various locations throughout Alberta and Saskatchewan before settling in Collingwood, Ontario. She is a genealogist who wrote two nonfiction books before turning her hand to historical fiction. Her talents as a researcher are reflected in novels chronicling two generations, starting with the journey of a child immigrant to Canada in the early 1900s.

A Pilgrim Passing Through (Rogdah Publishing)
A Pilgrim's Daughter (Rogdah Publishing)

Johanne E. Robertson

www.maranathanewspaper.com

Johanne E. Robertson is a writer, speaker and business consultant. She is co-founder and co-publisher of *Maranatha News*, a Canadian Christian newspaper celebrating 15 years of serving the community, and co-founder of Read for Life, a ministry encouraging Canadians to read life-changing books (www.readforlife.ca). Born in Montreal, Québec, and currently residing in Toronto, Ontario, Johanne serves on the board of directors for two national ministry organizations, The Word Guild and Women Alive.

Denise Budd Rumble

www.denisebuddrumble.com

Through her speaking and writing, Denise Budd Rumble shares her stories as a woman living in the real world with a real faith, and encourages others to see God at work in their lives too. Denise's blog, Midlife Odyssey, focuses on menopause, aging parents and other midlife challenges. Her articles have been published in newspapers and magazines across Canada, including *Faith Today* and *Focus on the Family Canada*. Born in England, Denise lives in southwestern Ontario and is the managing director of The Word Guild.

Jayne E. Self

www.jayneself.com

Jayne E. Self is a writer, speaker and church musician. Her work includes mysteries, short stories, nonfiction articles and devotionals. Her novel *Caught Dead: A Dean Constable Mystery* was shortlisted in the 2008 and 2009 Best New Canadian Christian Author contests. An active member of The Word Guild, Jayne has lived coast to coast in Canada and presently resides in Orangeville, Ontario.

Adele Simmons

http://adelesimmons.wordpress.com

Adele Simmons is an award-winning writer and editor who has published in many media, including books, journalism, television, scriptwriting, songwriting, and poetry. Also a professional singer and speaker, recording artist, and worship leader, she teaches music, public speaking, and creative ministries. Adele hails from British Columbia and Alberta, but spent her career life in Québec and Ontario, in business management, mental health, special education, and college teaching. She lives near Whitby, Ontario. Watch for Adele's upcoming memoir, *The Cabin: No Ordinary Miracle*.

Janet Sketchley

http://janetsketchley.wordpress.com

Janet Sketchley is an East Coast writer working to break into print in novel-length Christian women's suspense. Her unpublished novel *Praying for the Enemy* was shortlisted for the Best New Canadian Christian Author Award in 2008. She has published more than 100 short articles, columns, stories, and reviews. Stop by her blog, God With Us: Finding Joy, for book reviews, inspirational articles, and features. Janet lives in Dartmouth, Nova Scotia.

Jeannie Lockerbie Stephenson

http://jeanniestephenson.wordpress.com

Jeannie Lockerbie Stephenson opened a Literature Centre while a missionary in Bangladesh. She has written 28 books translated into Bengali and nine in English. The latest is *By Ones and Twos: Building Successful Relationships*. She was her mission's director of publications, producing *The Message* magazine (circulation 100,000) and editing 25 books.

Jeannie conducts writing conferences overseas and in North America. Born in Hamilton, she lives in London, Ontario and is available for speaking engagements.

By Ones and Twos: Building Successful Relationships (ABWE Publishing)

T. L. Wiens

http://tlwiens.wordpress.com

T. L. Wiens is a writer and speaker with an emphasis on youth. Living in the beauty of the hills along Lake Diefenbaker, Saskatchewan forms a stark contrast to T. L.'s novels, which address difficult issues. She is an organizer and workshop leader at the His Imprint writers' conference and a member of The Word Guild, InScribe, and Saskatchewan Writers' Guild.

Making the Bitter Sweet (Xlibris Publishing)
Where a Little Rain Comes Down (Xlibris Publishing)

Acknowledgements

Once again, because of her passion for developing Canadian writers, Wendy Nelles has gone above and beyond the call of duty. She's poured tremendous effort into helping the writers hone their pieces, and ensuring that this collection showcases their varied themes, interests, and styles.

We appreciate the expertise of Ingrid Paulson of Ingrid Paulson Design, who designed the eye-catching cover.

Thank you to contributors Jayne Self and Janet Sketchley, who assisted with processing the manuscript submissions; to proofreader Cameron Wybrow, PhD; to contributors Marguerite Cummings, Heather McGillivray and Judi Peers, who did final reviews; and to That's Life! intern, Lisa Hall-Wilson, who is helping with promotion. We thank Read for Life for its efforts to get great Canadian books (including this one) into the hands of appreciative audiences.

Our gratitude goes to those who took time from their busy schedules to read advance copies of the book and provide endorsements. Special thanks to Ellen Vaughn for writing the foreword.

We thank The Word Guild, a national association of Canadian writers, editors and speakers who are Christian. The nearly 400 members are united in their common passion to positively influence individuals—and ultimately the Canadian culture—through life-changing words that bring God's message of hope (www.thewordguild.com). Particular thanks to Denise Rumble, managing director, and to all the members of the prayer team.

Thanks to World Vision, a Christian relief, development and advocacy organization dedicated to working with children, families and communities to overcome poverty and injustice (www.worldvision.ca). Special thanks to Eric Spath, manager of speakers and events for World Vision Canada, who, in the fall of 2007, took a risk that we could produce a great book (*Hot Apple Cider*), and who was more than willing to trust us a second time.

We thank the 37 writers, all of whom are members of The Word Guild, who supported this project by donating much of the money needed to produce an additional 30,000 copies of the book, which World Vision will use in its ministry.

And we thank the many fans of Canadian writers for their support.

Most important, we thank God for His grace, guidance and wisdom. We pray that you will find encouragement, hope, and faith through the words on these pages—all of which are inspired by the One who is the Word:

> "In the beginning was the Word, and the Word was with
> God, and the Word was God" (John 1:1).

Les and *N. J. Lindquist*, Publishers, That's Life! Communications

That's Life! Communications is a niche publisher committed to finding innovative ways to produce quality books written by Canadians with a Christian faith perspective.

http://thatslifecommunications.com

We'd love to hear your comments about this book or any of our other books.

Write to us at:
comments@thatslifecommunications.com